KILL 6 BILLION DEMONS

KILL SIX BILLION DEMONS, BOOK FOUR.
First printing. August 2021. Published by Image Comics, Inc.
Office of publication: PO BOX 14457, Portland, OR 97293.

Interior book design by Hye Mardikian.

Printed in the USA.

For international rights, contact:
foreignlicensing@imagecomics.com.
ISBN: 978-1-5343-1913-4.

KILL 6 BILLION DEMONS

WAS FIRST PUBLISHED AS A WEBCOMIC.

IT CAN BE FOUND AT

KILL6BILLIONDEMONS.COM

CREATED BY

TOM PARKINSON-MORGAN

[**IV**]

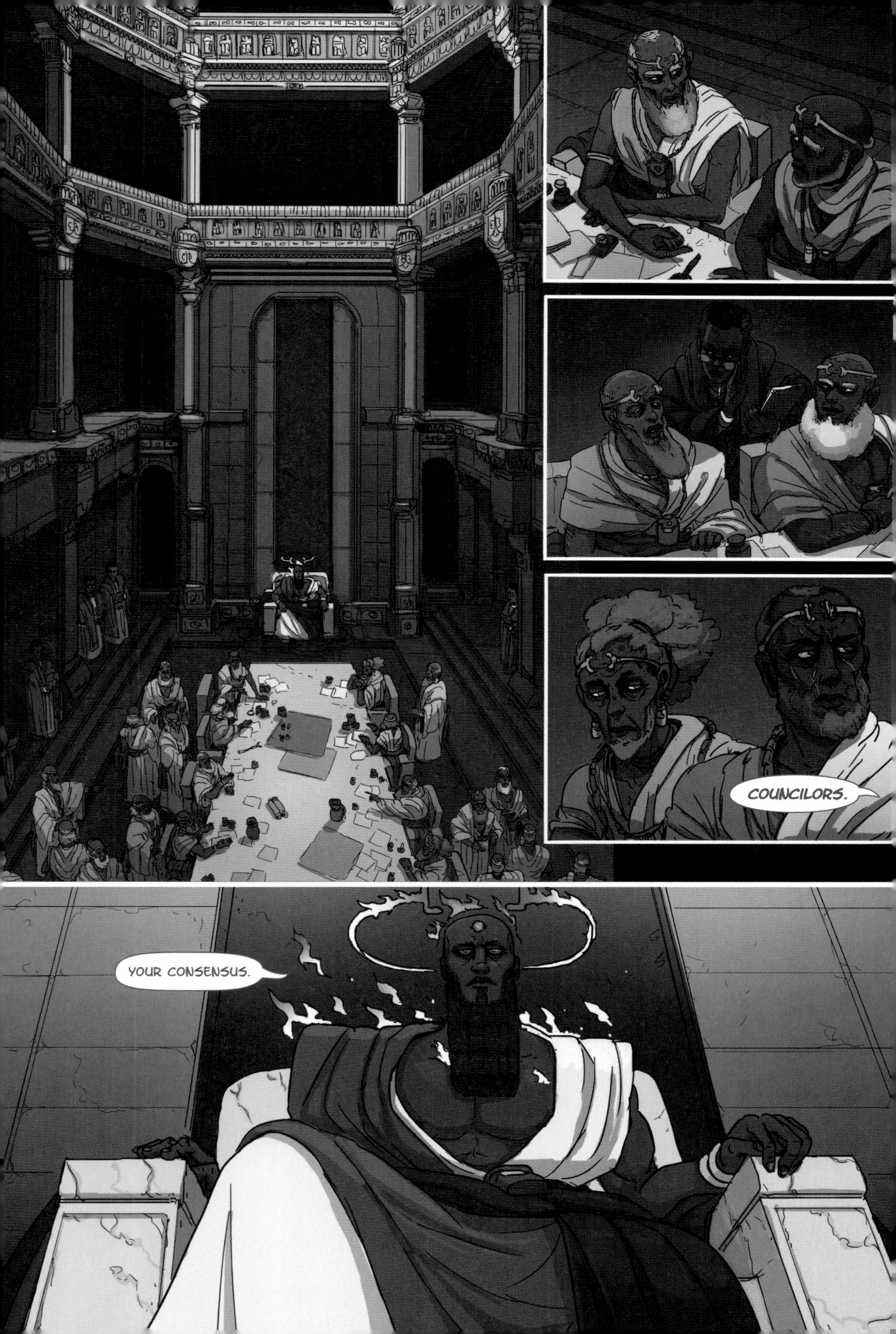
COUNCILORS.
YOUR CONSENSUS.

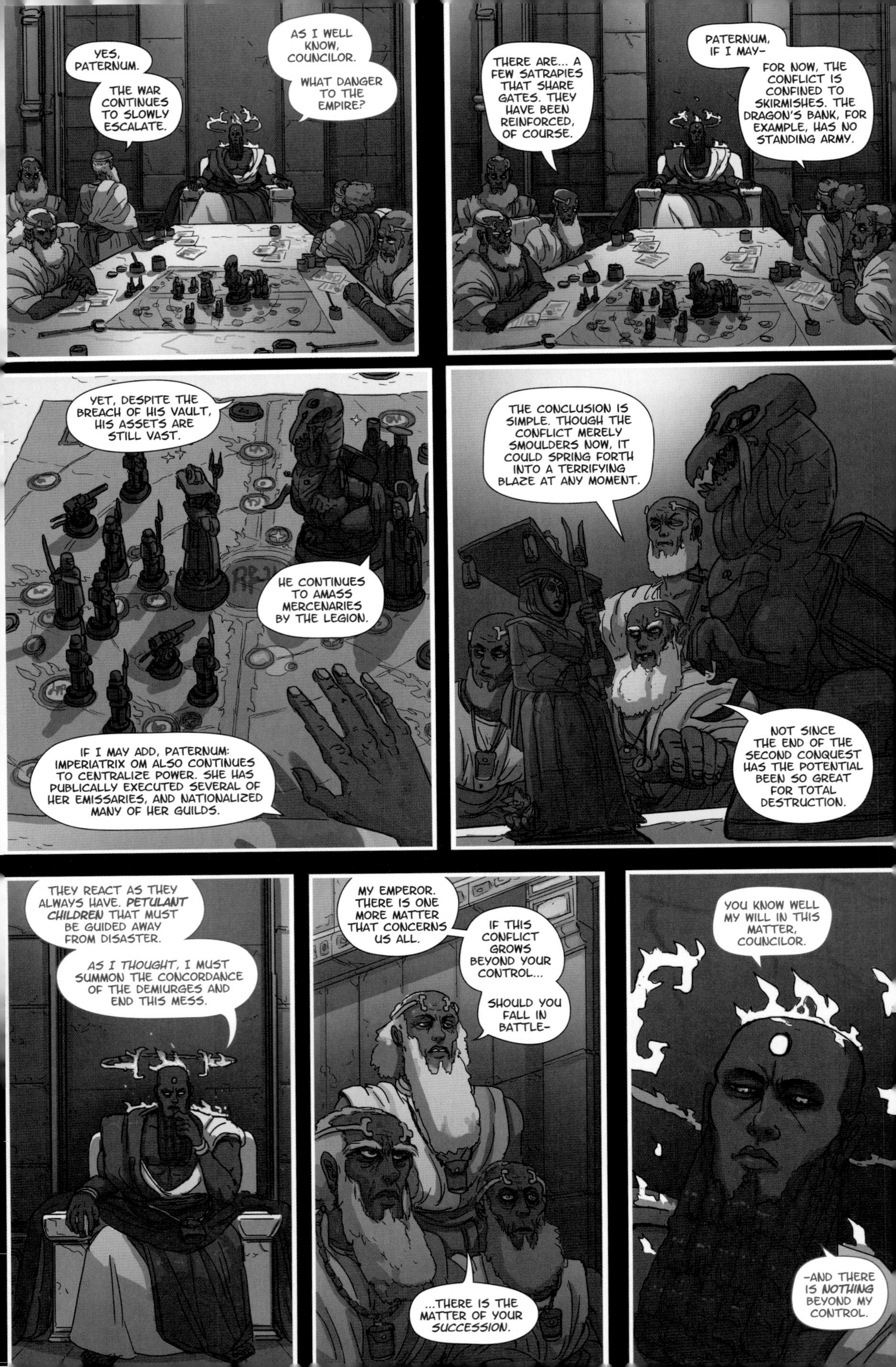
YES, PATERNUM.
THE WAR CONTINUES TO SLOWLY ESCALATE.
AS I WELL KNOW, COUNCILOR.
WHAT DANGER TO THE EMPIRE?
THERE ARE... A FEW SATRAPIES THAT SHARE GATES. THEY HAVE BEEN REINFORCED, OF COURSE.
PATERNUM, IF I MAY-
FOR NOW, THE CONFLICT IS CONFINED TO SKIRMISHES. THE DRAGON'S BANK, FOR EXAMPLE, HAS NO STANDING ARMY.
YET, DESPITE THE BREACH OF HIS VAULT, HIS ASSETS ARE STILL VAST.
HE CONTINUES TO AMASS MERCENARIES BY THE LEGION.
IF I MAY ADD, PATERNUM: IMPERIATRIX OM ALSO CONTINUES TO CENTRALIZE POWER. SHE HAS PUBLICALLY EXECUTED SEVERAL OF HER EMISSARIES, AND NATIONALIZED MANY OF HER GUILDS.
THE CONCLUSION IS SIMPLE. THOUGH THE CONFLICT MERELY SMOULDERS NOW, IT COULD SPRING FORTH INTO A TERRIFYING BLAZE AT ANY MOMENT.
NOT SINCE THE END OF THE SECOND CONQUEST HAS THE POTENTIAL BEEN SO GREAT FOR TOTAL DESTRUCTION.
THEY REACT AS THEY ALWAYS HAVE. *PETULANT CHILDREN* THAT MUST BE GUIDED AWAY FROM DISASTER.
AS I *THOUGHT*, I MUST SUMMON THE CONCORDANCE OF THE DEMIURGES AND END THIS MESS.
MY EMPEROR. THERE IS ONE MORE MATTER THAT CONCERNS US ALL.
IF THIS CONFLICT GROWS BEYOND YOUR CONTROL...
SHOULD YOU FALL IN BATTLE-
...THERE IS THE MATTER OF YOUR *SUCCESSION*.
YOU KNOW WELL MY WILL IN THIS MATTER, COUNCILOR.
-AND THERE IS *NOTHING* BEYOND MY CONTROL.

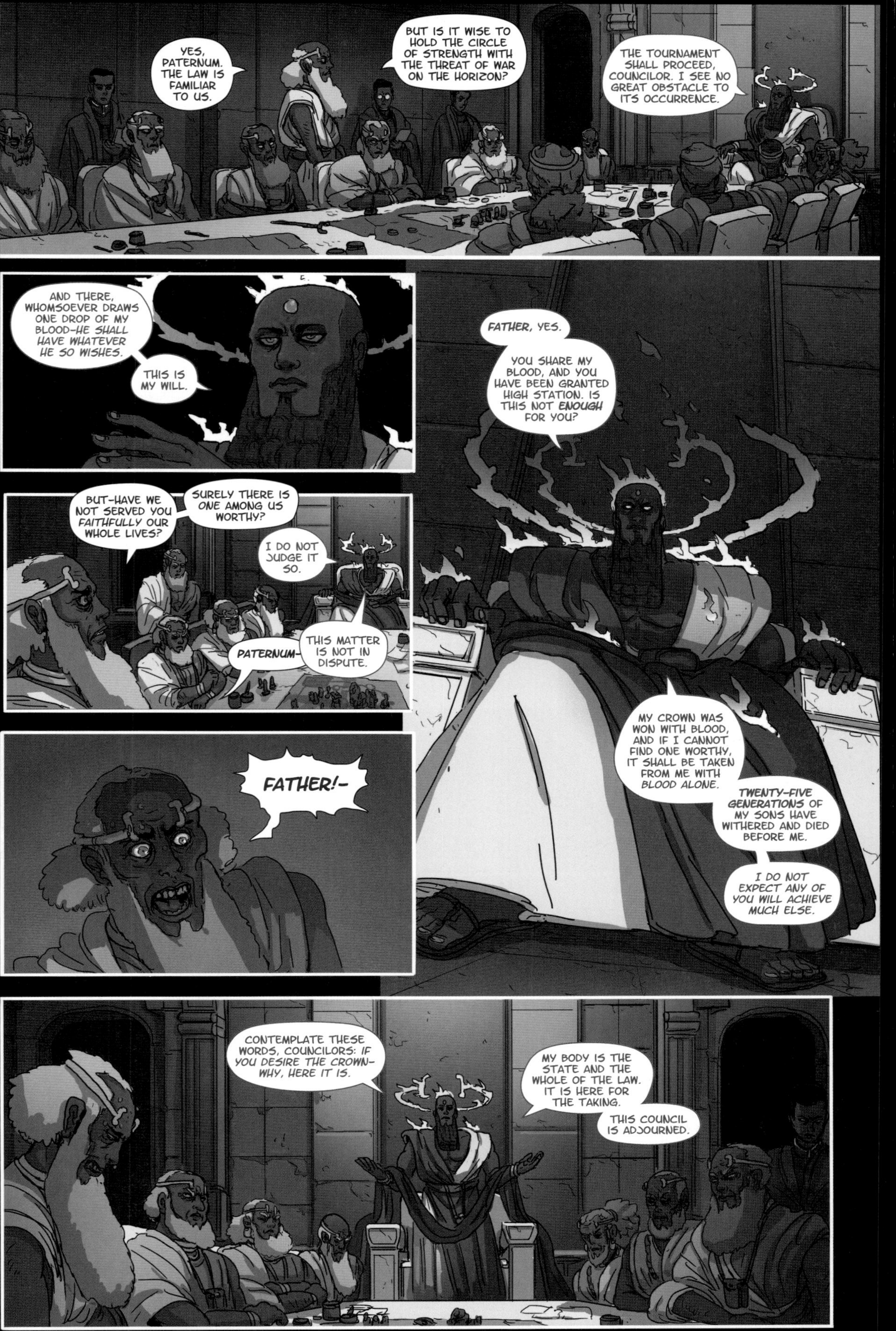
YES, PATERNUM. THE LAW IS FAMILIAR TO US.
BUT IS IT WISE TO HOLD THE CIRCLE OF STRENGTH WITH THE THREAT OF WAR ON THE HORIZON?
THE TOURNAMENT SHALL PROCEED, COUNCILOR. I SEE NO GREAT OBSTACLE TO ITS OCCURRENCE.
AND THERE, WHOMSOEVER DRAWS ONE DROP OF MY BLOOD—HE SHALL HAVE WHATEVER HE SO WISHES.
THIS IS MY WILL.
BUT—HAVE WE NOT SERVED YOU FAITHFULLY OUR WHOLE LIVES?
SURELY THERE IS ONE AMONG US WORTHY?
I DO NOT JUDGE IT SO.
PATERNUM—
THIS MATTER IS NOT IN DISPUTE.
FATHER!—
FATHER, YES.
YOU SHARE MY BLOOD, AND YOU HAVE BEEN GRANTED HIGH STATION. IS THIS NOT ENOUGH FOR YOU?
MY CROWN WAS WON WITH BLOOD, AND IF I CANNOT FIND ONE WORTHY, IT SHALL BE TAKEN FROM ME WITH BLOOD ALONE.
TWENTY-FIVE GENERATIONS OF MY SONS HAVE WITHERED AND DIED BEFORE ME.
I DO NOT EXPECT ANY OF YOU WILL ACHIEVE MUCH ELSE.
CONTEMPLATE THESE WORDS, COUNCILORS: IF YOU DESIRE THE CROWN—WHY, HERE IT IS.
MY BODY IS THE STATE AND THE WHOLE OF THE LAW. IT IS HERE FOR THE TAKING.
THIS COUNCIL IS ADJOURNED.

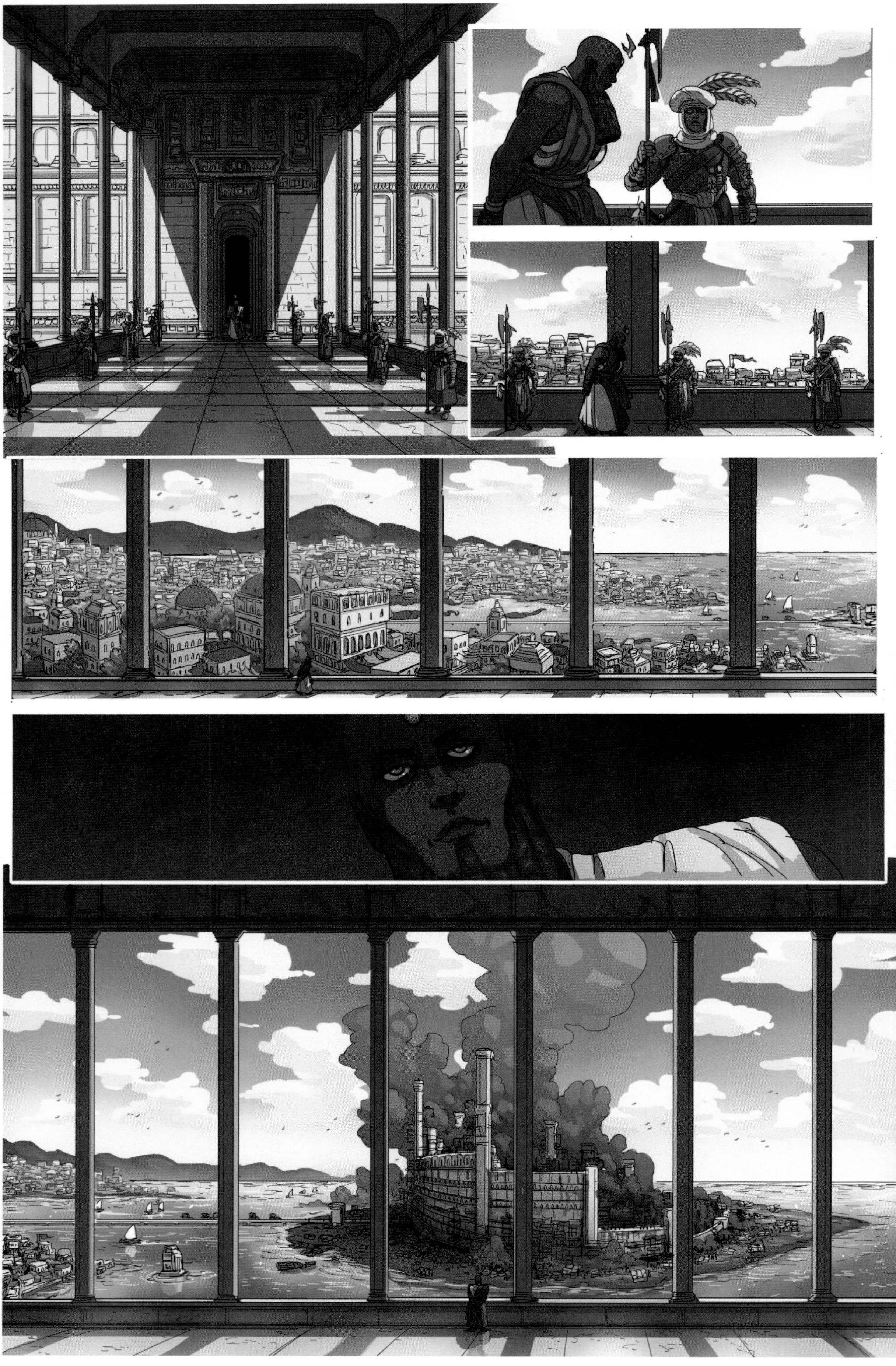

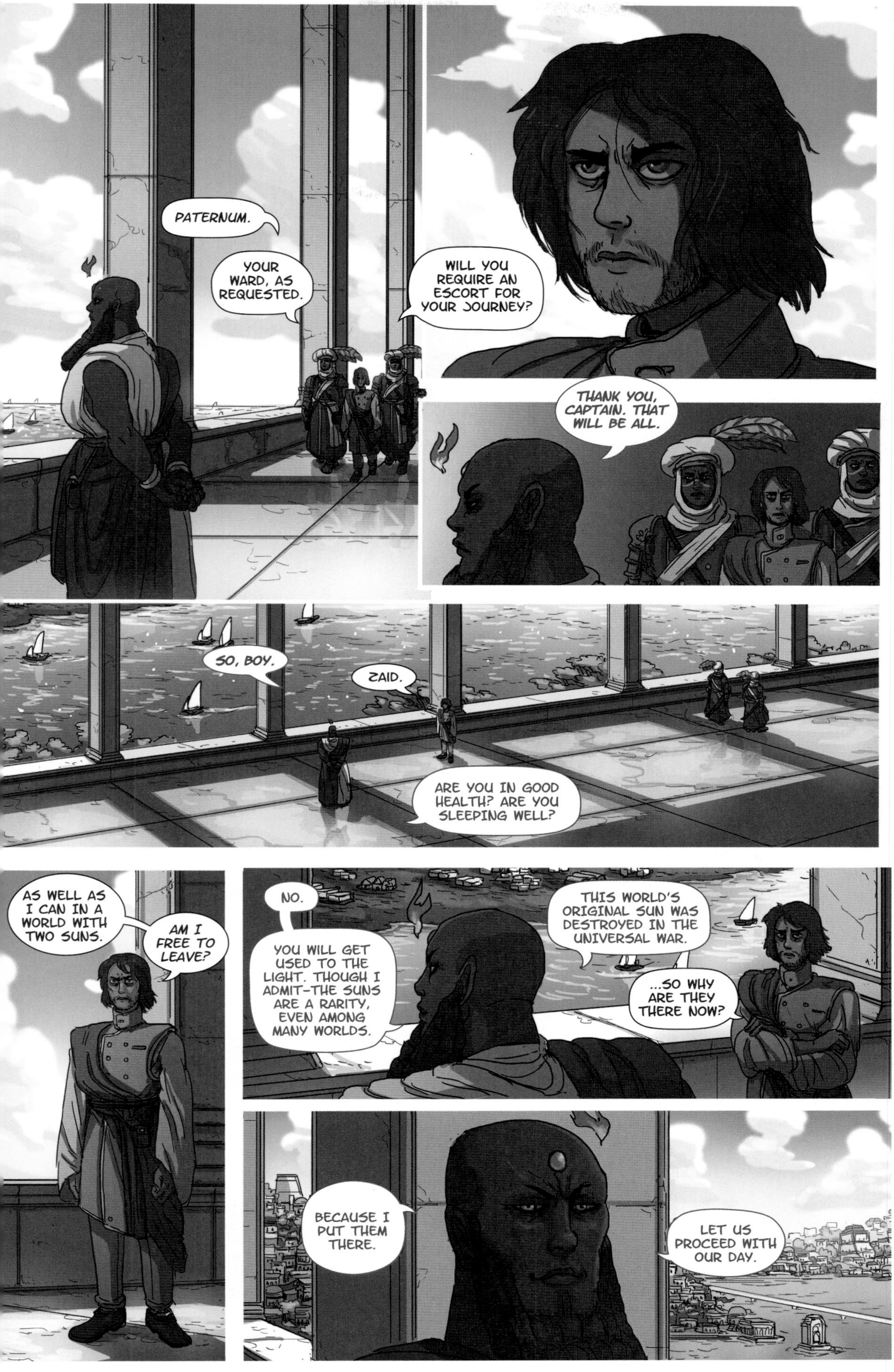
PATERNUM.
YOUR WARD, AS REQUESTED.
WILL YOU REQUIRE AN ESCORT FOR YOUR JOURNEY?
THANK YOU, CAPTAIN. THAT WILL BE ALL.
SO, BOY.
ZAID.
ARE YOU IN GOOD HEALTH? ARE YOU SLEEPING WELL?
AS WELL AS I CAN IN A WORLD WITH TWO SUNS.
AM I FREE TO LEAVE?
NO.
YOU WILL GET USED TO THE LIGHT. THOUGH I ADMIT–THE SUNS ARE A RARITY, EVEN AMONG MANY WORLDS.
THIS WORLD'S ORIGINAL SUN WAS DESTROYED IN THE UNIVERSAL WAR.
...SO WHY ARE THEY THERE NOW?
BECAUSE I PUT THEM THERE.
LET US PROCEED WITH OUR DAY.

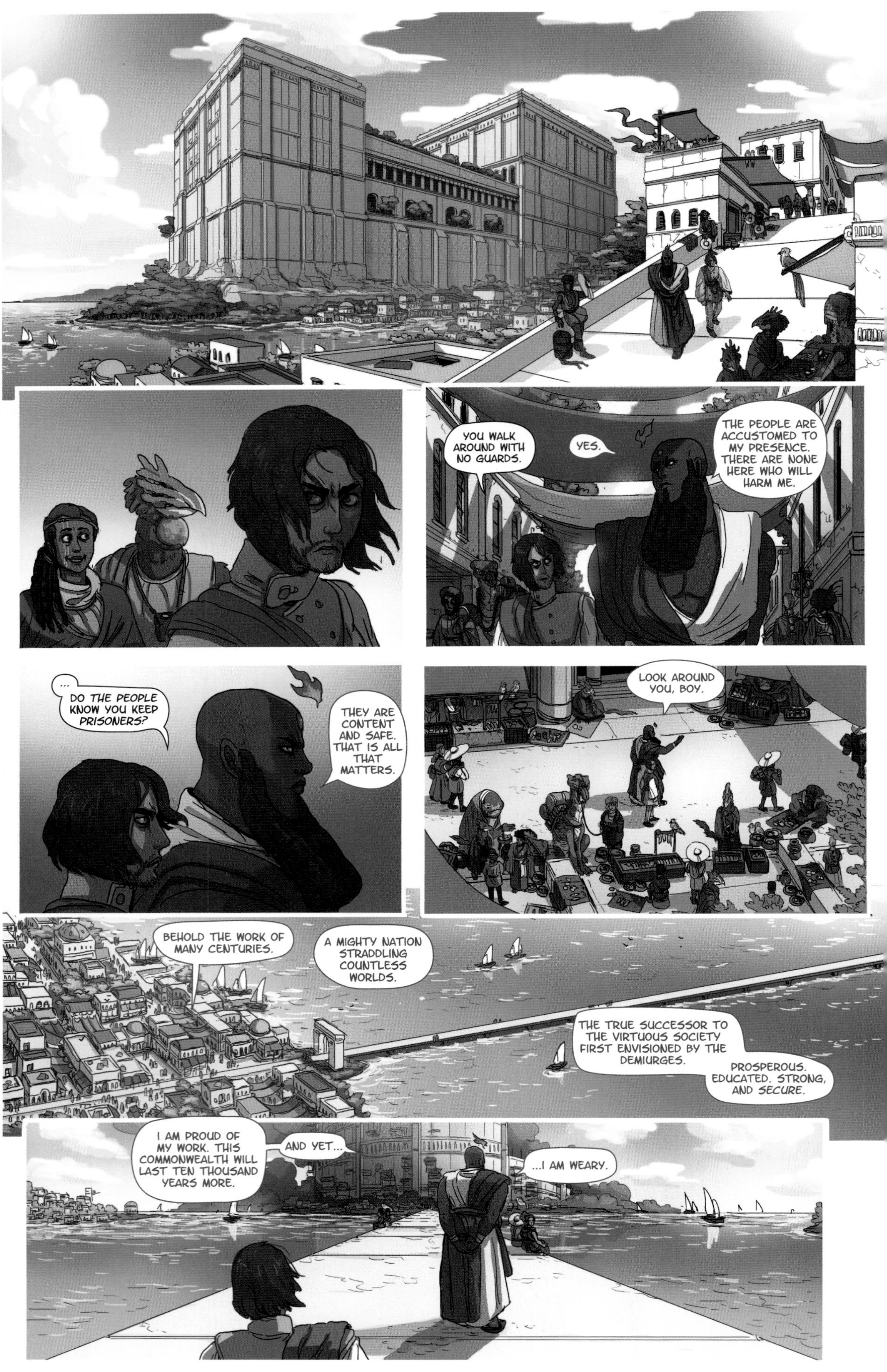
YOU WALK AROUND WITH NO GUARDS.
YES.
THE PEOPLE ARE ACCUSTOMED TO MY PRESENCE. THERE ARE NONE HERE WHO WILL HARM ME.
... DO THE PEOPLE KNOW YOU KEEP *PRISONERS?*
THEY ARE CONTENT AND SAFE. THAT IS ALL THAT MATTERS.
LOOK AROUND YOU, BOY.
BEHOLD THE WORK OF MANY CENTURIES.
A MIGHTY NATION STRADDLING COUNTLESS WORLDS.
THE TRUE SUCCESSOR TO THE VIRTUOUS SOCIETY FIRST ENVISIONED BY THE DEMIURGES.
PROSPEROUS. EDUCATED. STRONG, AND *SECURE.*
I AM PROUD OF MY WORK. THIS COMMONWEALTH WILL LAST TEN THOUSAND YEARS MORE.
AND YET...
...I AM WEARY.

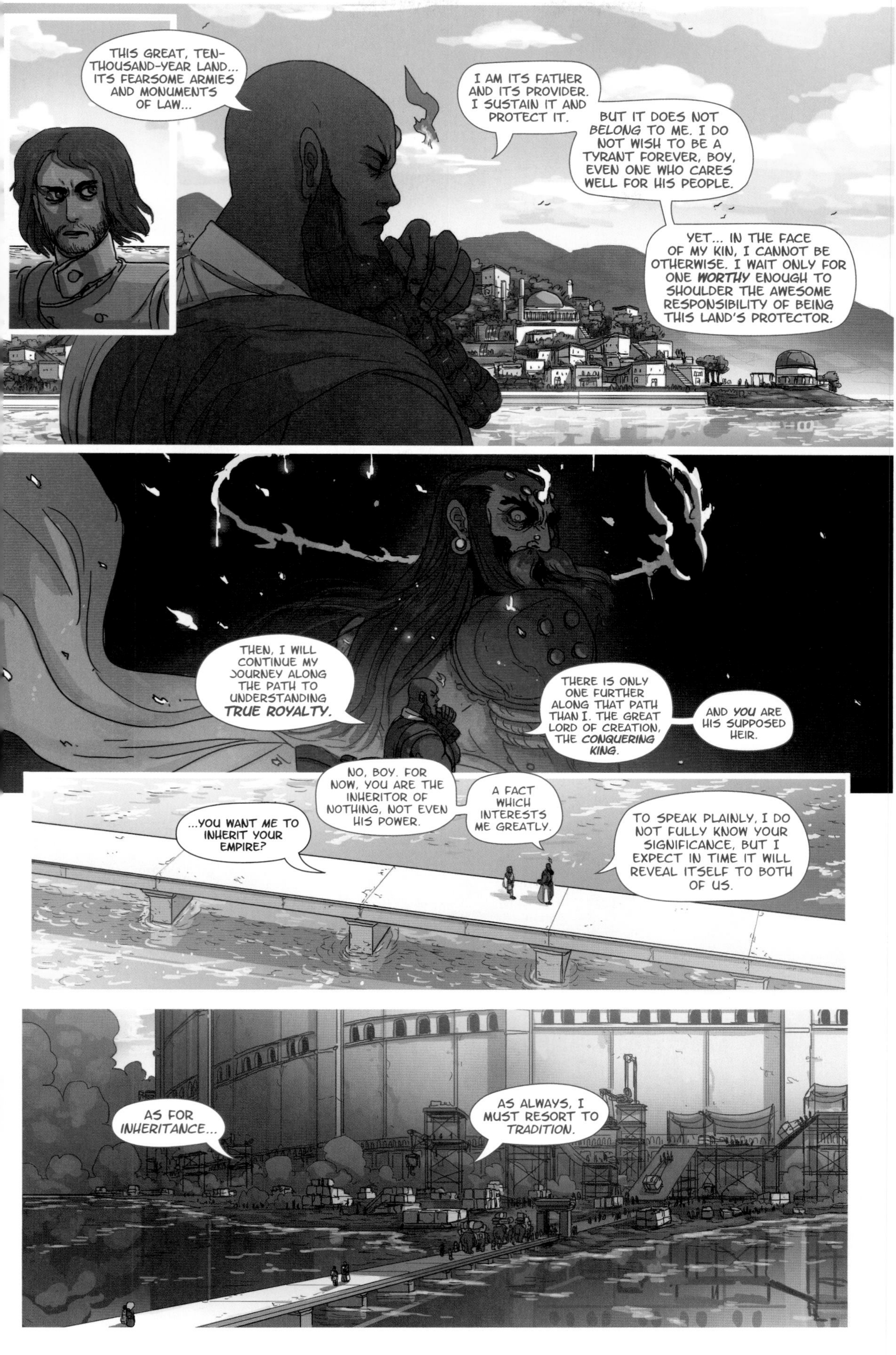

THIS GREAT, TEN-THOUSAND-YEAR LAND... ITS FEARSOME ARMIES AND MONUMENTS OF LAW...
I AM ITS FATHER AND ITS PROVIDER. I SUSTAIN IT AND PROTECT IT.
BUT IT DOES NOT *BELONG* TO ME. I DO NOT WISH TO BE A TYRANT FOREVER, BOY, EVEN ONE WHO CARES WELL FOR HIS PEOPLE.
YET... IN THE FACE OF MY KIN, I CANNOT BE OTHERWISE. I WAIT ONLY FOR ONE ***WORTHY*** ENOUGH TO SHOULDER THE AWESOME RESPONSIBILITY OF BEING THIS LAND'S PROTECTOR.
THEN, I WILL CONTINUE MY JOURNEY ALONG THE PATH TO UNDERSTANDING ***TRUE ROYALTY.***
THERE IS ONLY ONE FURTHER ALONG THAT PATH THAN I. THE GREAT LORD OF CREATION, THE ***CONQUERING KING***.
AND ***YOU*** ARE HIS SUPPOSED HEIR.
NO, BOY. FOR NOW, YOU ARE THE INHERITOR OF NOTHING, NOT EVEN HIS POWER.
A FACT WHICH INTERESTS ME GREATLY.
...YOU WANT ME TO INHERIT YOUR EMPIRE?
TO SPEAK PLAINLY, I DO NOT FULLY KNOW YOUR SIGNIFICANCE, BUT I EXPECT IN TIME IT WILL REVEAL ITSELF TO BOTH OF US.
AS FOR *INHERITANCE*...
AS ALWAYS, I MUST RESORT TO *TRADITION*.

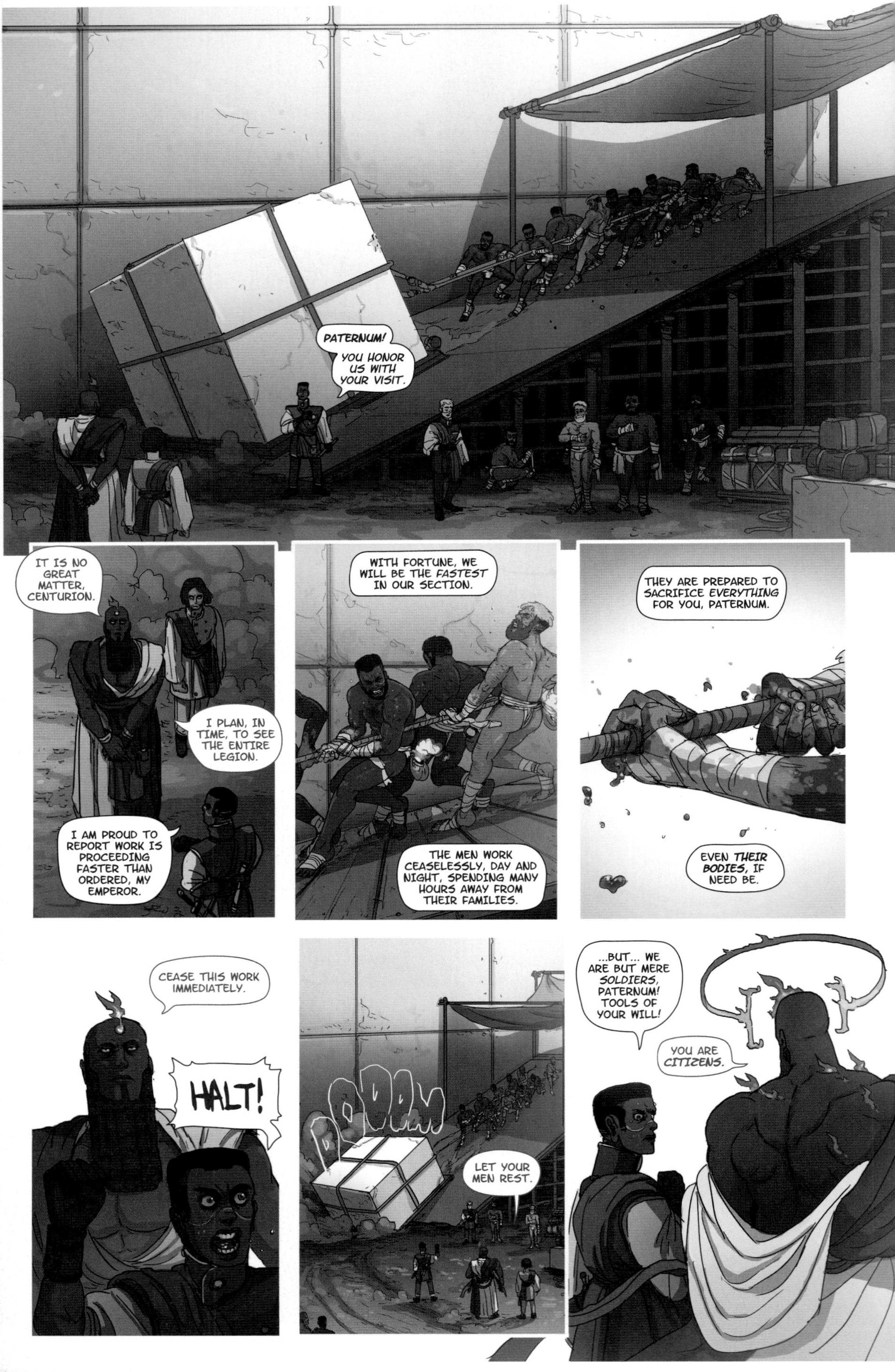
PATERNUM!
YOU HONOR US WITH YOUR VISIT.
IT IS NO GREAT MATTER, CENTURION.
I PLAN, IN TIME, TO SEE THE ENTIRE LEGION.
I AM PROUD TO REPORT WORK IS PROCEEDING FASTER THAN ORDERED, MY EMPEROR.
WITH FORTUNE, WE WILL BE THE FASTEST IN OUR SECTION.
THE MEN WORK CEASELESSLY, DAY AND NIGHT, SPENDING MANY HOURS AWAY FROM THEIR FAMILIES.
THEY ARE PREPARED TO SACRIFICE EVERYTHING FOR YOU, PATERNUM.
EVEN THEIR BODIES, IF NEED BE.
CEASE THIS WORK IMMEDIATELY.
HALT!
BOOOM
LET YOUR MEN REST.
...BUT... WE ARE BUT MERE SOLDIERS, PATERNUM! TOOLS OF YOUR WILL!
YOU ARE CITIZENS.

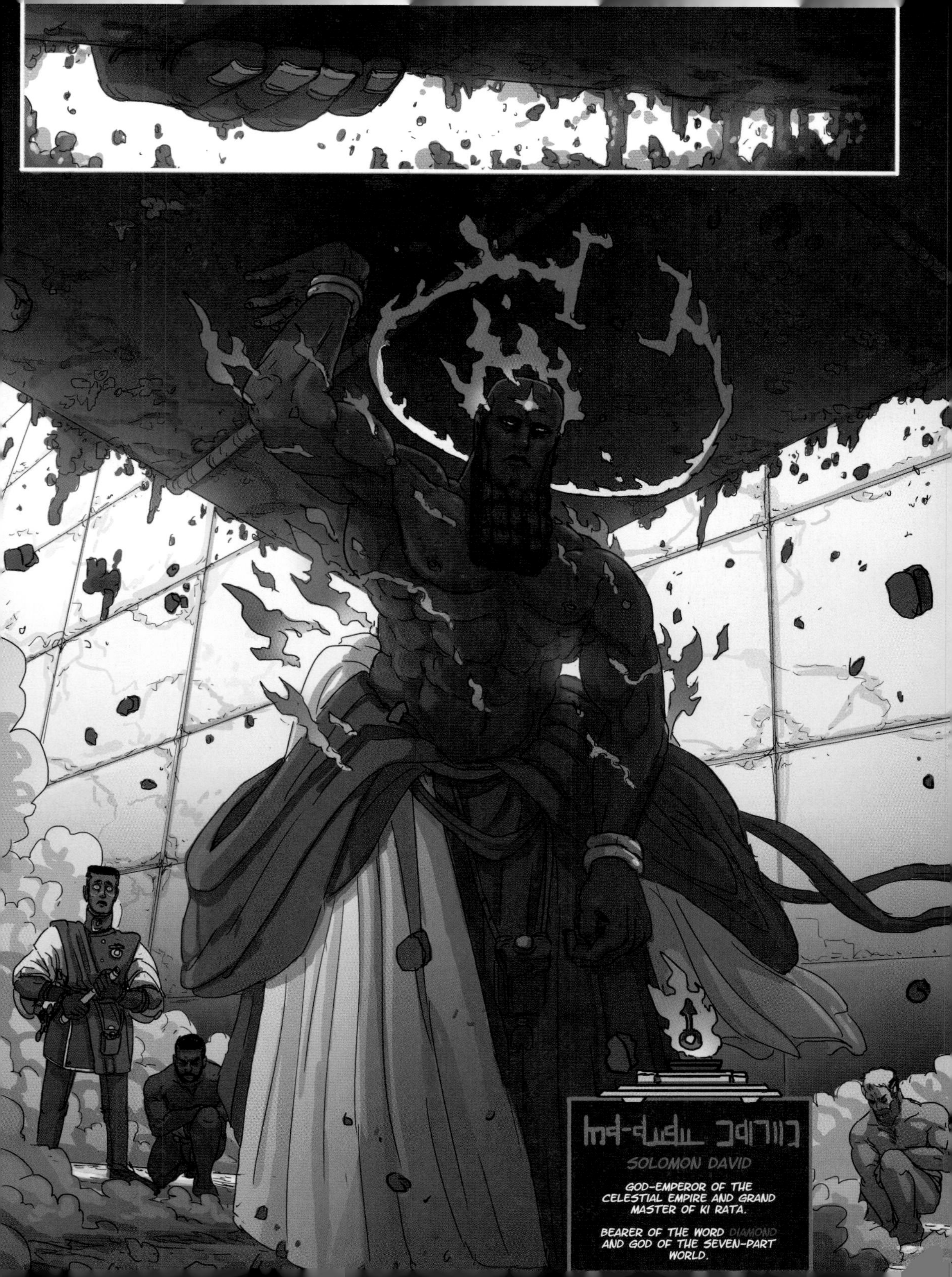
SOLOMON DAVID
GOD-EMPEROR OF THE CELESTIAL EMPIRE AND GRAND MASTER OF KI RATA.
BEARER OF THE WORD DIAMOND AND GOD OF THE SEVEN-PART WORLD.

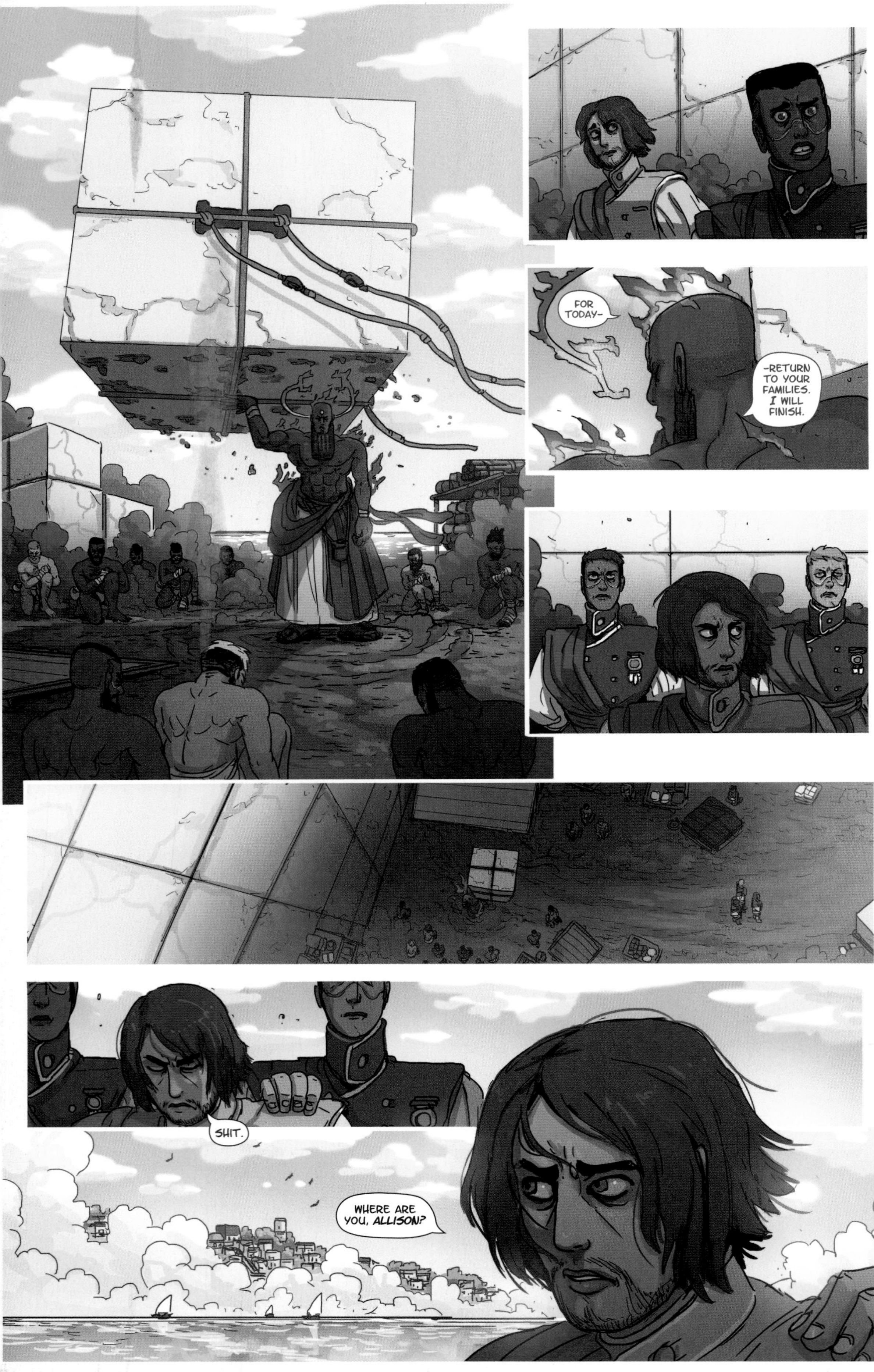
FOR TODAY-
-RETURN TO YOUR FAMILIES. I WILL FINISH.
SHIT.
WHERE ARE YOU, ALLISON?

I.

IN THE DAYS when the King's Road was scarred with the tramping of soldier's boots and littered with the detritus they left behind, there was Het, who was a watchman. Het was very tall and straight, and she had arms like sinewy boughs. She was very good with a staff but very poor with a straight sword, which drew her constant disapproving looks from the Sergeant, since the staff was a peasant's weapon, and not befitting a proper executioner of the Old Law.

The Sergeant's name was Ramys, but that is neither here nor there, for he was a proper Sergeant. He was very calm, and very handsome, and he had a flawless Watchman's Eye – that's why he was promoted. Het pined for him piteously but in vain, for it was astounding how completely dry he was of anything that could possibly resemble love. He took his morning tea bitter, he sat rod-straight, and his nails were exceptionally clean. He was an excellent policeman.

Het and the Sergeant traveled together with a third person, who was very uninteresting. He was the Centurion, and he was a blunt instrument that had been hammered into the shape of a person. He had a neck the size of a tree trunk, and about as knotted. He loved his sword, and the shape of his sword, and most of all, he loved to use it. He was masterful at killing with the sword, which made him a very poor swordsman.

So it was that Het, the Sergeant, and the Centurion were summoned to kill a demon, for that was the job of watchmen in those days. The demon was a Rakshasa, which was a special kind that crawled down a person's throat or nostrils when he was sleeping and filled him up with bile. Since it

wore a person about it like a skin, it was exceptionally hard to find and root out. It fed on blood, stole milk, and abhorred the sound of lying. This was known to Het, who was studious, and the Sergeant, who was very intelligent, but not the Centurion, who cared only about swords.

The Road was on fire with war most of those days, so their travel was exceptionally slow, and the Sergeant kept them to the back paths. It was no place for men of the Law, for the Law had abandoned heaven. So it was a full six turns before Het, the Sergeant, and the Centurion reached their destination.

When they arrived, they saw at once that the Rakshasa had been exceptionally cunning. For this was a land of mires and muck, a low, sulfurous land where people eked out their living in filth. So covered head to toe were they that everyone looked almost exactly alike. Passing her gaze from person to person, Het could scarcely tell the young from the old, the man from the woman, or anyone at all, and she shivered, for she was exceptionally clean, as all watchmen were. Watchmen were men of class and stature in those days. They wore shiny boots and spotless uniforms with gleaming buttons.

They were met by the lord of that place, who lived in a palace built on a promontory rising out of the muck (the only promontory around, in fact). The lord was exceptionally beautiful, and had perfect nails, just like the Sergeant. He was borne aloft by four servants who sweated and heaved his palanquin far above the filth below, even though they themselves were often buried up to the waist. It was necessary, in those days.

The lord expounded to them at length about the trouble he was in. "Oh please," he said, fanning himself with great consternation, "Do something about this filthy Rakshasa! Why, just the other day, it broke into the palace and left a terrible mess. A flock of my prized doves were all torn apart, and its muddy footprints were everywhere!"

"You've not to worry," said the Sergeant, with the utmost confidence, "I rarely fail in my quest to root out evil. We'll smash your Rakshasa within the week, in the name of the Old Law and the fourth name of God." Het could attest to the Sergeant's efficiency, and gave her firm affirmation.

The Sergeant, indeed, seemed to have a terrifyingly strong sense for evil, a preternatural ability to sniff out even the tiniest bit of its stench clinging to a person. This was his Watchman's Eye. It was a fine instrument of justice, and a great source of admiration for Het, who still thought herself a rough-spun peasant girl in braids. In fact, she was a head taller than the Sergeant, and twice as brawny, but that's a tale for later. For now, she saw the Sergeant's perfect fingernails, and his handsome mustaches, and his dramatic brow, and felt a strong swell of pride and longing.

The lord was very happy. He promised to give them proper accommodations at his high palace and a bath every day to clean them from the muck of the land and keep them in proper watchmen shape, as long as they returned by the time the gates closed.

AND SO IT WAS THAT **HET,** THE **SERGEANT,** AND THE **CENTURION** SET ABOUT THE LAND ON THE FIRST DAY, LOOKING FOR **THE RAKSHASA.**

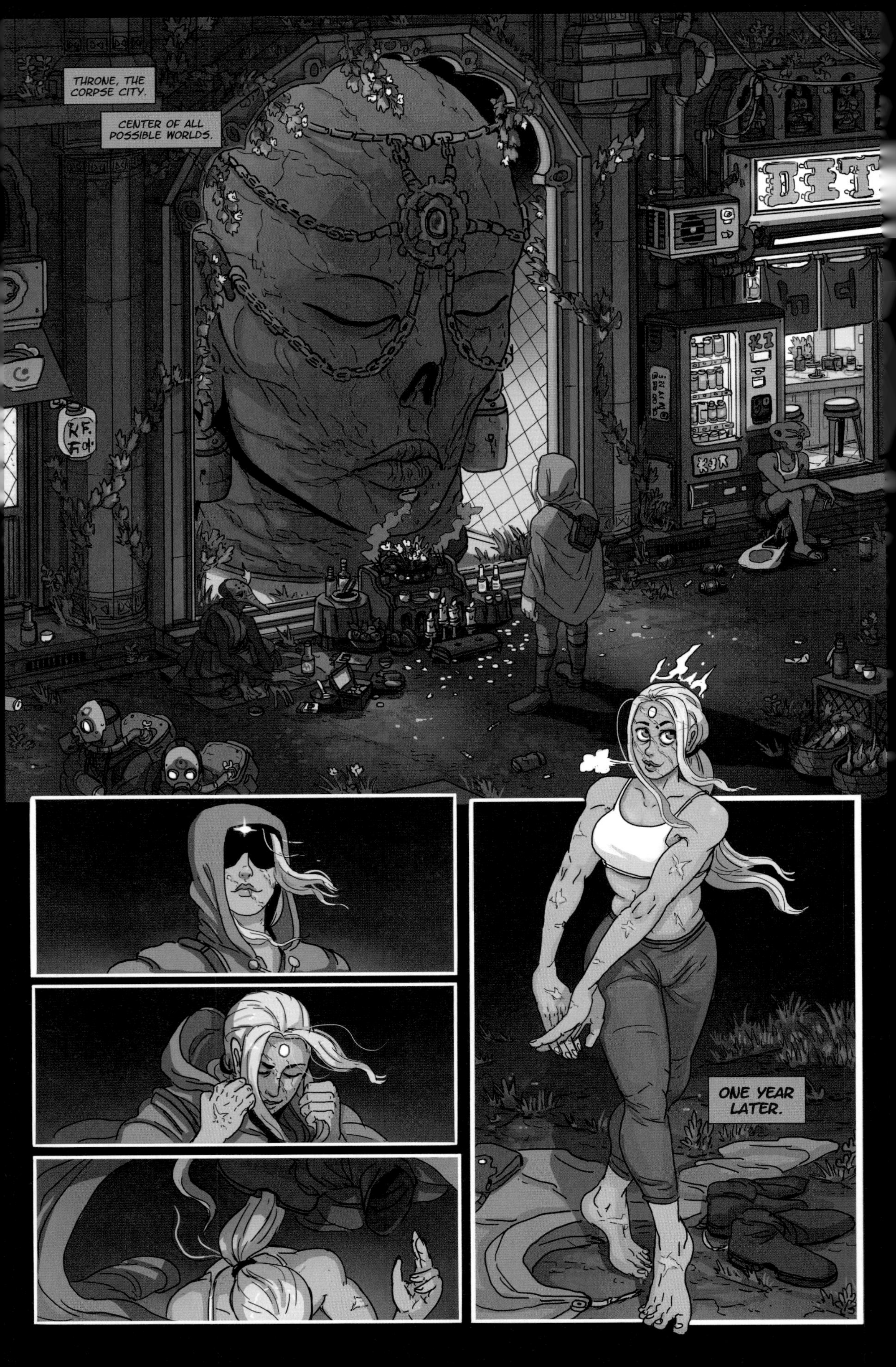
THRONE, THE CORPSE CITY.
CENTER OF ALL POSSIBLE WORLDS.
ONE YEAR LATER.

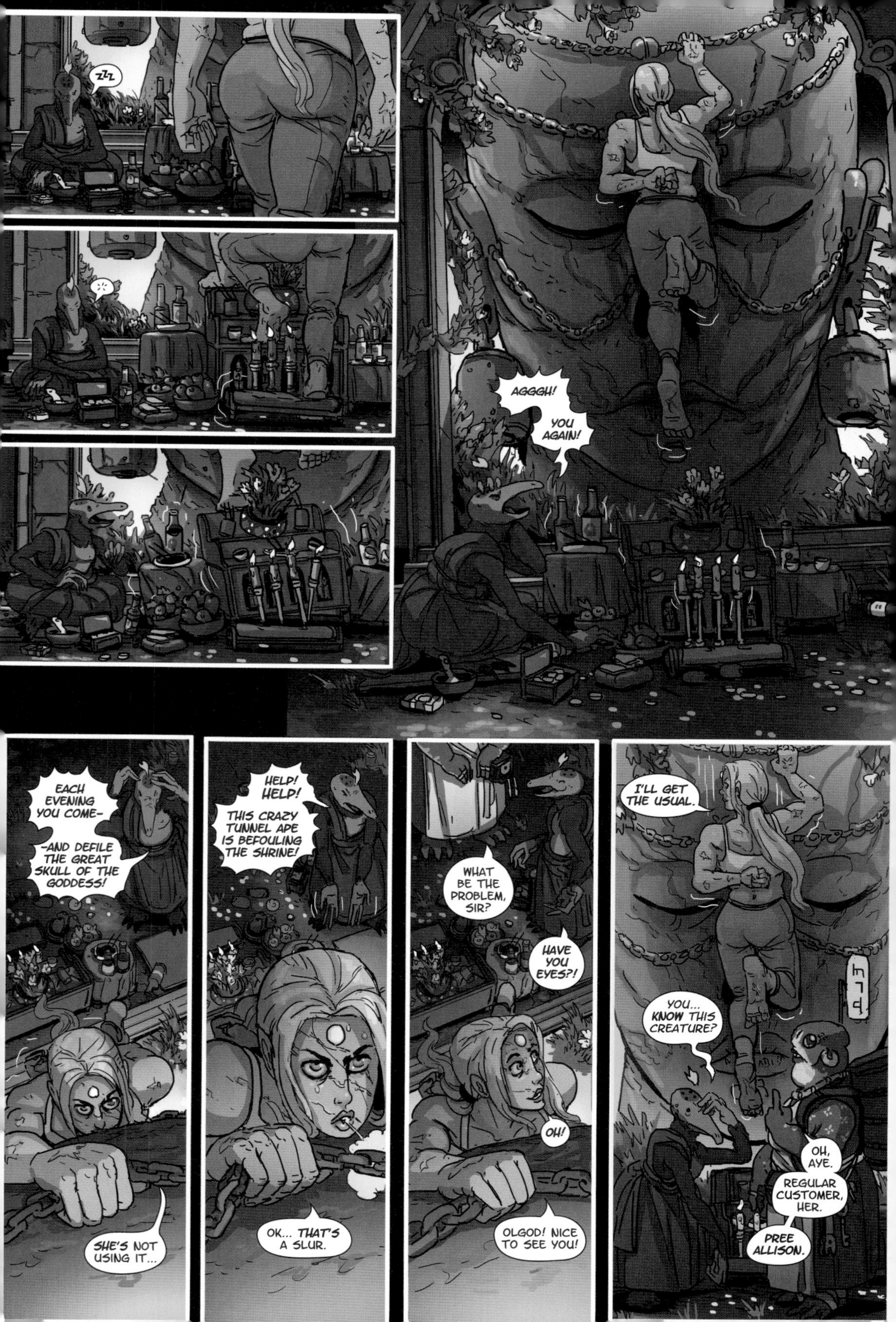
ZZZ
AGGGH!
YOU AGAIN!
EACH EVENING YOU COME-
-AND DEFILE THE GREAT SKULL OF THE GODDESS!
SHE'S NOT USING IT...
HELP! HELP!
THIS CRAZY TUNNEL APE IS BEFOULING THE SHRINE!
OK... THAT'S A SLUR.
WHAT BE THE PROBLEM, SIR?
HAVE YOU EYES?!
OH!
OLGOD! NICE TO SEE YOU!
I'LL GET THE USUAL.
YOU... KNOW THIS CREATURE?
OH, AYE.
REGULAR CUSTOMER, HER.
PREE ALLISON.

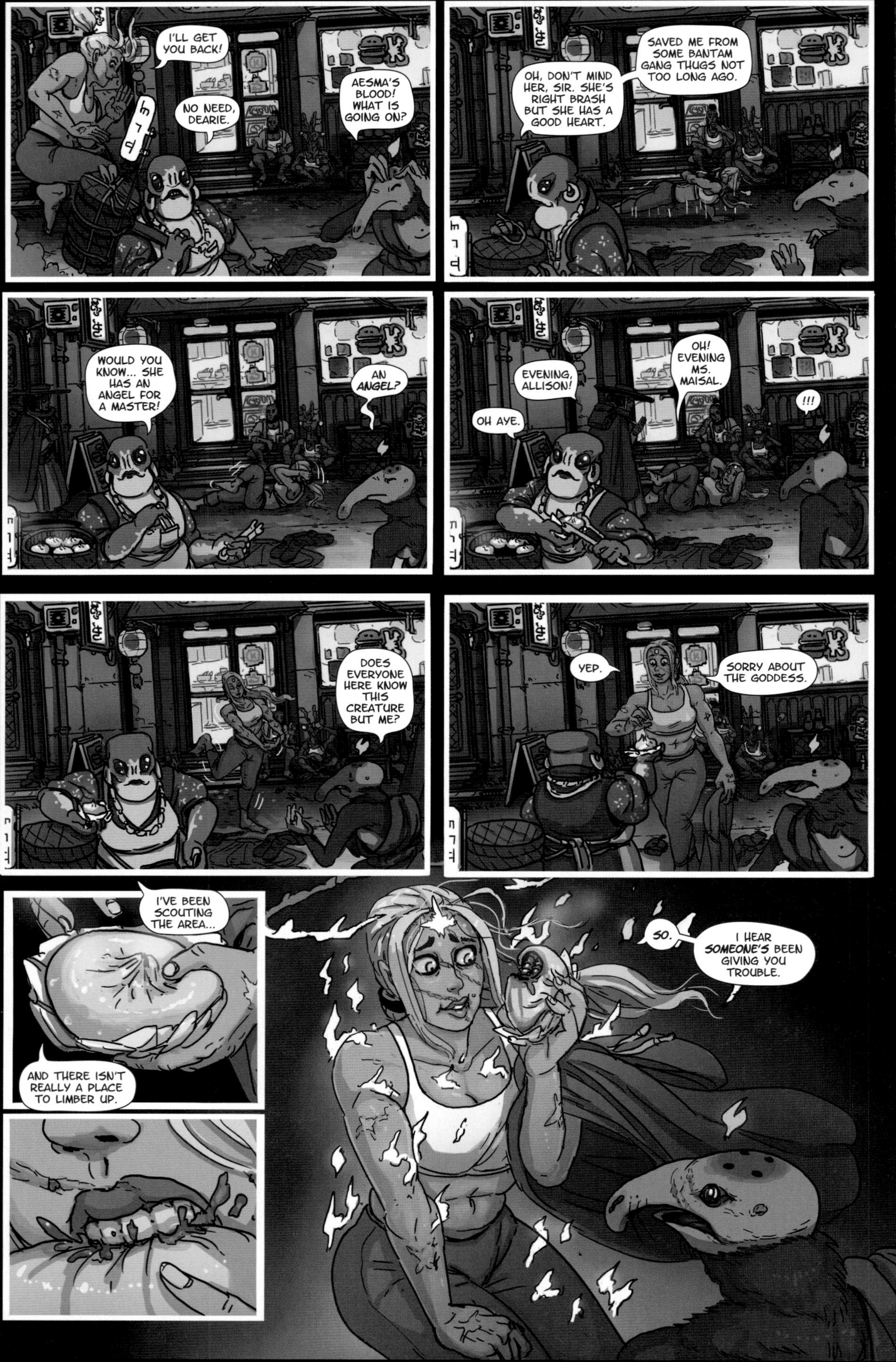

I'LL GET YOU BACK!
NO NEED, DEARIE.
AESMA'S BLOOD! WHAT IS GOING ON?
OH, DON'T MIND HER, SIR. SHE'S RIGHT BRASH BUT SHE HAS A GOOD HEART.
SAVED ME FROM SOME BANTAM GANG THUGS NOT TOO LONG AGO.
WOULD YOU KNOW... SHE HAS AN ANGEL FOR A MASTER!
AN ANGEL?
EVENING, ALLISON!
OH AYE.
OH! EVENING MS. MAISAL.
!!!
DOES EVERYONE HERE KNOW THIS CREATURE BUT ME?
YEP.
SORRY ABOUT THE GODDESS.
I'VE BEEN SCOUTING THE AREA...
AND THERE ISN'T REALLY A PLACE TO LIMBER UP.
SO.
I HEAR SOMEONE'S BEEN GIVING YOU TROUBLE.

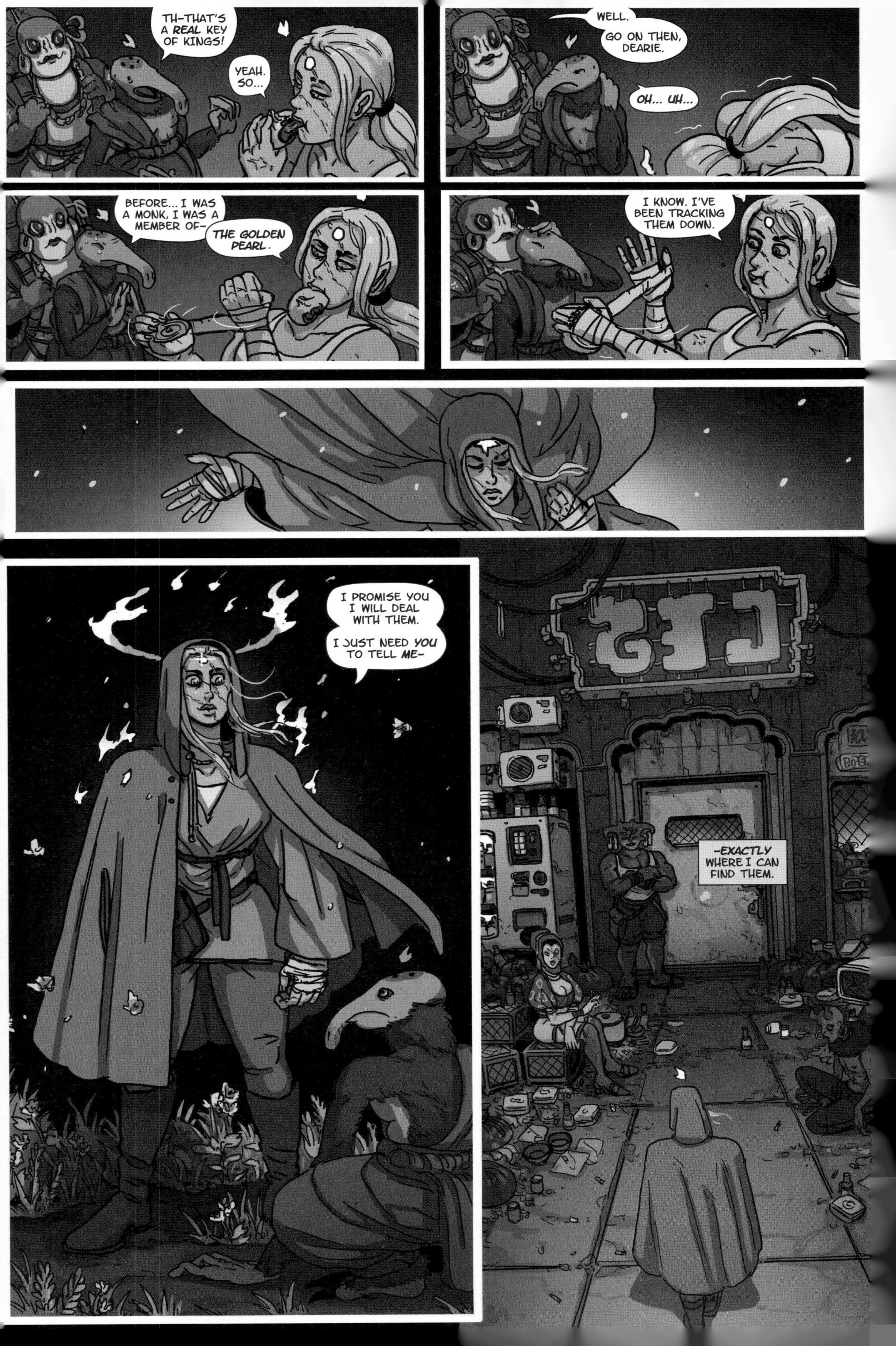
TH-THAT'S A REAL KEY OF KINGS!
YEAH. SO...
WELL.
GO ON THEN, DEARIE.
OH... UH...
BEFORE... I WAS A MONK, I WAS A MEMBER OF-
THE GOLDEN PEARL.
I KNOW. I'VE BEEN TRACKING THEM DOWN.
I PROMISE YOU I WILL DEAL WITH THEM.
I JUST NEED YOU TO TELL ME-
-EXACTLY WHERE I CAN FIND THEM.

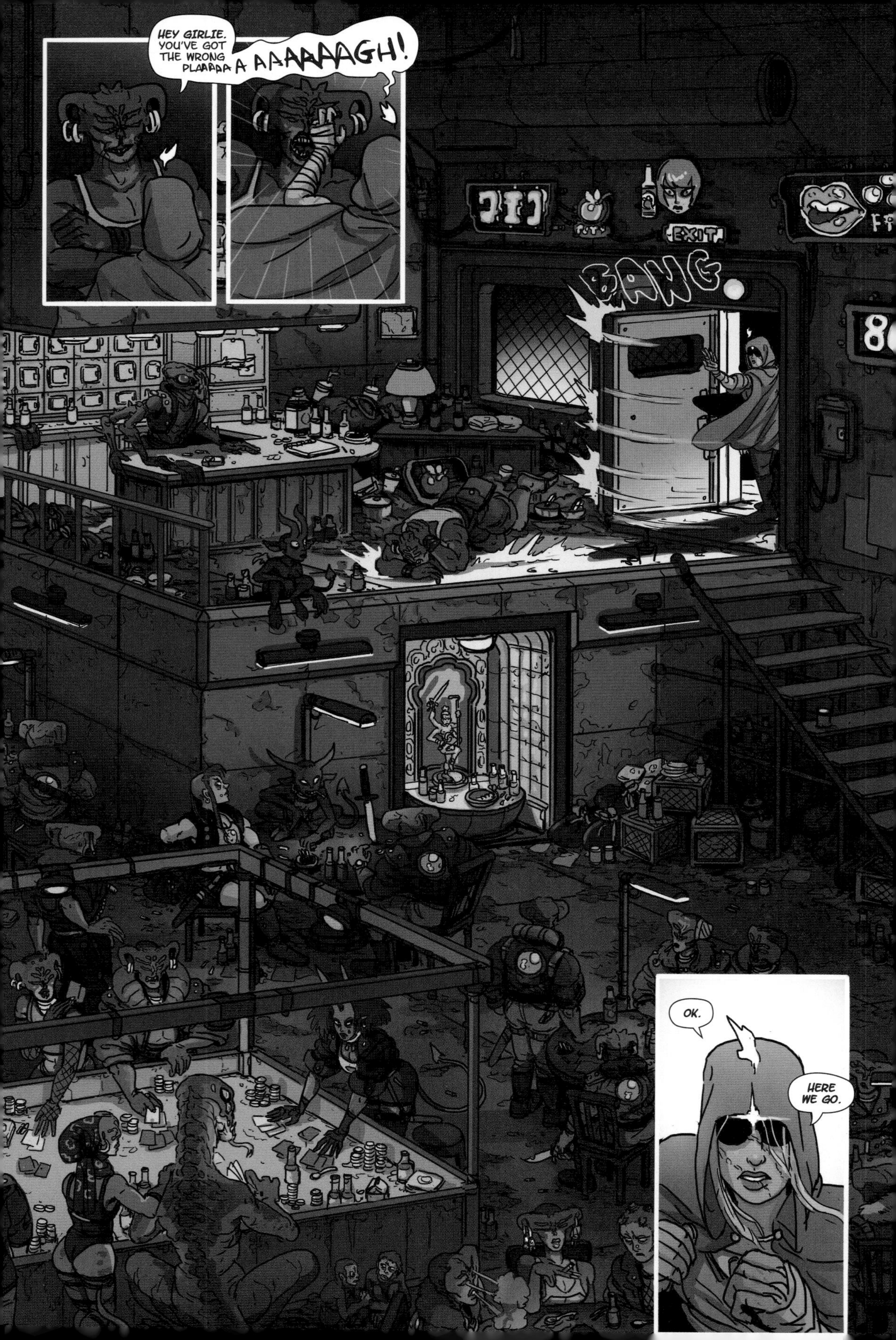
HEY GIRLIE. YOU'VE GOT THE WRONG PLAAAAA A AAARRAAGH!
EXIT
BANG
OK.
HERE WE GO.

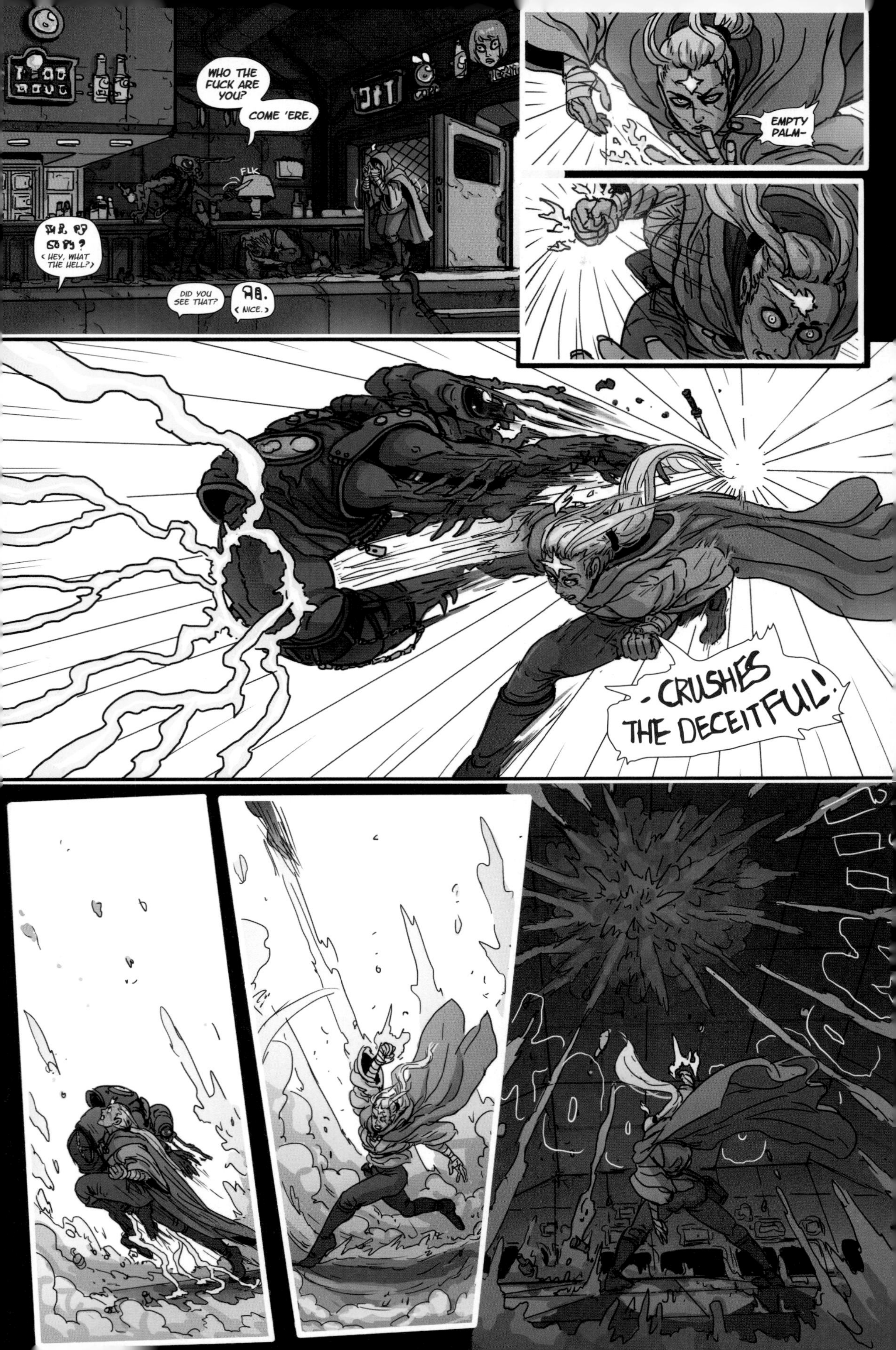

WHO THE FUCK ARE YOU?
COME 'ERE.
FLK
< HEY, WHAT THE HELL? >
DID YOU SEE THAT?
< NICE. >
EMPTY PALM-
-CRUSHES THE DECEITFUL!

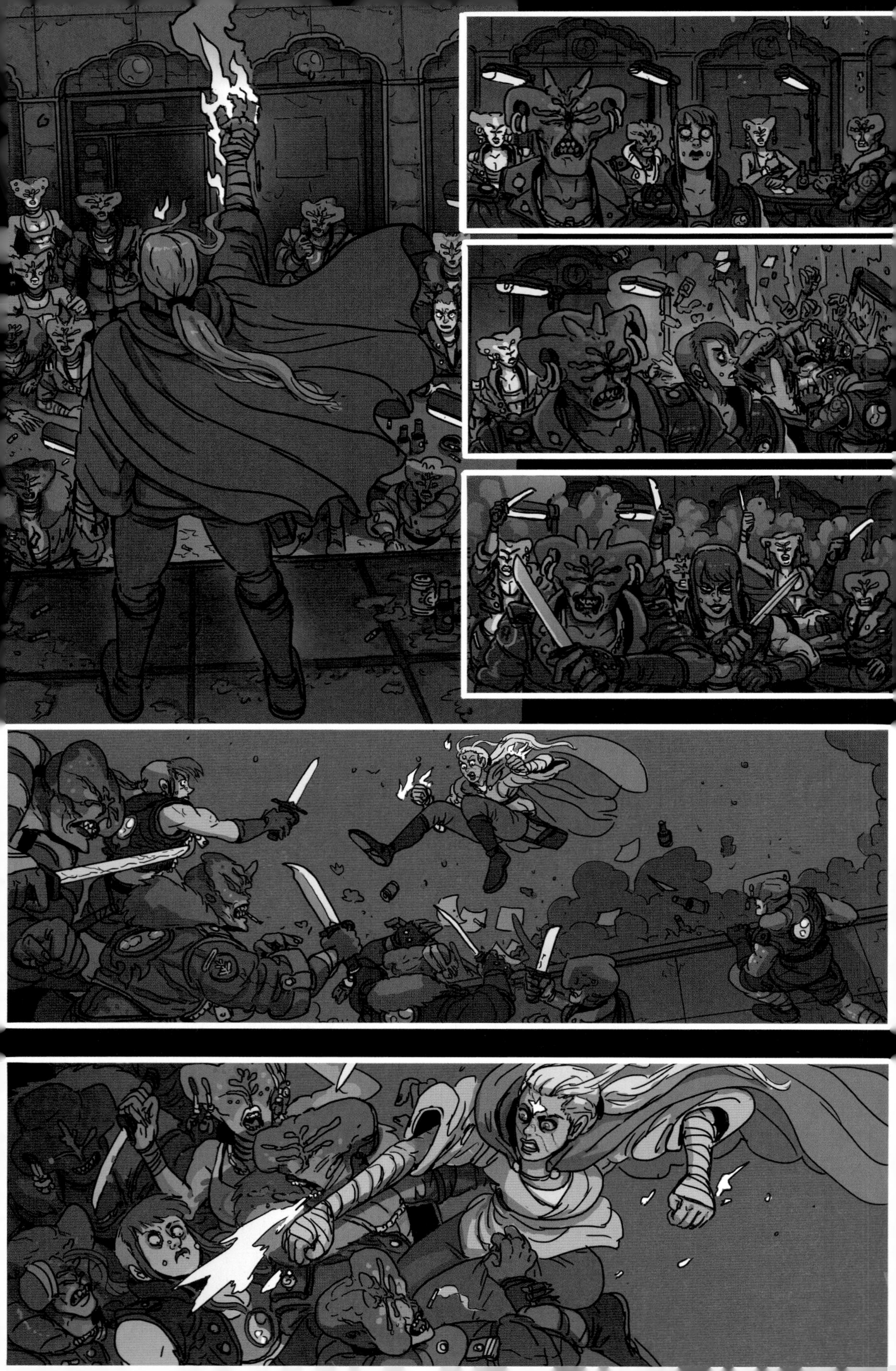

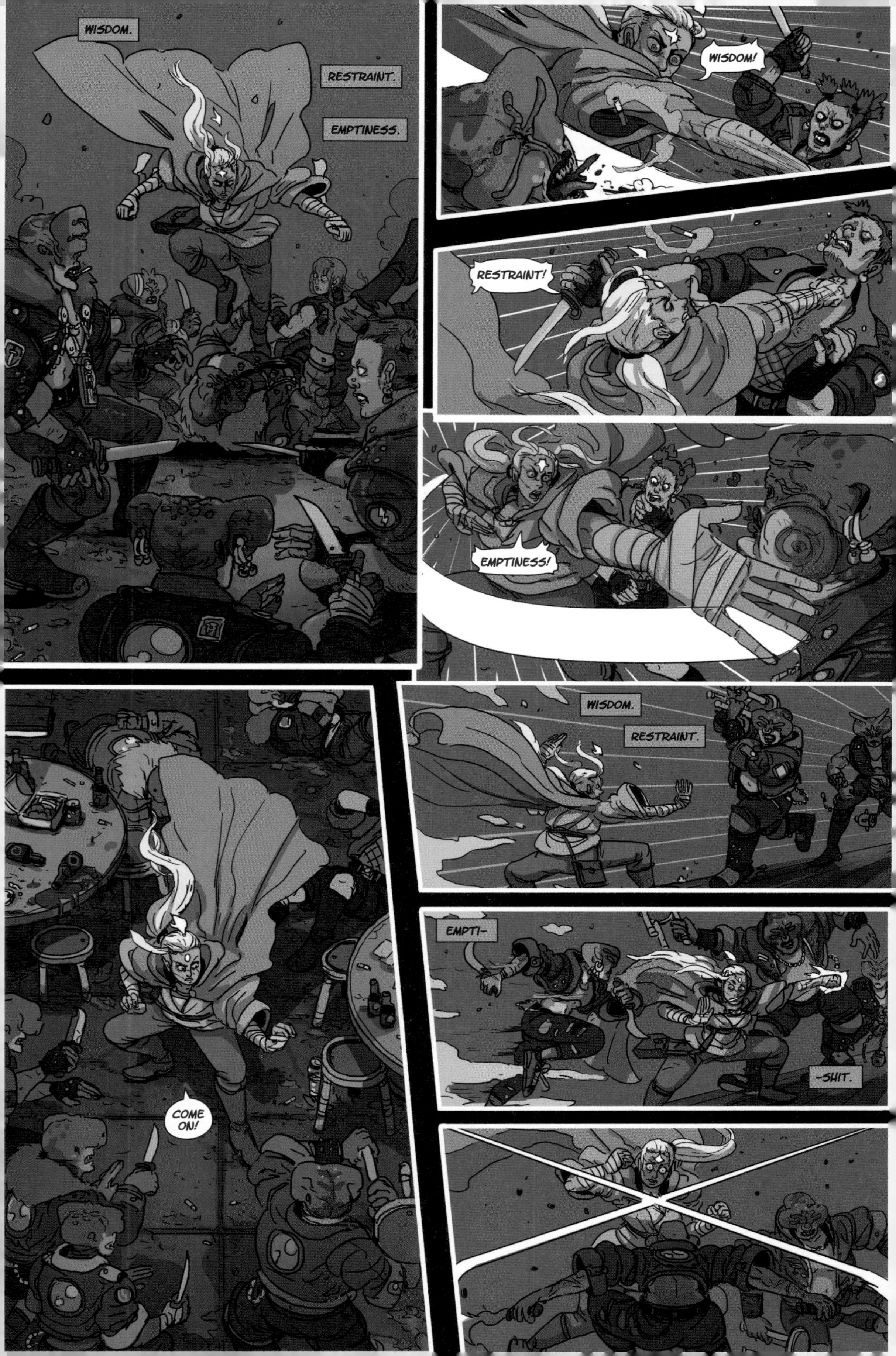
WISDOM.
RESTRAINT.
EMPTINESS.
WISDOM!
RESTRAINT!
EMPTINESS!
COME ON!
WISDOM.
RESTRAINT.
EMPTI-
-SHIT.

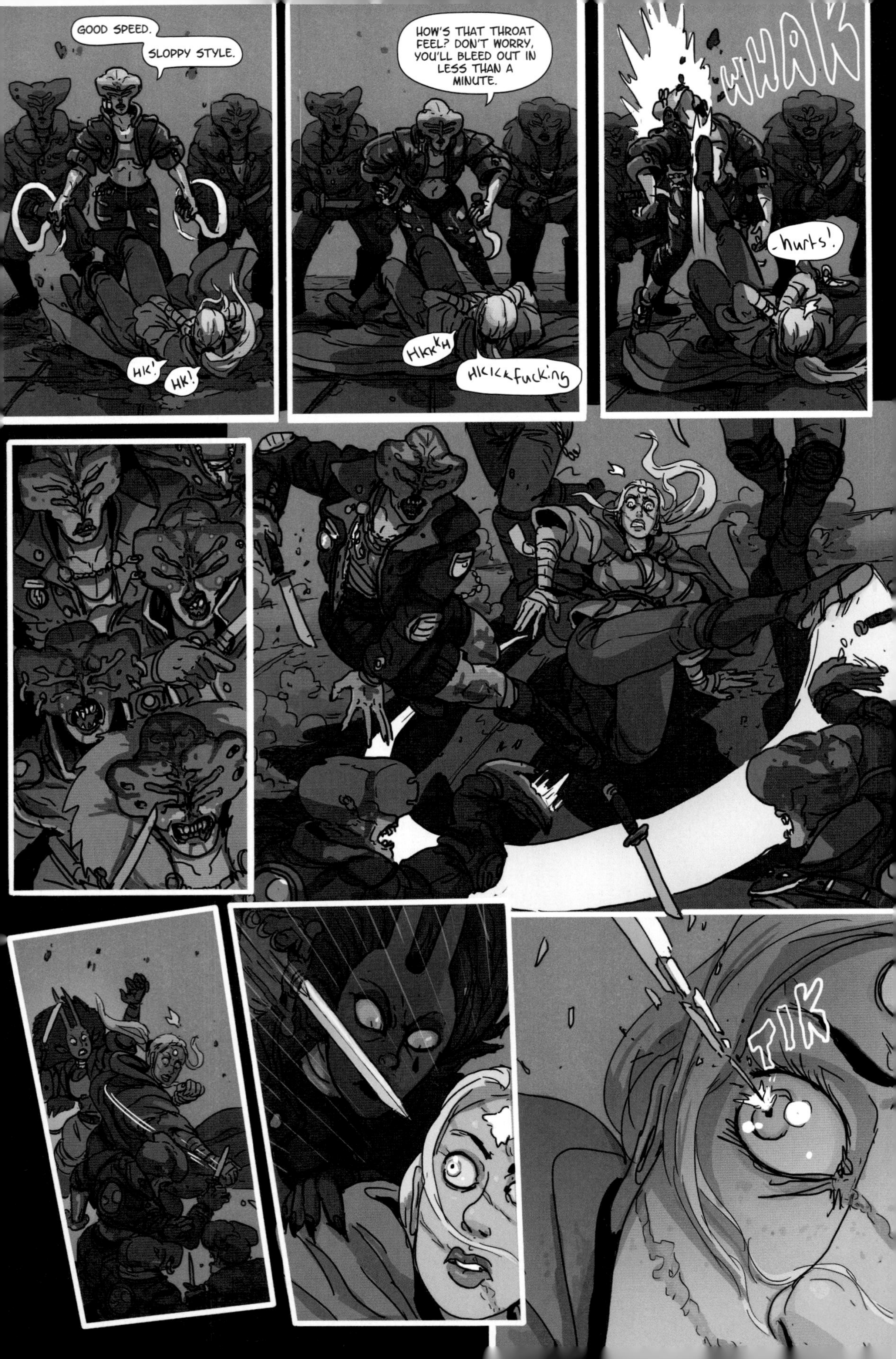
GOOD SPEED.
SLOPPY STYLE.
HK!
HK!
HOW'S THAT THROAT FEEL? DON'T WORRY, YOU'LL BLEED OUT IN LESS THAN A MINUTE.
HkkKH
HKKKfucking
WHAK
-hurts!
TIK

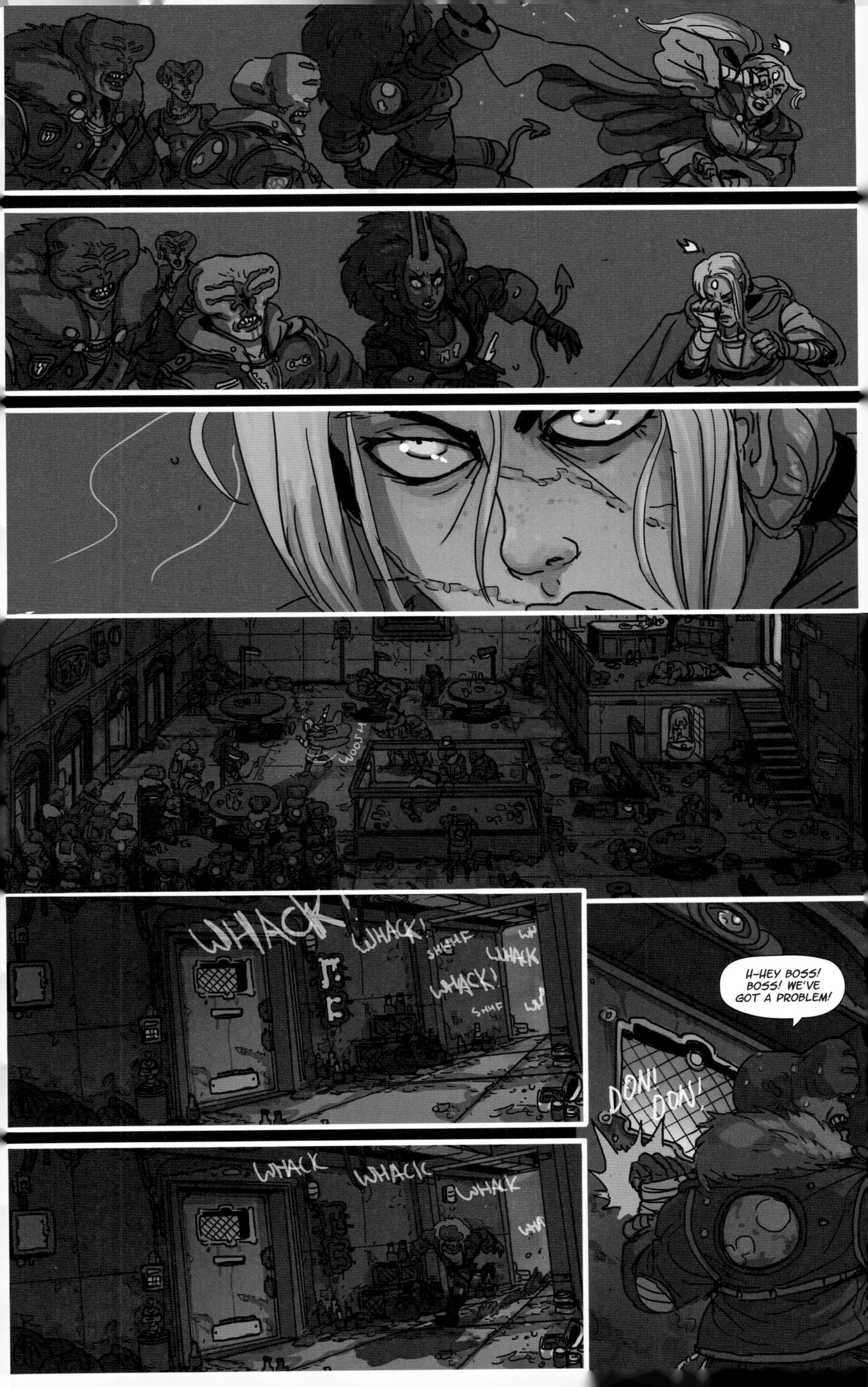
WHACK!
WHACK!
WHACK
WHACK!
H-HEY BOSS! BOSS! WE'VE GOT A PROBLEM!
DON! DON!
WHACK
WHACK
WHACK

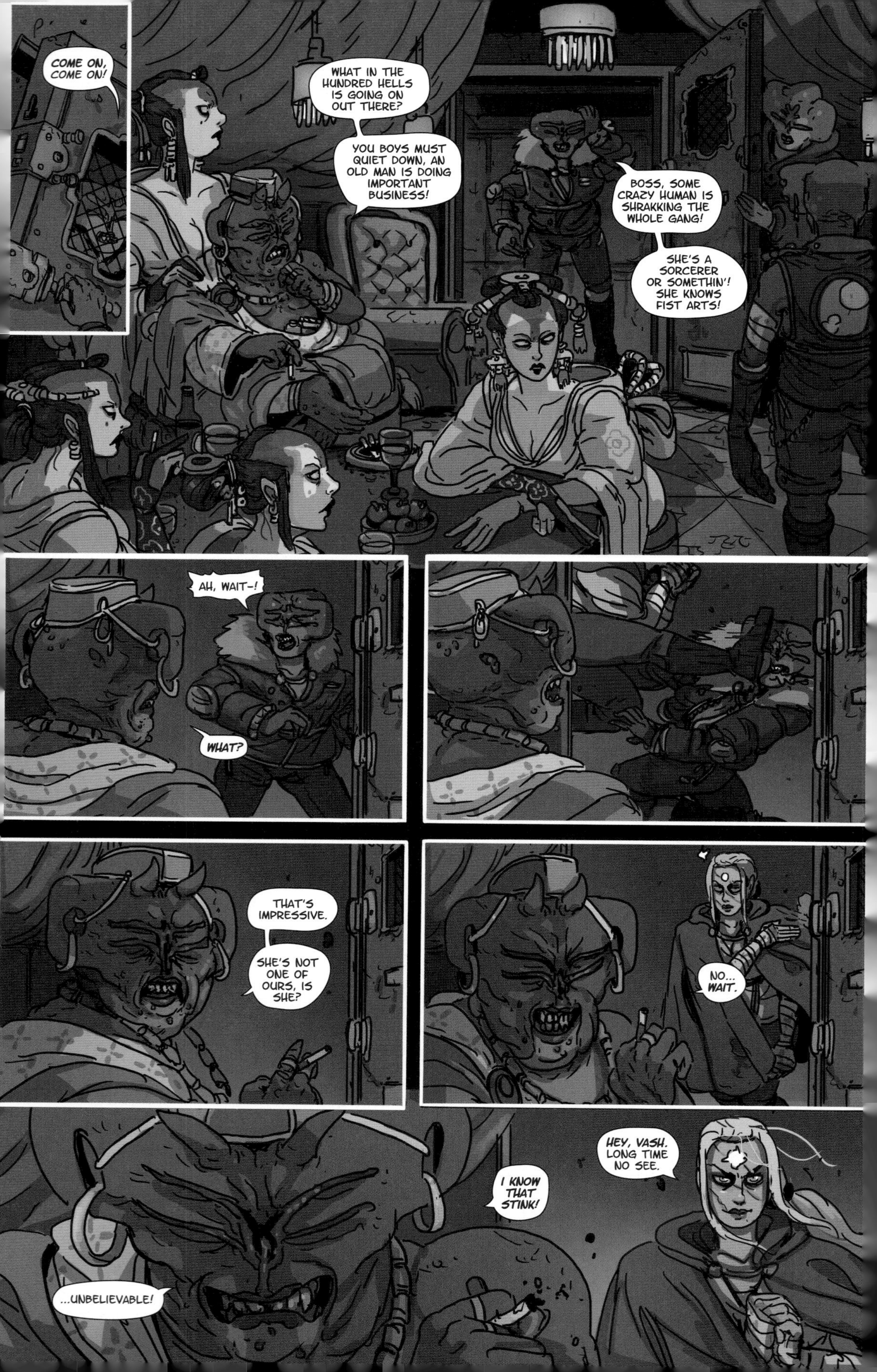
COME ON, COME ON!
WHAT IN THE HUNDRED HELLS IS GOING ON OUT THERE?
YOU BOYS MUST QUIET DOWN, AN OLD MAN IS DOING IMPORTANT BUSINESS!
BOSS, SOME CRAZY HUMAN IS SHRAKKING THE WHOLE GANG!
SHE'S A SORCERER OR SOMETHIN'! SHE KNOWS FIST ARTS!
AH, WAIT-!
WHAT?
THAT'S IMPRESSIVE.
SHE'S NOT ONE OF OURS, IS SHE?
NO... WAIT.
HEY, VASH. LONG TIME NO SEE.
I KNOW THAT STINK!
...UNBELIEVABLE!

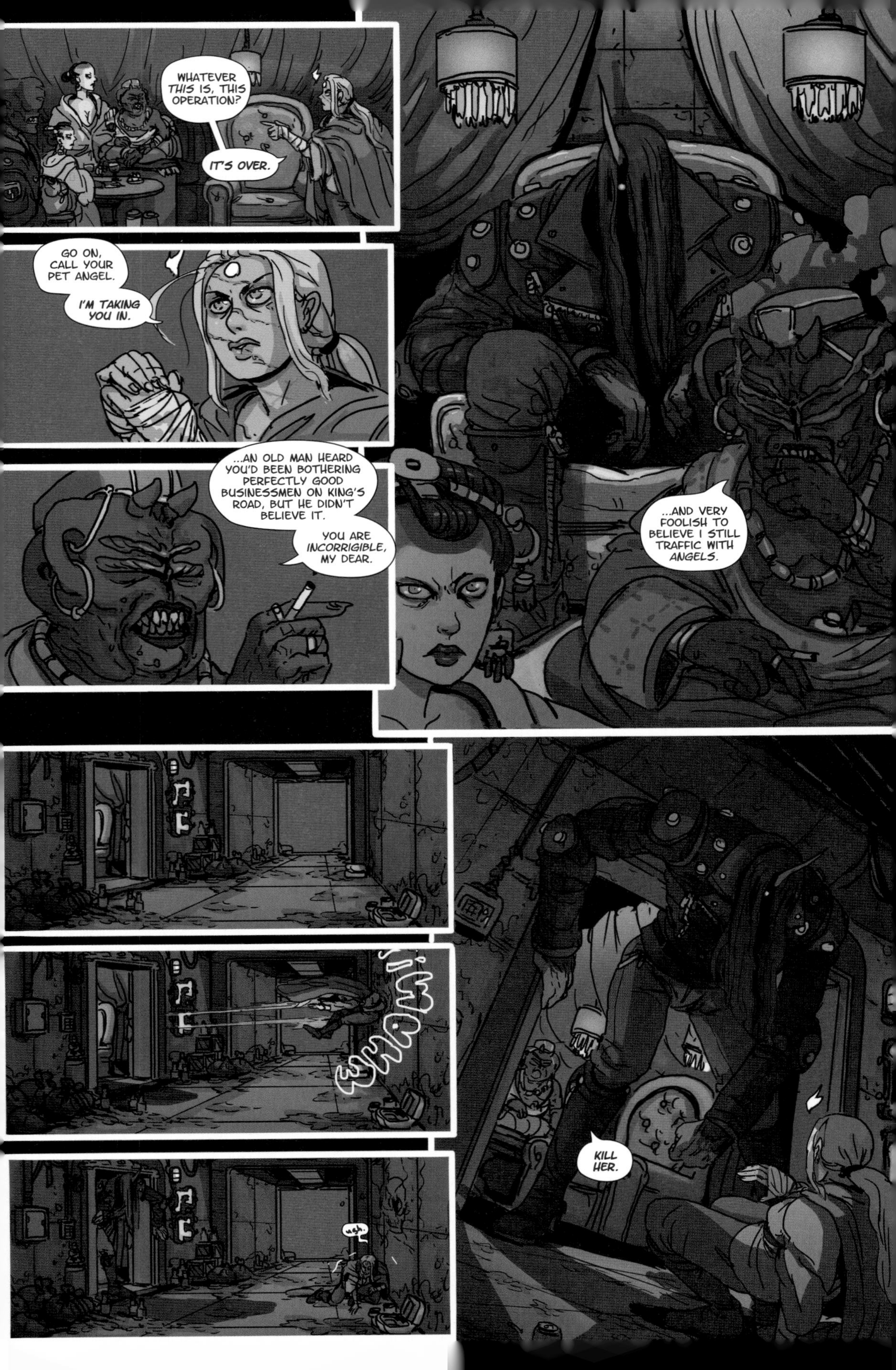
WHATEVER THIS IS, THIS OPERATION?
IT'S OVER.
GO ON, CALL YOUR PET ANGEL.
I'M TAKING YOU IN.
...AN OLD MAN HEARD YOU'D BEEN BOTHERING PERFECTLY GOOD BUSINESSMEN ON KING'S ROAD, BUT HE DIDN'T BELIEVE IT.
YOU ARE INCORRIGIBLE, MY DEAR.
...AND VERY FOOLISH TO BELIEVE I STILL TRAFFIC WITH ANGELS.
WHOM!
ugh.
KILL HER.

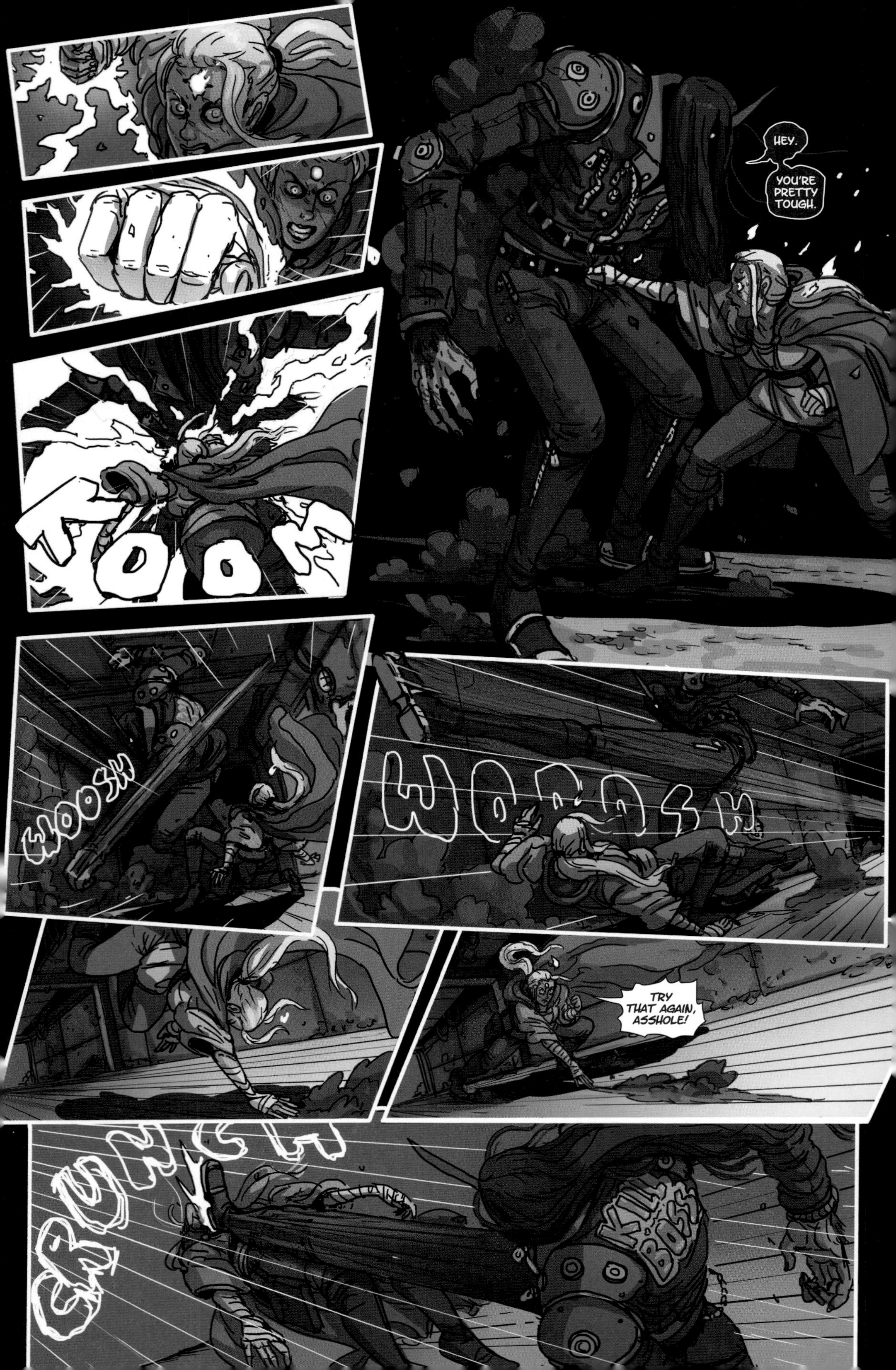
HEY.
YOU'RE PRETTY TOUGH.
WOOSH
WOOOSH
TRY THAT AGAIN, ASSHOLE!
CRUNCH
KILL BOSS

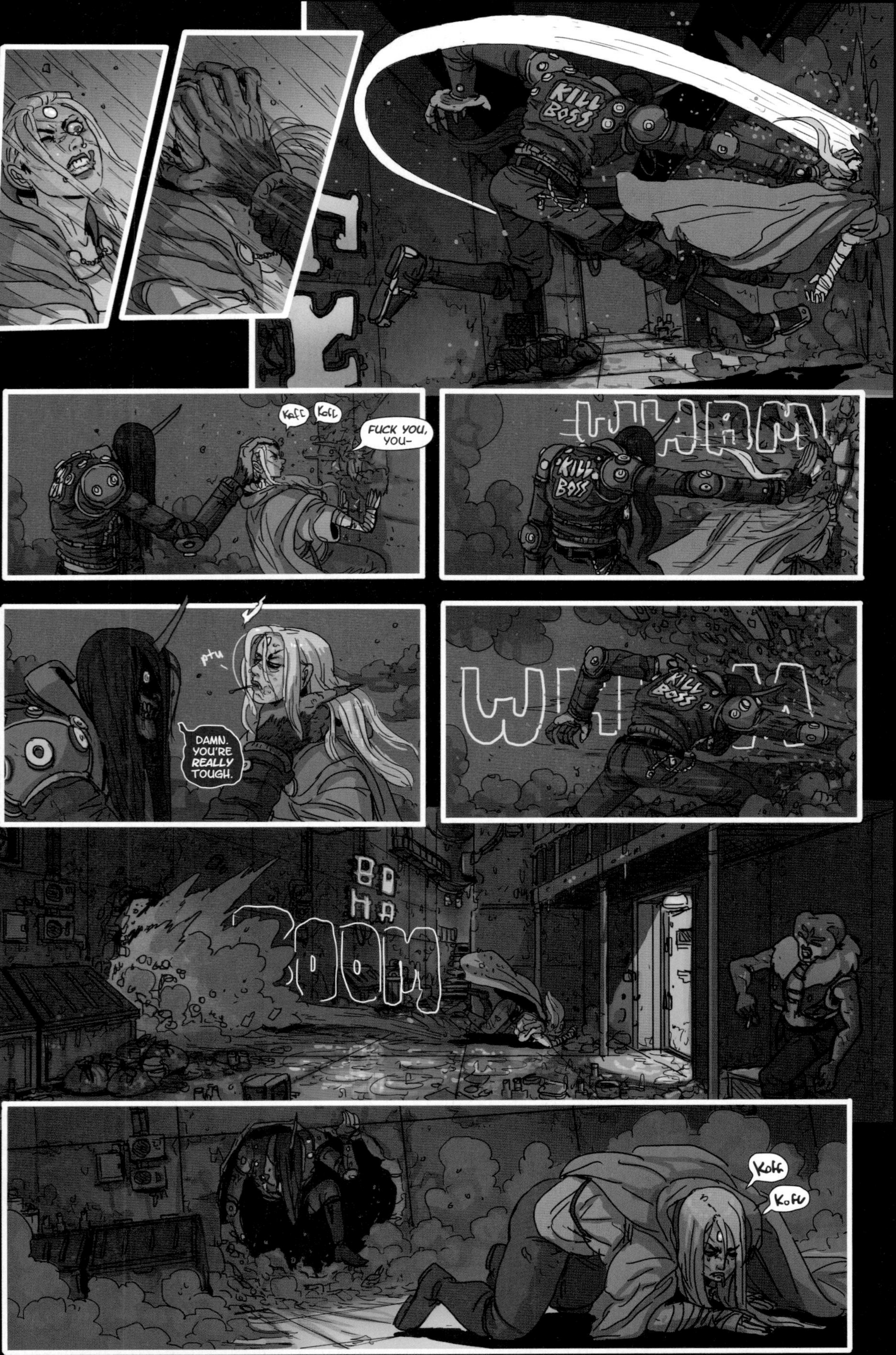
KILL BOSS
Koff
Koff
FUCK YOU, YOU-
ptu
DAMN. YOU'RE REALLY TOUGH.
BOOM
Koff
Koff

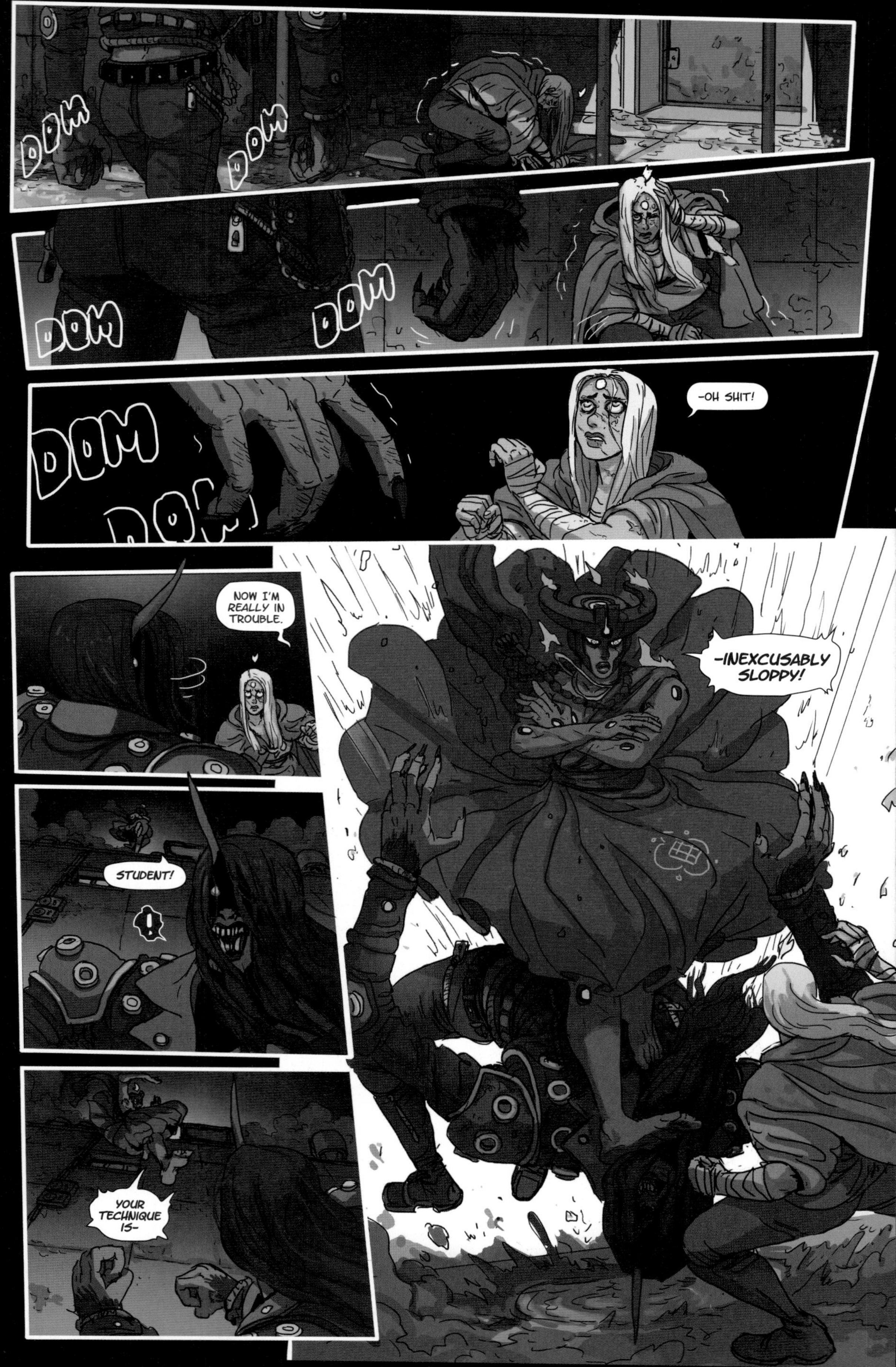
DOM
DOM
DOM
DOM
DOM
-OH SHIT!
DOM
NOW I'M REALLY IN TROUBLE.
STUDENT!
!
YOUR TECHNIQUE IS-
-INEXCUSABLY SLOPPY!

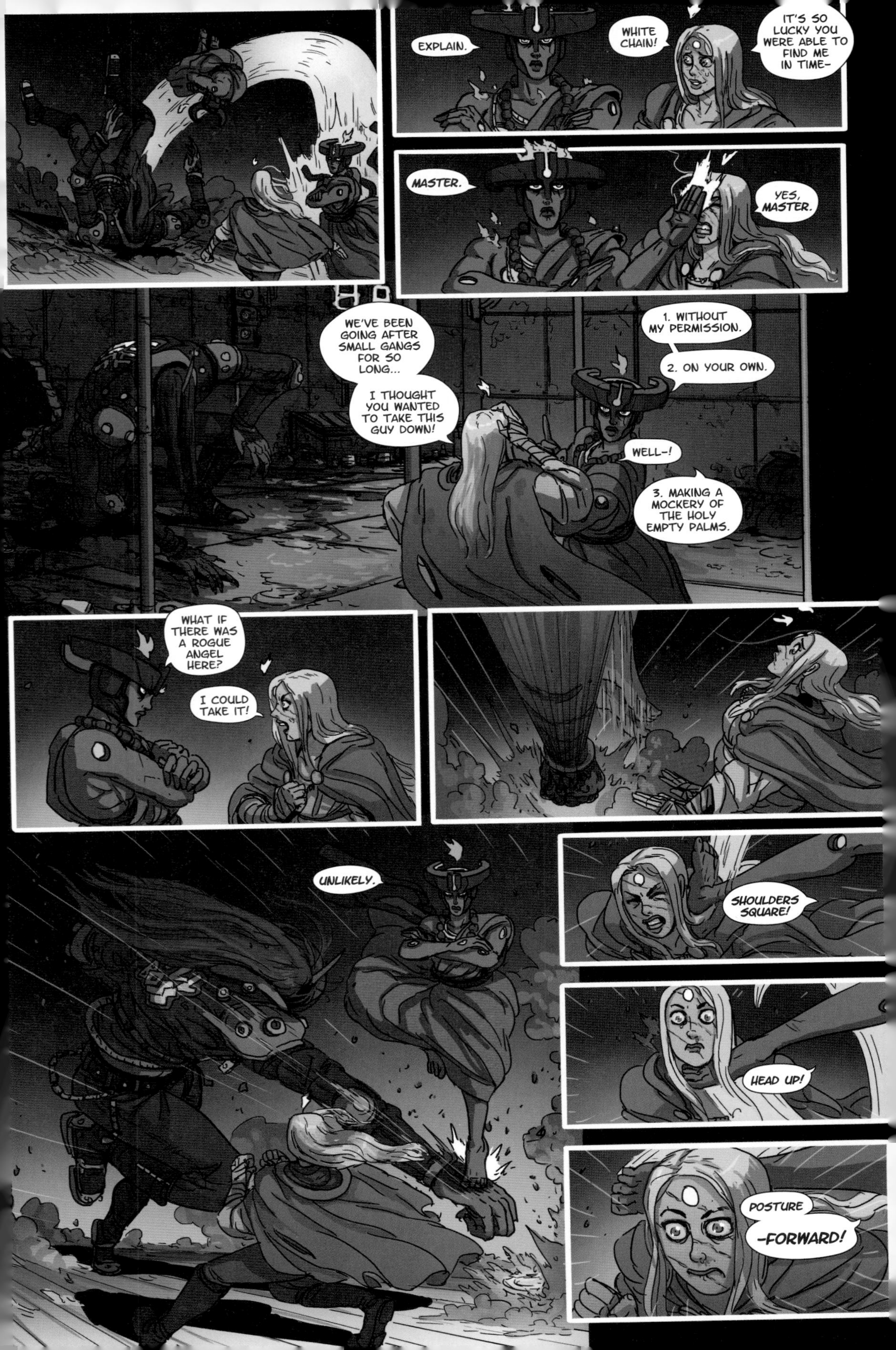
EXPLAIN.
WHITE CHAIN!
IT'S SO LUCKY YOU WERE ABLE TO FIND ME IN TIME-
MASTER.
YES, MASTER.
WE'VE BEEN GOING AFTER SMALL GANGS FOR SO LONG...
I THOUGHT YOU WANTED TO TAKE THIS GUY DOWN!
1. WITHOUT MY PERMISSION.
2. ON YOUR OWN.
WELL-!
3. MAKING A MOCKERY OF THE HOLY EMPTY PALMS.
WHAT IF THERE WAS A ROGUE ANGEL HERE?
I COULD TAKE IT!
UNLIKELY.
SHOULDERS SQUARE!
HEAD UP!
POSTURE
-FORWARD!

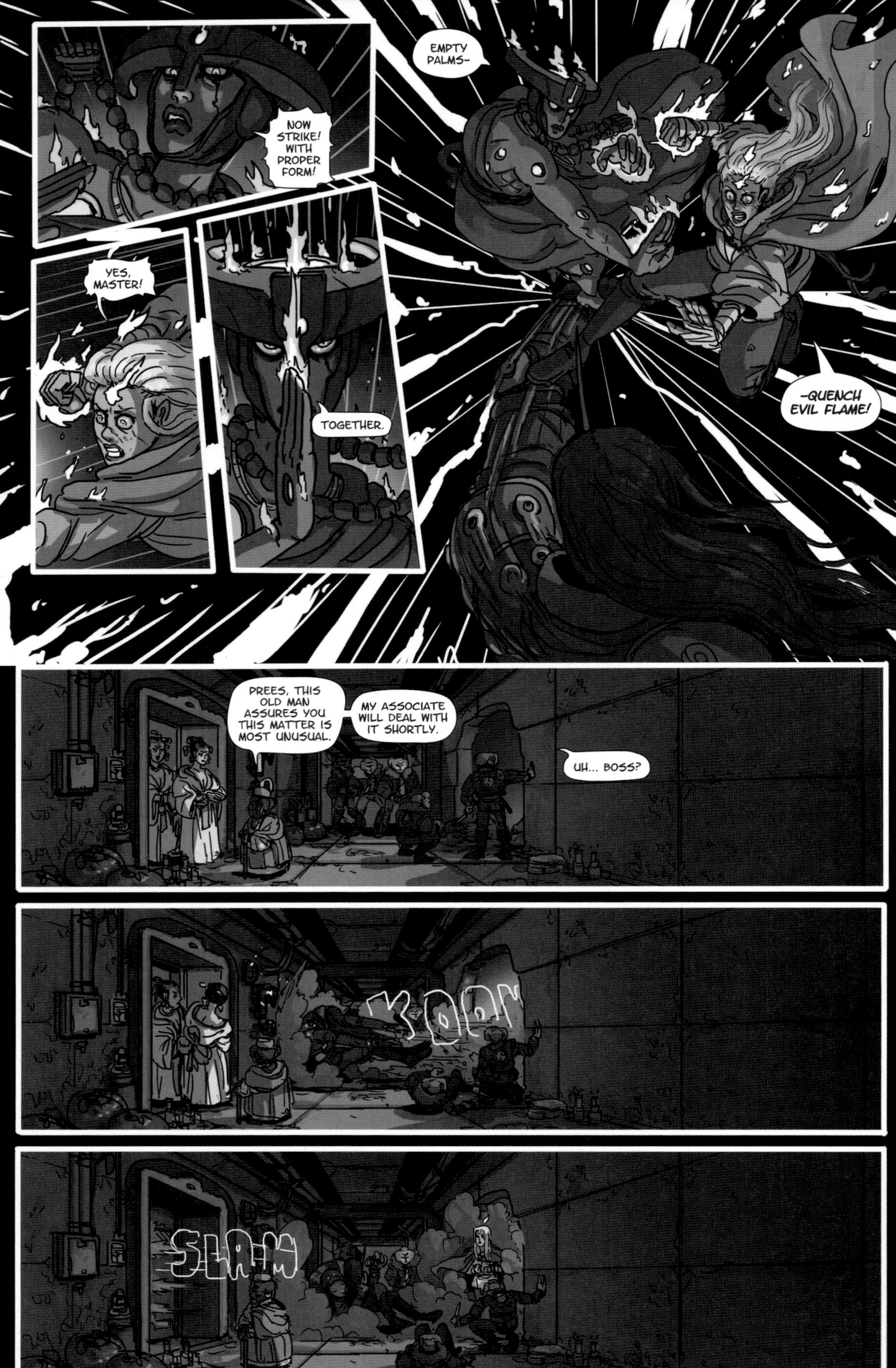
NOW STRIKE! WITH PROPER FORM!
YES, MASTER!
TOGETHER.
EMPTY PALMS-
-QUENCH EVIL FLAME!
PREES, THIS OLD MAN ASSURES YOU THIS MATTER IS MOST UNUSUAL.
MY ASSOCIATE WILL DEAL WITH IT SHORTLY.
UH... BOSS?
KOOM
SLAM

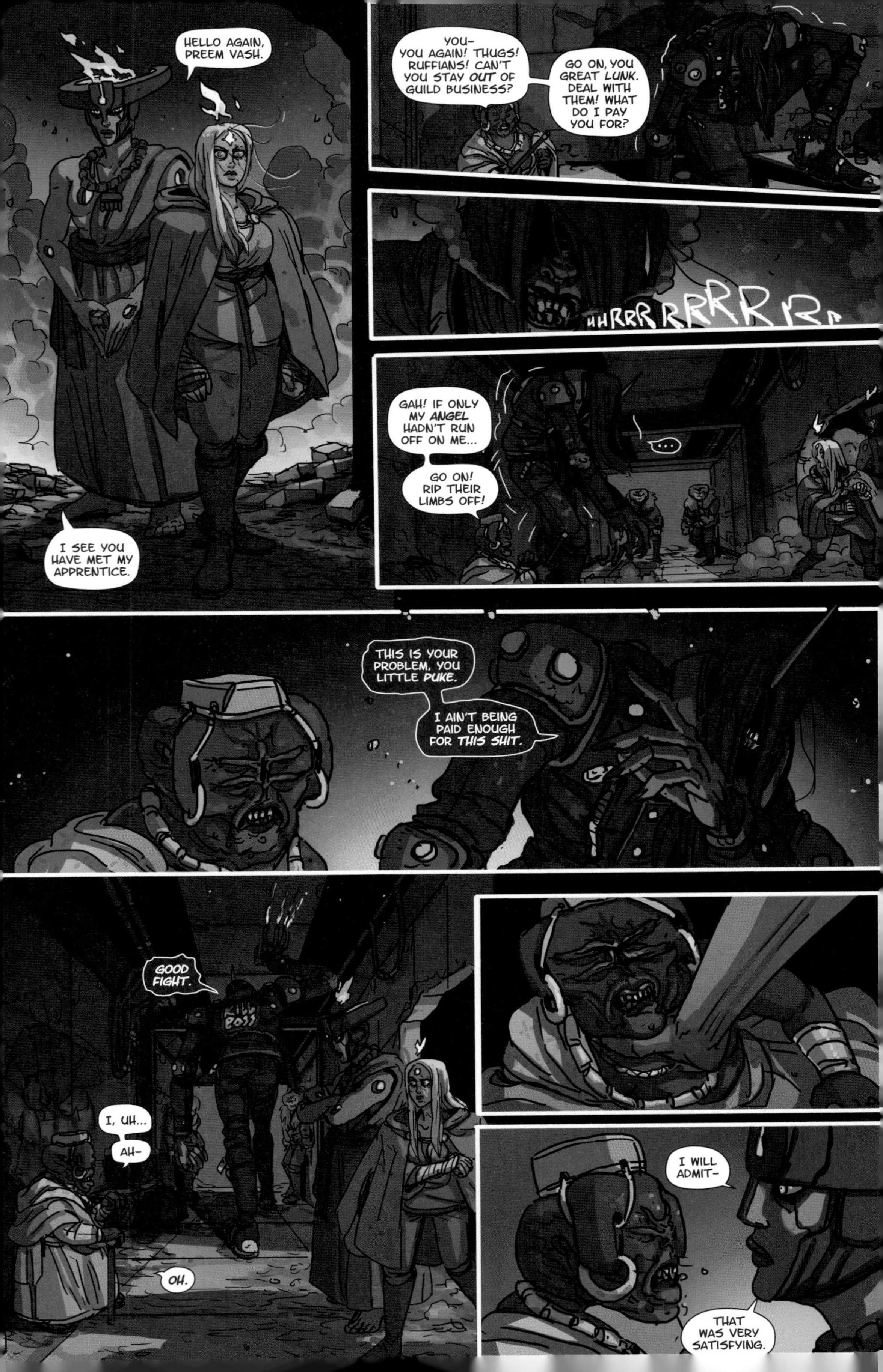
HELLO AGAIN, PREEM VASH.
I SEE YOU HAVE MET MY APPRENTICE.
YOU- YOU AGAIN! THUGS! RUFFIANS! CAN'T YOU STAY OUT OF GUILD BUSINESS?
GO ON, YOU GREAT LUNK. DEAL WITH THEM! WHAT DO I PAY YOU FOR?
HHRRRRRRRRR
GAH! IF ONLY MY ANGEL HADN'T RUN OFF ON ME...
GO ON! RIP THEIR LIMBS OFF!
...
THIS IS YOUR PROBLEM, YOU LITTLE PUKE.
I AIN'T BEING PAID ENOUGH FOR THIS SHIT.
GOOD FIGHT.
I, UH...
AH-
OH.
I WILL ADMIT-
THAT WAS VERY SATISFYING.

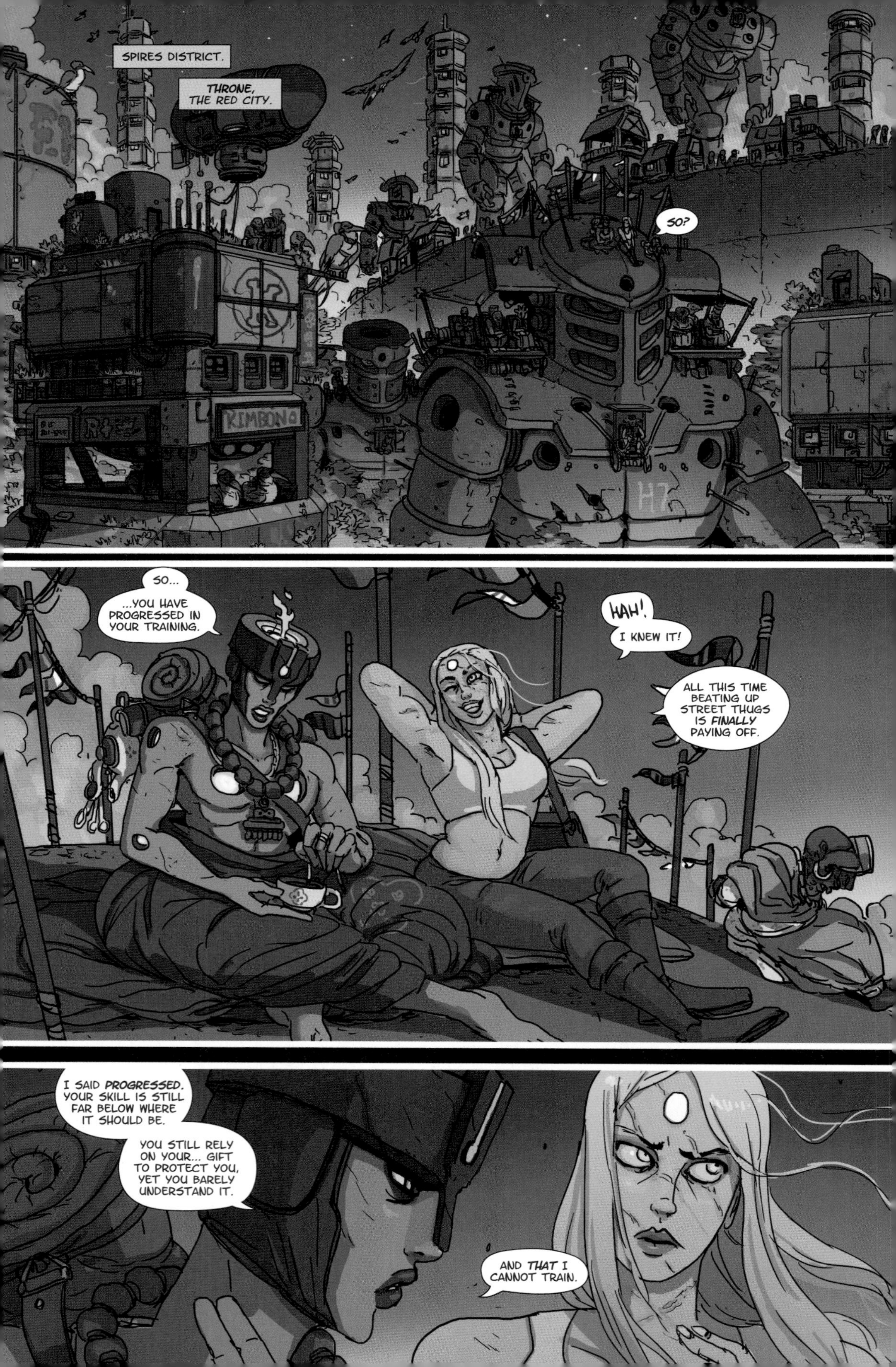
SPIRES DISTRICT.
THRONE, THE RED CITY.
KIMBONO
H7
SO?
SO...
...YOU HAVE PROGRESSED IN YOUR TRAINING.
HAH!
I KNEW IT!
ALL THIS TIME BEATING UP STREET THUGS IS FINALLY PAYING OFF.
I SAID PROGRESSED. YOUR SKILL IS STILL FAR BELOW WHERE IT SHOULD BE.
YOU STILL RELY ON YOUR... GIFT TO PROTECT YOU, YET YOU BARELY UNDERSTAND IT.
AND THAT I CANNOT TRAIN.

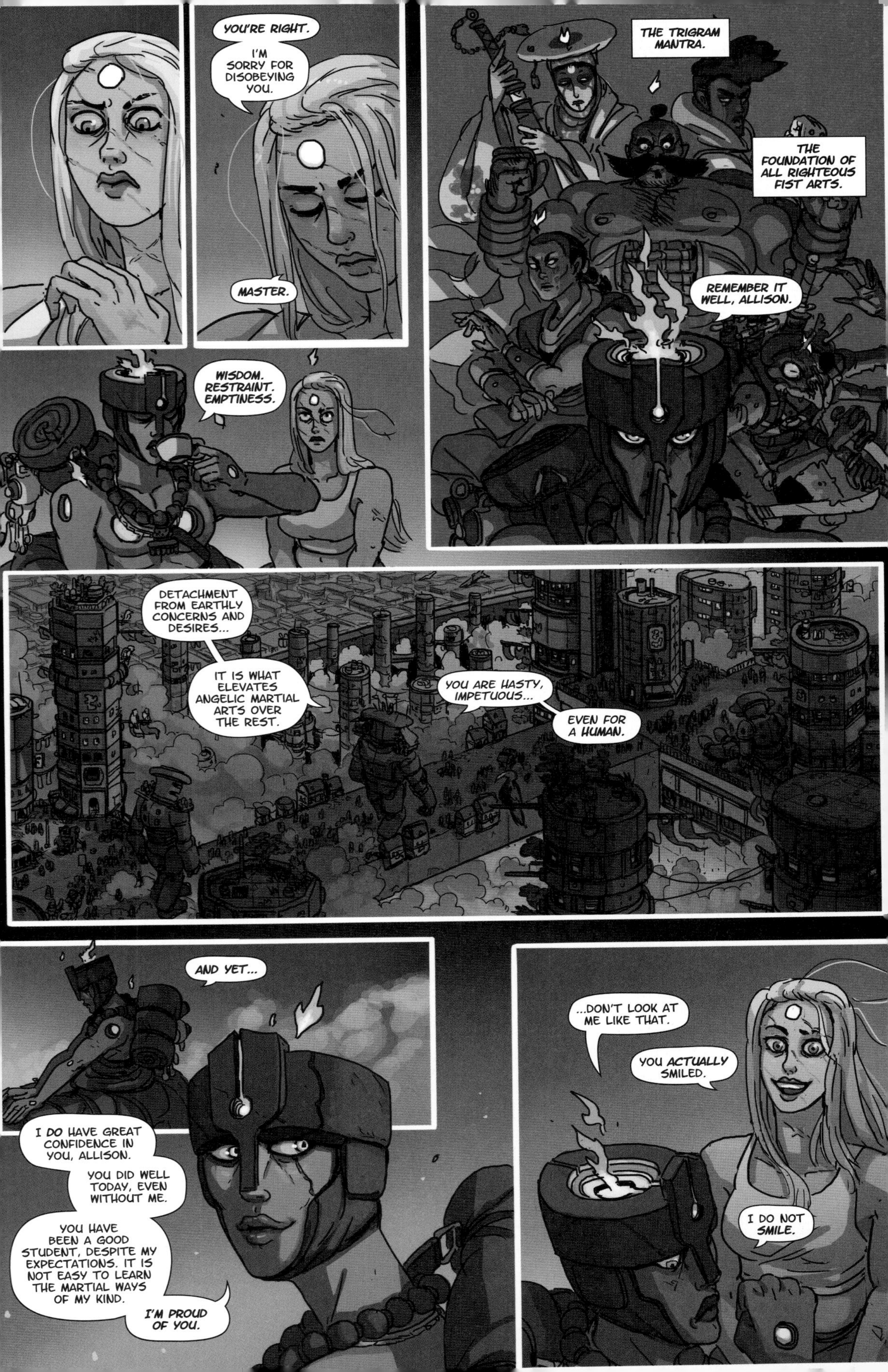
YOU'RE RIGHT.
I'M SORRY FOR DISOBEYING YOU.
MASTER.
THE TRIGRAM MANTRA.
THE FOUNDATION OF ALL RIGHTEOUS FIST ARTS.
REMEMBER IT WELL, ALLISON.
WISDOM. RESTRAINT. EMPTINESS.
DETACHMENT FROM EARTHLY CONCERNS AND DESIRES...
IT IS WHAT ELEVATES ANGELIC MARTIAL ARTS OVER THE REST.
YOU ARE HASTY, IMPETUOUS...
EVEN FOR A HUMAN.
AND YET...
I DO HAVE GREAT CONFIDENCE IN YOU, ALLISON.
YOU DID WELL TODAY, EVEN WITHOUT ME.
YOU HAVE BEEN A GOOD STUDENT, DESPITE MY EXPECTATIONS. IT IS NOT EASY TO LEARN THE MARTIAL WAYS OF MY KIND.
I'M PROUD OF YOU.
...DON'T LOOK AT ME LIKE THAT.
YOU ACTUALLY SMILED.
I DO NOT SMILE.

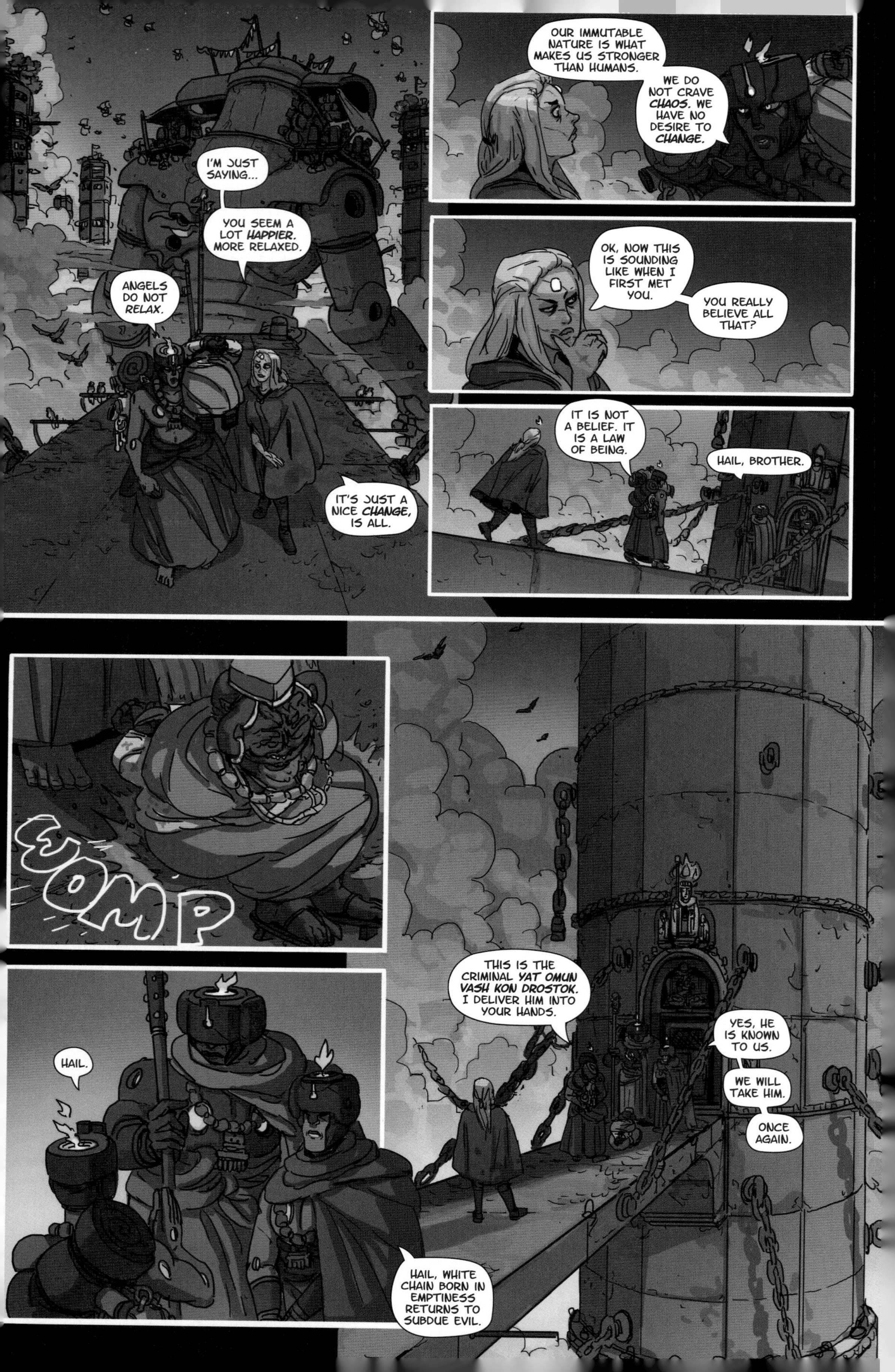
I'M JUST SAYING...
YOU SEEM A LOT HAPPIER. MORE RELAXED.
ANGELS DO NOT RELAX.
IT'S JUST A NICE CHANGE, IS ALL.
OUR IMMUTABLE NATURE IS WHAT MAKES US STRONGER THAN HUMANS.
WE DO NOT CRAVE CHAOS. WE HAVE NO DESIRE TO CHANGE.
OK, NOW THIS IS SOUNDING LIKE WHEN I FIRST MET YOU.
YOU REALLY BELIEVE ALL THAT?
IT IS NOT A BELIEF. IT IS A LAW OF BEING.
HAIL, BROTHER.
WOMP
HAIL.
HAIL, WHITE CHAIN BORN IN EMPTINESS RETURNS TO SUBDUE EVIL.
THIS IS THE CRIMINAL YAT OMUN VASH KON DROSTOK. I DELIVER HIM INTO YOUR HANDS.
YES, HE IS KNOWN TO US.
WE WILL TAKE HIM.
ONCE AGAIN.

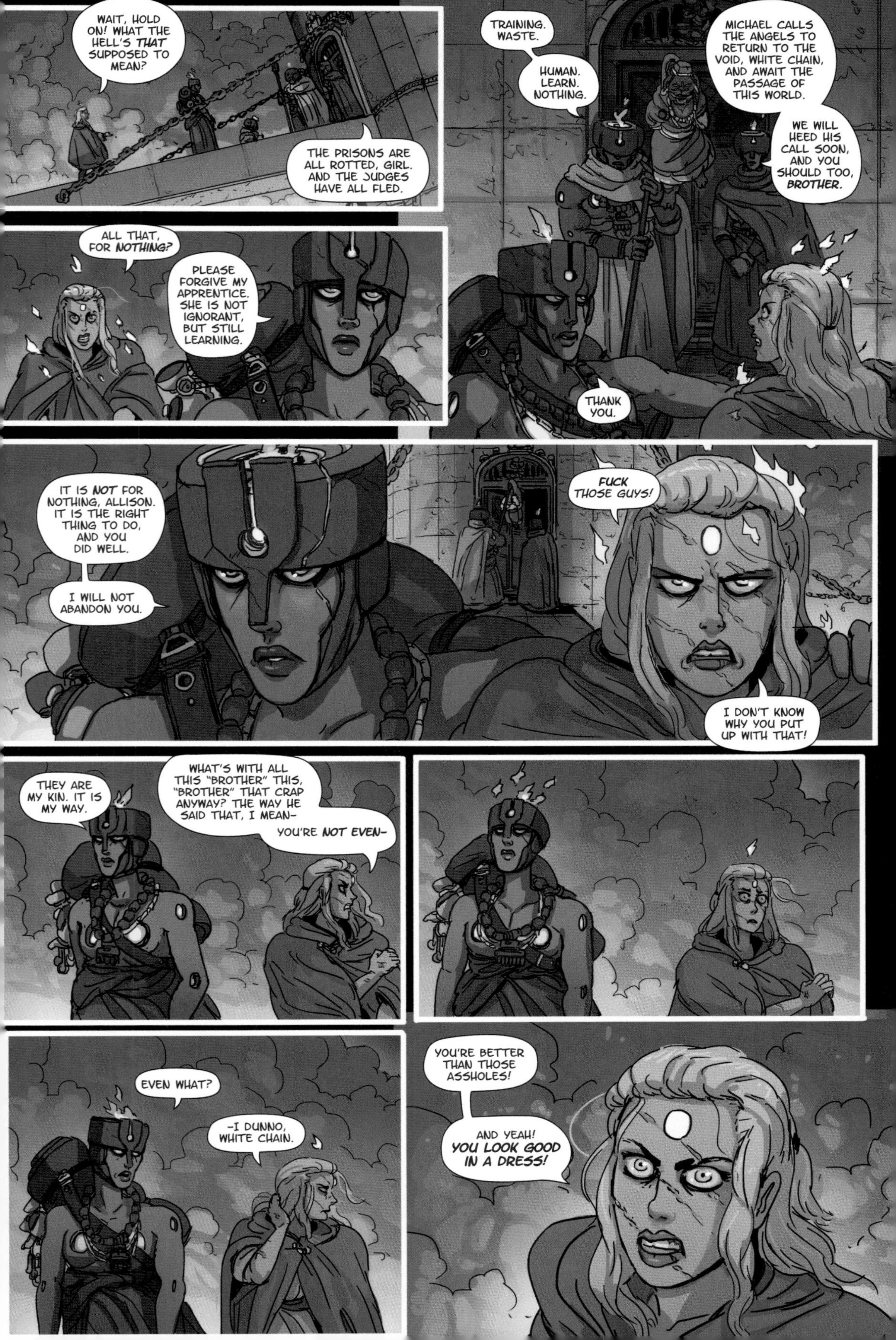
WAIT, HOLD ON! WHAT THE HELL'S *THAT* SUPPOSED TO MEAN?
THE PRISONS ARE ALL ROTTED, GIRL. AND THE JUDGES HAVE ALL FLED.
TRAINING. WASTE.
HUMAN. LEARN. NOTHING.
MICHAEL CALLS THE ANGELS TO RETURN TO THE VOID, WHITE CHAIN, AND AWAIT THE PASSAGE OF THIS WORLD.
WE WILL HEED HIS CALL SOON, AND YOU SHOULD TOO, ***BROTHER.***
ALL THAT, FOR ***NOTHING?***
PLEASE FORGIVE MY APPRENTICE. SHE IS NOT IGNORANT, BUT STILL LEARNING.
THANK YOU.
IT IS ***NOT*** FOR NOTHING, ALLISON. IT IS THE RIGHT THING TO DO, AND YOU DID WELL.
I WILL NOT ABANDON YOU.
FUCK THOSE GUYS!
I DON'T KNOW WHY YOU PUT UP WITH THAT!
THEY ARE MY KIN. IT IS MY WAY.
WHAT'S WITH ALL THIS "BROTHER" THIS, "BROTHER" THAT CRAP ANYWAY? THE WAY HE SAID THAT, I MEAN-
YOU'RE ***NOT EVEN-***
EVEN WHAT?
-I DUNNO, WHITE CHAIN.
YOU'RE BETTER THAN THOSE ASSHOLES!
AND YEAH! ***YOU LOOK GOOD IN A DRESS!***

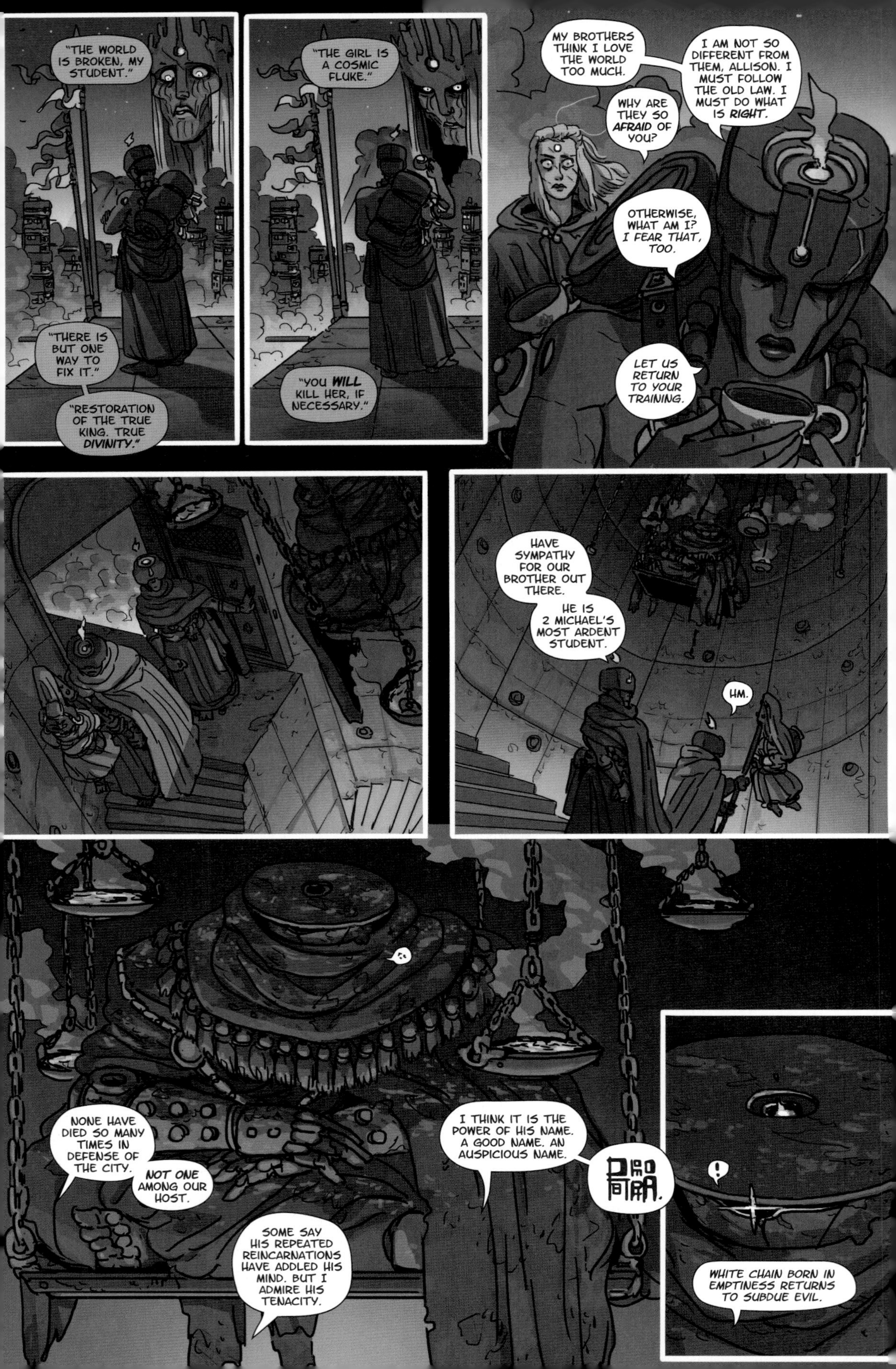
"THE WORLD IS BROKEN, MY STUDENT."
"THERE IS BUT ONE WAY TO FIX IT."
"RESTORATION OF THE TRUE KING. TRUE *DIVINITY*."
"THE GIRL IS A COSMIC FLUKE."
"YOU **WILL** KILL HER, IF NECESSARY."
MY BROTHERS THINK I LOVE THE WORLD TOO MUCH.
I AM NOT SO DIFFERENT FROM THEM, ALLISON. I MUST FOLLOW THE OLD LAW. I MUST DO WHAT IS ***RIGHT***.
WHY ARE THEY SO ***AFRAID*** OF YOU?
OTHERWISE, WHAT AM I? I FEAR THAT, TOO.
LET US RETURN TO YOUR TRAINING.
HAVE SYMPATHY FOR OUR BROTHER OUT THERE.
HE IS 2 MICHAEL'S MOST ARDENT STUDENT.
HM.
NONE HAVE DIED SO MANY TIMES IN DEFENSE OF THE CITY.
NOT ONE AMONG OUR HOST.
SOME SAY HIS REPEATED REINCARNATIONS HAVE ADDLED HIS MIND. BUT I ADMIRE HIS TENACITY.
I THINK IT IS THE POWER OF HIS NAME. A GOOD NAME. AN AUSPICIOUS NAME.
!
WHITE CHAIN BORN IN EMPTINESS RETURNS TO SUBDUE EVIL.

II.

THE LAND WAS foreign to Het and she held her stave tightly to her as they wandered about the mires that passed for streets in that place. People slept on the street, or with animals, to her great shock. The buildings were low and hunched, and covered in the muck of the earth, and in that respect, they were just like the people. Here and there she could peer into their smoky interiors and see a woman bent and crooked over a fire, a man picking through junk, a youth carrying a lashed and heavy bundle over her back. But that was about as much as Het could tell apart, for the muck that covered them made them all look alike. Their eyes were white and hungry, and Het shivered as she passed the listless clusters of them lining the street.

The day passed and the Sergeant asked many fine questions, as his perfect fingernails tapped the polished hilt of his straight sword. Het and the Centurion followed him to and fro, from dwelling to dwelling. The Sergeant would knock, and bend his handsome head just a little inside. He would step his great policeman's strides, and in his polite way, inquire about the terrible happenings in the community. Het was very impressed, for the dwellers were

sullen and hard to read with their faces covered in muck. They spoke very little and Het was sure they were hiding some dark secret away.

The Sergeant, however, was nonplussed. "I am piecing together little by little the location of our monster," he said to Het and the Centurion. His back was very straight, and he was utterly confident. Het saw that his Watchman's Eye was working very well indeed, and longed to know its secrets. The day grew very late and Het was very anxious to get back to the palace and her bath, for the eyes of the populace followed their party like hungry beads, and the muck had piled up around her shiny boots. But as they drew up in front of the last low and sloping dwelling, the Sergeant gave them a knowing look. As he knocked, there was a tremendous noise as a man stumbled out of a side alley in a dead run. The Sergeant gave out a cry, and before Het could even ready her stave, the Centurion had closed thirty paces and struck the man down with a single horrifying blow.

The Centurion was extremely happy, but Het was not, for as she drew closer, she saw among the man's scattered entrails there was scarcely a demon to be found. In

his outstretched hand was a purse of silver coins. "He shouldn't have run," said the Sergeant sadly, and wiped his brow, "A common thief, no more." Het felt repulsed and regretful, for the punishment for thievery was not death. But then the Sergeant noted the hour, and Het thought of the palace and her bath, and they returned at speed.

The Sergeant's confidence was hardly dented at all. "The poor sap was just a criminal, not a demon as I suspected! The information was very poor, but I'll keep at it," he said. "The people of this land are sullen and poorly spoken, but that doesn't mean they don't deserve our protection!" The lord of the land agreed. They had a pheasant dinner and a fine bath, and slept well. Het, however, could scarcely sleep and spent her night staring out at the muck below.

In the morning came tales of dead livestock and stolen milk. This made the Sergeant more resolute, and gave Het hope as they set about the town. The Centurion followed along eagerly. He had cleaned his sword.

This time, a strange familiarity came over Het. Having seen the town and its inhabitants before, passing through a second time her curiosity got the better of her.

II.

As they passed through the bent, filthy streets, she peered once again into their cramped interiors. Here again was the woman bent over a fire. But Het saw that the fire was a kind of kiln or oven, and the woman had a long stick she was stoking it with. Here again, was the man bent over junk, but here and there Het saw glimmers. And here again, was the youth bent low by her heavy load, but Het suddenly saw that her load was a cloth of interesting texture.

The Sergeant again passed from dwelling to dwelling, relentless. "I am very sure this time," said the Sergeant, "For these leads have the stench of evil about them. Where dwelleth evil, dwelleth demons, don't you think?"

As the hour was growing late, the Sergeant's inquiries drew them close to a dwelling by a choked and polluted river. And as soon as the Sergeant rapped on the door, a woman scrambled out the window and dove into the river. Once again, the Sergeant cried out, and once again, the Centurion sprang eagerly forth. He leapt into the water and speared the woman through the belly like a fish. She spent a long-time dying as the Centurion cleaned his sword.

She did not have a Rakshasa inside her: just the rotted teeth of a long time Glass addict. The Sergeant wiped his brow. "She shouldn't have run," he said, his eyes sad. Het was despondent, for the punishment for using Glass was not death. She was glad that they were rooting out evil in this land, no matter how small, but it still weighed heavily on her as they trudged through the mud back to the palace and their bath.

The lord was very happy with their progress, even if they hadn't caught the Rakshasa, and Het lost no confidence in the Sergeant's Watchman's Eye, for it had indeed detected evil, even though the dwellers of that land were uncooperative. But a bath could not clear her mind, nor could clean clothes.

Once again, she spent her night staring at the muck below. This time, a strange impulse struck her.

SHE DONNED HER UNIFORM, PUT ON HER SHINY BOOTS, AND CLAMBERED OUT THE WINDOW.

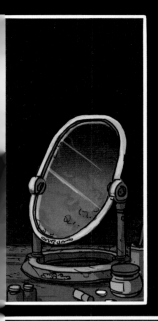

GRRRN

MY HAIR HAS GONE TOTALLY WHITE.

MY FACE SWELLED UP, THEN MY WOUNDS CONGEALED INTO SCARS. THEY NEVER PROPERLY HEALED.

CIO NEVER SAID ANYTHING, BUT SHE TRIED TO LEAVE. I KNEW SHE FELT GUILTY.

I CRIED A LOT. I FELT HIDEOUS.

I STILL DO, SOMETIMES. IT HURTS.

TOO FAT, TOO THIN, TOO MUSCULAR, TOO UGLY.

YET... DESPITE EVERYTHING...

...MAYBE FOR THE FIRST TIME...

...IT FEELS LIKE ME.

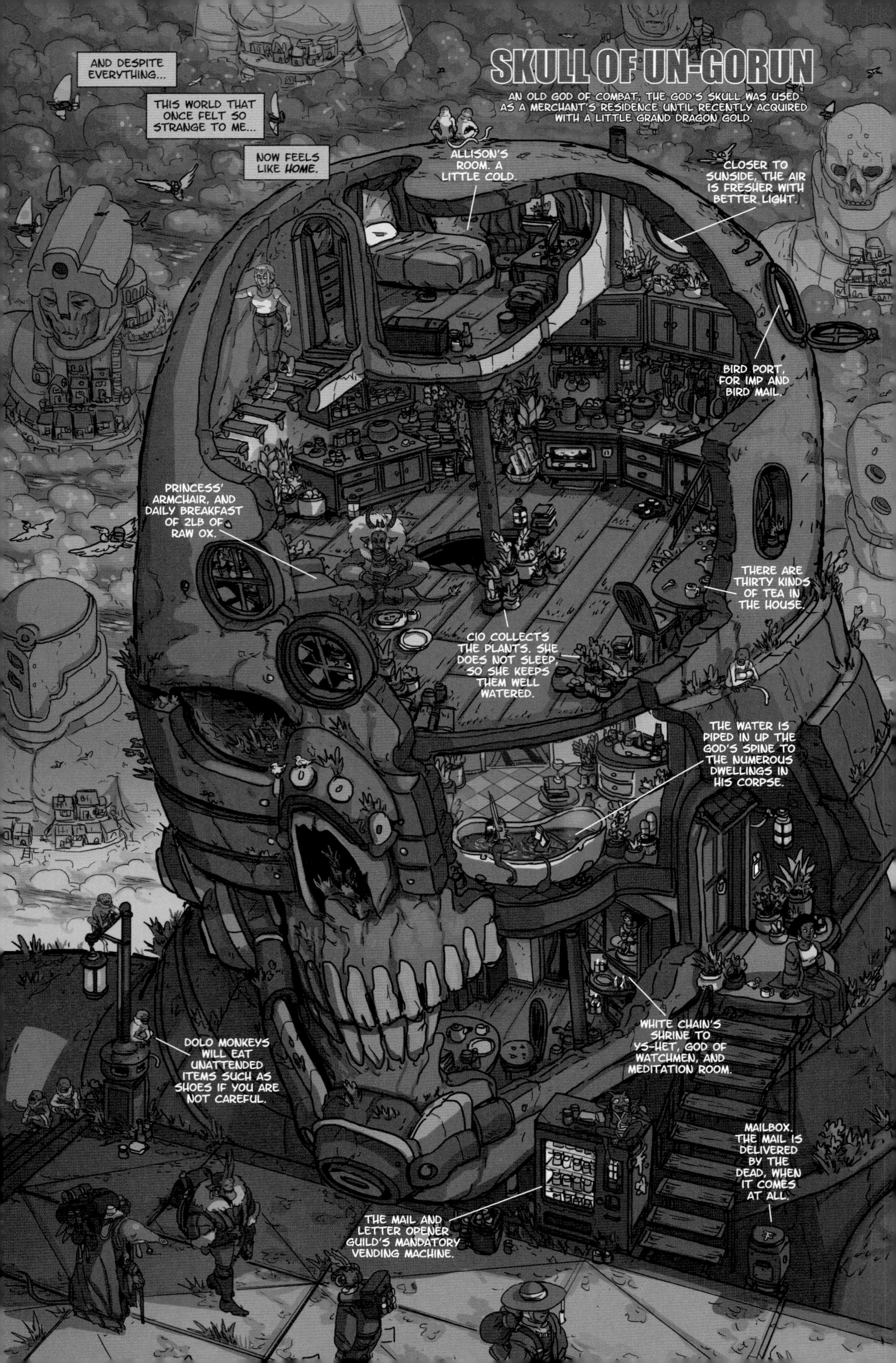

AND DESPITE EVERYTHING...
THIS WORLD THAT ONCE FELT SO STRANGE TO ME...
NOW FEELS LIKE *HOME*.
SKULL OF UN-GORUN
AN OLD GOD OF COMBAT, THE GOD'S SKULL WAS USED AS A MERCHANT'S RESIDENCE UNTIL RECENTLY ACQUIRED WITH A LITTLE GRAND DRAGON GOLD.
ALLISON'S ROOM. A LITTLE COLD.
CLOSER TO SUNSIDE, THE AIR IS FRESHER WITH BETTER LIGHT.
BIRD PORT, FOR IMP AND BIRD MAIL.
PRINCESS' ARMCHAIR, AND DAILY BREAKFAST OF 2LB OF RAW OX.
THERE ARE THIRTY KINDS OF TEA IN THE HOUSE.
CIO COLLECTS THE PLANTS. SHE DOES NOT SLEEP, SO SHE KEEPS THEM WELL WATERED.
THE WATER IS PIPED IN UP THE GOD'S SPINE TO THE NUMEROUS DWELLINGS IN HIS CORPSE.
WHITE CHAIN'S SHRINE TO YS-HET, GOD OF WATCHMEN, AND MEDITATION ROOM.
DOLO MONKEYS WILL EAT UNATTENDED ITEMS SUCH AS SHOES IF YOU ARE NOT CAREFUL.
MAILBOX. THE MAIL IS DELIVERED BY THE DEAD, WHEN IT COMES AT ALL.
THE MAIL AND LETTER OPENER GUILD'S MANDATORY VENDING MACHINE.

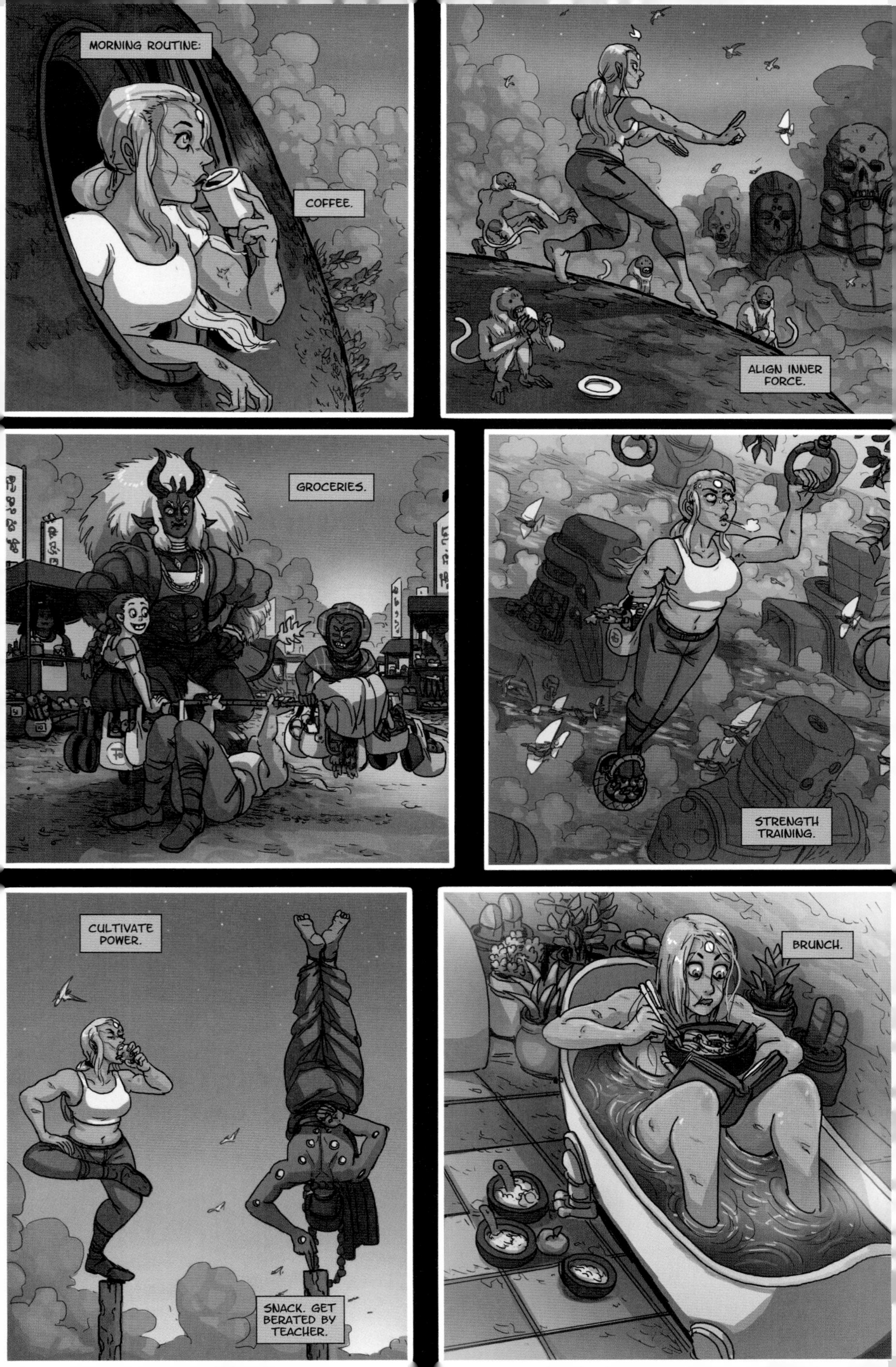

MORNING ROUTINE:
COFFEE.
ALIGN INNER FORCE.
GROCERIES.
STRENGTH TRAINING.
CULTIVATE POWER.
SNACK. GET BERATED BY TEACHER.
BRUNCH.

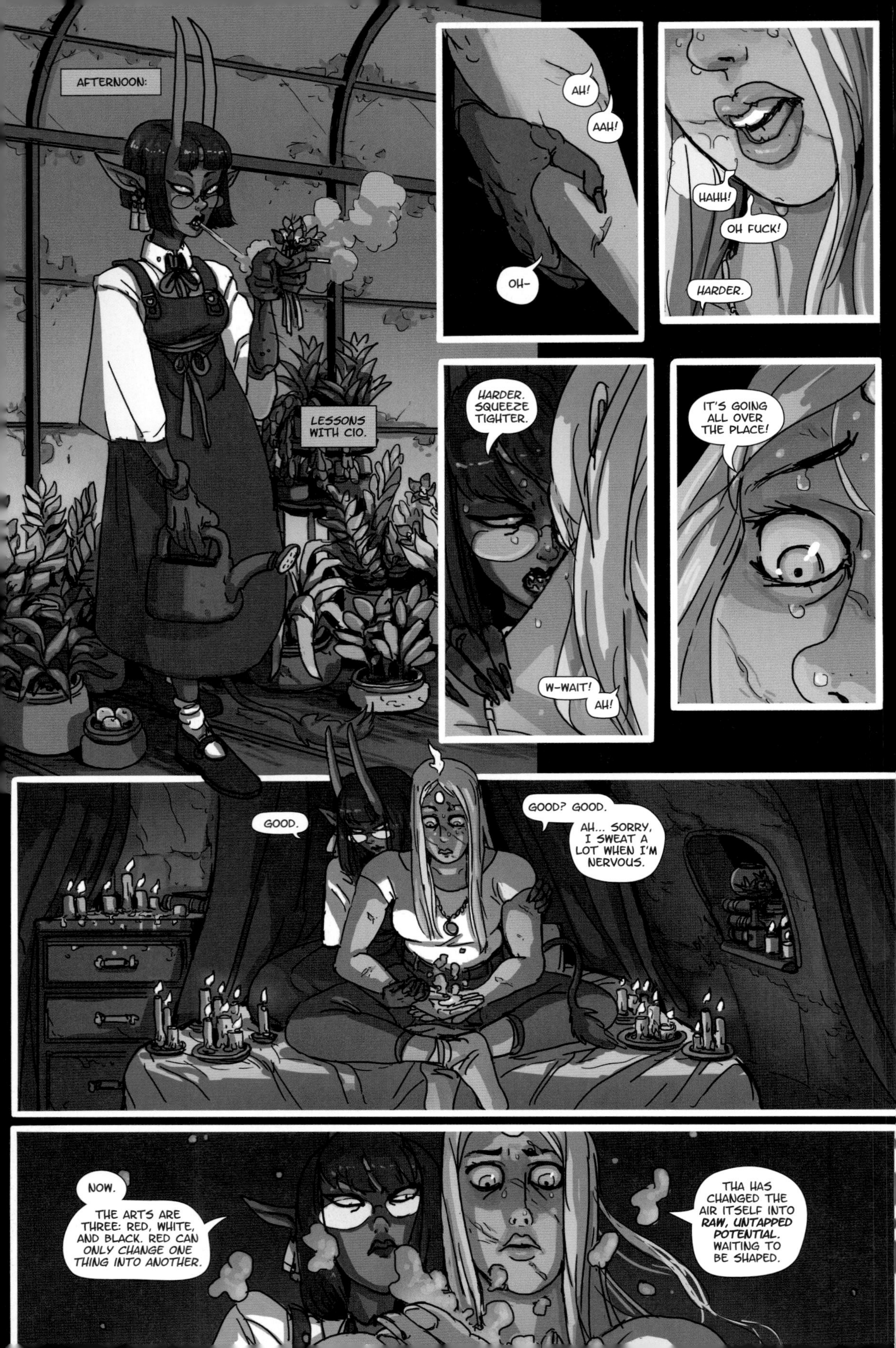
AFTERNOON:
LESSONS WITH CIO.
AH!
AAH!
OH-
HAHH!
OH FUCK!
HARDER.
HARDER. SQUEEZE TIGHTER.
W-WAIT!
AH!
IT'S GOING ALL OVER THE PLACE!
GOOD.
GOOD? GOOD.
AH... SORRY, I SWEAT A LOT WHEN I'M NERVOUS.
NOW.
THE ARTS ARE THREE: RED, WHITE, AND BLACK. RED CAN ONLY CHANGE ONE THING INTO ANOTHER.
THA HAS CHANGED THE AIR ITSELF INTO ***RAW, UNTAPPED POTENTIAL.*** WAITING TO BE SHAPED.

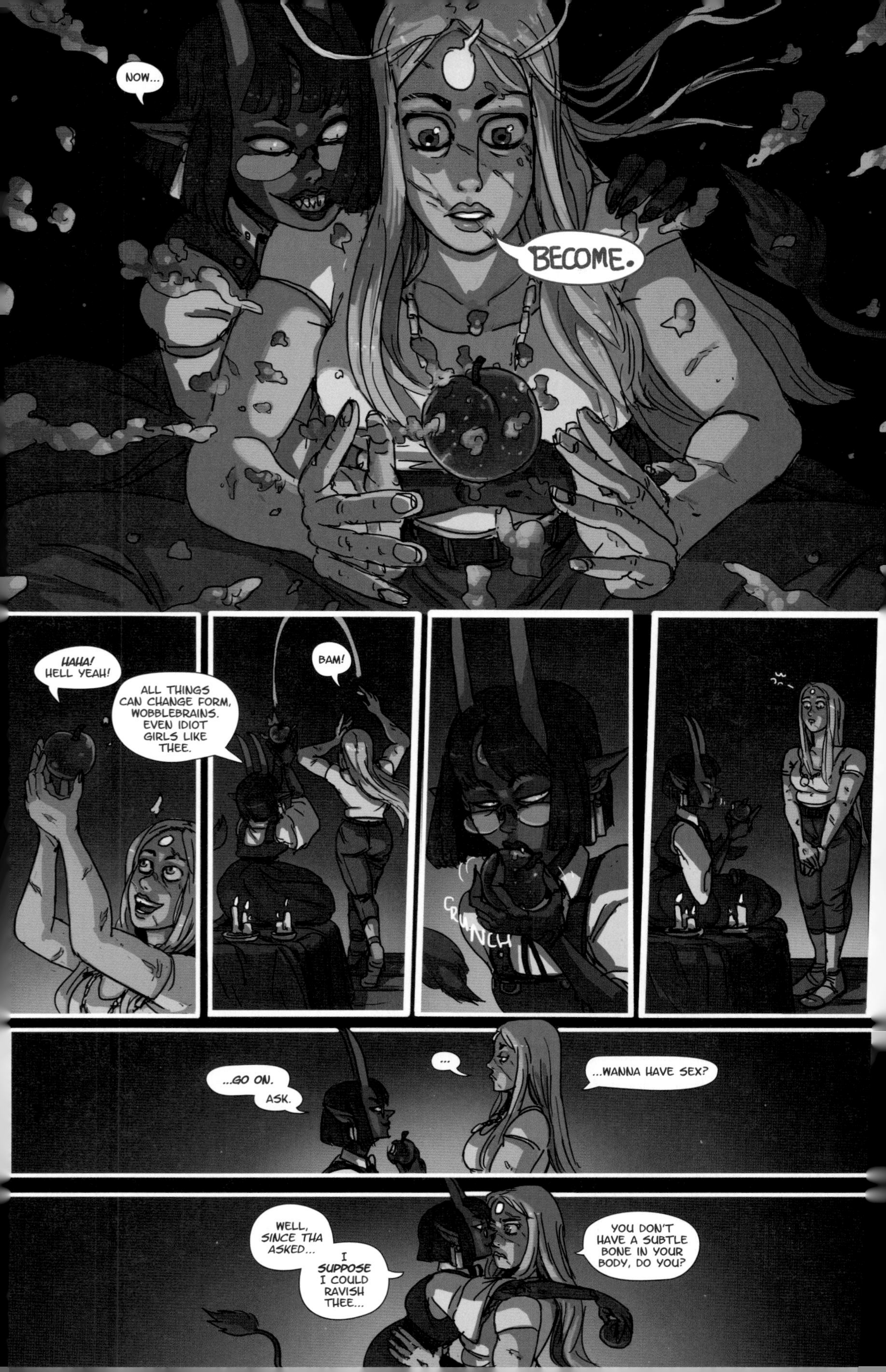
NOW...
BECOME.
HAHA! HELL YEAH!
ALL THINGS CAN CHANGE FORM, WOBBLEBRAINS. EVEN IDIOT GIRLS LIKE THEE.
BAM!
CRUNCH
...
...GO ON.
ASK.
...WANNA HAVE SEX?
WELL, SINCE THA ASKED...
I SUPPOSE I COULD RAVISH THEE...
YOU DON'T HAVE A SUBTLE BONE IN YOUR BODY, DO YOU?

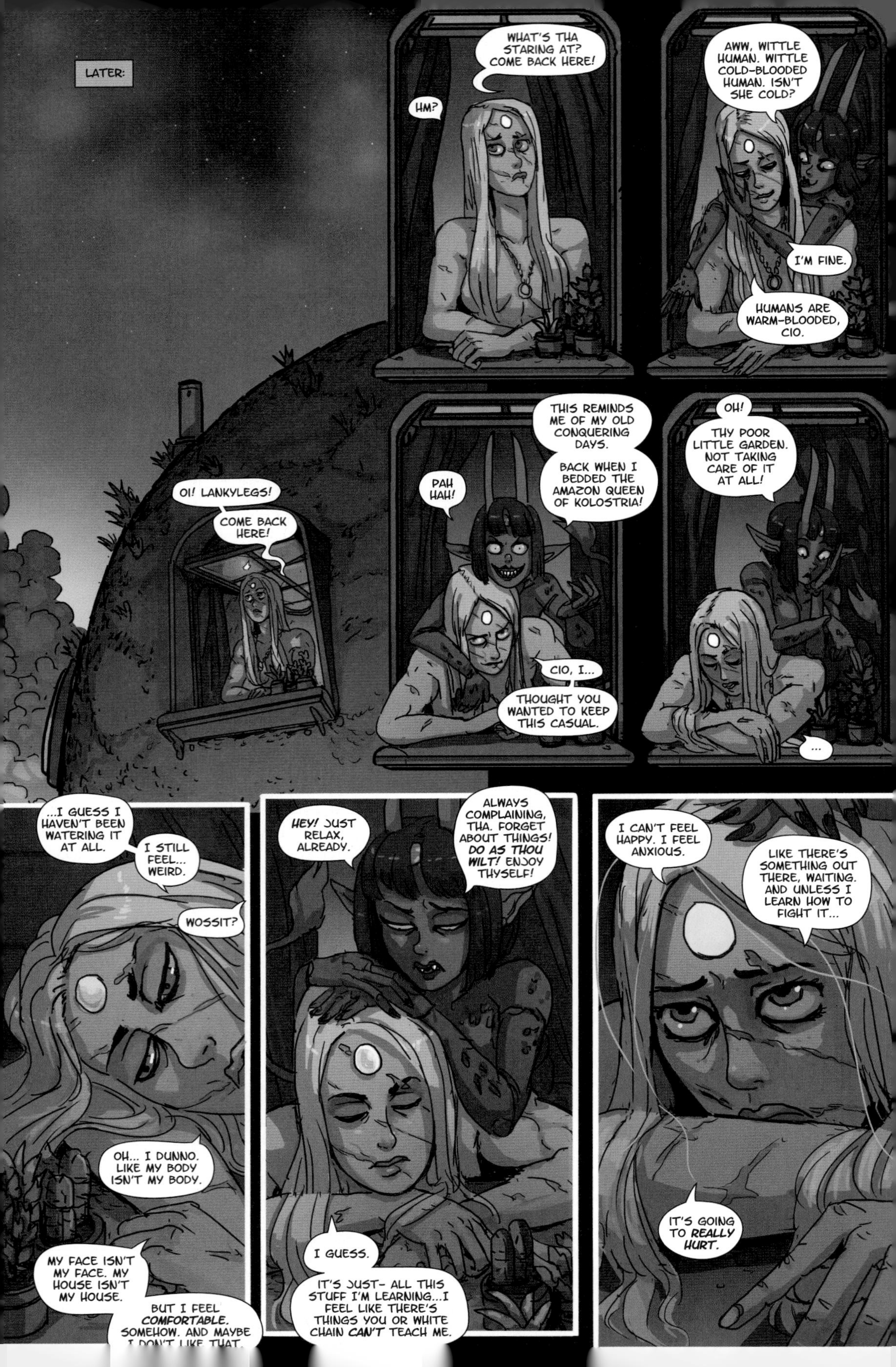
LATER:
WHAT'S THA STARING AT? COME BACK HERE!
HM?
AWW, WITTLE HUMAN. WITTLE COLD-BLOODED HUMAN. ISN'T SHE COLD?
I'M FINE.
HUMANS ARE WARM-BLOODED, CIO.
OI! LANKYLEGS!
COME BACK HERE!
THIS REMINDS ME OF MY OLD CONQUERING DAYS.
BACK WHEN I BEDDED THE AMAZON QUEEN OF KOLOSTRIA!
PAH HAH!
CIO, I...
THOUGHT YOU WANTED TO KEEP THIS CASUAL.
OH!
THY POOR LITTLE GARDEN. NOT TAKING CARE OF IT AT ALL!
...
...I GUESS I HAVEN'T BEEN WATERING IT AT ALL.
I STILL FEEL... WEIRD.
WOSSIT?
OH... I DUNNO. LIKE MY BODY ISN'T MY BODY.
MY FACE ISN'T MY FACE. MY HOUSE ISN'T MY HOUSE.
BUT I FEEL COMFORTABLE. SOMEHOW. AND MAYBE I DON'T LIKE THAT.
HEY! JUST RELAX, ALREADY.
ALWAYS COMPLAINING, THA. FORGET ABOUT THINGS! DO AS THOU WILT! ENJOY THYSELF!
I GUESS.
IT'S JUST- ALL THIS STUFF I'M LEARNING...I FEEL LIKE THERE'S THINGS YOU OR WHITE CHAIN CAN'T TEACH ME.
I CAN'T FEEL HAPPY. I FEEL ANXIOUS.
LIKE THERE'S SOMETHING OUT THERE, WAITING. AND UNLESS I LEARN HOW TO FIGHT IT...
IT'S GOING TO REALLY HURT.

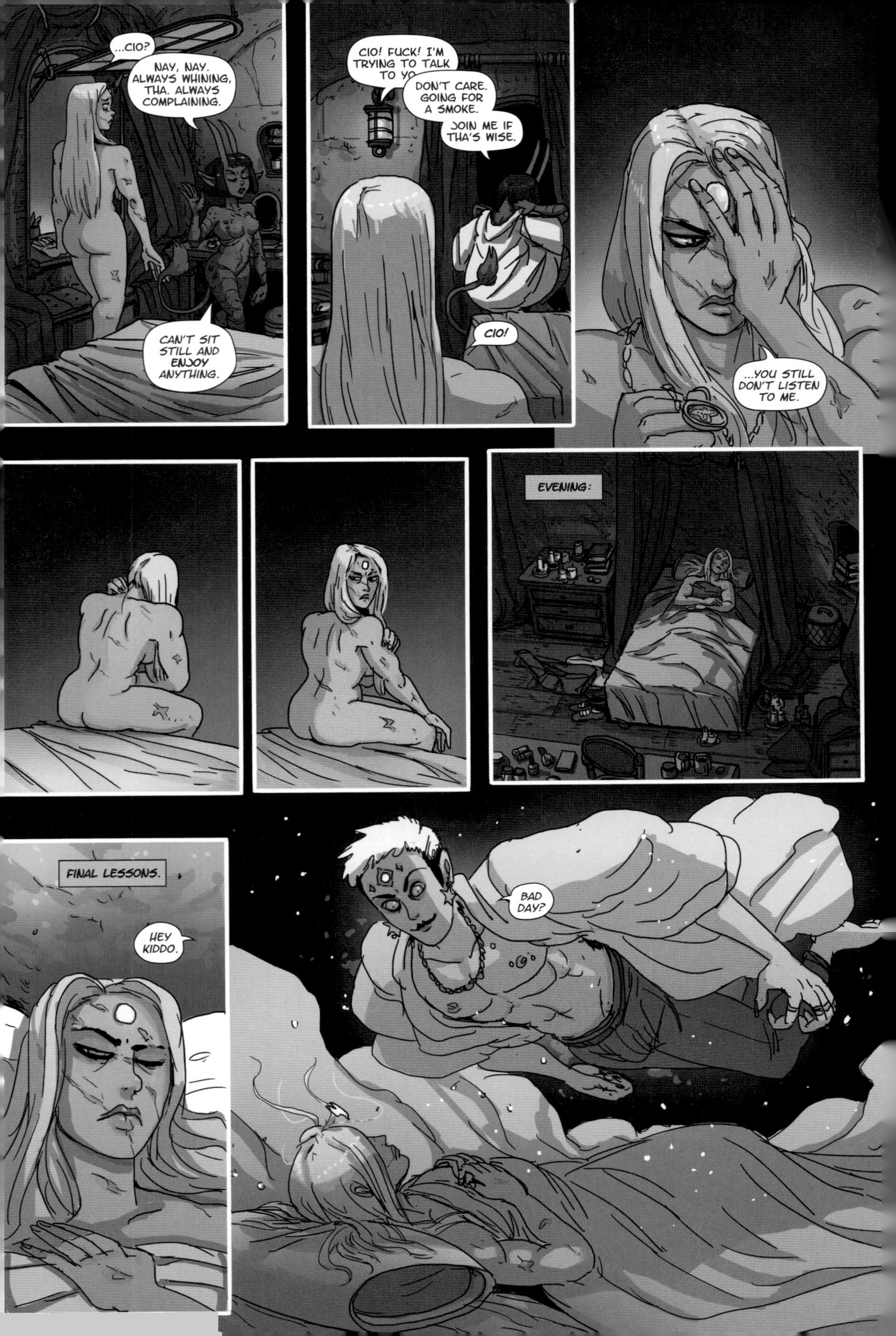

...CIO?
NAY, NAY. ALWAYS WHINING, THA. ALWAYS COMPLAINING.
CAN'T SIT STILL AND ENJOY ANYTHING.
CIO! FUCK! I'M TRYING TO TALK TO YO
DON'T CARE. GOING FOR A SMOKE.
JOIN ME IF THA'S WISE.
CIO!
...YOU STILL DON'T LISTEN TO ME.
EVENING:
FINAL LESSONS.
HEY KIDDO.
BAD DAY?

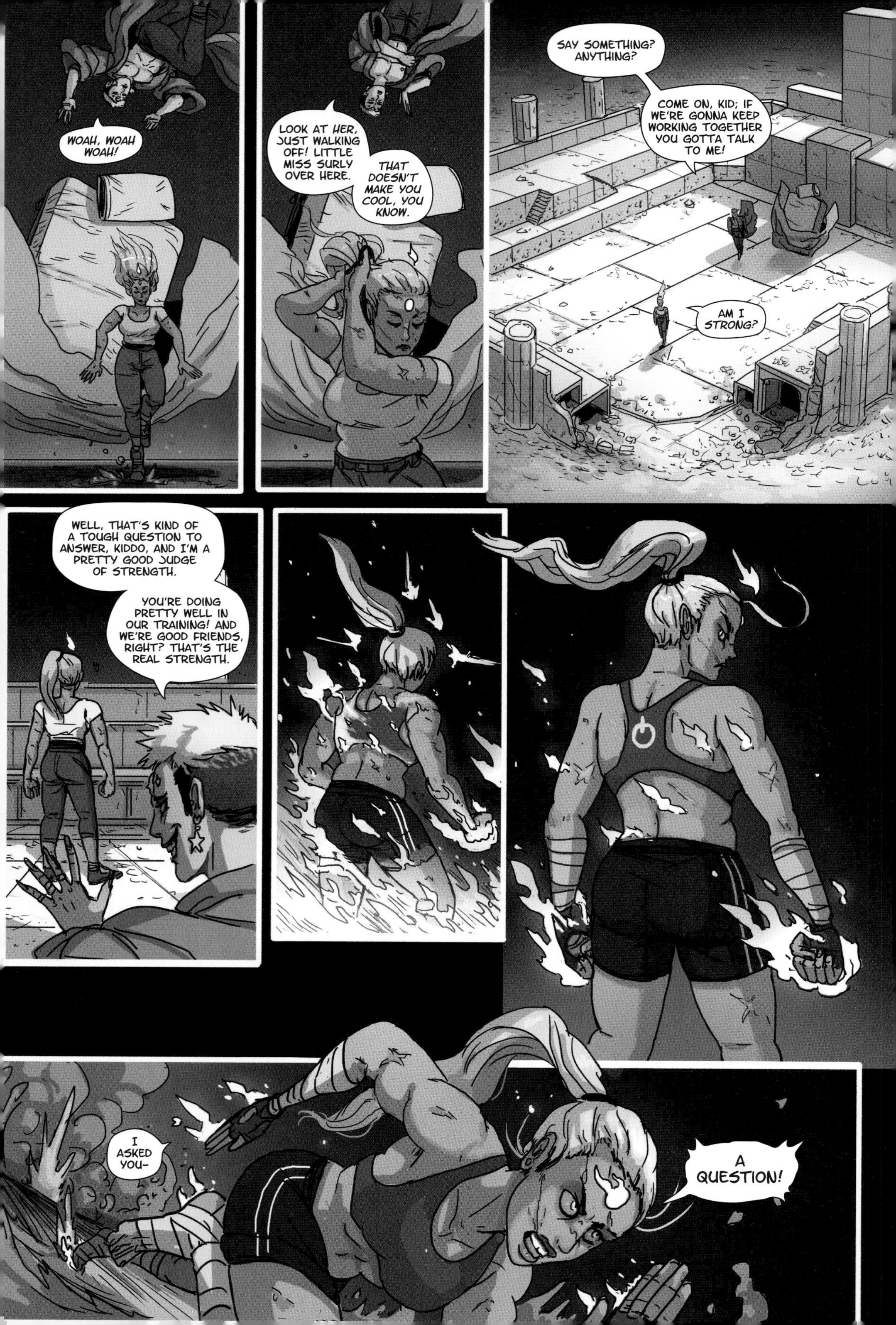
WOAH, WOAH WOAH!
LOOK AT HER, JUST WALKING OFF! LITTLE MISS SURLY OVER HERE.
THAT DOESN'T MAKE YOU COOL, YOU KNOW.
SAY SOMETHING? ANYTHING?
COME ON, KID; IF WE'RE GONNA KEEP WORKING TOGETHER YOU GOTTA TALK TO ME!
AM I STRONG?
WELL, THAT'S KIND OF A TOUGH QUESTION TO ANSWER, KIDDO, AND I'M A PRETTY GOOD JUDGE OF STRENGTH.
YOU'RE DOING PRETTY WELL IN OUR TRAINING! AND WE'RE GOOD FRIENDS, RIGHT? THAT'S THE REAL STRENGTH.
I ASKED YOU-
A QUESTION!

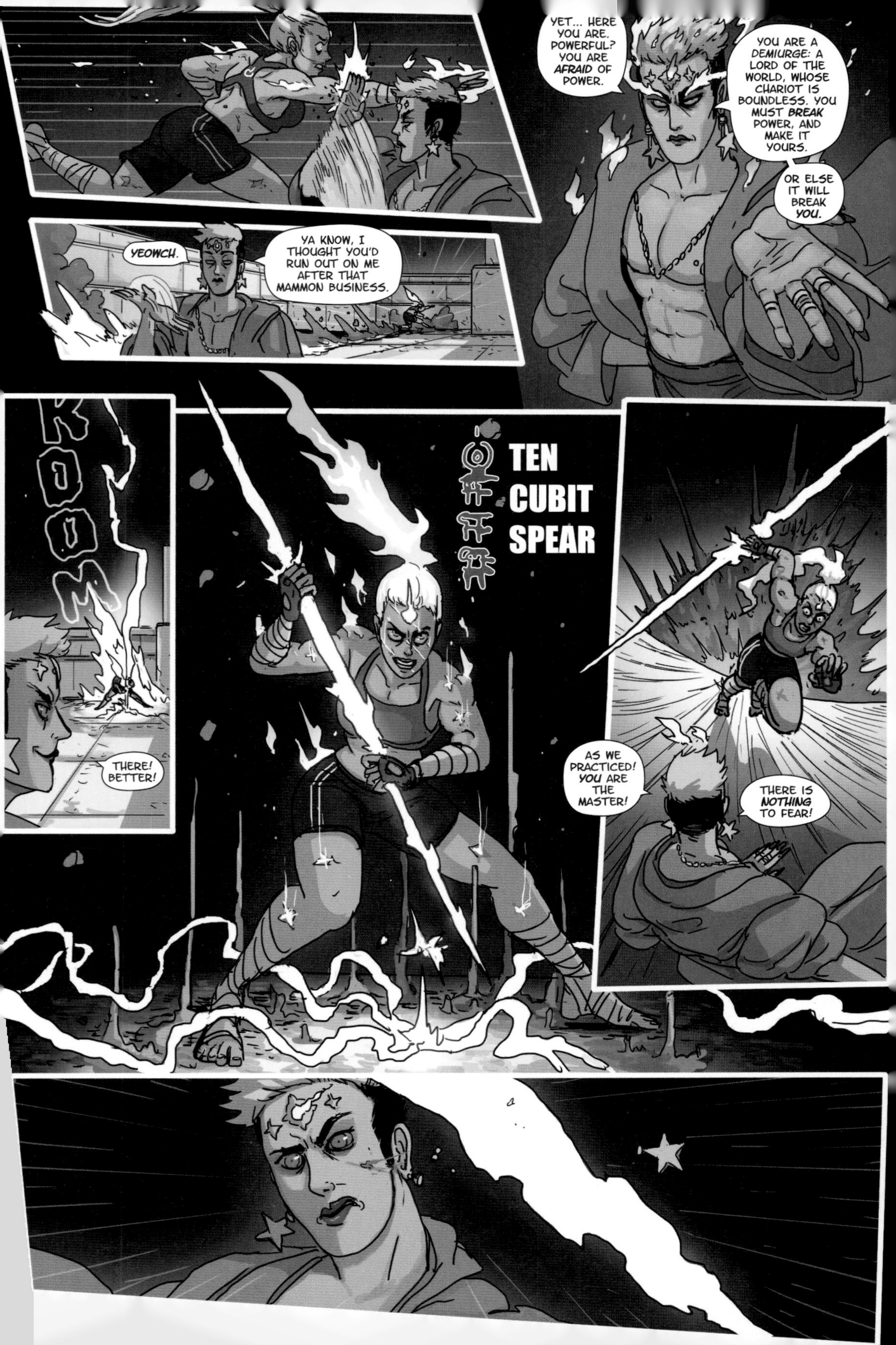
YEOWCH.
YA KNOW, I THOUGHT YOU'D RUN OUT ON ME AFTER THAT MAMMON BUSINESS.
YET... HERE YOU ARE. POWERFUL? YOU ARE AFRAID OF POWER.
YOU ARE A DEMIURGE: A LORD OF THE WORLD, WHOSE CHARIOT IS BOUNDLESS. YOU MUST BREAK POWER, AND MAKE IT YOURS.
OR ELSE IT WILL BREAK YOU.
ROOM
THERE! BETTER!
TEN CUBIT SPEAR
AS WE PRACTICED! YOU ARE THE MASTER!
THERE IS NOTHING TO FEAR!

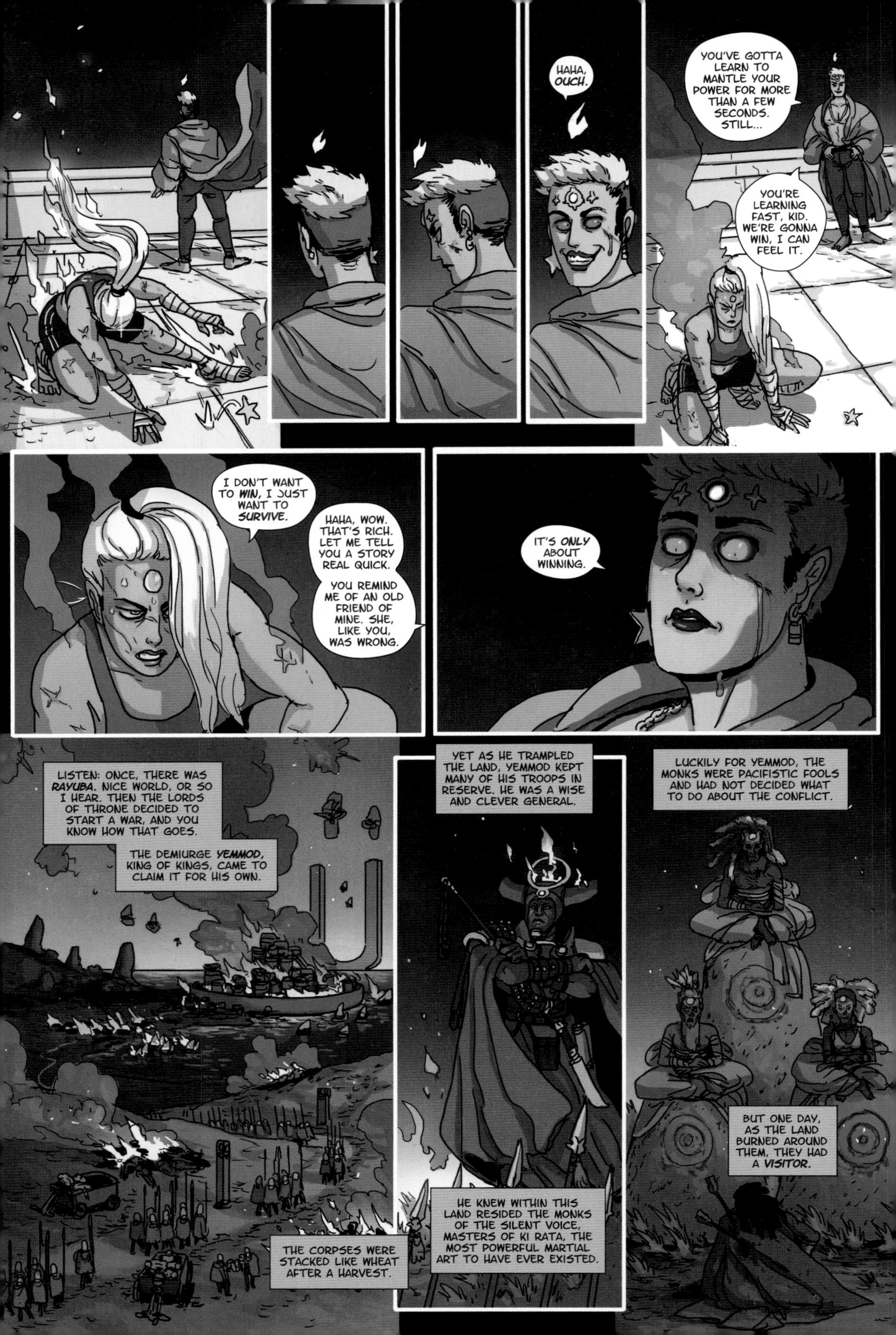
HAHA, OUCH.
YOU'VE GOTTA LEARN TO MANTLE YOUR POWER FOR MORE THAN A FEW SECONDS. STILL...
YOU'RE LEARNING FAST, KID. WE'RE GONNA WIN, I CAN FEEL IT.
I DON'T WANT TO WIN, I JUST WANT TO SURVIVE.
HAHA, WOW. THAT'S RICH. LET ME TELL YOU A STORY REAL QUICK.
YOU REMIND ME OF AN OLD FRIEND OF MINE. SHE, LIKE YOU, WAS WRONG.
IT'S ONLY ABOUT WINNING.
LISTEN: ONCE, THERE WAS RAYUBA. NICE WORLD, OR SO I HEAR. THEN THE LORDS OF THRONE DECIDED TO START A WAR, AND YOU KNOW HOW THAT GOES.
THE DEMIURGE YEMMOD, KING OF KINGS, CAME TO CLAIM IT FOR HIS OWN.
THE CORPSES WERE STACKED LIKE WHEAT AFTER A HARVEST.
YET AS HE TRAMPLED THE LAND, YEMMOD KEPT MANY OF HIS TROOPS IN RESERVE. HE WAS A WISE AND CLEVER GENERAL.
HE KNEW WITHIN THIS LAND RESIDED THE MONKS OF THE SILENT VOICE, MASTERS OF KI RATA, THE MOST POWERFUL MARTIAL ART TO HAVE EVER EXISTED.
LUCKILY FOR YEMMOD, THE MONKS WERE PACIFISTIC FOOLS AND HAD NOT DECIDED WHAT TO DO ABOUT THE CONFLICT.
BUT ONE DAY, AS THE LAND BURNED AROUND THEM, THEY HAD A VISITOR.

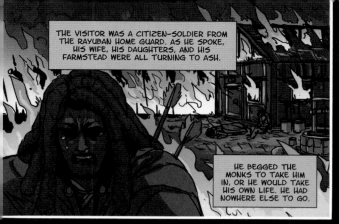

THE VISITOR WAS A CITIZEN-SOLDIER FROM THE RAYUBAN HOME GUARD. AS HE SPOKE, HIS WIFE, HIS DAUGHTERS, AND HIS FARMSTEAD WERE ALL TURNING TO ASH.

HE BEGGED THE MONKS TO TAKE HIM IN, OR HE WOULD TAKE HIS OWN LIFE. HE HAD NOWHERE ELSE TO GO.

THE MONKS WERE WARY, FOR THEY SENSED REVENGE IN HIS HEART.

BUT SINCE THEY HAD ALREADY RESOLVED THAT THEY WOULD NOT STOP RAYUBA'S DEATH, THEY DEICDED TO AT LEAST SAVE THIS ONE MAN.

THEY KNEW IT WOULD BE MANY, MANY YEARS BEFORE THE MAN COULD MASTER KI RATA.

BY THEN, THEY KNEW HE WOULD BE AT PEACE WITH HIS REVENGE.

SO, THEY TOOK ON AN APPRENTICE.

THE SOLDIER WAS A RESOLUTE AND DUTIFUL STUDENT. WHILE HE TRAINED OVER THE YEARS, RAYUBA DIED, PART BY PART. THE EARTH WAS SCOURED AND SALTED. THE CITIZENS WERE SLAUGHTERED OR ENSLAVED.

EVEN THE GREAT STONES OF ITS CITIES WERE TAKEN AWAY.

MANY MORE YEARS PASSED, BEFORE THE MAN FINISHED HIS TRAINING.

BY THEN, NOTHING REMAINED ON RAYUBA. EVEN THE SUN HAD BEEN DESTROYED.

THE MONKS WERE SATISFIED.

"YOU HAVE REACHED THE PINNACLE OF YOUR STRENGTH," SAID THE LEAD MONK.

"YOU, LIKE US, UNDERSTAND THAT VIOLENCE IS A PERPETUAL CYCLE YOU HAVE ESCAPED FROM."

"I AM PROUD OF YOU, MY SON."

... HEH.

...AND?

COME ON, ALLISON. HAVE YOU BEEN PAYING ATTENTION?

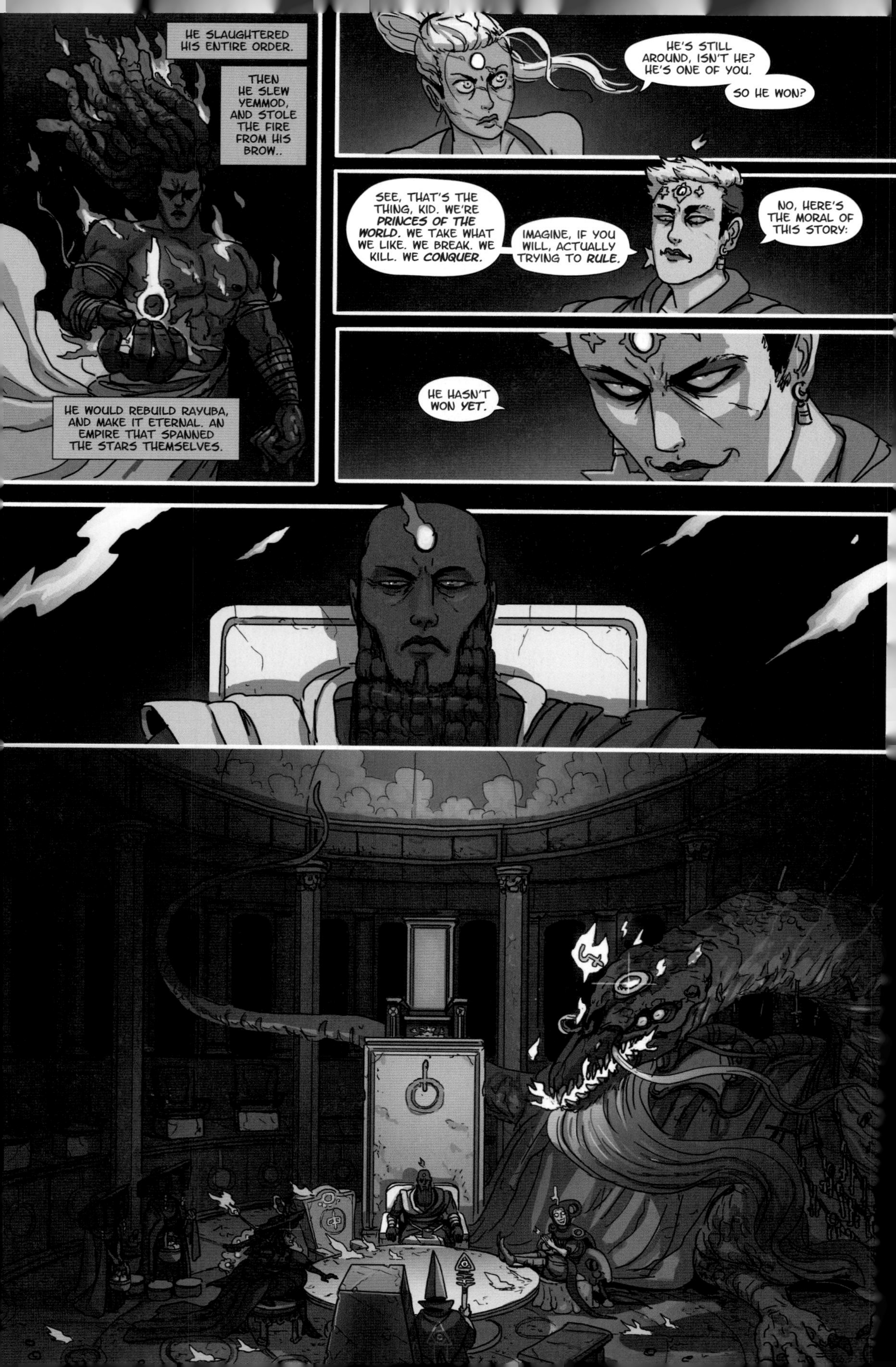
HE SLAUGHTERED HIS ENTIRE ORDER.
THEN HE SLEW YEMMOD, AND STOLE THE FIRE FROM HIS BROW..
HE WOULD REBUILD RAYUBA, AND MAKE IT ETERNAL. AN EMPIRE THAT SPANNED THE STARS THEMSELVES.
HE'S STILL AROUND, ISN'T HE? HE'S ONE OF YOU.
SO HE WON?
NO, HERE'S THE MORAL OF THIS STORY:
IMAGINE, IF YOU WILL, ACTUALLY TRYING TO RULE.
SEE, THAT'S THE THING, KID. WE'RE PRINCES OF THE WORLD. WE TAKE WHAT WE LIKE. WE BREAK. WE KILL. WE CONQUER.
HE HASN'T WON YET.

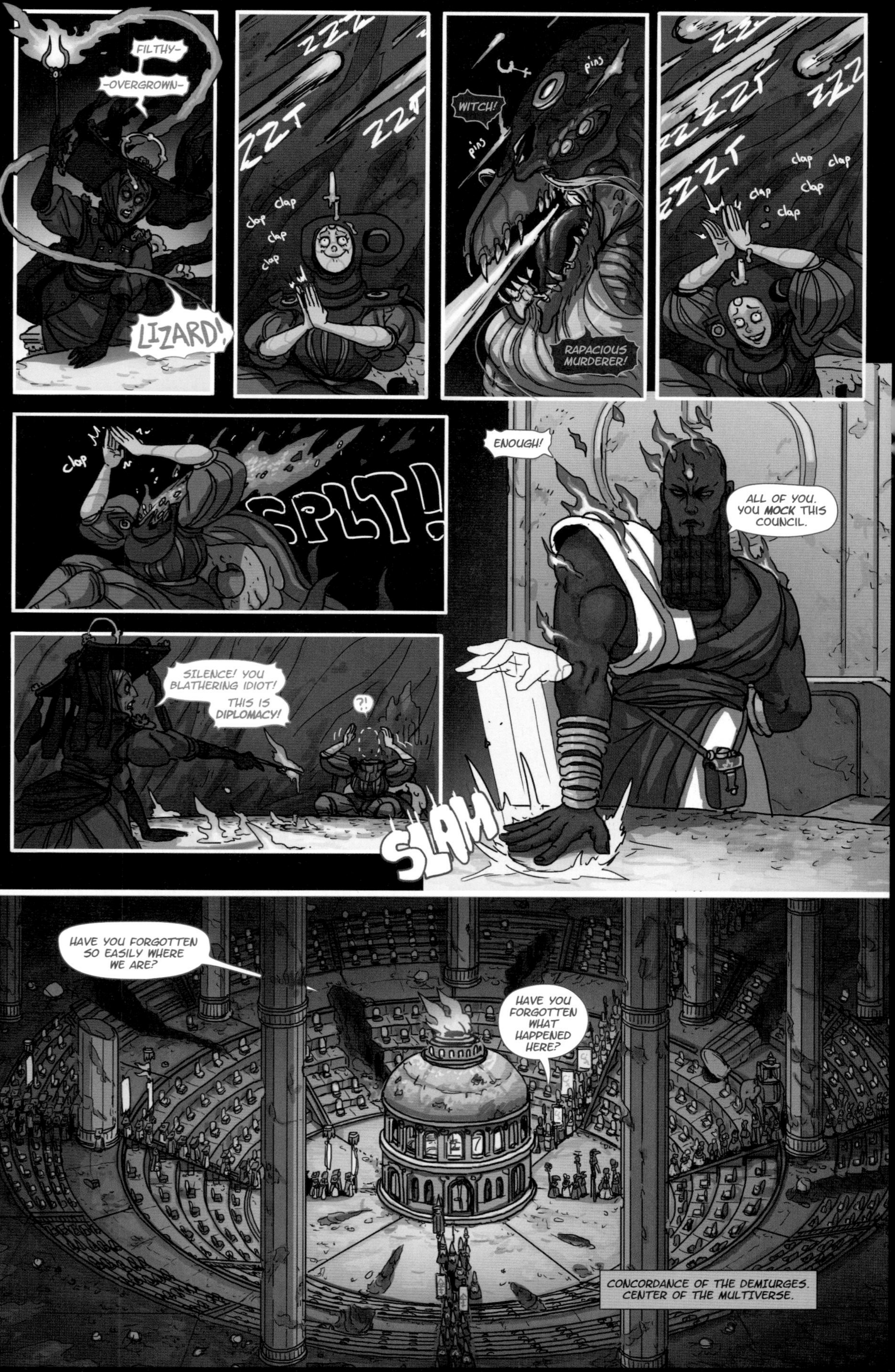
FILTHY-
-OVERGROWN-
LIZARD!
ZZZT
ZZZT
clap clap
clap
clap
WITCH!
pins
pins
RAPACIOUS MURDERER!
ZZZZT
ZZZT
clap clap
clap clap
clap
clap
SPLT!
ENOUGH!
ALL OF YOU. YOU MOCK THIS COUNCIL.
SILENCE! YOU BLATHERING IDIOT!
THIS IS DIPLOMACY!
?!
SLAM
HAVE YOU FORGOTTEN SO EASILY WHERE WE ARE?
HAVE YOU FORGOTTEN WHAT HAPPENED HERE?
CONCORDANCE OF THE DEMIURGES. CENTER OF THE MULTIVERSE.

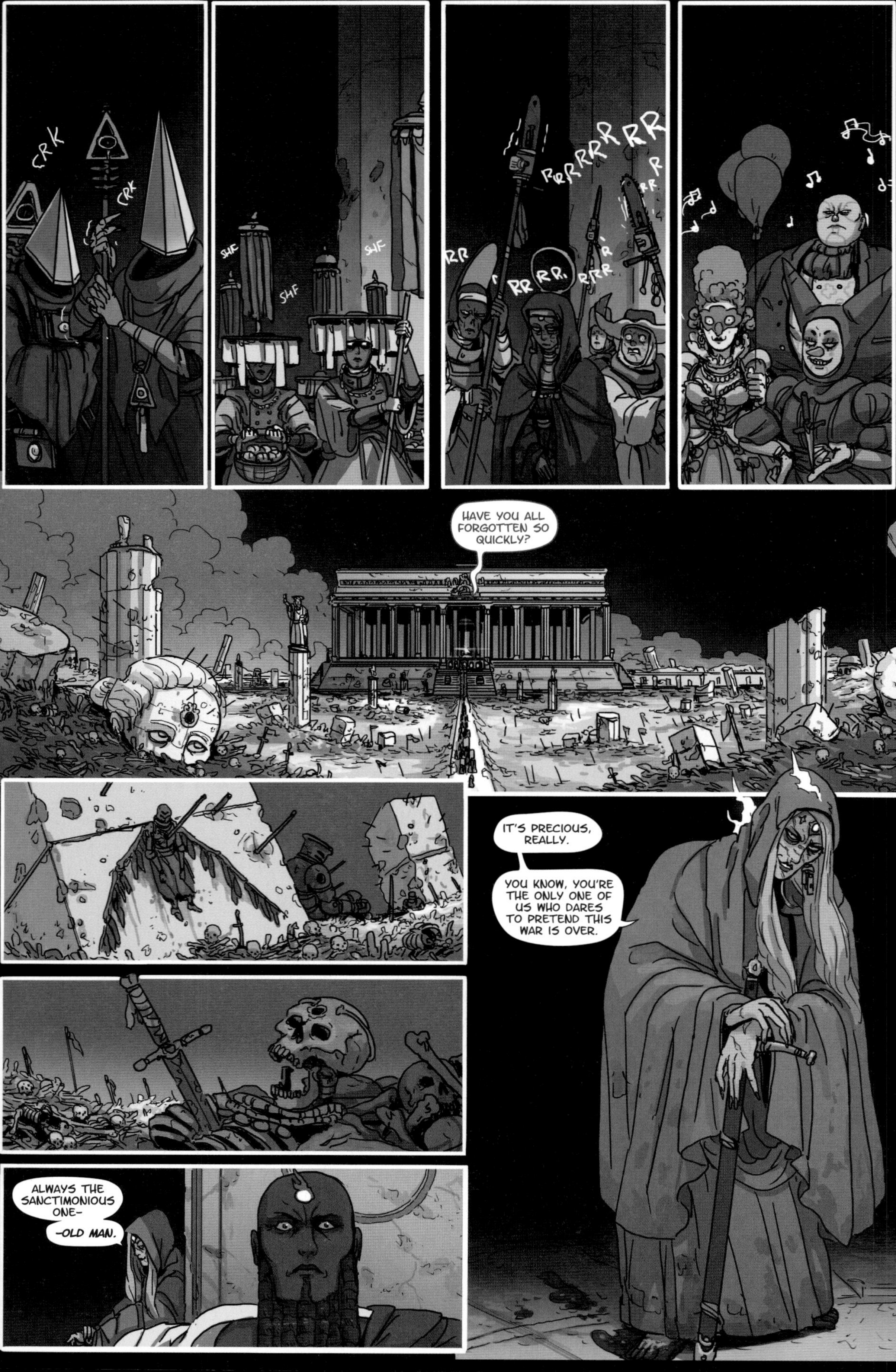
CRK
CRK
SHF
SHF
SHF
RRRRRRRRR
RR
RR
RR RR.
RRR
HAVE YOU ALL FORGOTTEN SO QUICKLY?
IT'S PRECIOUS, REALLY.
YOU KNOW, YOU'RE THE ONLY ONE OF US WHO DARES TO PRETEND THIS WAR IS OVER.
ALWAYS THE SANCTIMONIOUS ONE-
-OLD MAN.

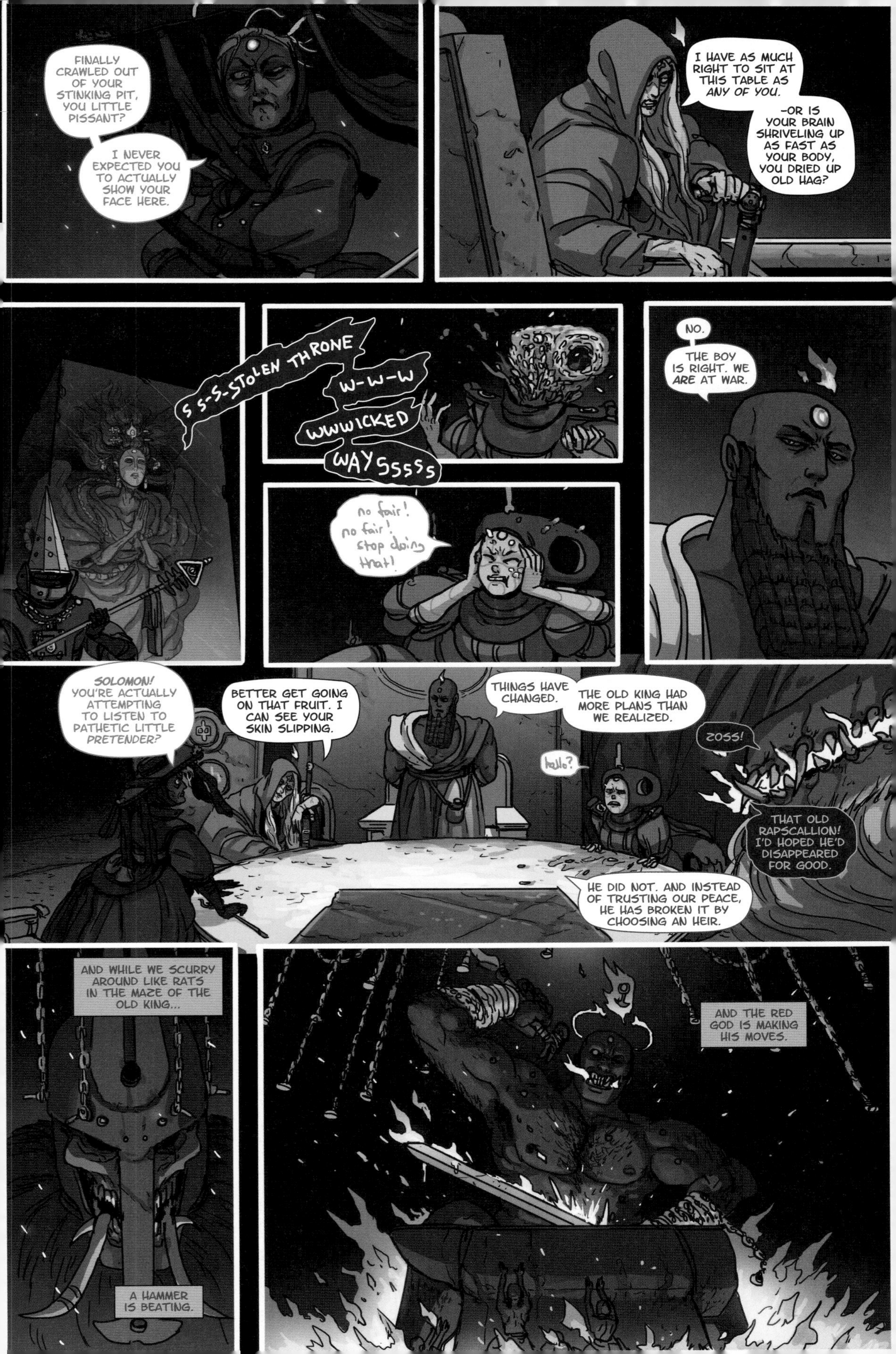
FINALLY CRAWLED OUT OF YOUR STINKING PIT, YOU LITTLE PISSANT?
I NEVER EXPECTED YOU TO ACTUALLY SHOW YOUR FACE HERE.
I HAVE AS MUCH RIGHT TO SIT AT THIS TABLE AS ANY OF YOU.
-OR IS YOUR BRAIN SHRIVELING UP AS FAST AS YOUR BODY, YOU DRIED UP OLD HAG?
S S-S-STOLEN THRONE
W-W-W
WWWICKED
WAYSSSSS
no fair! no fair! stop doing that!
NO.
THE BOY IS RIGHT. WE ARE AT WAR.
SOLOMON! YOU'RE ACTUALLY ATTEMPTING TO LISTEN TO PATHETIC LITTLE PRETENDER?
BETTER GET GOING ON THAT FRUIT. I CAN SEE YOUR SKIN SLIPPING.
THINGS HAVE CHANGED.
THE OLD KING HAD MORE PLANS THAN WE REALIZED.
hello?
ZOSS!
THAT OLD RAPSCALLION! I'D HOPED HE'D DISAPPEARED FOR GOOD.
HE DID NOT. AND INSTEAD OF TRUSTING OUR PEACE, HE HAS BROKEN IT BY CHOOSING AN HEIR.
AND WHILE WE SCURRY AROUND LIKE RATS IN THE MAZE OF THE OLD KING...
A HAMMER IS BEATING.
AND THE RED GOD IS MAKING HIS MOVES.

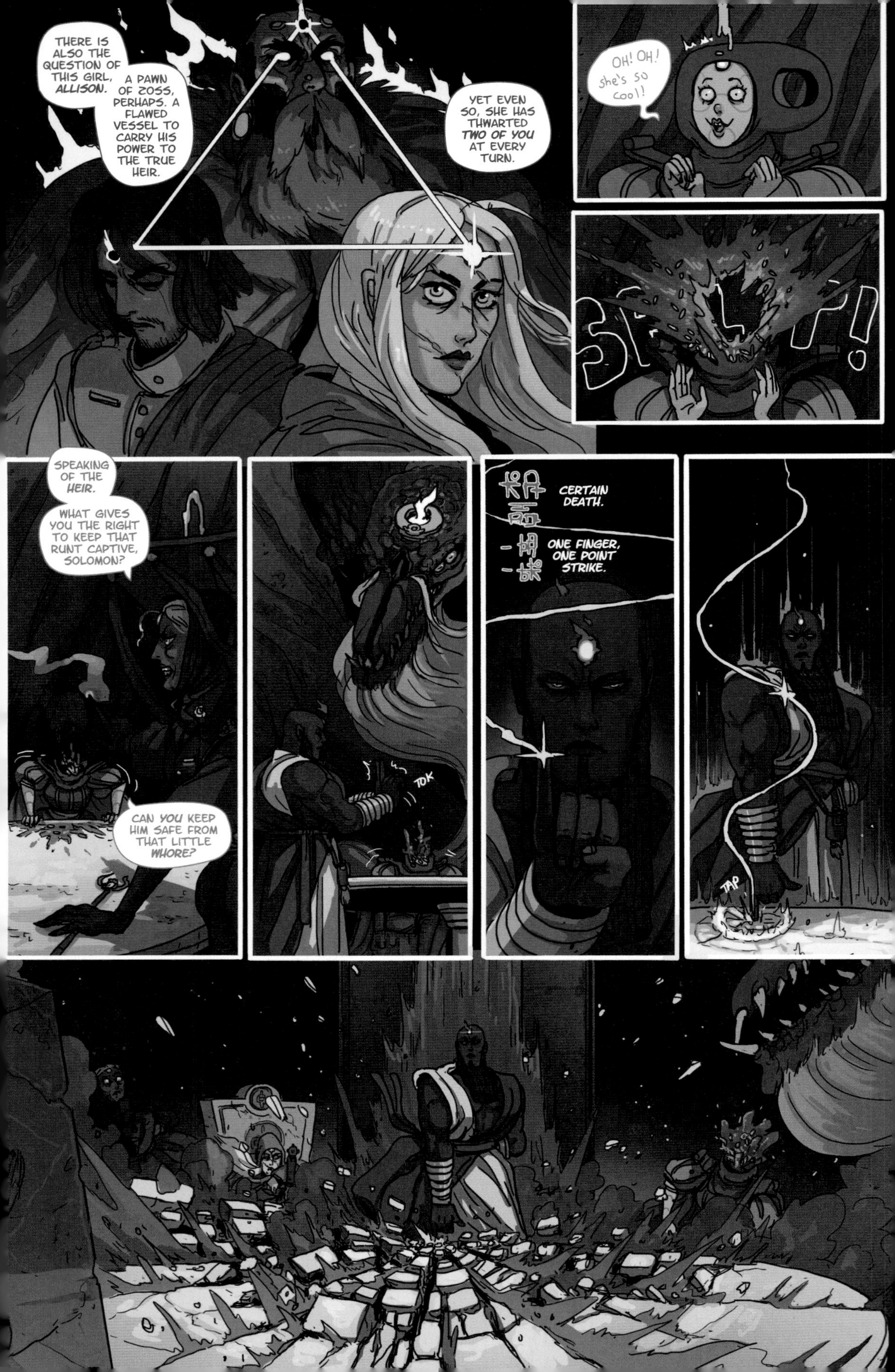
THERE IS ALSO THE QUESTION OF THIS GIRL, *ALLISON.*
A PAWN OF ZOSS, PERHAPS. A FLAWED VESSEL TO CARRY HIS POWER TO THE TRUE HEIR.
YET EVEN SO, SHE HAS THWARTED *TWO OF YOU* AT EVERY TURN.
OH! OH! she's so cool!
SPEAKING OF THE *HEIR.*
WHAT GIVES YOU THE RIGHT TO KEEP THAT RUNT CAPTIVE, SOLOMON?
CAN *YOU* KEEP HIM SAFE FROM THAT LITTLE *WHORE?*
TOK
CERTAIN DEATH.
ONE FINGER, ONE POINT STRIKE.
TAP

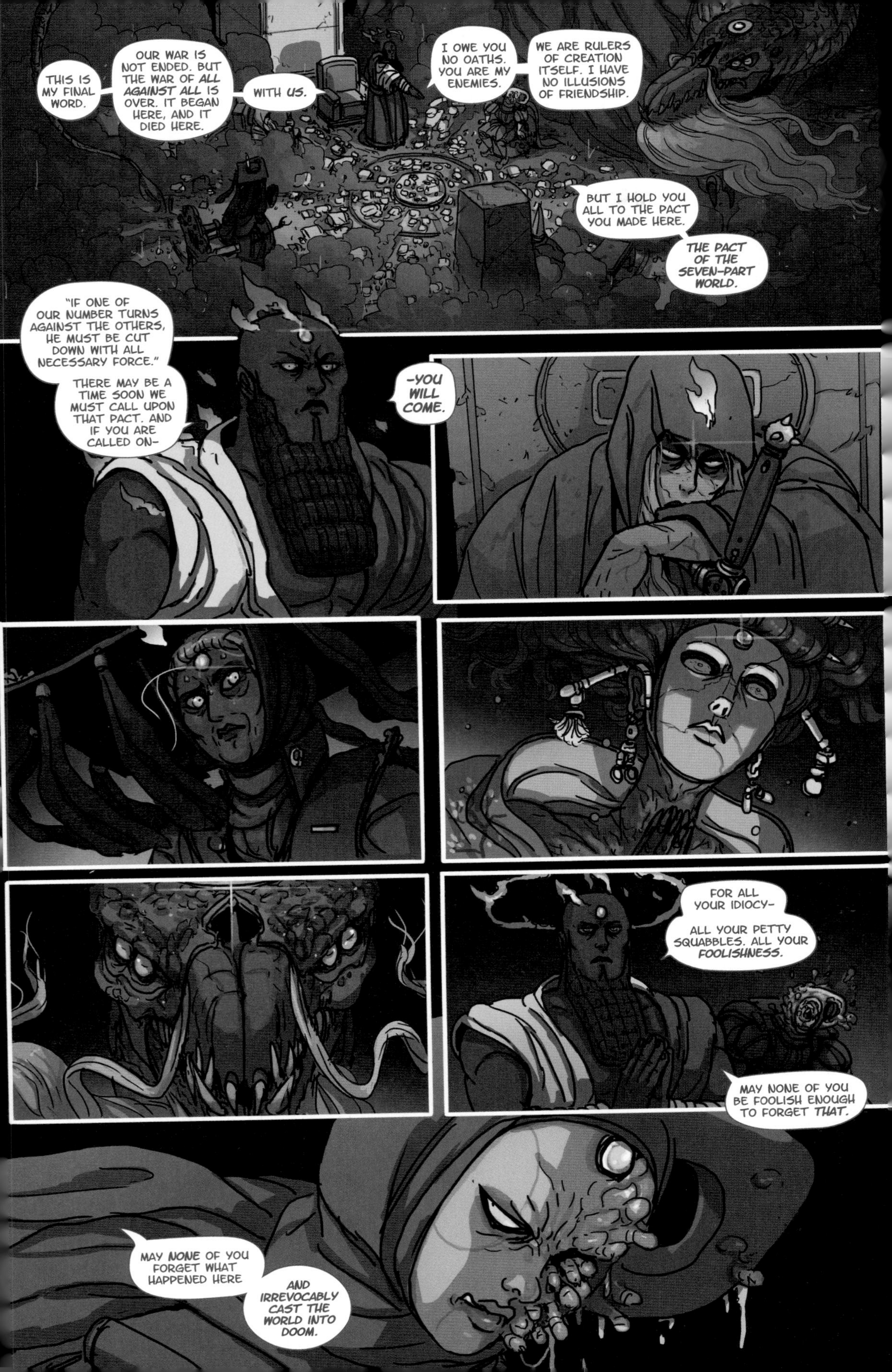
THIS IS MY FINAL WORD.
OUR WAR IS NOT ENDED. BUT THE WAR OF ALL AGAINST ALL IS OVER. IT BEGAN HERE, AND IT DIED HERE.
WITH US.
I OWE YOU NO OATHS. YOU ARE MY ENEMIES.
WE ARE RULERS OF CREATION ITSELF. I HAVE NO ILLUSIONS OF FRIENDSHIP.
BUT I HOLD YOU ALL TO THE PACT YOU MADE HERE.
THE PACT OF THE SEVEN-PART WORLD.
"IF ONE OF OUR NUMBER TURNS AGAINST THE OTHERS, HE MUST BE CUT DOWN WITH ALL NECESSARY FORCE."
THERE MAY BE A TIME SOON WE MUST CALL UPON THAT PACT. AND IF YOU ARE CALLED ON-
-YOU WILL COME.
FOR ALL YOUR IDIOCY-
ALL YOUR PETTY SQUABBLES. ALL YOUR FOOLISHNESS.
MAY NONE OF YOU BE FOOLISH ENOUGH TO FORGET THAT.
MAY NONE OF YOU FORGET WHAT HAPPENED HERE
AND IRREVOCABLY CAST THE WORLD INTO DOOM.

Resolute, Her she could find some new information for the Sergeant (and perhaps impress him), Het truggled down the muddy slope into he land below. And when she arrived here, she saw a strange and terrifying ight indeed.

n the square there was a great gathering of the dwellers of that land. A long and warped table had been aid out, and all the dwellers were all gathered around a terrible fire, which hrew ghastly light upon their dark and white-eyed faces. Het saw there he fire-stoking woman, and the junk-sifting man, and the bundle-bearing youth. The entire gathering was giving forth an unearthly wail, their hands outstretched in claw-like shapes, their aces upturned and monstrous. A great lightning bolt of fear struck Het about the heart and she fled at once back to the palace.

Early in the morning, she told the Sergeant of what she had seen, and he congratulated her for her find, and promised to redouble his investigation given the new evidence of wrongdoing. So it was that even though Het's boots and uniform were already muddy from the night before, hat morning she set out warm with pride and her chin thrust in the air, he Centurion ahead of her with his word hand flexing.

Het's discovery seemed to invigorate the Sergeant. He set about questioning the dwellers at twice the speed he had before, and very shortly they had a suspect, who the Centurion cut down with incredible speed before they could even ask him a question. He did not have a Rakshasa inside him, but, n fact, turned out to be simply a bad debtor. So it was with the next person he Centurion slaughtered, a woman who turned out to be a forger of the king's coin. "We'll have a very busy day," said the Sergeant, cleaning his perfect fingernails.

Het was roiling with frustration and guilt. How could they have been so misled? Petty criminals were not what they had come for. Surely the dwellers of this land had some awful secret they were hiding away, especially given the dark gathering Het had stumbled on the night before. Perhaps there was an entire clan of Rakshasa, scheming away at their demise. The mud-daubed faces of the hunched and twisted people around Het looked more similar than ever. They seemed to be laughing.

With great intent, Het excused herself from the Sergeant and Centurion, and rushed to the hut of the fire-stoking woman, knocking her door open with the butt of her stave. "You there!" said Het accusingly, "What are you doing?"

"I am making bread," said the astonished woman, "For this land is harsh and scarce, but it gives to us all the same. It's what we have." Het was suspicious and took three fine steps into the room, in the way she'd seen the Sergeant step. But the woman showed her the oven, and the way it was stoked, and the thin and flimsy-looking bread that she was baking there. And since Het could find no fault with baking bread, she left and ran to the dwelling of the junk-sifting man.

"You there!" she said as she reached his dwelling. She gripped her stave tightly, for she feared trouble. "What is your business?" The junk-sifter turned to her, astonished. "I am preparing amulets, made by the townspeople," he said. "For this land is harsh and bleak, but its people are resourceful." Het took two great steps inside the dwelling and saw that he was telling the truth. The amulets weren't terribly well made, but they had a certain crude beauty to them that was undeniable. Growing increasingly uneasy, Het took up her stave and fled to find the bundle-bearing youth.

It took her very little time, for Het was in a great hurry. A terrible suspicion that she was being deceived had taken hold of her, and she began to walk square shouldered and narrow-eyed like the Centurion. Her hand ever hovered around her sword handle, but never touched it, for she was terrible with the sword.

She accosted the youth, who turned to her wide eyed. "You there!" barked Het, and she took a single step and grasped the youth's shoulder. "What are you scheming? I know there's something your people are hiding from me!" The youth gaped at Het and said, "Please! I'm carrying the burial cloths! For this land is harsh and its rulers cruel, but its people are resilient." It was then that Het realized she was crushing the youth's shoulder and let go. The trembling youth unfurled the cloth, and explained how the cloth was dyed and folded. Het saw its intricate pattern, but still her suspicions were not quenched. She shoved the terrified youth aside and ran in a panic to where the Sergeant and the Centurion were executing a root seller who was selling their produce over-price. "A terrible shame," said the Sergeant, and wiped his brow.

As Het approached him, she told him of her suspicions. "A conspiracy is boiling here!" she said, breathless. "I am certain now the dwellers of this land are hiding the Rakshasa!"

"I thought as much," said the Sergeant, "which is why I have stepped up our investigations once again."

The Centurion said nothing, but only cleaned the viscera off his sword in well-practiced motions.

HE HAD BUTCHERED SEVEN DWELLERS THAT DAY, AND WAS EXCEPTIONALLY HAPPY FOR IT.

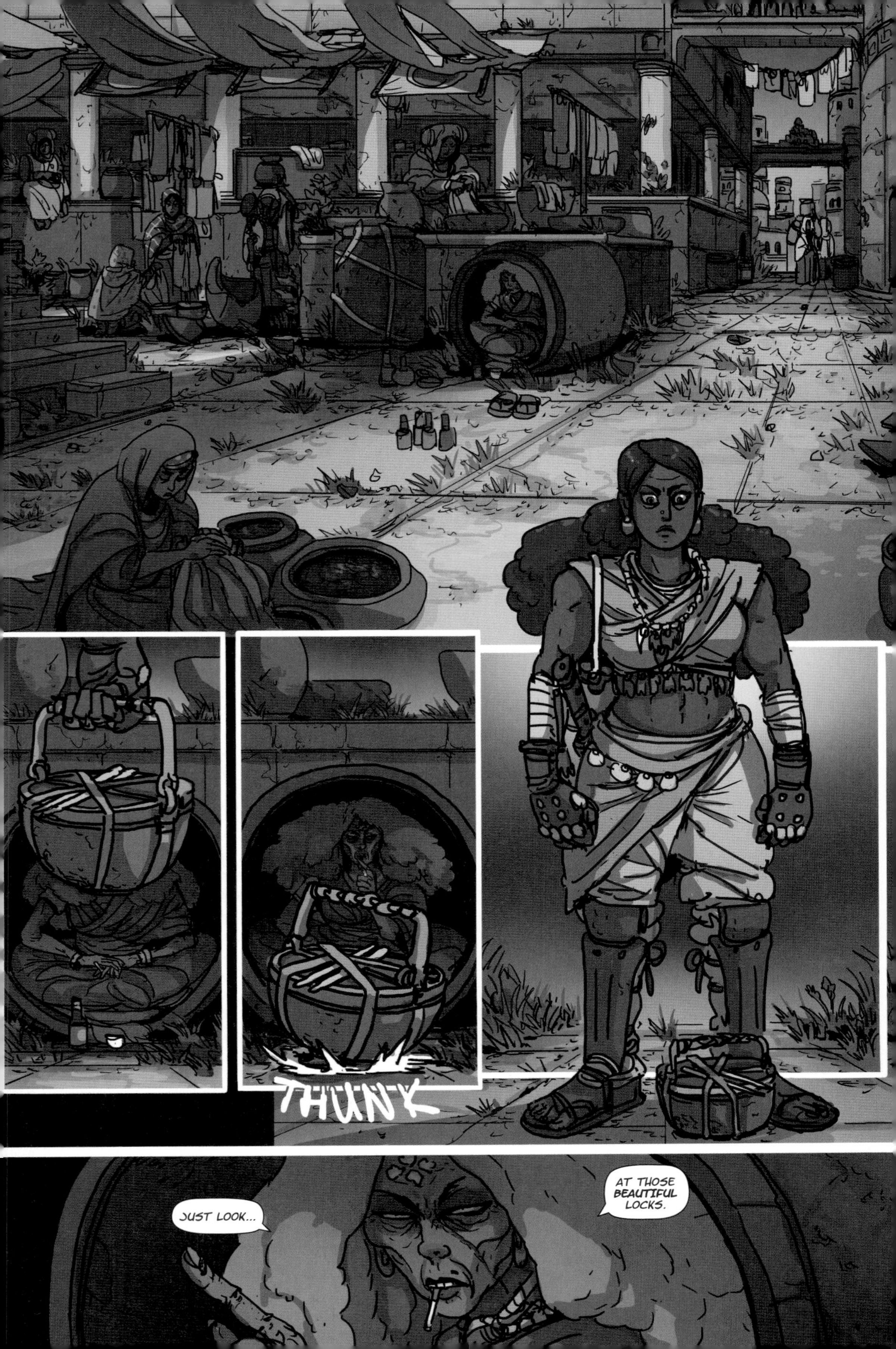
THUNK
JUST LOOK...
AT THOSE BEAUTIFUL LOCKS.

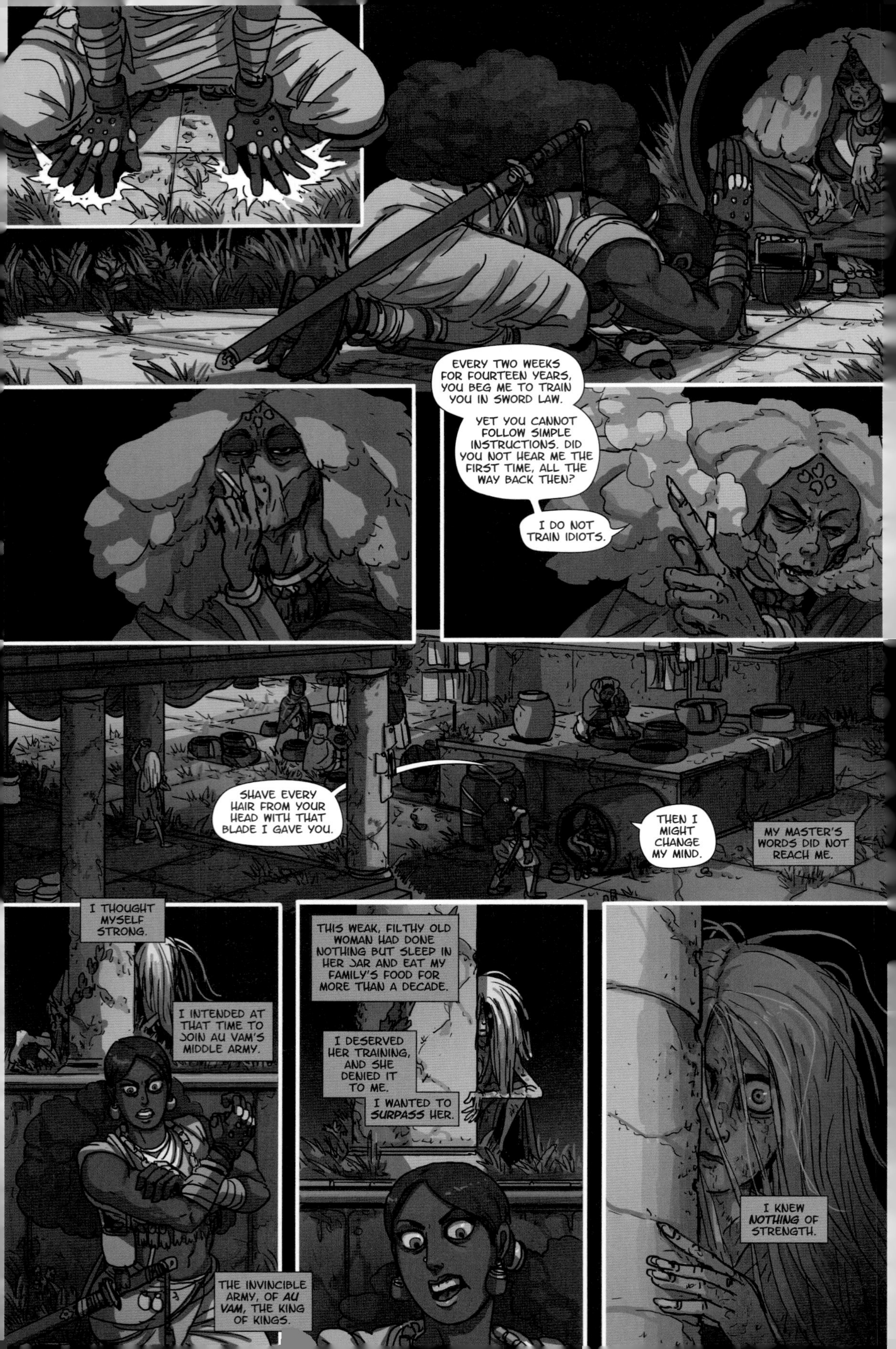
EVERY TWO WEEKS FOR FOURTEEN YEARS, YOU BEG ME TO TRAIN YOU IN SWORD LAW.
YET YOU CANNOT FOLLOW SIMPLE INSTRUCTIONS. DID YOU NOT HEAR ME THE FIRST TIME, ALL THE WAY BACK THEN?
I DO NOT TRAIN IDIOTS.
SHAVE EVERY HAIR FROM YOUR HEAD WITH THAT BLADE I GAVE YOU.
THEN I MIGHT CHANGE MY MIND.
MY MASTER'S WORDS DID NOT REACH ME.
I THOUGHT MYSELF STRONG.
I INTENDED AT THAT TIME TO JOIN AU VAM'S MIDDLE ARMY.
THE INVINCIBLE ARMY, OF *AU VAM*, THE KING OF KINGS.
THIS WEAK, FILTHY OLD WOMAN HAD DONE NOTHING BUT SLEEP IN HER JAR AND EAT MY FAMILY'S FOOD FOR MORE THAN A DECADE.
I DESERVED HER TRAINING, AND SHE DENIED IT TO ME.
I WANTED TO *SURPASS* HER.
I KNEW *NOTHING* OF STRENGTH.

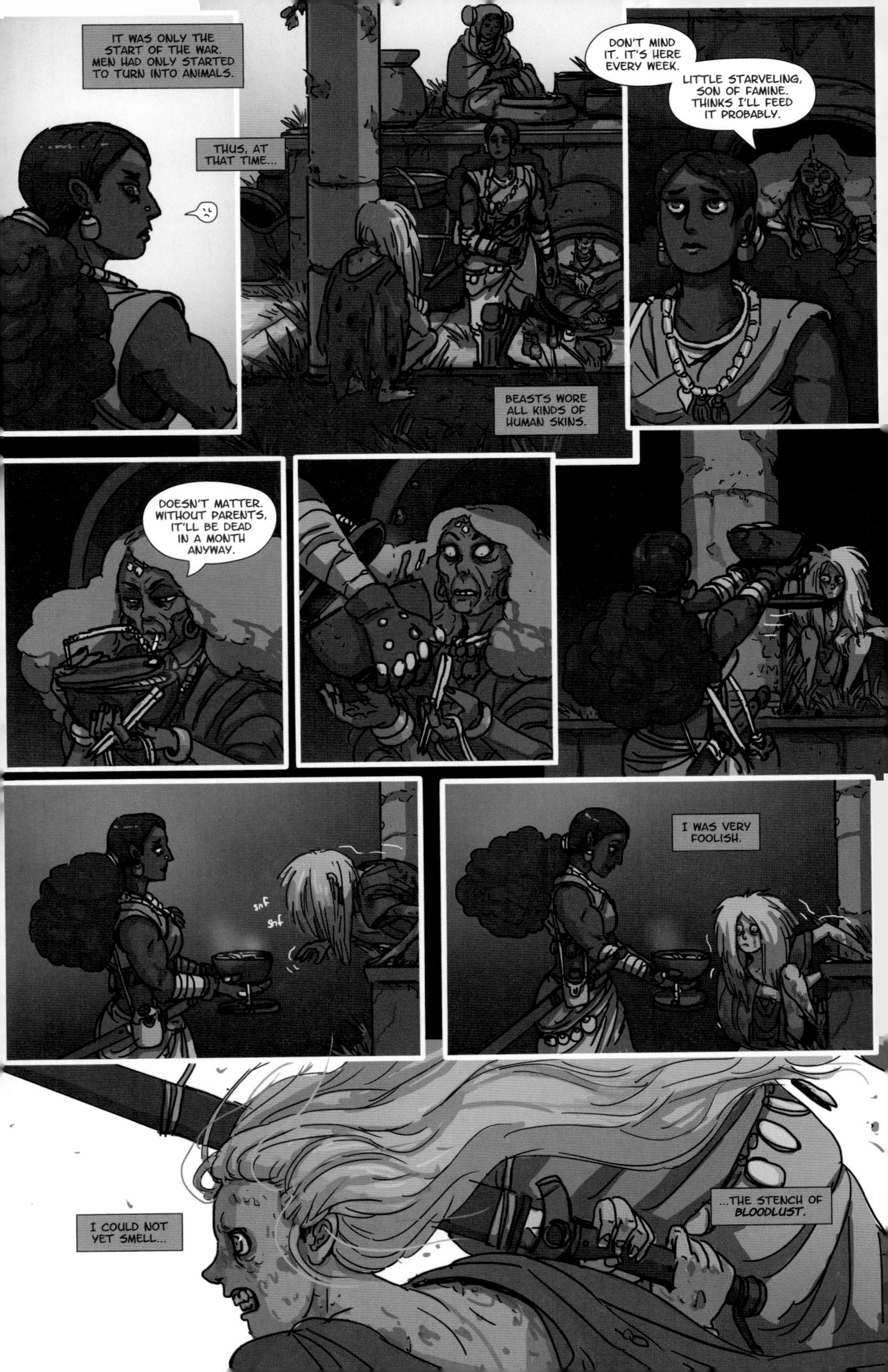
IT WAS ONLY THE START OF THE WAR. MEN HAD ONLY STARTED TO TURN INTO ANIMALS.
THUS, AT THAT TIME...
BEASTS WORE ALL KINDS OF HUMAN SKINS.
DON'T MIND IT. IT'S HERE EVERY WEEK.
LITTLE STARVELING, SON OF FAMINE. THINKS I'LL FEED IT PROBABLY.
DOESN'T MATTER. WITHOUT PARENTS, IT'LL BE DEAD IN A MONTH ANYWAY.
snf
snf
I WAS VERY FOOLISH.
I COULD NOT YET SMELL...
...THE STENCH OF *BLOODLUST*.

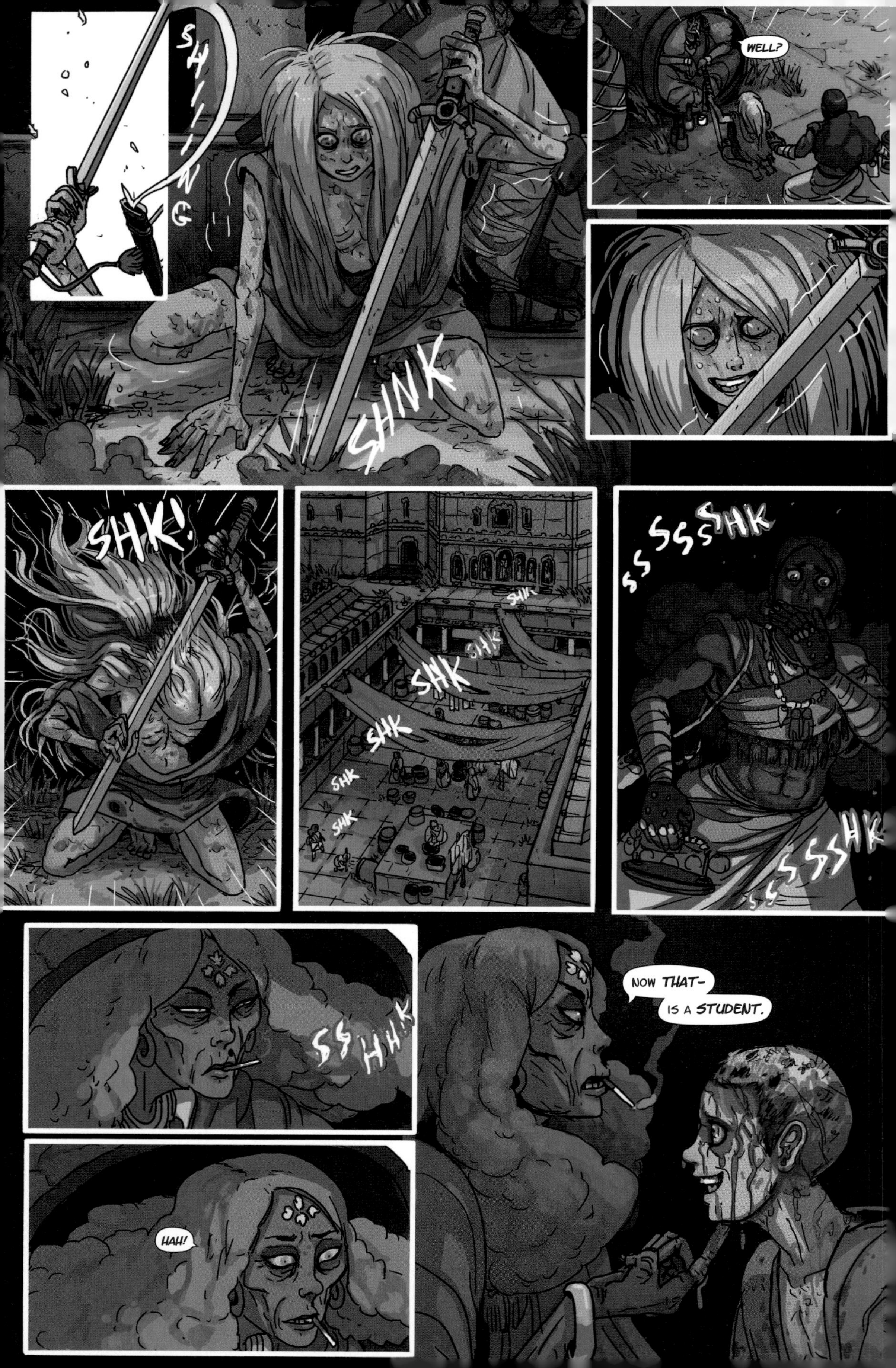
SHIIIING
SHNK
WELL?
SHK!
SHK
SHK
SHK
SHK
SHK
SHK
SSSSHK
SSSSSHK
SSHHK
HAH!
NOW THAT-
IS A STUDENT.

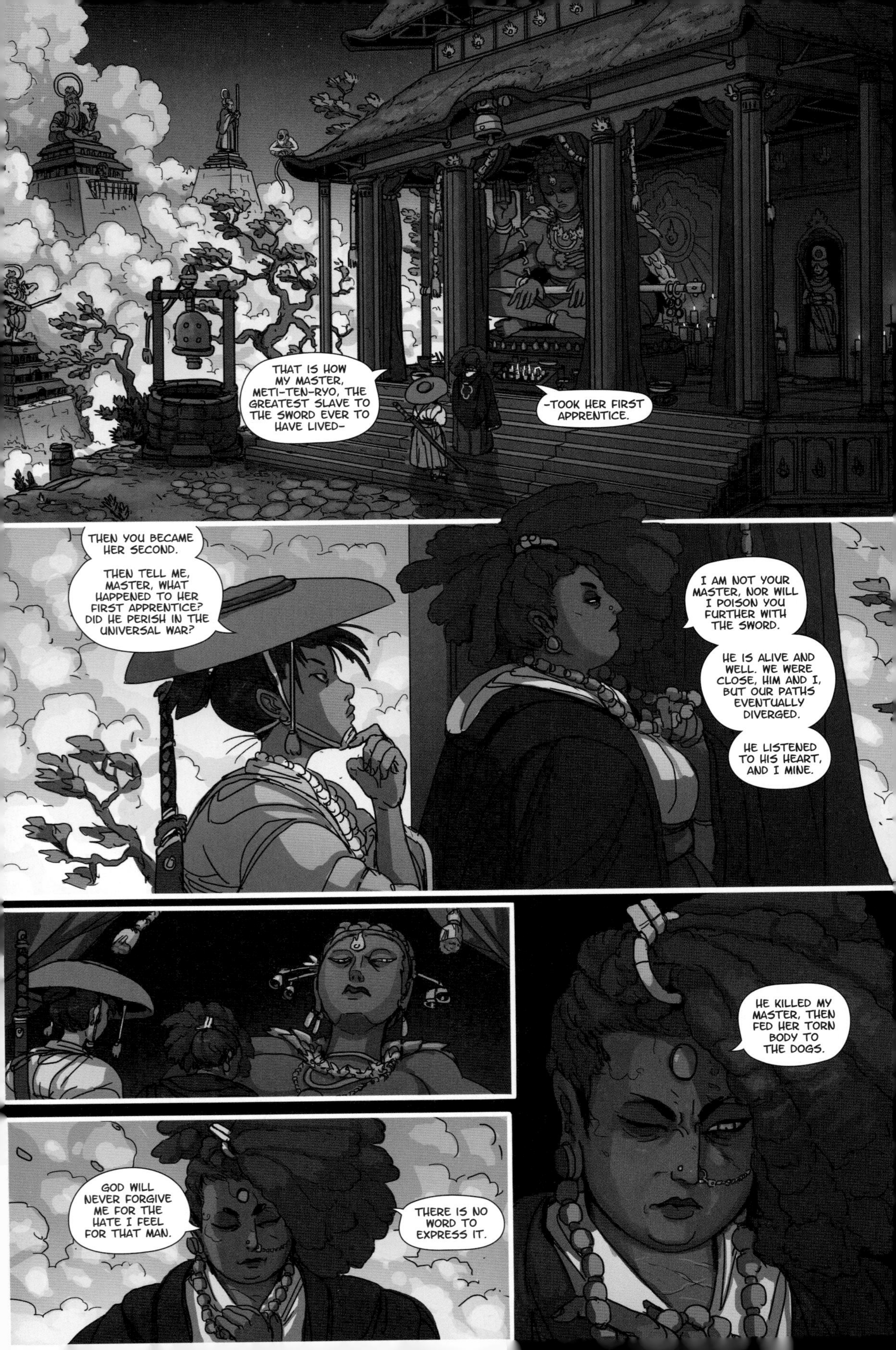
THAT IS HOW MY MASTER, METI-TEN-RYO, THE GREATEST SLAVE TO THE SWORD EVER TO HAVE LIVED-
-TOOK HER FIRST APPRENTICE.
THEN YOU BECAME HER SECOND.
THEN TELL ME, MASTER, WHAT HAPPENED TO HER FIRST APPRENTICE? DID HE PERISH IN THE UNIVERSAL WAR?
I AM NOT YOUR MASTER, NOR WILL I POISON YOU FURTHER WITH THE SWORD.
HE IS ALIVE AND WELL. WE WERE CLOSE, HIM AND I, BUT OUR PATHS EVENTUALLY DIVERGED.
HE LISTENED TO HIS HEART, AND I MINE.
HE KILLED MY MASTER, THEN FED HER TORN BODY TO THE DOGS.
GOD WILL NEVER FORGIVE ME FOR THE HATE I FEEL FOR THAT MAN.
THERE IS NO WORD TO EXPRESS IT.

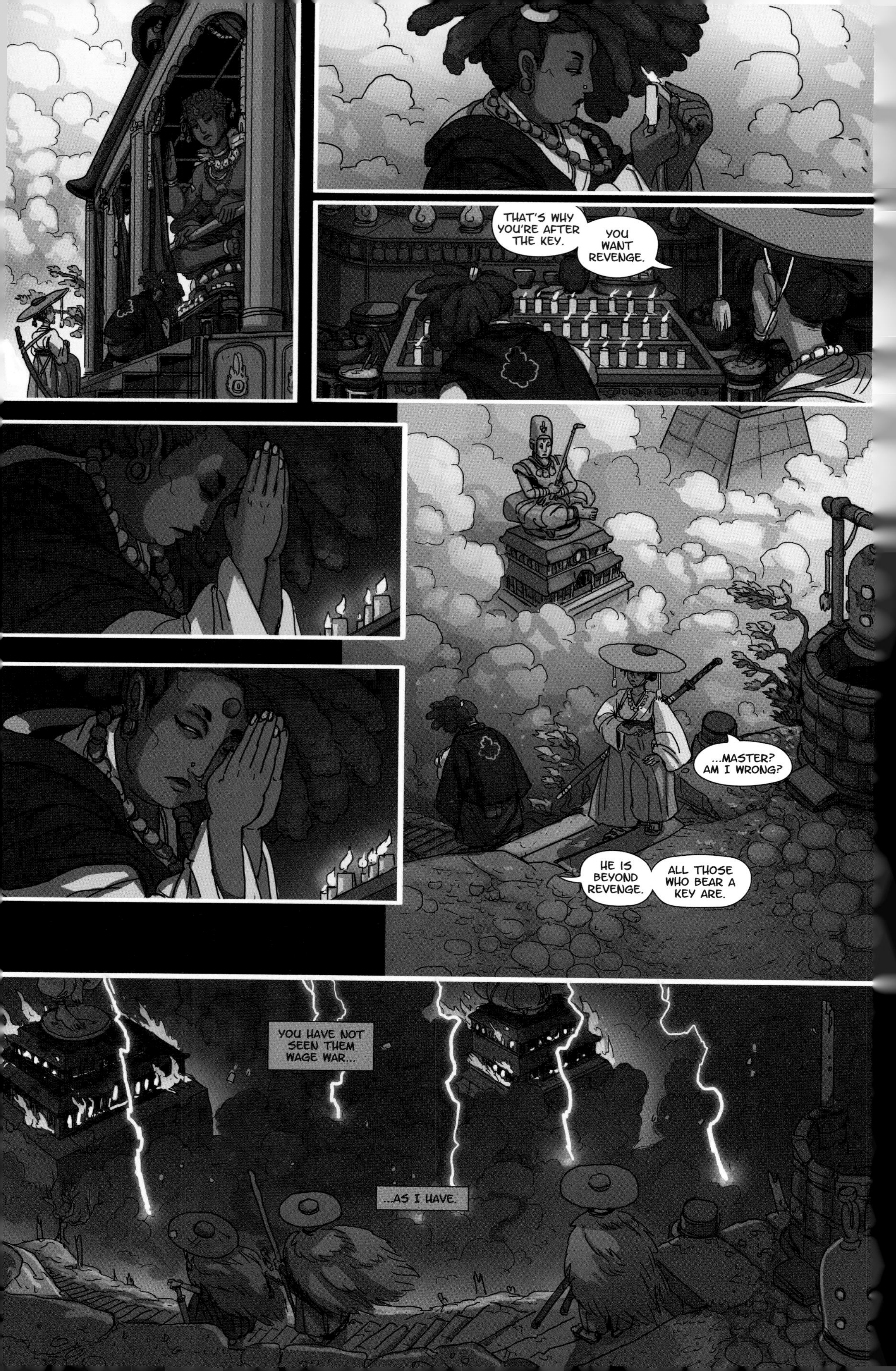
THAT'S WHY YOU'RE AFTER THE KEY.
YOU WANT REVENGE.
...MASTER? AM I WRONG?
HE IS BEYOND REVENGE.
ALL THOSE WHO BEAR A KEY ARE.
YOU HAVE NOT SEEN THEM WAGE WAR...
...AS I HAVE.

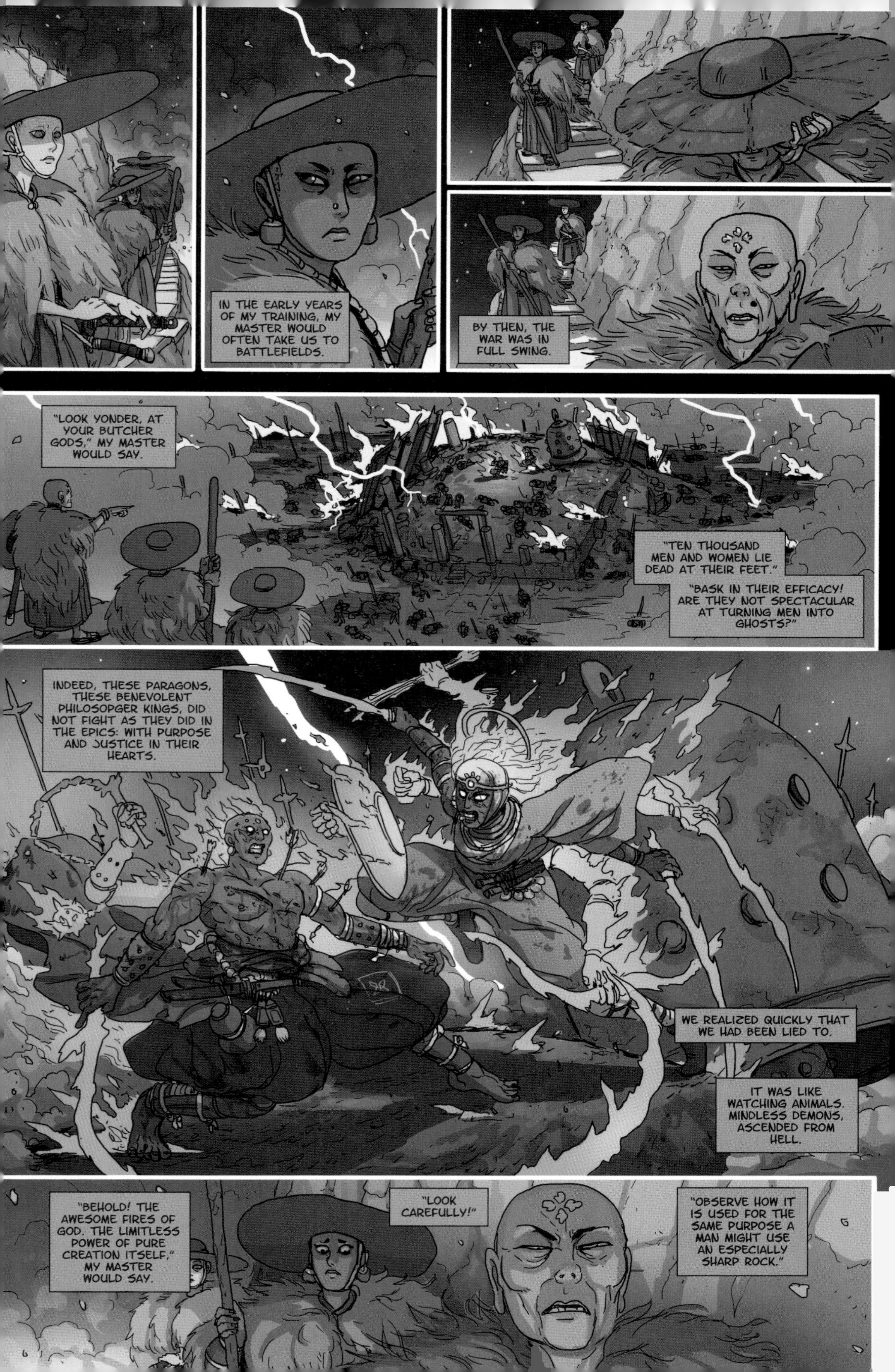

IN THE EARLY YEARS OF MY TRAINING, MY MASTER WOULD OFTEN TAKE US TO BATTLEFIELDS.
BY THEN, THE WAR WAS IN FULL SWING.
"LOOK YONDER, AT YOUR BUTCHER GODS," MY MASTER WOULD SAY.
"TEN THOUSAND MEN AND WOMEN LIE DEAD AT THEIR FEET."
"BASK IN THEIR EFFICACY! ARE THEY NOT SPECTACULAR AT TURNING MEN INTO GHOSTS?"
INDEED, THESE PARAGONS, THESE BENEVOLENT PHILOSOPGER KINGS, DID NOT FIGHT AS THEY DID IN THE EPICS: WITH PURPOSE AND JUSTICE IN THEIR HEARTS.
WE REALIZED QUICKLY THAT WE HAD BEEN LIED TO.
IT WAS LIKE WATCHING ANIMALS. MINDLESS DEMONS, ASCENDED FROM HELL.
"BEHOLD! THE AWESOME FIRES OF GOD. THE LIMITLESS POWER OF PURE CREATION ITSELF," MY MASTER WOULD SAY.
"LOOK CAREFULLY!"
"OBSERVE HOW IT IS USED FOR THE SAME PURPOSE A MAN MIGHT USE AN ESPECIALLY SHARP ROCK."

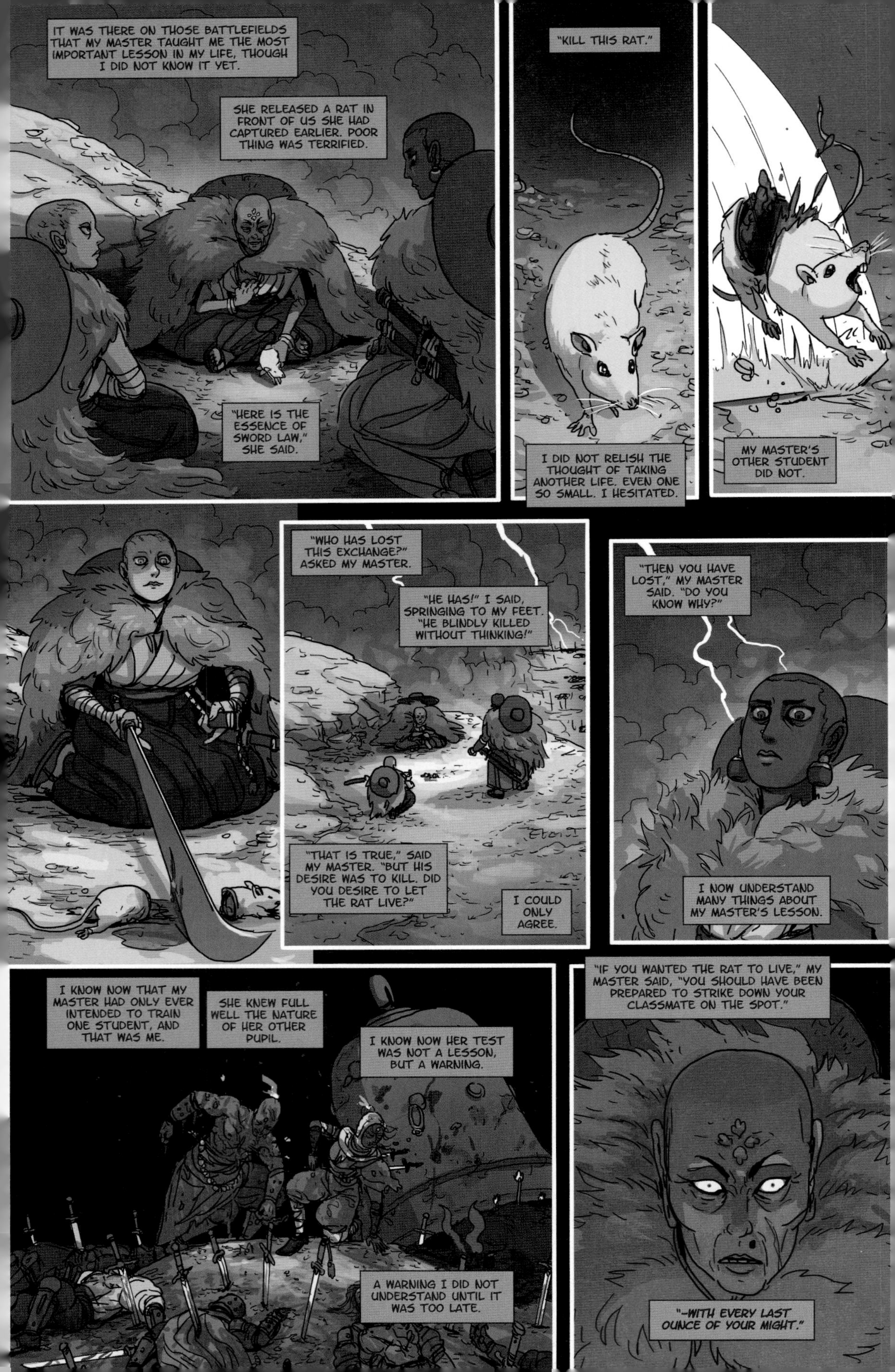
IT WAS THERE ON THOSE BATTLEFIELDS THAT MY MASTER TAUGHT ME THE MOST IMPORTANT LESSON IN MY LIFE, THOUGH I DID NOT KNOW IT YET.
SHE RELEASED A RAT IN FRONT OF US SHE HAD CAPTURED EARLIER. POOR THING WAS TERRIFIED.
"HERE IS THE ESSENCE OF SWORD LAW," SHE SAID.
"KILL THIS RAT."
I DID NOT RELISH THE THOUGHT OF TAKING ANOTHER LIFE. EVEN ONE SO SMALL. I HESITATED.
MY MASTER'S OTHER STUDENT DID NOT.
"WHO HAS LOST THIS EXCHANGE?" ASKED MY MASTER.
"HE HAS!" I SAID, SPRINGING TO MY FEET. "HE BLINDLY KILLED WITHOUT THINKING!"
"THAT IS TRUE," SAID MY MASTER. "BUT HIS DESIRE WAS TO KILL. DID YOU DESIRE TO LET THE RAT LIVE?"
I COULD ONLY AGREE.
"THEN YOU HAVE LOST," MY MASTER SAID. "DO YOU KNOW WHY?"
I NOW UNDERSTAND MANY THINGS ABOUT MY MASTER'S LESSON.
I KNOW NOW THAT MY MASTER HAD ONLY EVER INTENDED TO TRAIN ONE STUDENT, AND THAT WAS ME.
SHE KNEW FULL WELL THE NATURE OF HER OTHER PUPIL.
I KNOW NOW HER TEST WAS NOT A LESSON, BUT A WARNING.
A WARNING I DID NOT UNDERSTAND UNTIL IT WAS TOO LATE.
"IF YOU WANTED THE RAT TO LIVE," MY MASTER SAID, "YOU SHOULD HAVE BEEN PREPARED TO STRIKE DOWN YOUR CLASSMATE ON THE SPOT."
"—WITH EVERY LAST OUNCE OF YOUR MIGHT."

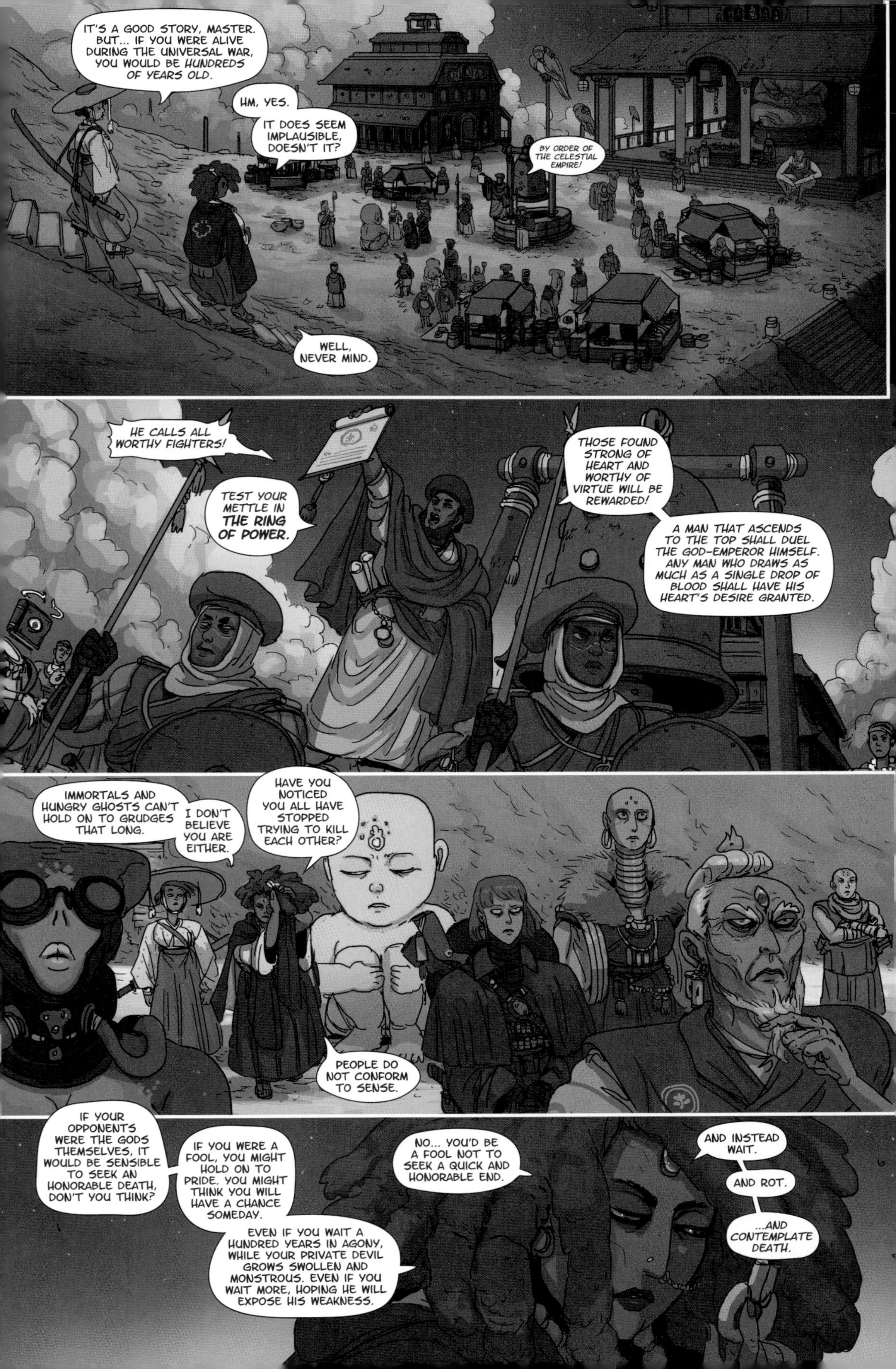
IT'S A GOOD STORY, MASTER. BUT... IF YOU WERE ALIVE DURING THE UNIVERSAL WAR, YOU WOULD BE HUNDREDS OF YEARS OLD.
HM, YES.
IT DOES SEEM IMPLAUSIBLE, DOESN'T IT?
BY ORDER OF THE CELESTIAL EMPIRE!
WELL, NEVER MIND.
HE CALLS ALL WORTHY FIGHTERS!
TEST YOUR METTLE IN THE RING OF POWER.
THOSE FOUND STRONG OF HEART AND WORTHY OF VIRTUE WILL BE REWARDED!
A MAN THAT ASCENDS TO THE TOP SHALL DUEL THE GOD-EMPEROR HIMSELF. ANY MAN WHO DRAWS AS MUCH AS A SINGLE DROP OF BLOOD SHALL HAVE HIS HEART'S DESIRE GRANTED.
IMMORTALS AND HUNGRY GHOSTS CAN'T HOLD ON TO GRUDGES THAT LONG.
I DON'T BELIEVE YOU ARE EITHER.
HAVE YOU NOTICED YOU ALL HAVE STOPPED TRYING TO KILL EACH OTHER?
PEOPLE DO NOT CONFORM TO SENSE.
IF YOUR OPPONENTS WERE THE GODS THEMSELVES, IT WOULD BE SENSIBLE TO SEEK AN HONORABLE DEATH, DON'T YOU THINK?
IF YOU WERE A FOOL, YOU MIGHT HOLD ON TO PRIDE. YOU MIGHT THINK YOU WILL HAVE A CHANCE SOMEDAY.
EVEN IF YOU WAIT A HUNDRED YEARS IN AGONY, WHILE YOUR PRIVATE DEVIL GROWS SWOLLEN AND MONSTROUS. EVEN IF YOU WAIT MORE, HOPING HE WILL EXPOSE HIS WEAKNESS.
NO... YOU'D BE A FOOL NOT TO SEEK A QUICK AND HONORABLE END.
AND INSTEAD WAIT.
AND ROT.
...AND CONTEMPLATE DEATH.

IV.

Het told the sergeant of her plan. She would stay behind and follow the dwellers to their night-time gathering, and get to the heart of the matter. Part of her daring plan, to be certain, was a desperate final bid to win the Sergeant's affection. But the large part of it was a deathly fear that the demons of this awful, muck-ridden land would surely get the better of them and they would be ripped apart.

"If you stay behind," said the Sergeant, matter-of-factly, "you shan't get in the palace in time. You will miss your bath and you'll be terribly filthy. I would think you'd have to sleep outside." He looked pointedly at Het's boots and uniform, doubly soiled with both the filth of that day and of her exploits the night before. Het's heart sunk, but she was resolute.

So it was that the Sergeant and the Centurion abandoned Het and returned to the palace. Het found a thin and dead tree and huddled under it, filled with fear and trepidation, and even touched her sword handle at some points. The bleak sun grew low in the sky and darkness swept across the land. Het crawled forth from her hiding place, trudging through the muck, until she saw the light of the great fire start up again in the distance. Her heart jumped as she grew closer, as once again she saw the dark forms of the dwellers gather together and lay out their table. But fear had made her feet unsteady, and all of a sudden she slipped and tumbled through the muck until she lay battered in the street, in plain view of the gathering.

Het struggled to her feet, gathered her staff close to her, and prepared to die. But the white eyes of the dwellers held looks of sadness and compassion, not of hate. "Come closer, stranger," they said, gathering her in and soothing her. And Het realized that she herself was so covered with filth at this point that she looked no different from anyone else standing around that great fire. Dazed, she was pulled into the gathering, and given water. And there, Het saw the fire-stoking woman. She was laying bread out upon the table, in roughly woven baskets.

Her mind racing, Het looked around, and found the junk-sifting man, and she saw him laying amulets upon the eyes of someone lying on the ground. The person was so still at first, that Het thought they were acting, but then Het saw the bundle-bearing youth wrap them in a burial cloth and realized it was one of the dwellers that the Sergeant and the Centurion had slaughtered earlier that day. That she had slaughtered. And she looked to the fire and saw the bodies burning there, and the wailing started, and there Het began to cry.

After Het had finished weeping, it was as though the tears had cleared her eyes of something dark and terrible. The people, who had looked so alike in their covering of dirt and their rough clothing now stood out stark as day. Here was a kindly woman with a lined face pulled tight in grief for her lost son. Here was a young and sun-worn man beating his chest for his dead sister. They were simple faces, dirty and weather-beaten, but in that moment, sublimely beautiful.

After the fire and its grim contents had burned down to coals, they sat around the great table and ate the thin bread that had been laid out there. As each person bit into it, they bowed their heads and loudly praised its fine taste. Het didn't touch it at first, but was urged on by the mourners. To her surprise, the bread was bitter and dry. "How can you praise this bread when the taste is so poor?" said Het, astonished. The dwellers looked at her strangely and said, "This land heaps pain and indignity upon us. We are small people, so we must be grateful for the small things. Otherwise, what do we have?"

Het was sickened by her own blindness. "In truth," she said, "I am a watchman come to town to hunt for the Rakshasa."

"We know," said the dwellers. "The Rakshasa has plagued us for some time. It steals what little livelihood we have and inflicts pain and malice upon us. At first, our funerals were only for those that it took in the night. Now we must work twice as hard to mourn those the Law takes as well. We resent it, but what can we do? It is the way of things."

Het thought of the Sergeant and his perfect fingernails, and felt a sudden and strong revulsion. "It is not the way of things," she said. An idea struck her then, as pure and clear as a bolt of lightning.

"Do all attend these gatherings?" she asked the dwellers. "No," said the dwellers, "there are some who stay silent in their grief, or resent our mourning." Het thought a moment, then planted her staff and stood up. "I will find this Rakshasa for you," she said, speaking to those assembled. "Are there dead that are not yet burned?" The dwellers showed her that there were, and Het bade them delay their final rites.

There was a great clamor among the dwellers, but Het planted her staff again, and they listened: partly in fear, and partly in awe.

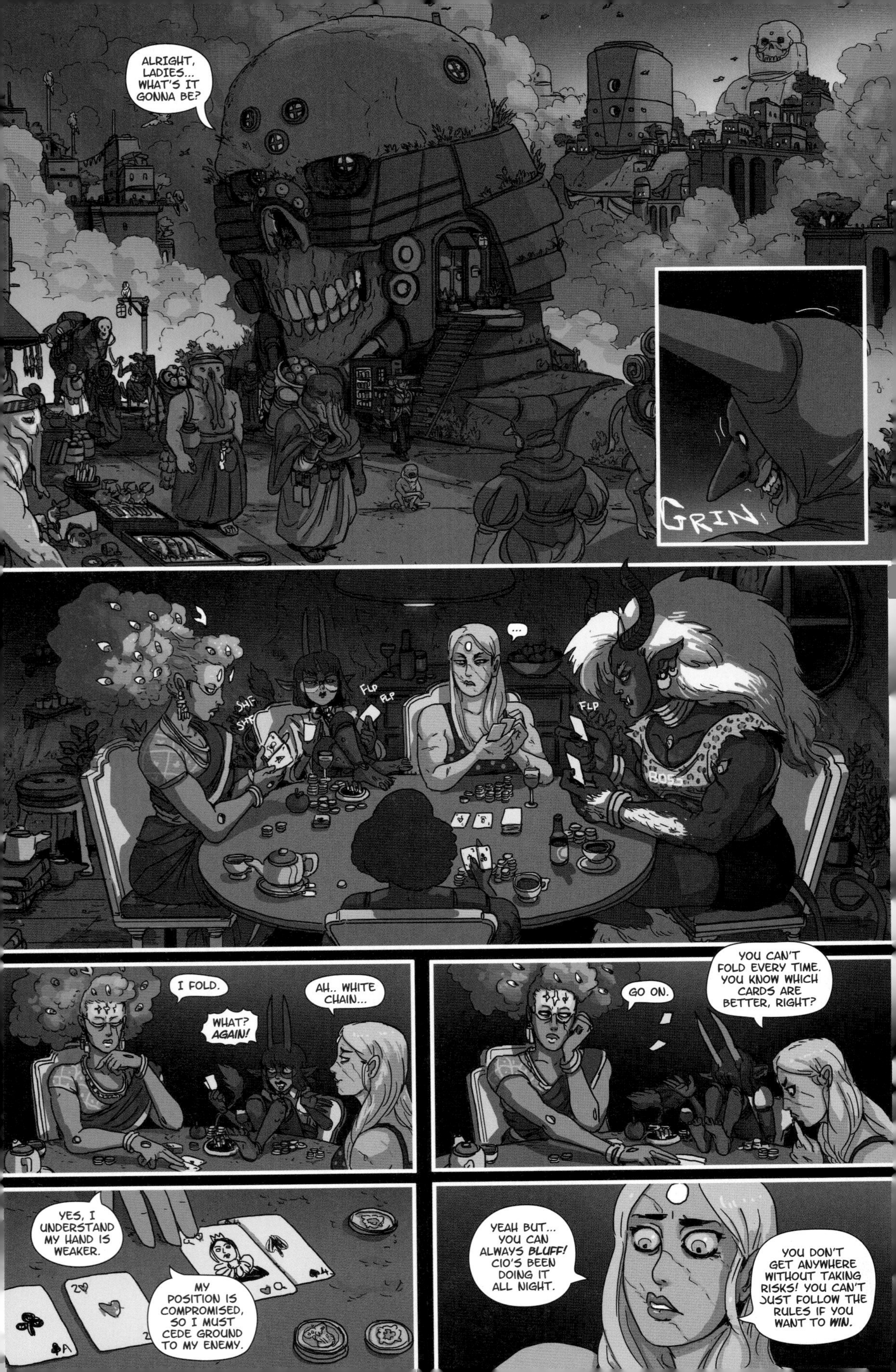

ALRIGHT, LADIES... WHAT'S IT GONNA BE?
GRIN
SHF SHF
FLP FLP
...
FLP
BOSS
I FOLD.
WHAT? AGAIN!
AH.. WHITE CHAIN...
GO ON.
YOU CAN'T FOLD EVERY TIME. YOU KNOW WHICH CARDS ARE BETTER, RIGHT?
YES, I UNDERSTAND MY HAND IS WEAKER.
MY POSITION IS COMPROMISED, SO I MUST CEDE GROUND TO MY ENEMY.
YEAH BUT... YOU CAN ALWAYS BLUFF! CIO'S BEEN DOING IT ALL NIGHT.
YOU DON'T GET ANYWHERE WITHOUT TAKING RISKS! YOU CAN'T JUST FOLLOW THE RULES IF YOU WANT TO WIN.

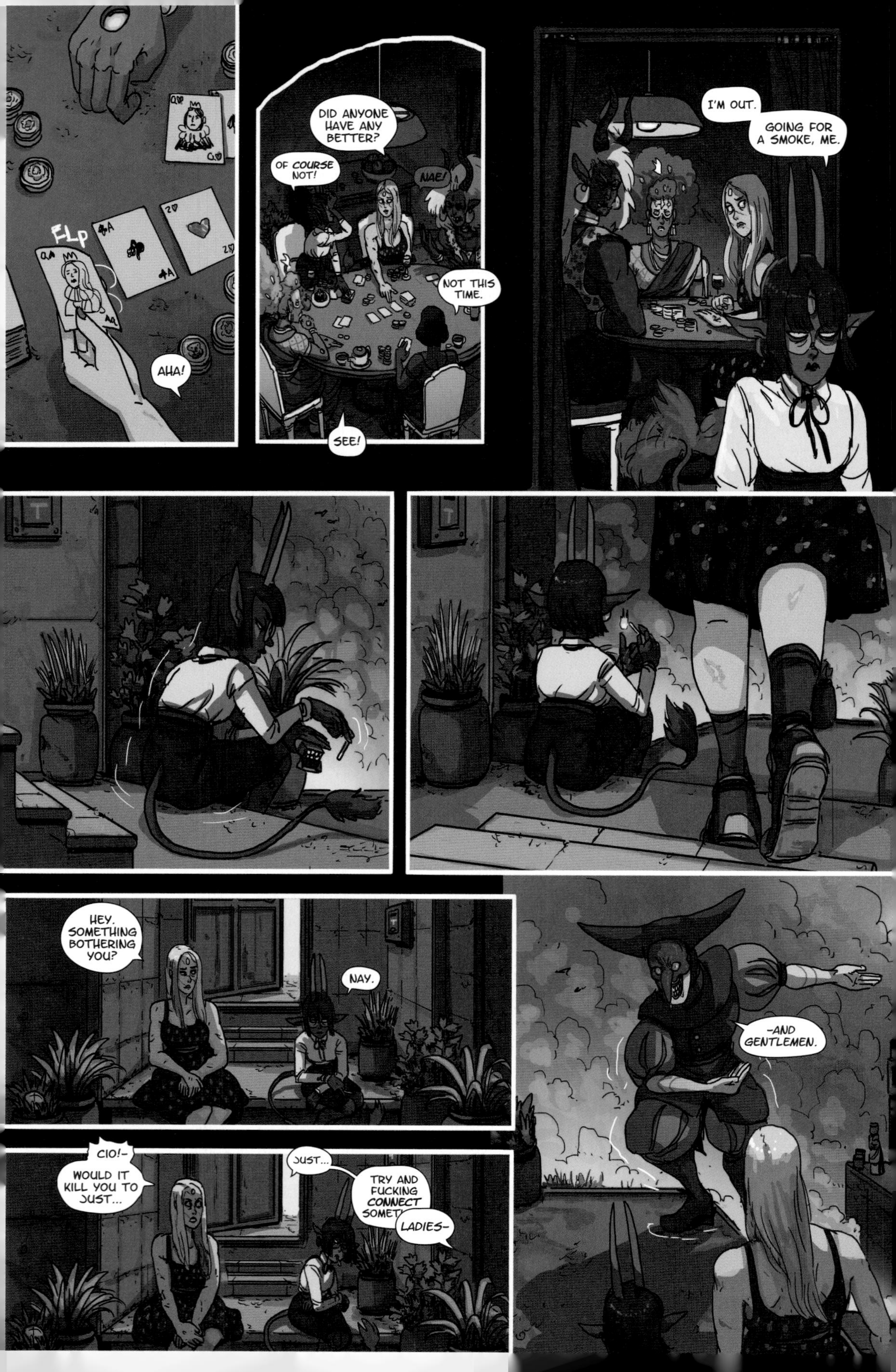

FLP
AHA!
DID ANYONE HAVE ANY BETTER?
OF COURSE NOT!
NAE!
NOT THIS TIME.
SEE!
I'M OUT.
GOING FOR A SMOKE, ME.
HEY. SOMETHING BOTHERING YOU?
NAY.
CIO!-
WOULD IT KILL YOU TO JUST...
JUST...
TRY AND FUCKING CONNECT SOMET-
LADIES-
-AND GENTLEMEN.

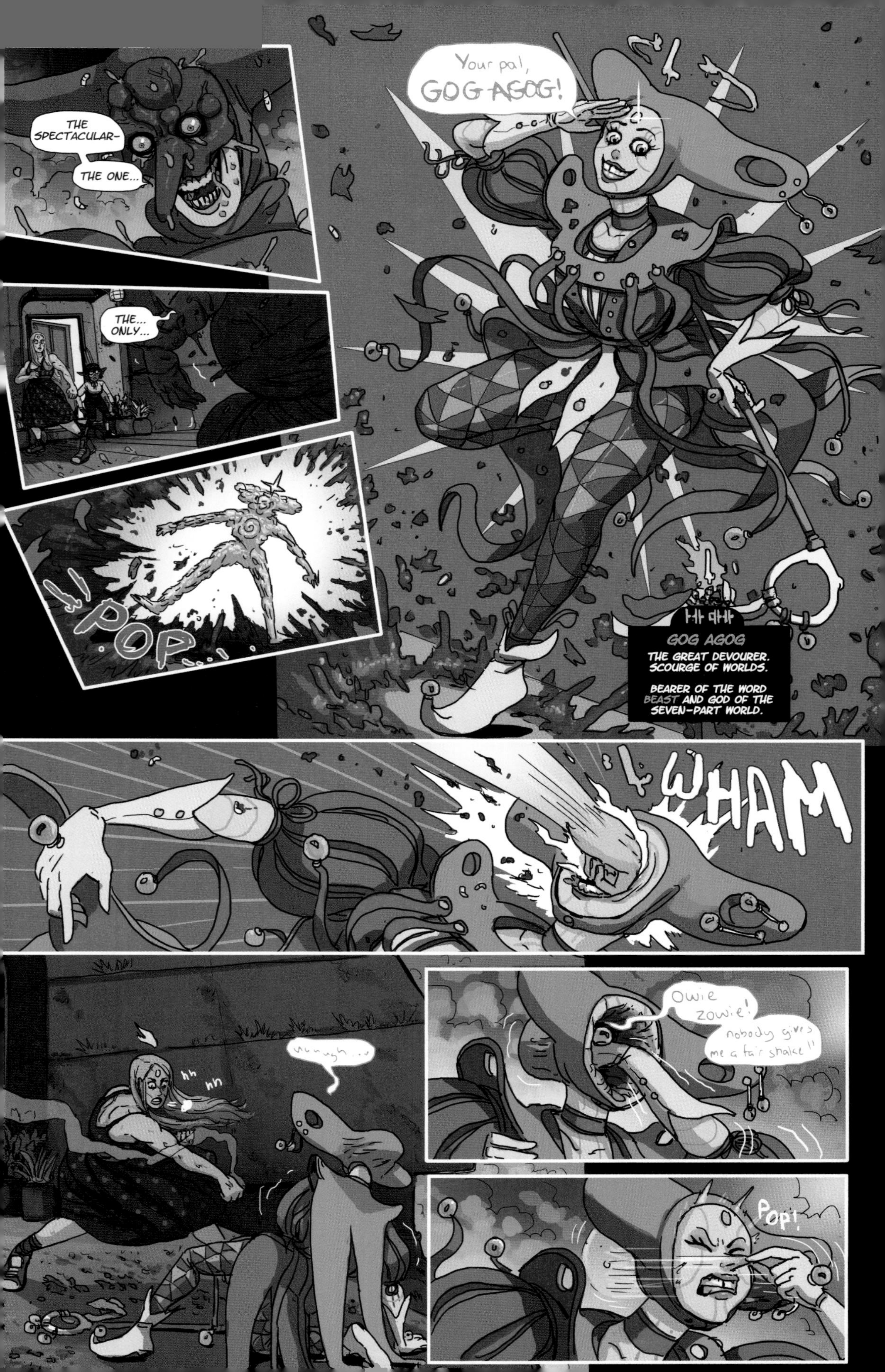
THE SPECTACULAR-
THE ONE...
THE... ONLY...
POP...
Your pal, GOG AGOG!
GOG AGOG
THE GREAT DEVOURER. SCOURGE OF WORLDS.
BEARER OF THE WORD BEAST AND GOD OF THE SEVEN-PART WORLD.
WHAM
hh hh
uuuugh...
Owie zowie!
nobody gives me a fair shake!!
POP!

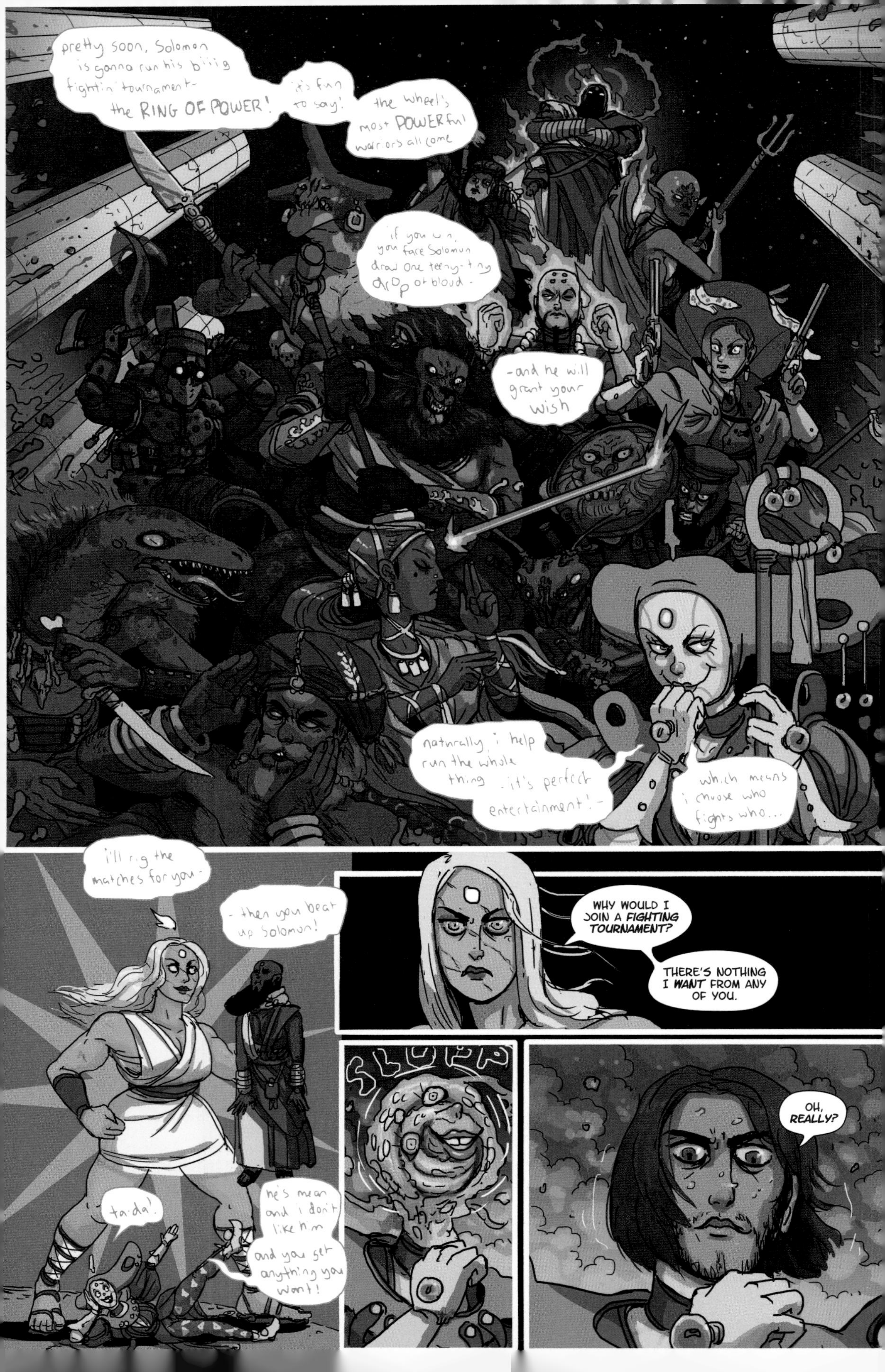
pretty soon, Solomon is gonna run his biiig fightin' tournament-
the RING OF POWER!
it's fun to say!
the wheel's most POWERful warriors all come
if you win, you face Solomon
draw one teeny-tiny drop of blood-
-and he will grant your wish
naturally i help run the whole thing. it's perfect entertainment!-
which means i choose who fights who...
i'll rig the matches for you-
-then you beat up Solomon!
ta-da!
he's mean and i don't like him
and you get anything you want!
WHY WOULD I JOIN A FIGHTING TOURNAMENT?
THERE'S NOTHING I WANT FROM ANY OF YOU.
OH, REALLY?

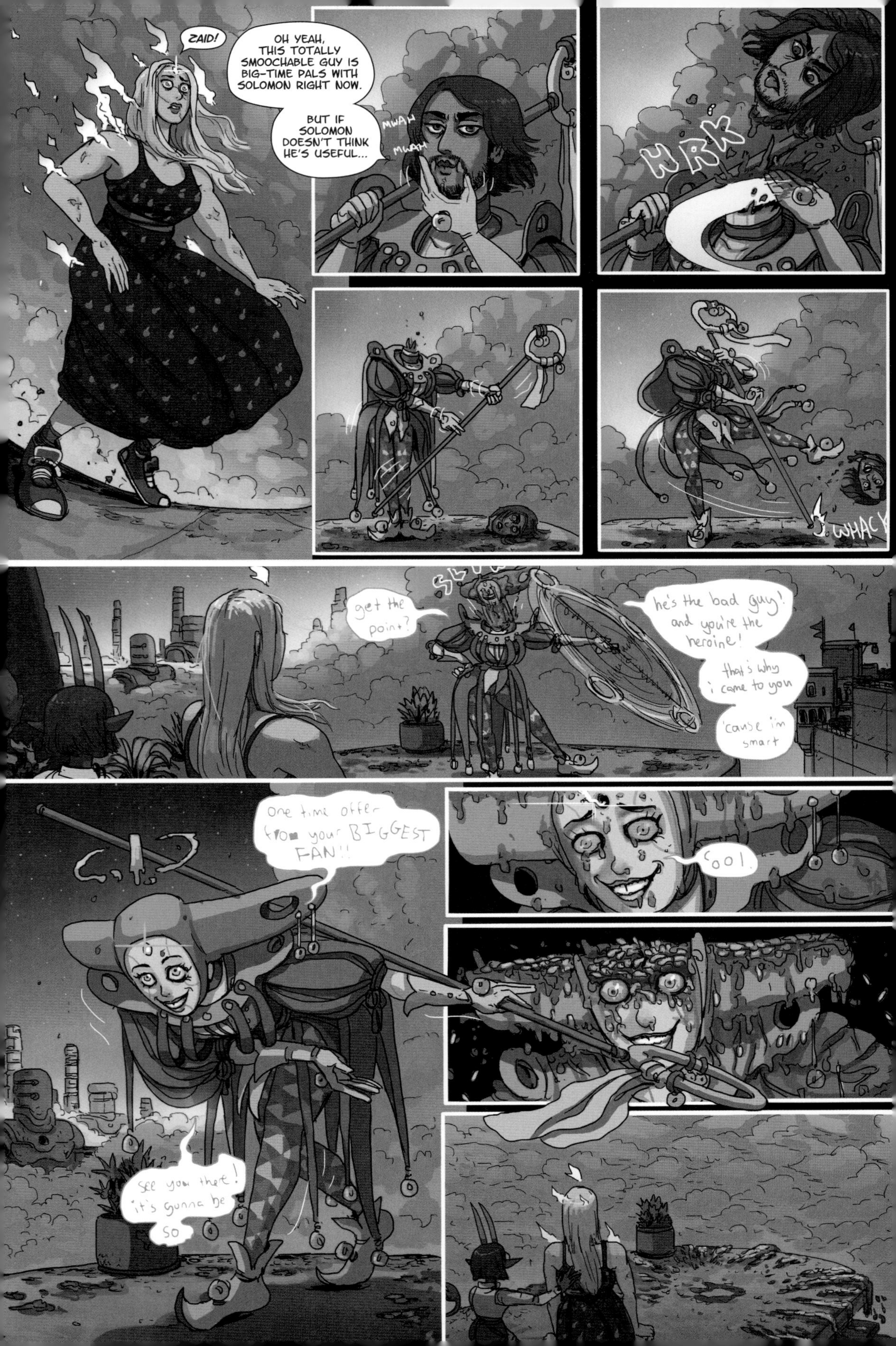
ZAID!
OH YEAH, THIS TOTALLY SMOOCHABLE GUY IS BIG-TIME PALS WITH SOLOMON RIGHT NOW.
BUT IF SOLOMON DOESN'T THINK HE'S USEFUL...
MWAH
MWAH
HRK
WHACK
get the point?
he's the bad guy! and you're the heroine!
that's why i came to you
'cause i'm smart
One time offer from your BIGGEST FAN!!
Cool.
See you there! it's gunna be so

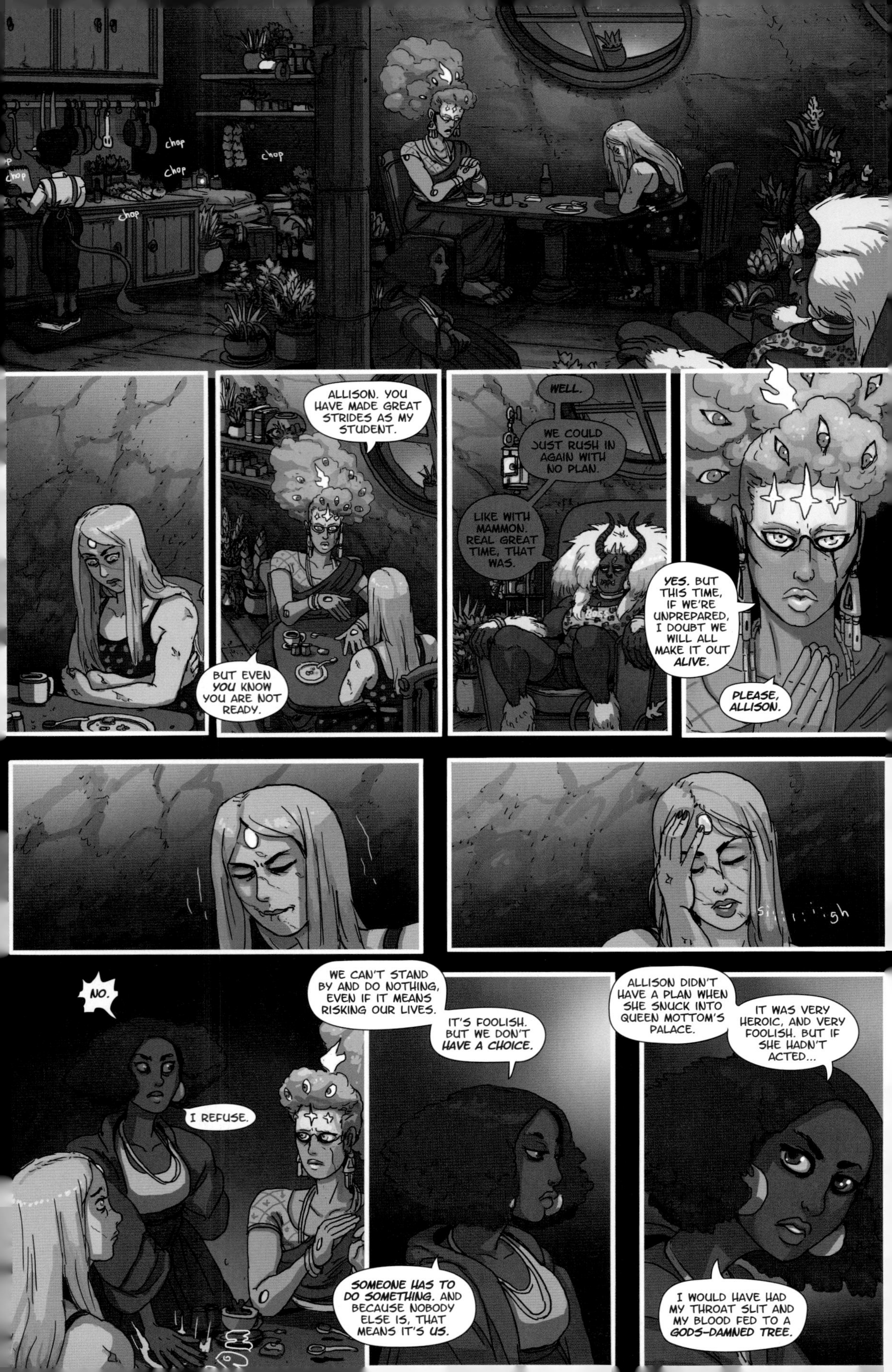
chop
chop
chop
chop
chop
ALLISON. YOU HAVE MADE GREAT STRIDES AS MY STUDENT.
BUT EVEN YOU KNOW YOU ARE NOT READY.
WELL.
WE COULD JUST RUSH IN AGAIN WITH NO PLAN.
LIKE WITH MAMMON. REAL GREAT TIME, THAT WAS.
YES. BUT THIS TIME, IF WE'RE UNPREPARED, I DOUBT WE WILL ALL MAKE IT OUT ALIVE.
PLEASE, ALLISON.
NO.
I REFUSE.
WE CAN'T STAND BY AND DO NOTHING, EVEN IF IT MEANS RISKING OUR LIVES.
IT'S FOOLISH. BUT WE DON'T HAVE A CHOICE.
SOMEONE HAS TO DO SOMETHING. AND BECAUSE NOBODY ELSE IS, THAT MEANS IT'S US.
ALLISON DIDN'T HAVE A PLAN WHEN SHE SNUCK INTO QUEEN MOTTOM'S PALACE.
IT WAS VERY HEROIC, AND VERY FOOLISH. BUT IF SHE HADN'T ACTED...
I WOULD HAVE HAD MY THROAT SLIT AND MY BLOOD FED TO A GODS-DAMNED TREE.

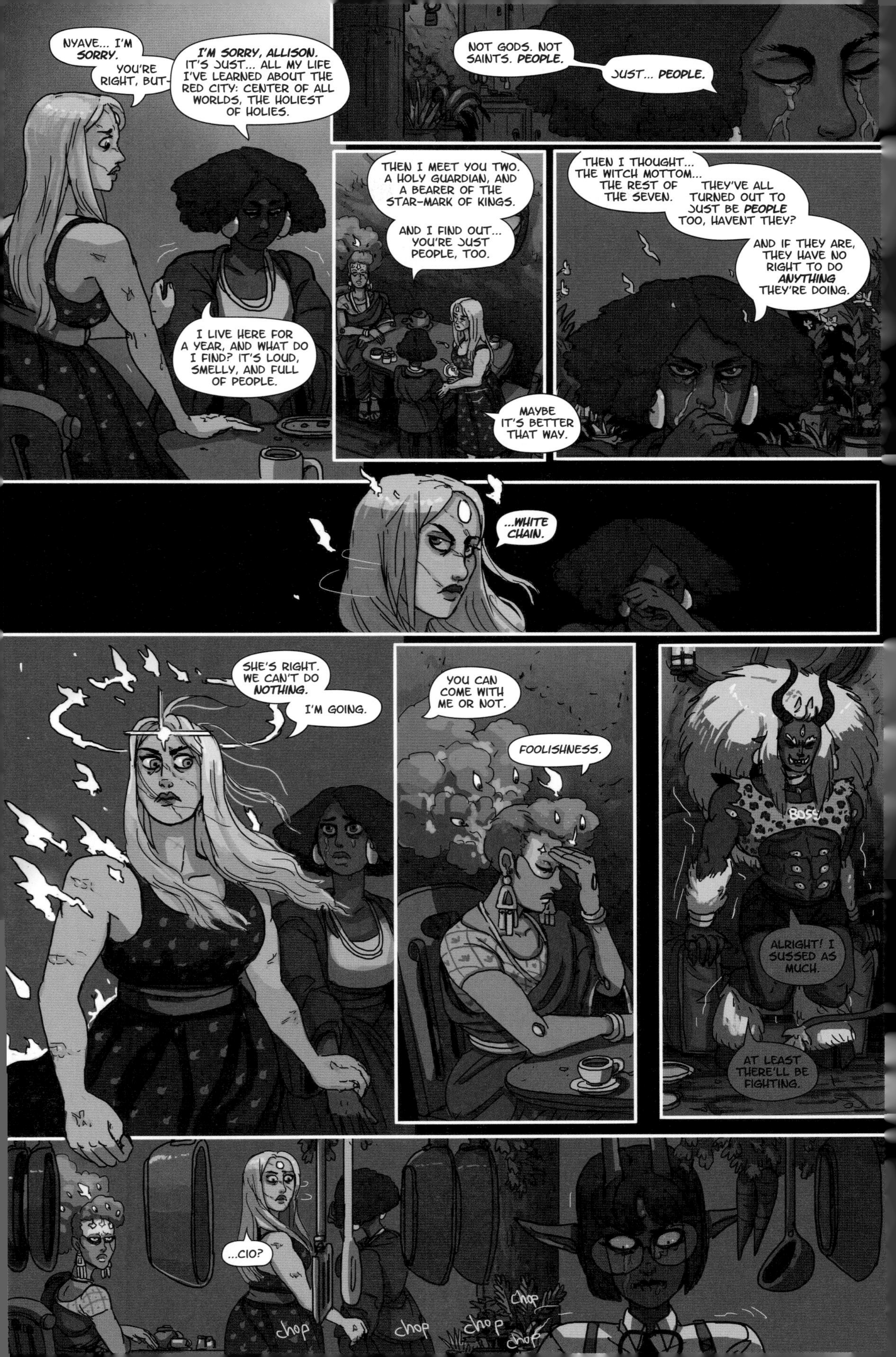

NYAVE... I'M SORRY.
YOU'RE RIGHT, BUT-
I'M SORRY, ALLISON. IT'S JUST... ALL MY LIFE I'VE LEARNED ABOUT THE RED CITY: CENTER OF ALL WORLDS, THE HOLIEST OF HOLIES.
I LIVE HERE FOR A YEAR, AND WHAT DO I FIND? IT'S LOUD, SMELLY, AND FULL OF PEOPLE.
NOT GODS. NOT SAINTS. PEOPLE.
JUST... PEOPLE.
THEN I MEET YOU TWO. A HOLY GUARDIAN, AND A BEARER OF THE STAR-MARK OF KINGS.
AND I FIND OUT... YOU'RE JUST PEOPLE, TOO.
MAYBE IT'S BETTER THAT WAY.
THEN I THOUGHT... THE WITCH MOTTOM... THE REST OF THE SEVEN.
THEY'VE ALL TURNED OUT TO JUST BE PEOPLE TOO, HAVENT THEY?
AND IF THEY ARE, THEY HAVE NO RIGHT TO DO ANYTHING THEY'RE DOING.
...WHITE CHAIN.
SHE'S RIGHT. WE CAN'T DO NOTHING.
I'M GOING.
YOU CAN COME WITH ME OR NOT.
FOOLISHNESS.
BOSS
ALRIGHT! I SUSSED AS MUCH.
AT LEAST THERE'LL BE FIGHTING.
...CIO?
chop
chop
chop
chop
chop

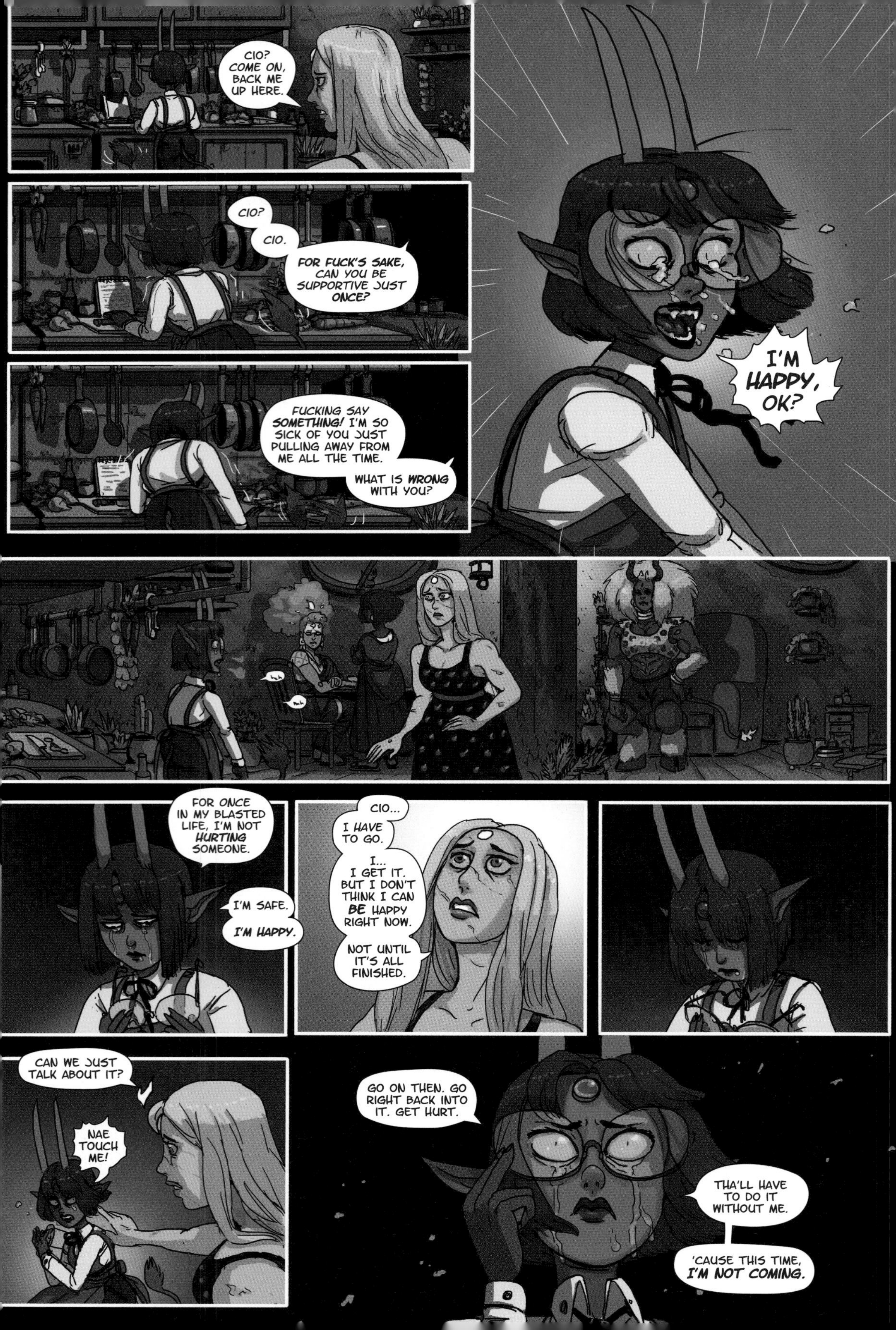
CIO? COME ON, BACK ME UP HERE.
CIO?
CIO.
FOR FUCK'S SAKE, CAN YOU BE SUPPORTIVE JUST ONCE?
FUCKING SAY SOMETHING! I'M SO SICK OF YOU JUST PULLING AWAY FROM ME ALL THE TIME.
WHAT IS WRONG WITH YOU?
I'M HAPPY, OK?
FOR ONCE IN MY BLASTED LIFE, I'M NOT HURTING SOMEONE.
I'M SAFE.
I'M HAPPY.
CIO...
I HAVE TO GO.
I... I GET IT. BUT I DON'T THINK I CAN BE HAPPY RIGHT NOW.
NOT UNTIL IT'S ALL FINISHED.
CAN WE JUST TALK ABOUT IT?
NAE TOUCH ME!
GO ON THEN. GO RIGHT BACK INTO IT. GET HURT.
THA'LL HAVE TO DO IT WITHOUT ME.
'CAUSE THIS TIME, I'M NOT COMING.

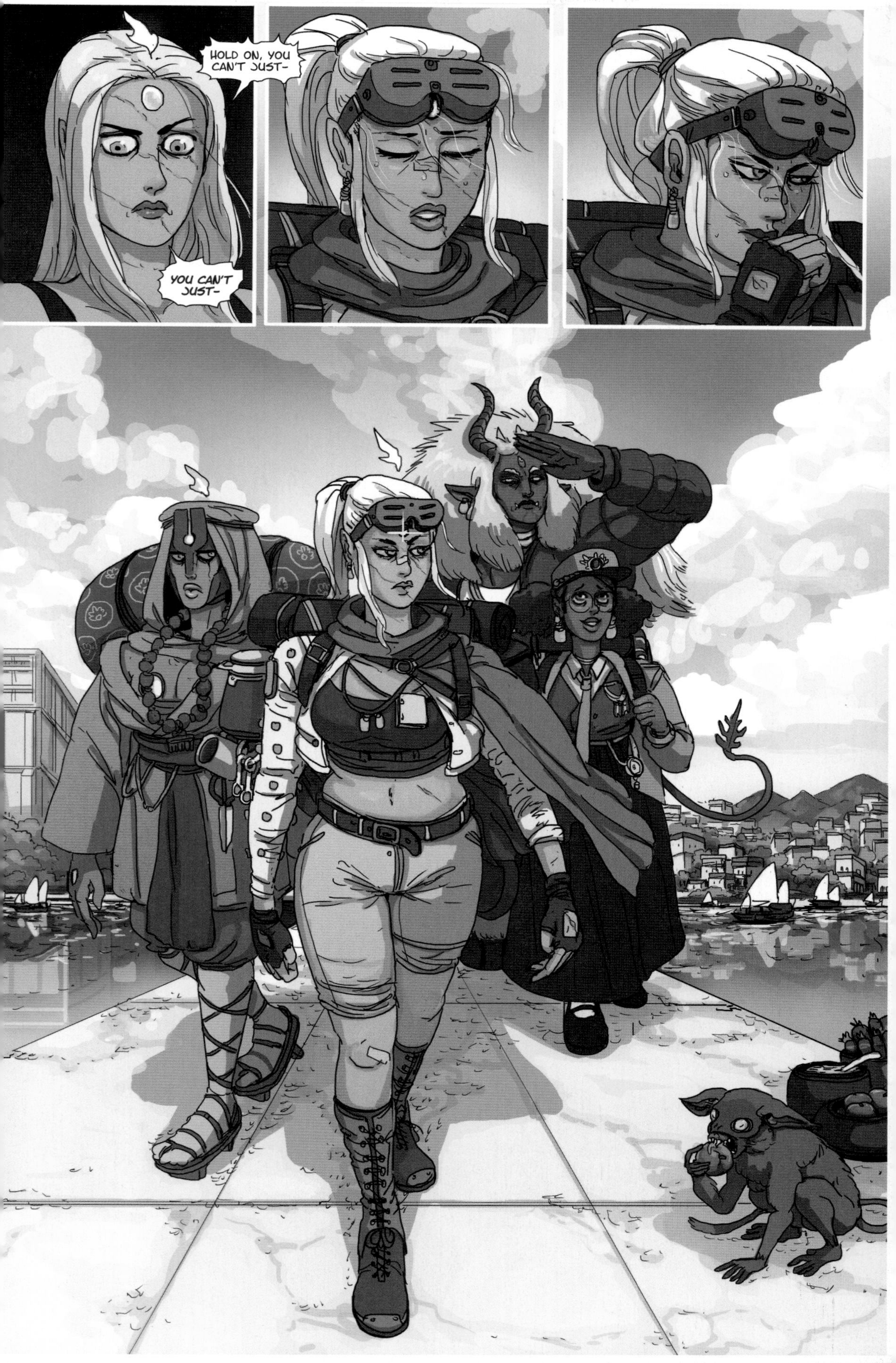
HOLD ON, YOU CAN'T JUST-
YOU CAN'T JUST-

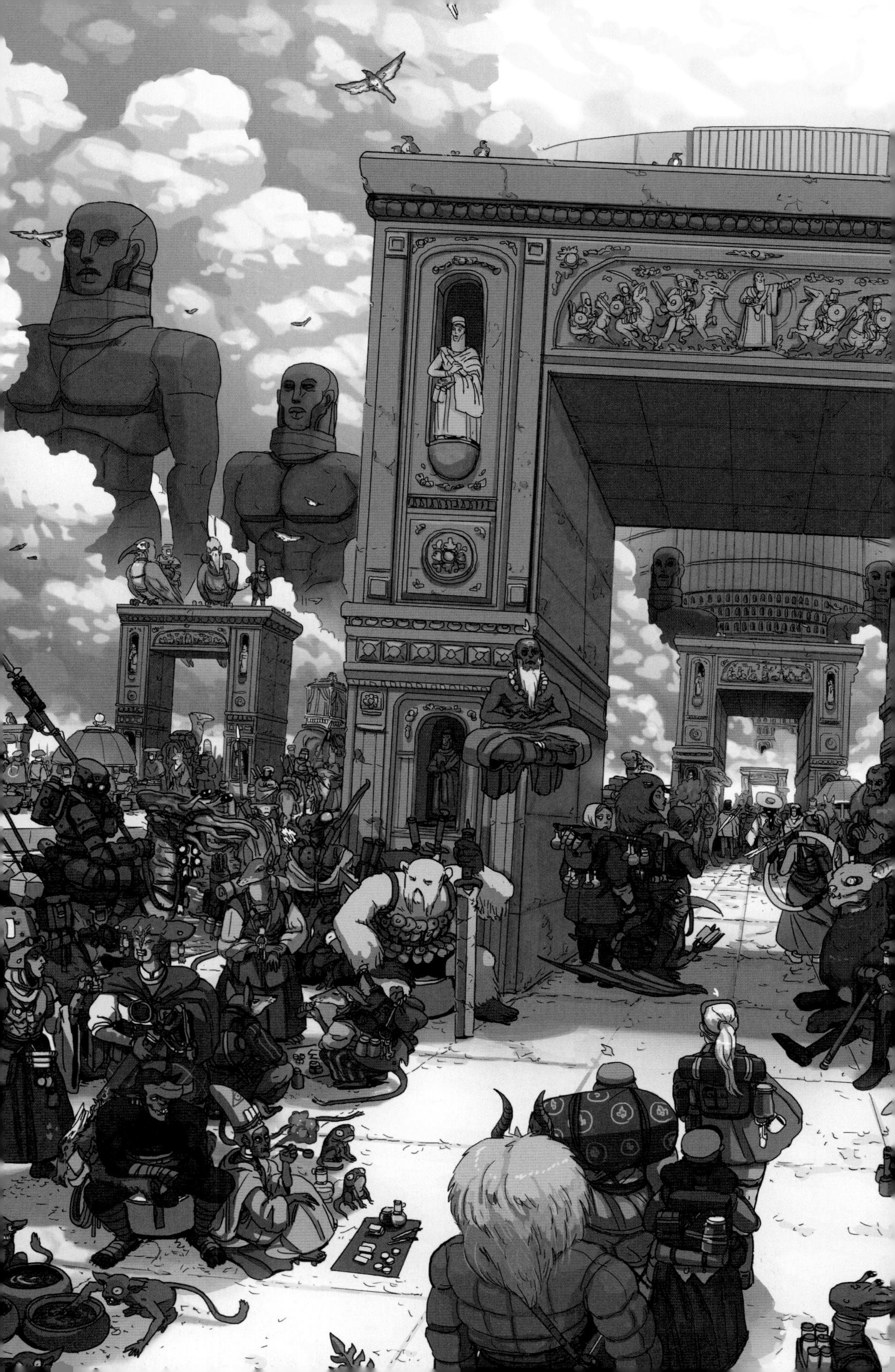

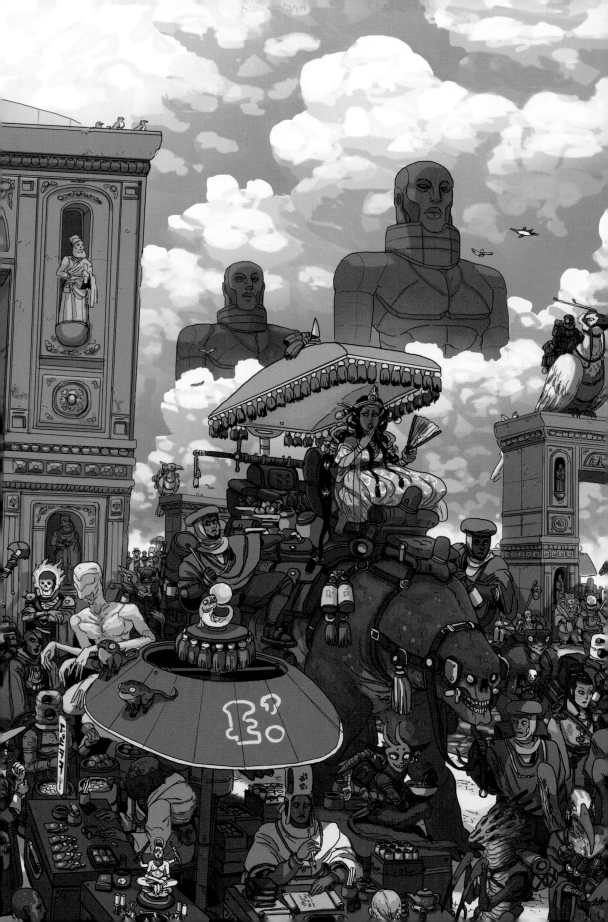

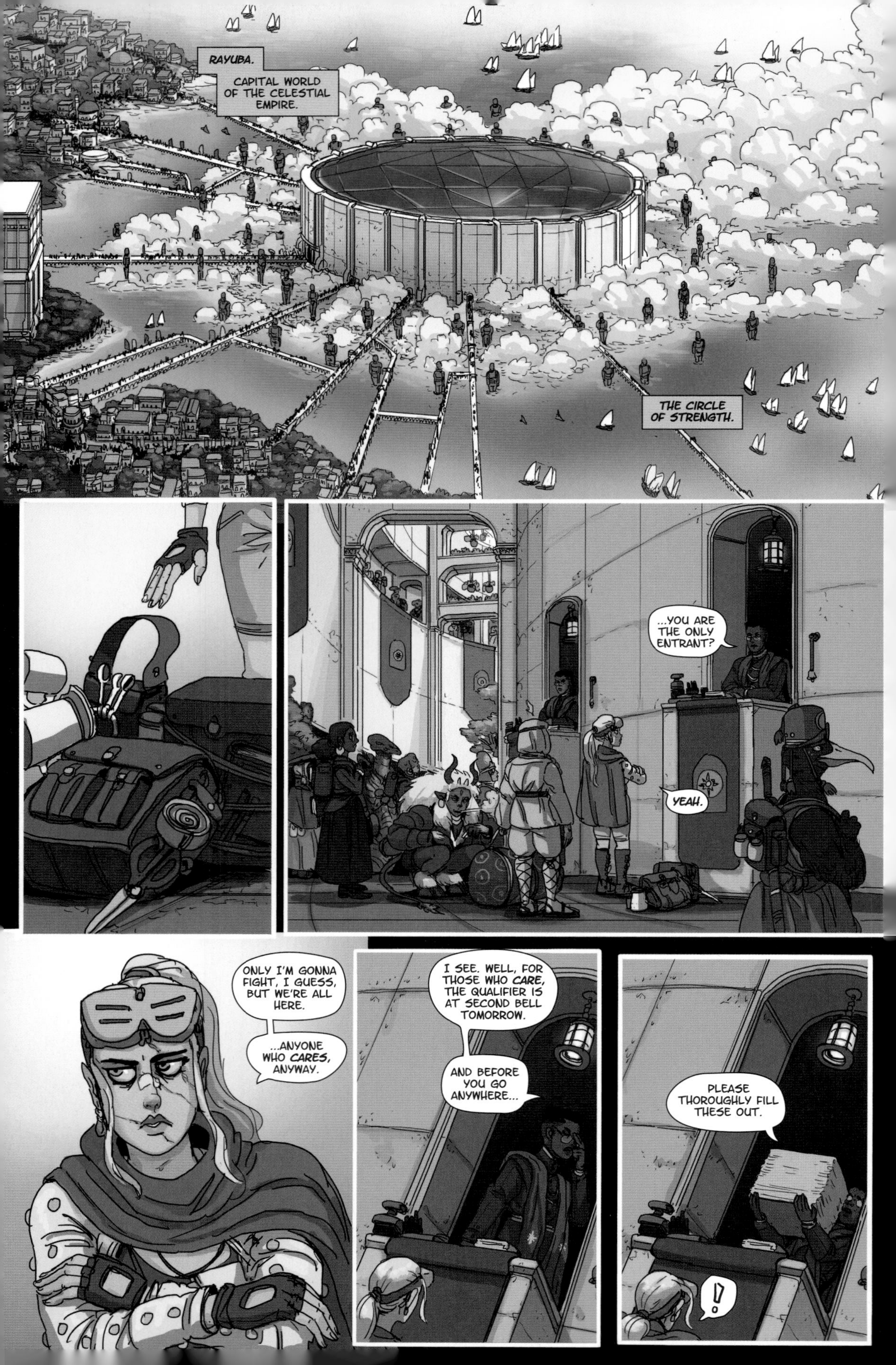
RAYUBA.
CAPITAL WORLD OF THE CELESTIAL EMPIRE.
THE CIRCLE OF STRENGTH.
...YOU ARE THE ONLY ENTRANT?
YEAH.
ONLY I'M GONNA FIGHT, I GUESS, BUT WE'RE ALL HERE.
...ANYONE WHO CARES, ANYWAY.
I SEE. WELL, FOR THOSE WHO CARE, THE QUALIFIER IS AT SECOND BELL TOMORROW.
AND BEFORE YOU GO ANYWHERE...
PLEASE THOROUGHLY FILL THESE OUT.
!?

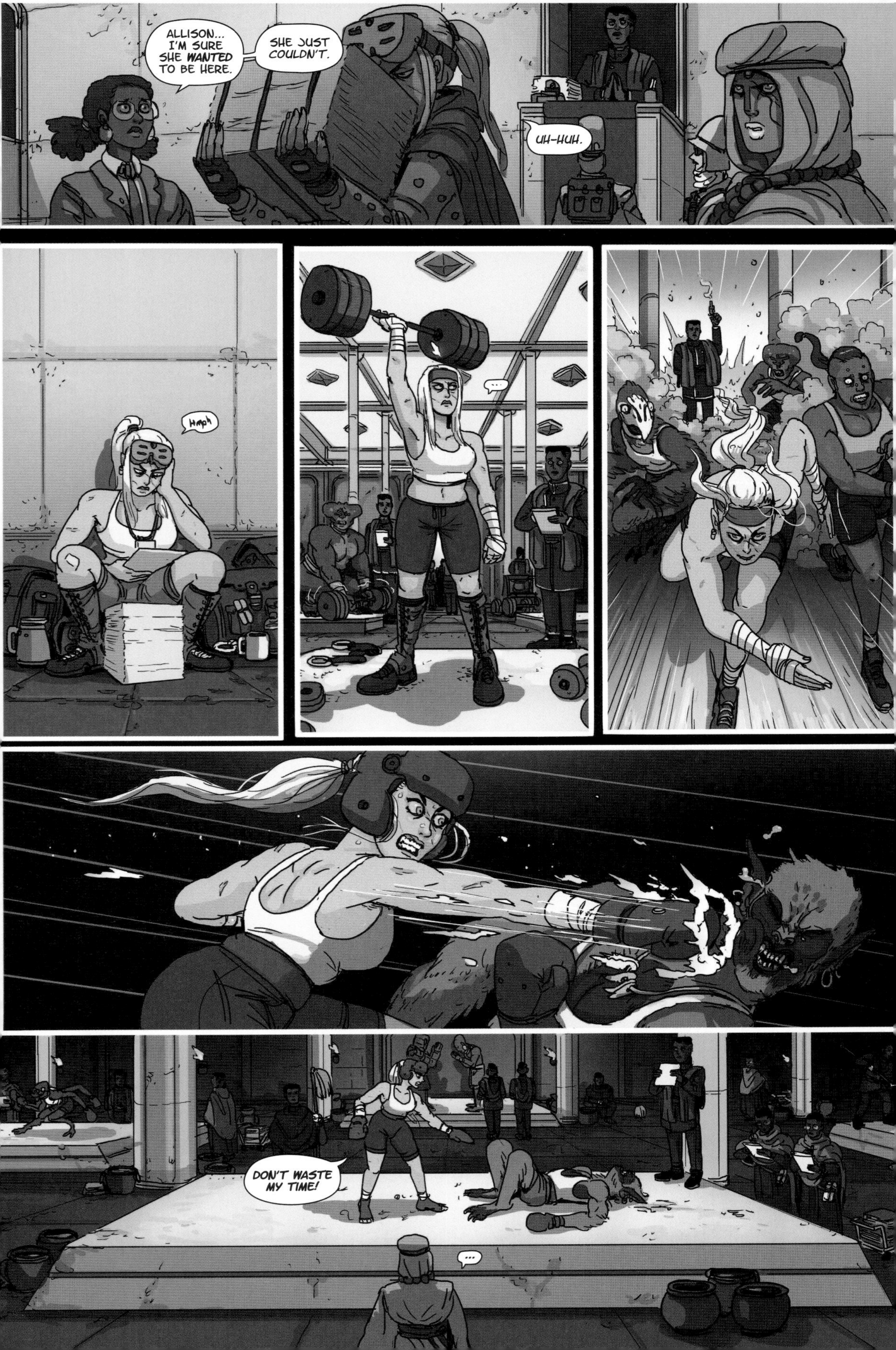
ALLISON... I'M SURE SHE WANTED TO BE HERE.
SHE JUST COULDN'T.
UH-HUH.
Hmph
...
DON'T WASTE MY TIME!
...

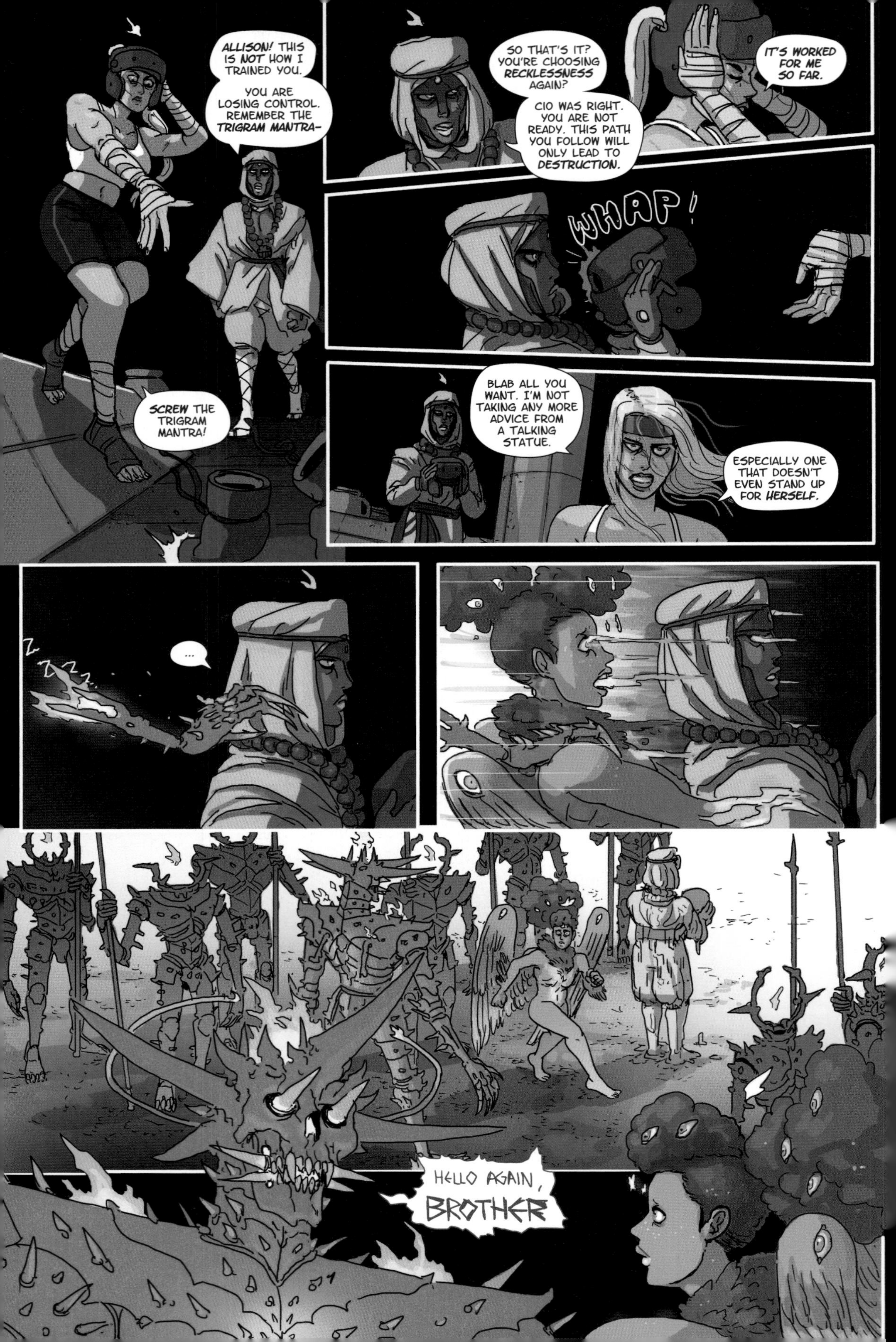
ALLISON! THIS IS NOT HOW I TRAINED YOU.
YOU ARE LOSING CONTROL. REMEMBER THE TRIGRAM MANTRA-
SCREW THE TRIGRAM MANTRA!
SO THAT'S IT? YOU'RE CHOOSING RECKLESSNESS AGAIN?
CIO WAS RIGHT. YOU ARE NOT READY. THIS PATH YOU FOLLOW WILL ONLY LEAD TO DESTRUCTION.
IT'S WORKED FOR ME SO FAR.
WHAP!
BLAB ALL YOU WANT. I'M NOT TAKING ANY MORE ADVICE FROM A TALKING STATUE.
ESPECIALLY ONE THAT DOESN'T EVEN STAND UP FOR HERSELF.
...
HELLO AGAIN, BROTHER

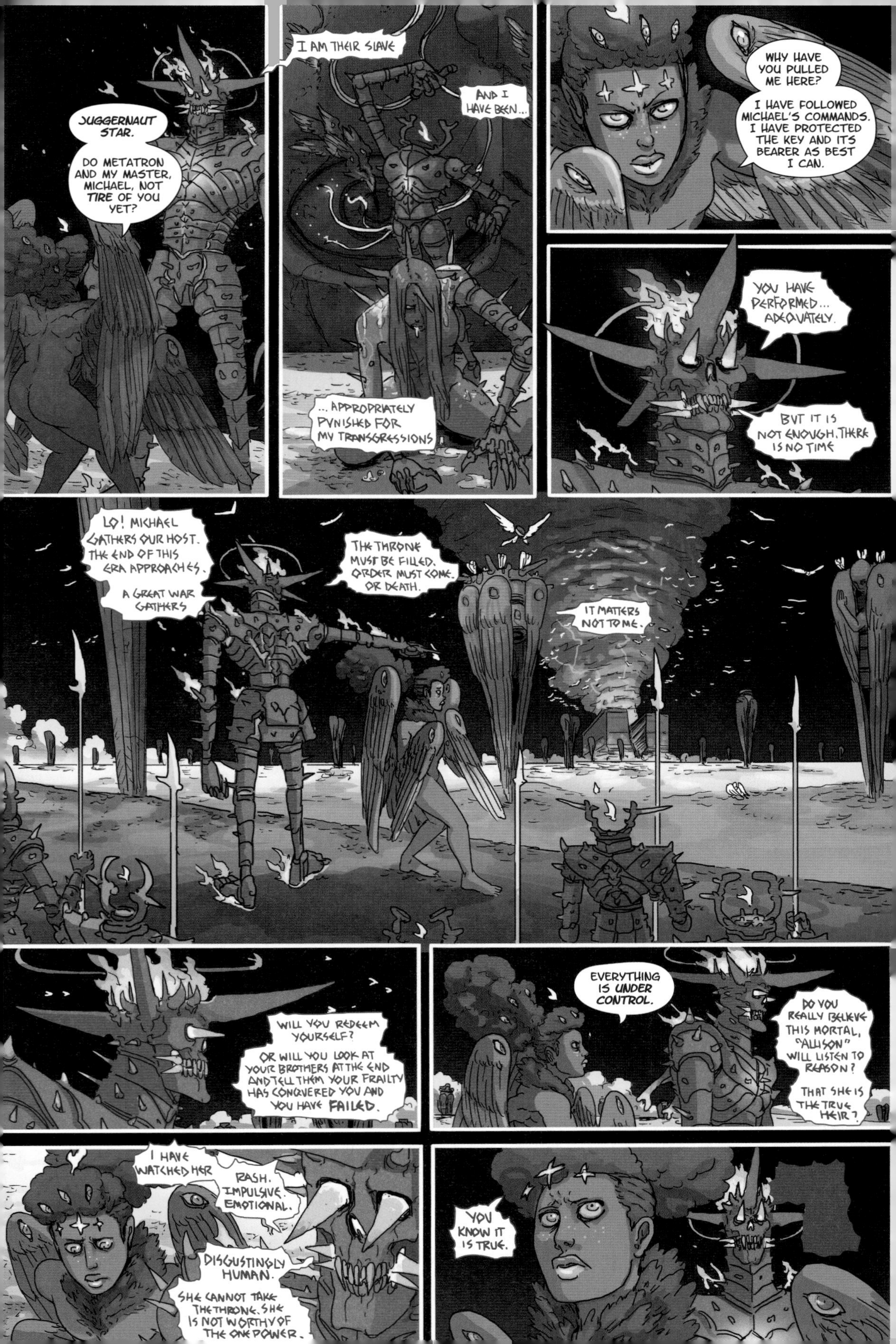
JUGGERNAUT STAR.
DO METATRON AND MY MASTER, MICHAEL, NOT TIRE OF YOU YET?
I AM THEIR SLAVE
AND I HAVE BEEN...
...APPROPRIATELY PUNISHED FOR MY TRANSGRESSIONS
WHY HAVE YOU PULLED ME HERE?
I HAVE FOLLOWED MICHAEL'S COMMANDS. I HAVE PROTECTED THE KEY AND ITS BEARER AS BEST I CAN.
YOU HAVE PERFORMED... ADEQUATELY.
BUT IT IS NOT ENOUGH. THERE IS NO TIME
LO! MICHAEL GATHERS OUR HOST. THE END OF THIS ERA APPROACHES.
A GREAT WAR GATHERS
THE THRONE MUST BE FILLED. ORDER MUST COME. OR DEATH.
IT MATTERS NOT TO ME.
WILL YOU REDEEM YOURSELF?
OR WILL YOU LOOK AT YOUR BROTHERS AT THE END AND TELL THEM YOUR FRAILTY HAS CONQUERED YOU AND YOU HAVE FAILED.
EVERYTHING IS UNDER CONTROL.
DO YOU REALLY BELIEVE THIS MORTAL, "ALLISON" WILL LISTEN TO REASON?
THAT SHE IS THE TRUE HEIR?
I HAVE WATCHED HER
RASH. IMPULSIVE. EMOTIONAL.
DISGUSTINGLY HUMAN.
SHE CANNOT TAKE THE THRONE. SHE IS NOT WORTHY OF THE ONE POWER.
YOU KNOW IT IS TRUE.

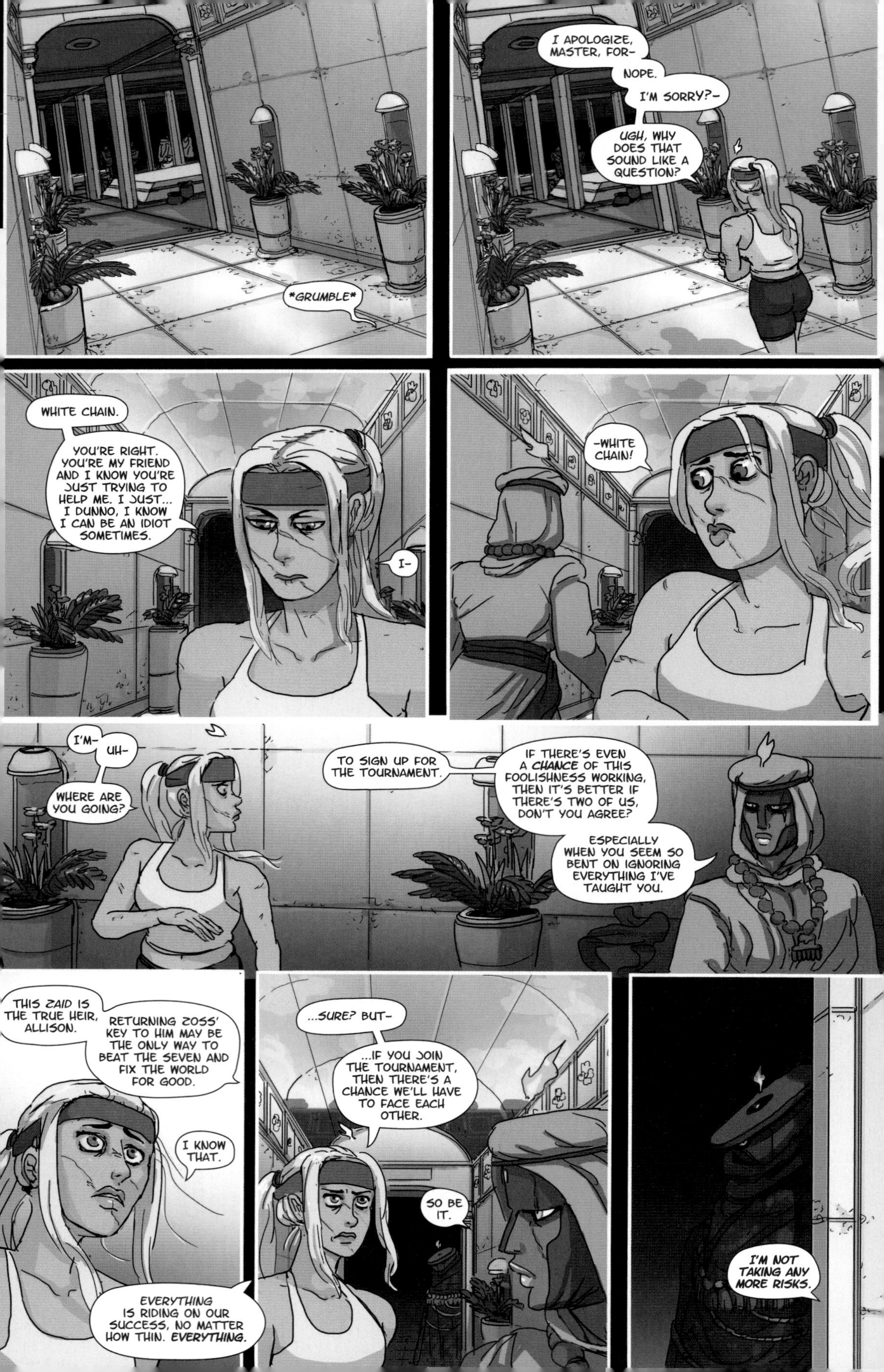
GRUMBLE
I APOLOGIZE, MASTER, FOR-
NOPE.
I'M SORRY?-
UGH, WHY DOES THAT SOUND LIKE A QUESTION?
WHITE CHAIN.
YOU'RE RIGHT. YOU'RE MY FRIEND AND I KNOW YOU'RE JUST TRYING TO HELP ME. I JUST... I DUNNO, I KNOW I CAN BE AN IDIOT SOMETIMES.
I-
-WHITE CHAIN!
I'M-
UH-
WHERE ARE YOU GOING?
TO SIGN UP FOR THE TOURNAMENT.
IF THERE'S EVEN A CHANCE OF THIS FOOLISHNESS WORKING, THEN IT'S BETTER IF THERE'S TWO OF US, DON'T YOU AGREE?
ESPECIALLY WHEN YOU SEEM SO BENT ON IGNORING EVERYTHING I'VE TAUGHT YOU.
THIS ZAID IS THE TRUE HEIR, ALLISON.
RETURNING ZOSS' KEY TO HIM MAY BE THE ONLY WAY TO BEAT THE SEVEN AND FIX THE WORLD FOR GOOD.
I KNOW THAT.
EVERYTHING IS RIDING ON OUR SUCCESS, NO MATTER HOW THIN. EVERYTHING.
...SURE? BUT-
...IF YOU JOIN THE TOURNAMENT, THEN THERE'S A CHANCE WE'LL HAVE TO FACE EACH OTHER.
SO BE IT.
I'M NOT TAKING ANY MORE RISKS.

V.

"THE SERGEANT WILL START his investigation again tomorrow," said Het in a voice she didn't knew she had yet. "You will burn your dead when the sun is high, instead of at night, and you will bid all the town come to the funeral. Those that are not at the gathering will surely be in danger, for the Sergeant has promised me he will step up his investigation. You will bake the bread, and make the amulets, and prepare the burial cloth, just as normal, and in turn, I will reveal to you a secret way to draw out and kill the Rakshasa."

The dwellers were in turmoil at Het's suggestion, for it was a grave breach of custom. But the Rakshasa had plagued them for a long time, and the suggestion of relief from its scourge was just enough to motivate them. They set about finishing their funeral rites, and preparing for the next day. Het, for her part, trudged in the cold and dark back to the palace. But, as promised, the palace gates were closed to her. She slept in the mud and awoke cold and wet, but full of purpose.

When the Sergeant and Centurion strode through the palace gates that morning clean and shiny, they reacted with a start when Het rose to greet them, for she was so covered in mud that she appeared just like the dwellers. But the Sergeant recognized her stave and questioned her at once about her inexcusable appearance.

"Delay your investigation," pleaded Het, "for we have treated these people with nothing but brutality and cruelty! Out of your love for the Law, please let the Centurion sheathe his sword today!" The Sergeant denied her of course, for there was not one ounce of anything resembling love in his whole body. As he denied her, Het found her longing for the Sergeant slip out of her like a cold liquid, and she felt deeply saddened, for it confirmed what she had known all along. But it was an expected loss, and resolution quickly filled its place.

The Sergeant immediately began his investigation, rapping on doors and even windows with his perfect fingernails The buttons of his uniform suddenly seemed too bright and sharp to Het, and the glint from them hurt her eyes. She heard the sweaty palm of the Centurion rubbing over his sword hilt. But true to their word, the dwellers had gathered absolutely everyone to the central square for the delayed funeral rites, and there was nary a soul to be found in any of the humble and stooped dwellings of that land. For once, Het saw the Sergeant taken aback.

"Well, this is awfully strange," he said to Het with a cold look in his eye, and the Centurion fumed. It was then that the funereal wailing started, and following its sound and the smoke from the fire, the group made their way to the central square.

But true to their word, the dwellers had gathered absolutely everyone to the central square for the delayed funeral rites, and there was nary a soul to be found in any of the humble and stooped dwellings of that land. For once, Het saw the Sergeant taken aback. "Well this is awfully strange," he said to Het with a cold look in his eye, and the Centurion fumed. It was then that the funereal wailing started, and following its sound and the smoke from the fire, the group made their way to the central square.

"Stop this nonsense!" said the Sergeant in his very reasonable policeman's voice as they strode amongst the gathered masses, but nobody listened. They were filled with grief and resentment at having to delay their funeral rites, and many of them threw spurious glances at Het as they wailed. "Hold a moment," said Het, and they held as the bread was laid out. "A little longer," said Het as the amulets were laid on the eyes of the dead. "Just a little longer," said Het, as the cloth was wrapped around the bodies.

OUT OF THE CORNER OF HER EYE SHE SAW THAT THE CENTURION'S EXPERT SWORD ARM WAS BULGING WITH UNRELEASED TENSION, AND THE CORDS OF HIS NECK WERE THICK AND RED.

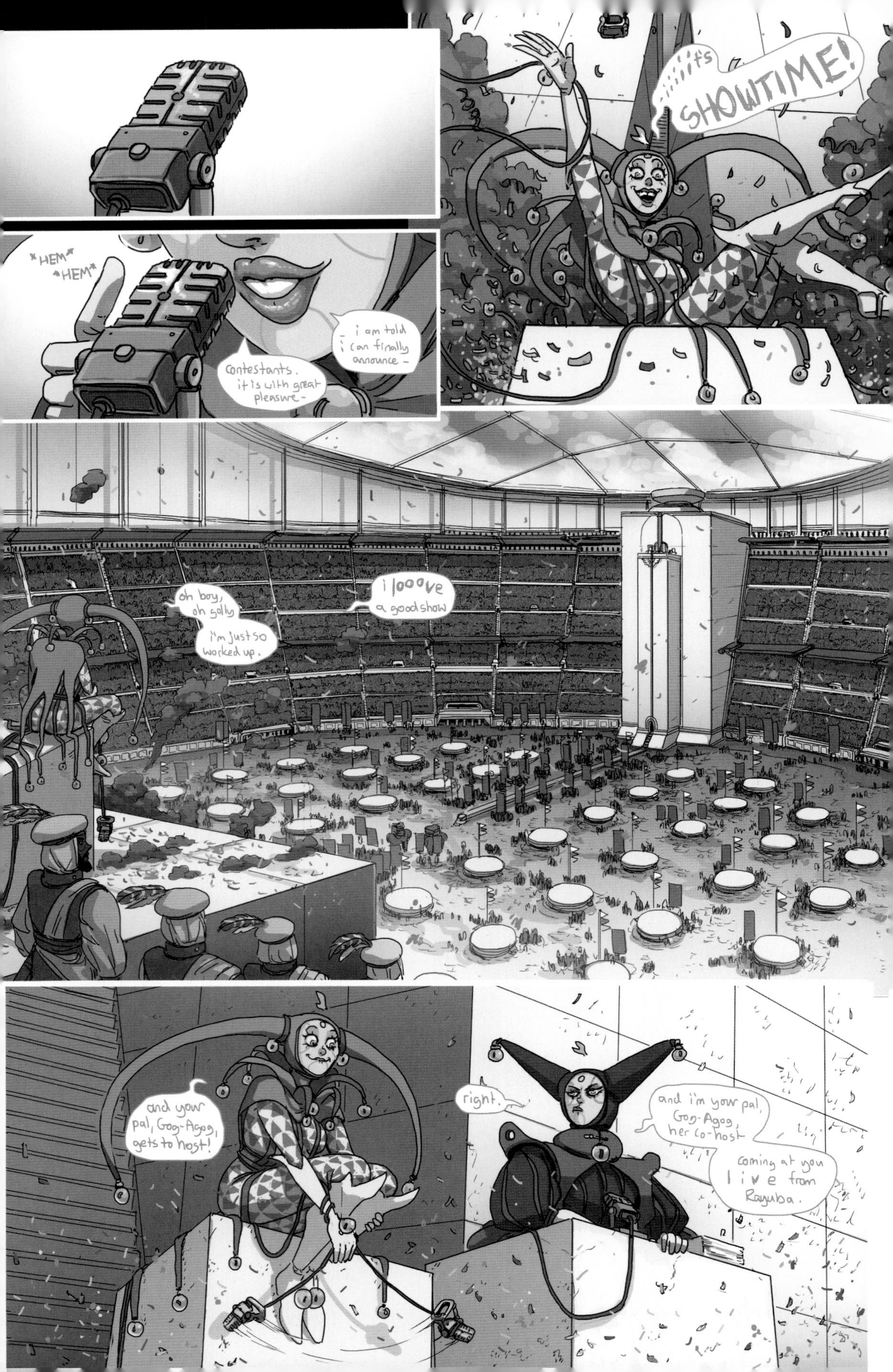
HEM
HEM
contestants. it is with great pleasure-
i am told i can finally announce-
it's SHOWTIME!
oh boy, oh golly
i'm just so worked up.
i looove a good show
and your pal, Gog-Agog, gets to host!
right.
and i'm your pal, Gog-Agog, her co-host
coming at you live from Rayuba.

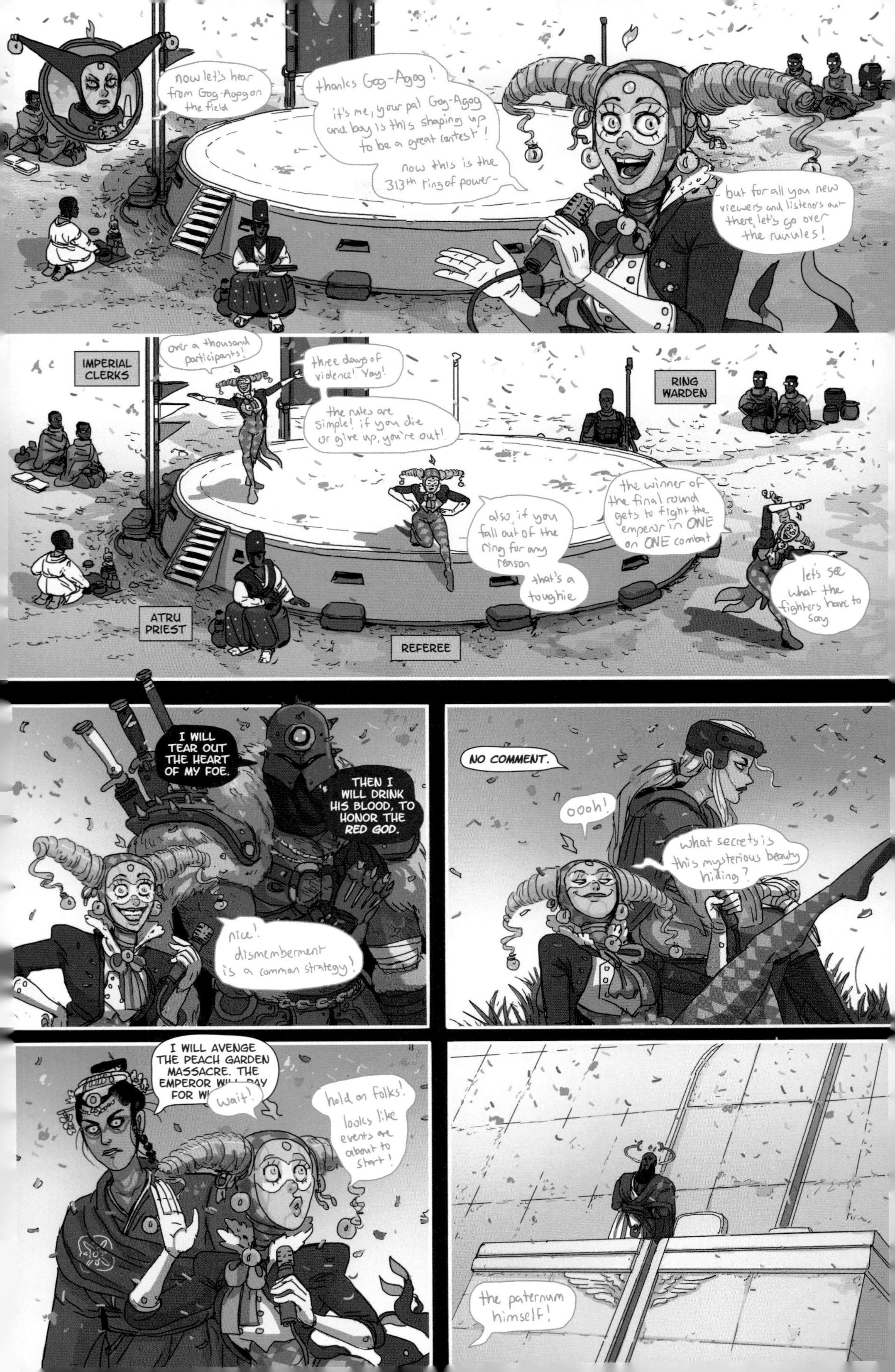
now let's hear from Gog-Agog on the field
thanks Gog-Agog!
it's me, your pal Gog-Agog and boy is this shaping up to be a great contest!
now this is the 313th ring of power-
-but for all you new viewers and listeners out there, let's go over the ruuules!
IMPERIAL CLERKS
over a thousand participants!
three days of violence! Yay!
the rules are simple! if you die or give up, you're out!
RING WARDEN
also, if you fall out of the ring for any reason
that's a toughie
the winner of the final round gets to fight the emperor in ONE on ONE combat
let's see what the fighters have to say
ATRU PRIEST
REFEREE
I WILL TEAR OUT THE HEART OF MY FOE.
THEN I WILL DRINK HIS BLOOD, TO HONOR THE RED GOD.
nice! dismemberment is a common strategy!
NO COMMENT.
oooh!
what secrets is this mysterious beauty hiding?
I WILL AVENGE THE PEACH GARDEN MASSACRE. THE EMPEROR WILL PAY FOR WI
wait!
hold on folks! looks like events are about to start!
the paternum himself!

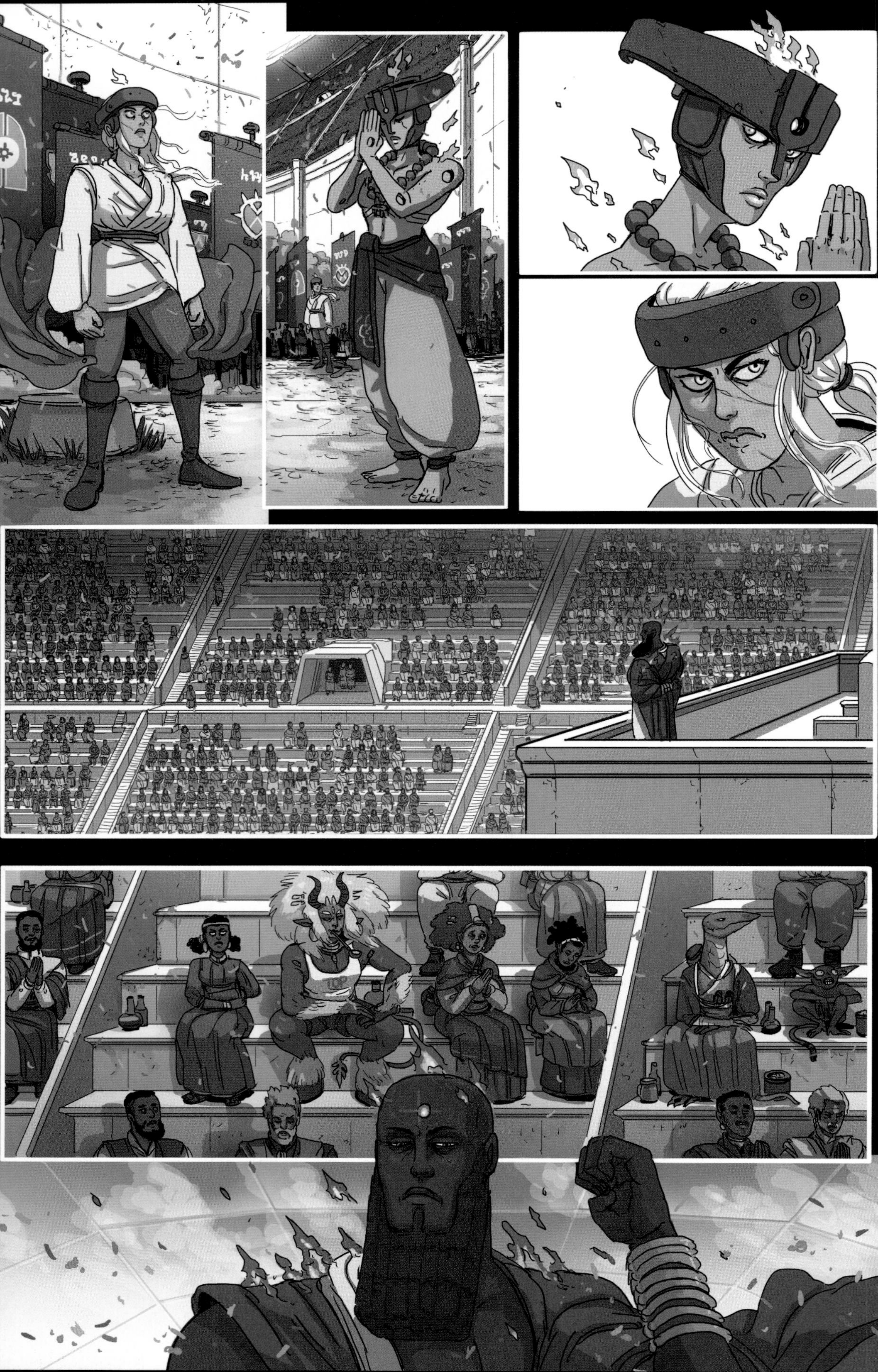
TOP

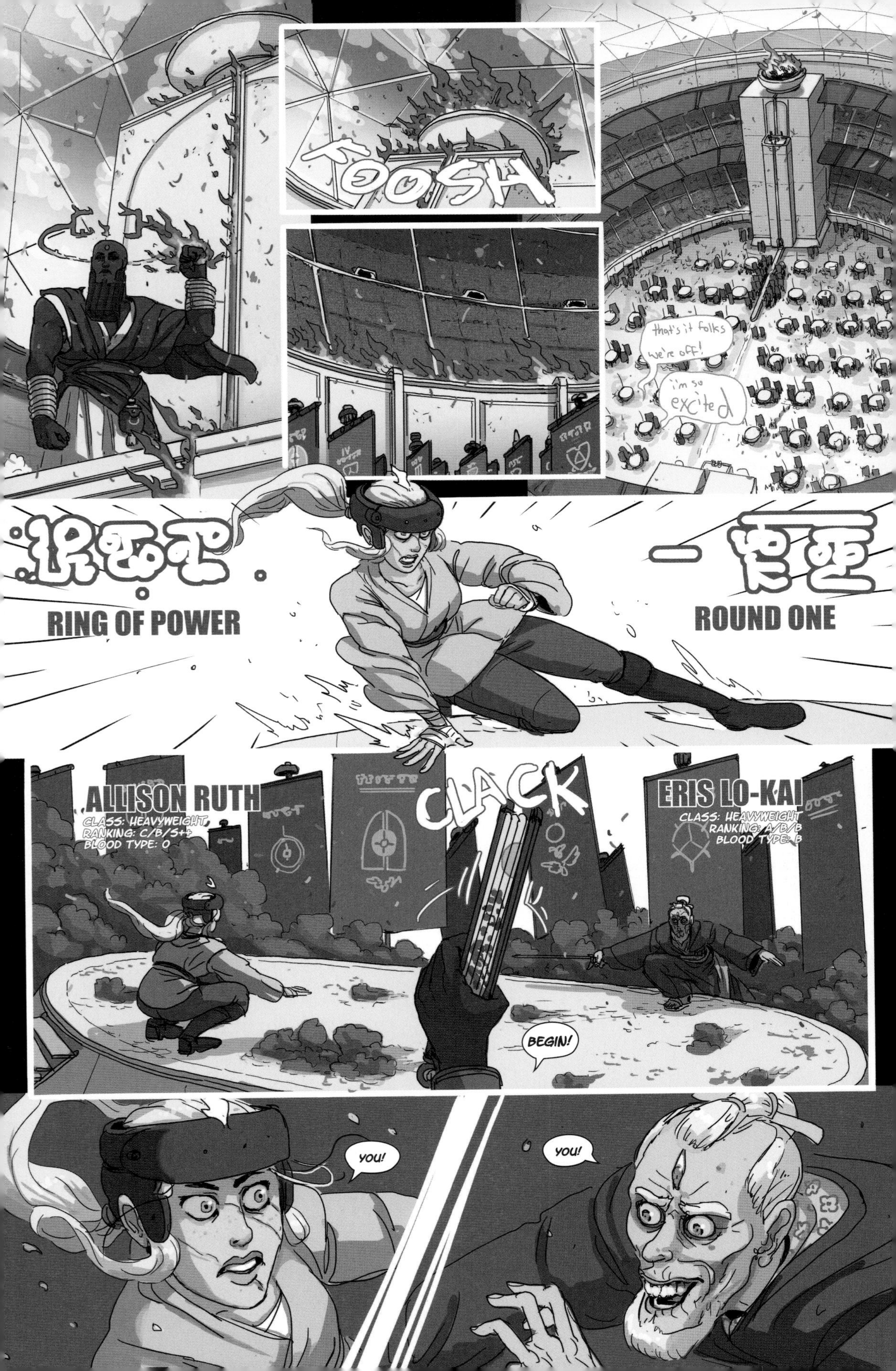
KOOSH
that's it folks we're off!
i'm so excited
RING OF POWER
ROUND ONE
CLACK
ALLISON RUTH
CLASS: HEAVYWEIGHT
RANKING: C/B/S++
BLOOD TYPE: O
ERIS LO-KAI
CLASS: HEAVYWEIGHT
RANKING: A/B/B
BLOOD TYPE: B
BEGIN!
YOU!
YOU!

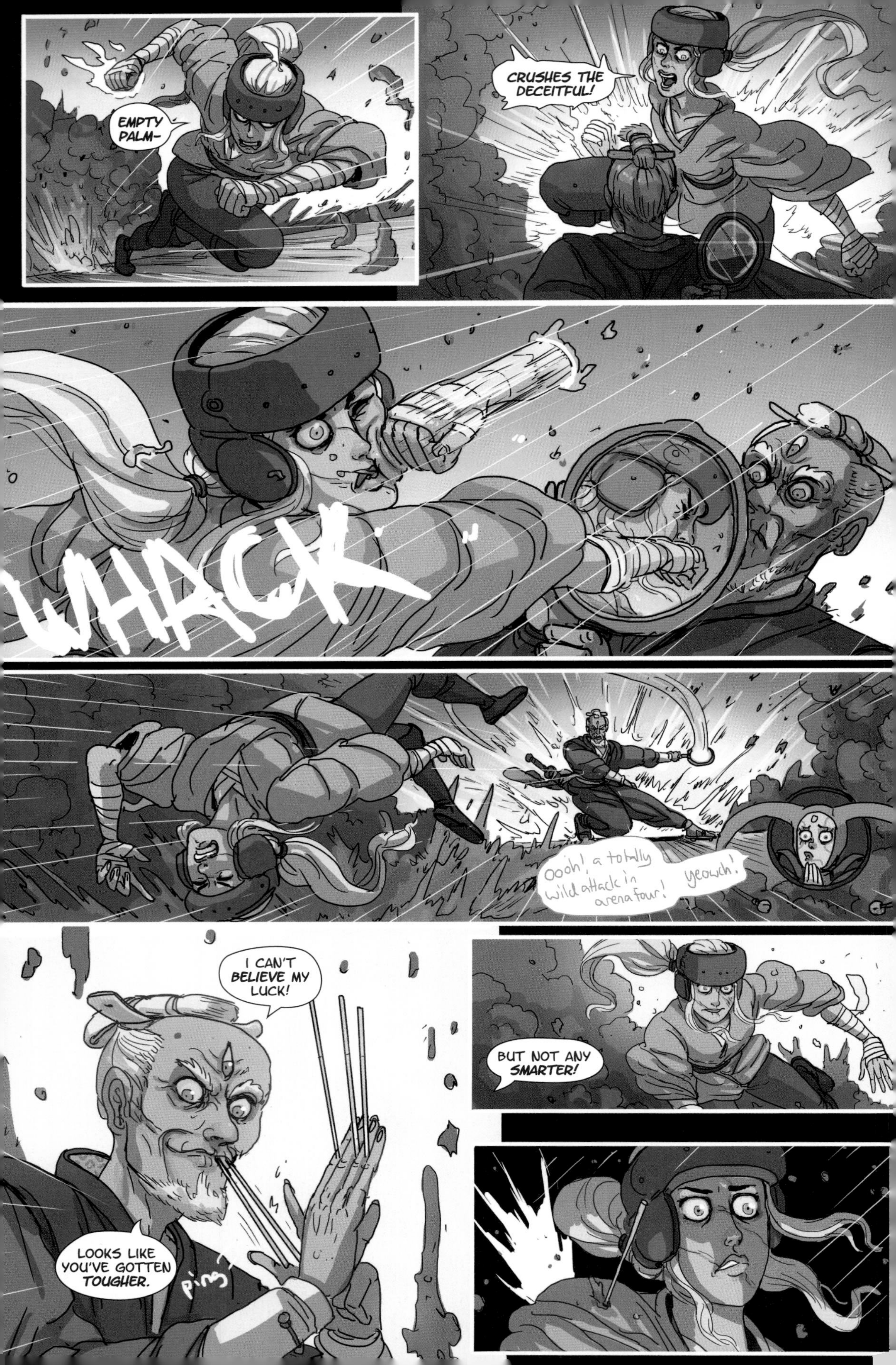
EMPTY PALM-
CRUSHES THE DECEITFUL!
WHACK
Oooh! a totally wild attack in arena four!
yeowch!
I CAN'T BELIEVE MY LUCK!
LOOKS LIKE YOU'VE GOTTEN TOUGHER.
ping
BUT NOT ANY SMARTER!

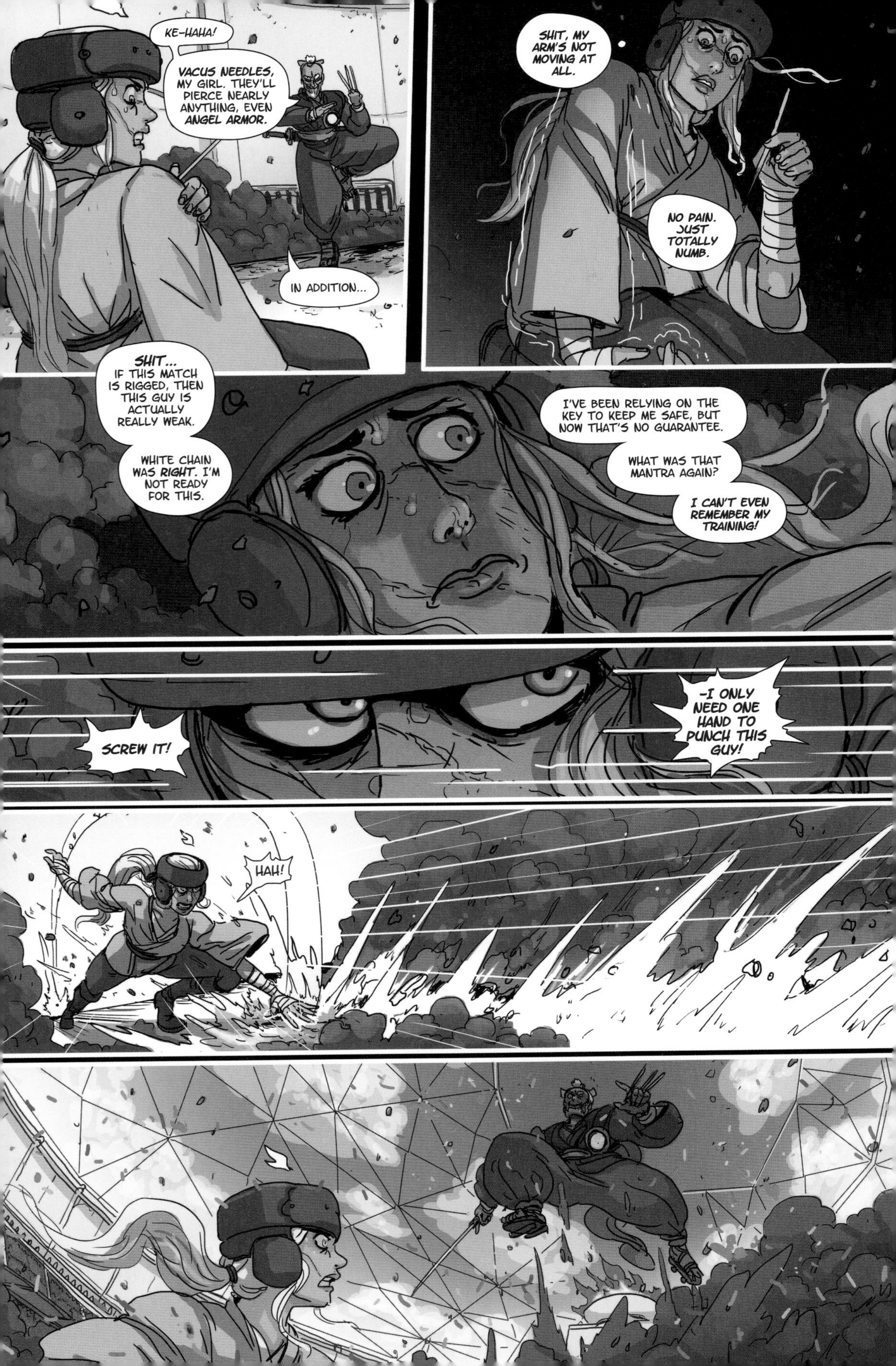
KE-HAHA!
VACUS NEEDLES, MY GIRL. THEY'LL PIERCE NEARLY ANYTHING, EVEN ANGEL ARMOR.
IN ADDITION...
SHIT, MY ARM'S NOT MOVING AT ALL.
NO PAIN. JUST TOTALLY NUMB.
SHIT... IF THIS MATCH IS RIGGED, THEN THIS GUY IS ACTUALLY REALLY WEAK.
WHITE CHAIN WAS RIGHT. I'M NOT READY FOR THIS.
I'VE BEEN RELYING ON THE KEY TO KEEP ME SAFE, BUT NOW THAT'S NO GUARANTEE.
WHAT WAS THAT MANTRA AGAIN?
I CAN'T EVEN REMEMBER MY TRAINING!
SCREW IT!
-I ONLY NEED ONE HAND TO PUNCH THIS GUY!
HAH!

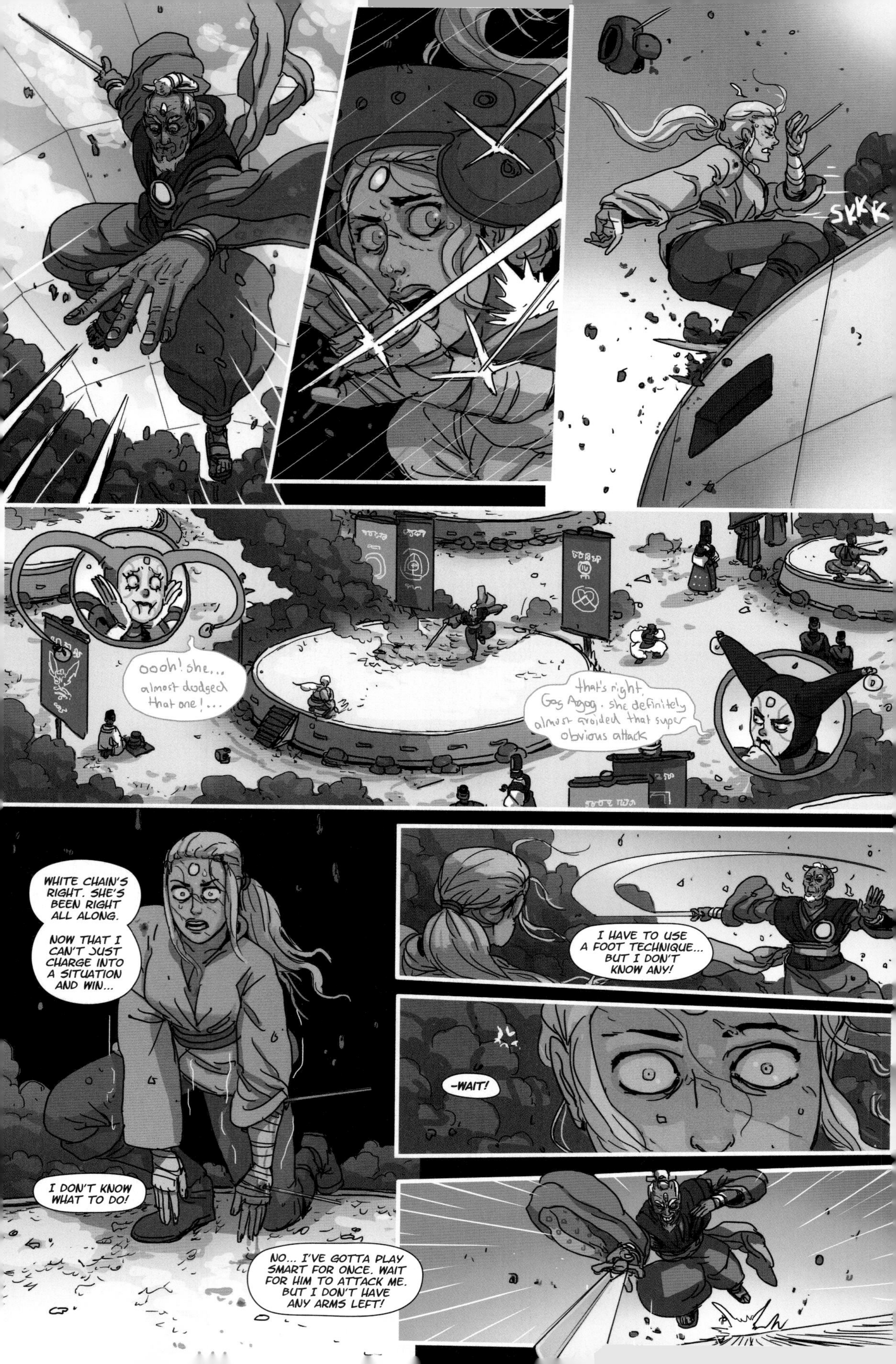
SKKK
oooh! she... almost dodged that one!...
that's right, Gas Agog. she definitely almost avoided that super obvious attack
WHITE CHAIN'S RIGHT. SHE'S BEEN RIGHT ALL ALONG.
NOW THAT I CAN'T JUST CHARGE INTO A SITUATION AND WIN...
I DON'T KNOW WHAT TO DO!
I HAVE TO USE A FOOT TECHNIQUE... BUT I DON'T KNOW ANY!
-WAIT!
NO... I'VE GOTTA PLAY SMART FOR ONCE. WAIT FOR HIM TO ATTACK ME. BUT I DON'T HAVE ANY ARMS LEFT!

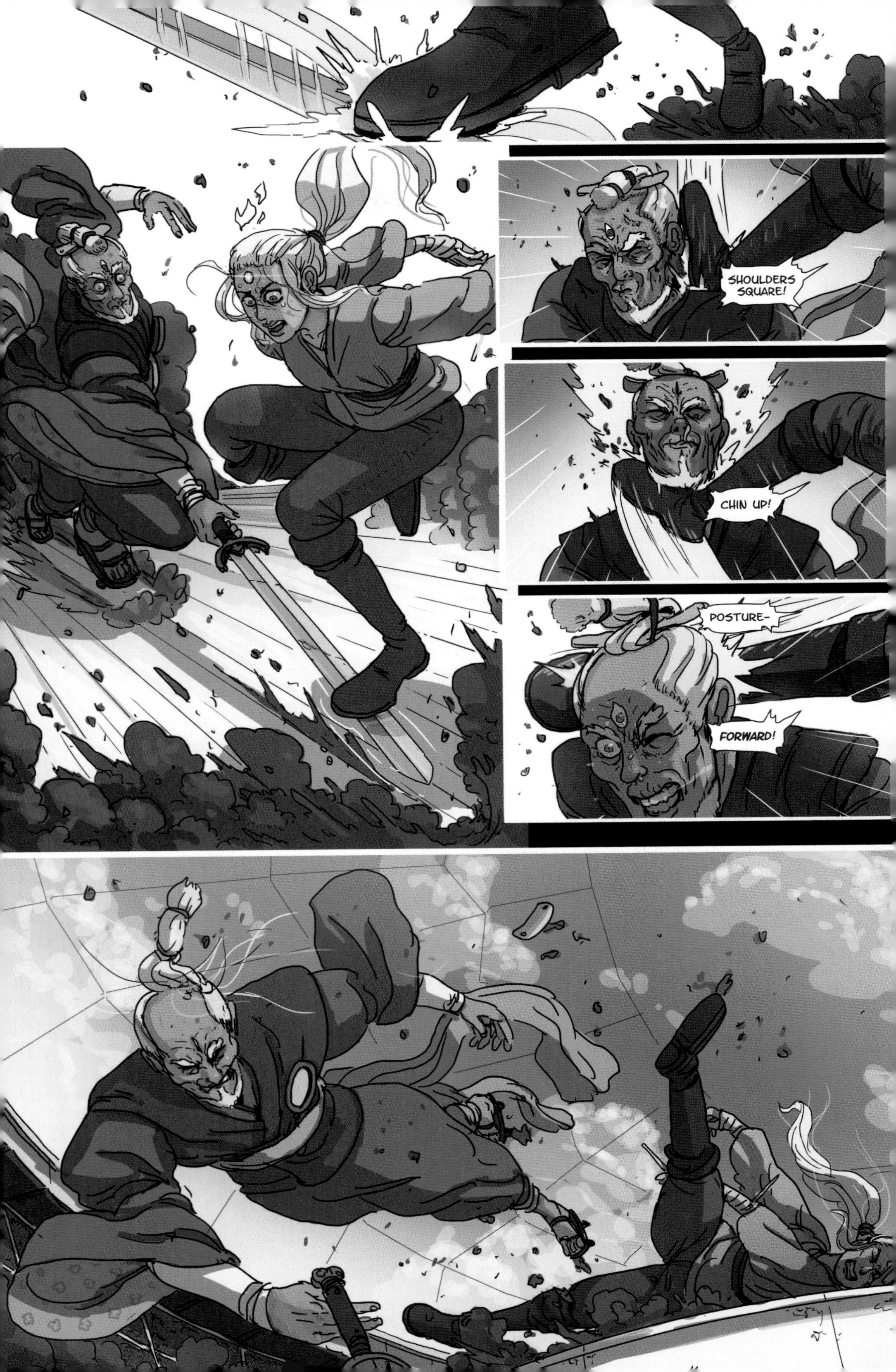
SHOULDERS SQUARE!
CHIN UP!
POSTURE-
FORWARD!

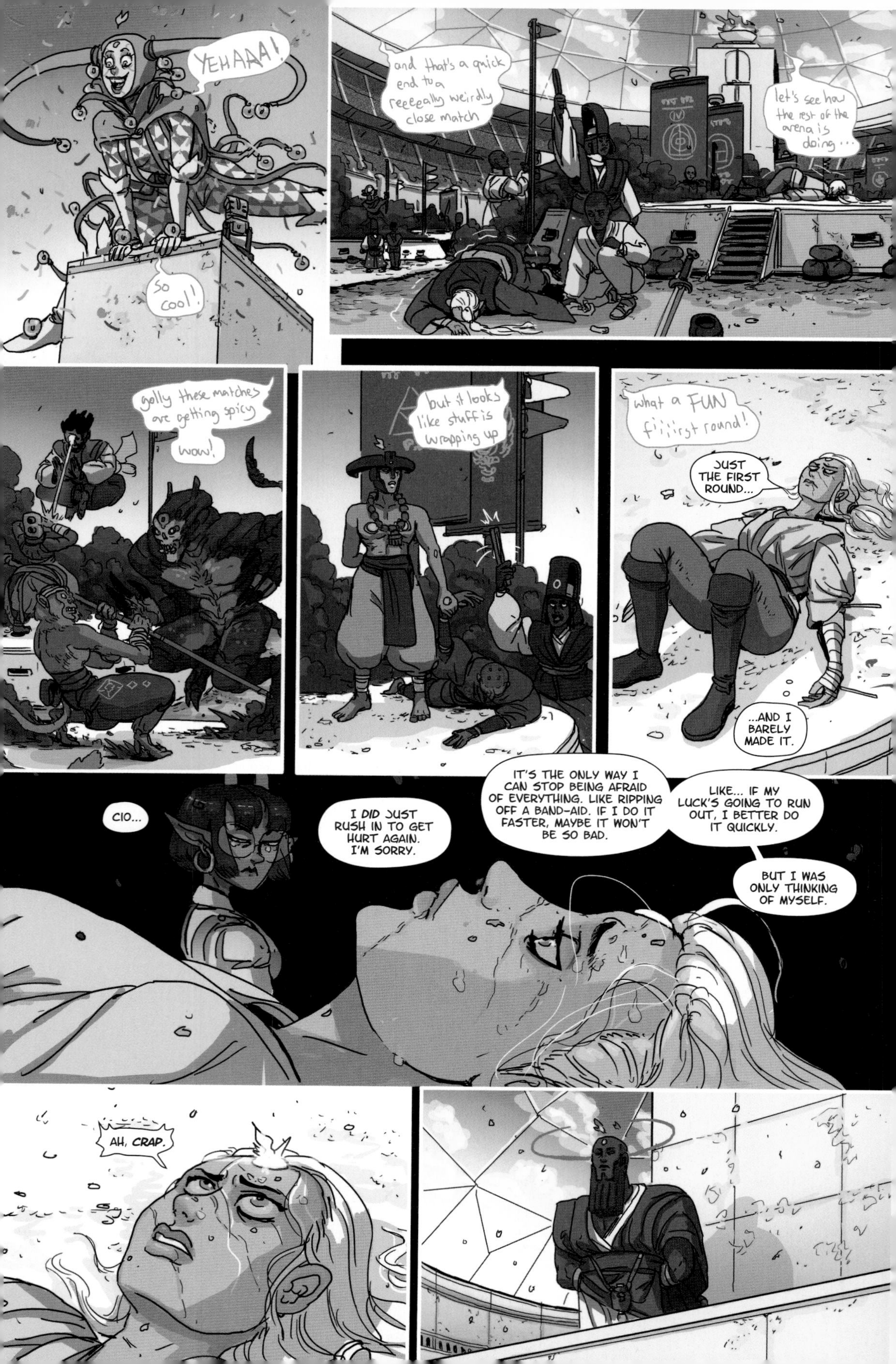

YEHAAA!
So cool!
and that's a quick end to a reeeeally weirdly close match
let's see how the rest of the arena is doing...
golly these matches are getting spicy
wow!
but it looks like stuff is wrapping up
what a FUN fiiiirst round!
JUST THE FIRST ROUND...
...AND I BARELY MADE IT.
CIO...
I DID JUST RUSH IN TO GET HURT AGAIN. I'M SORRY.
IT'S THE ONLY WAY I CAN STOP BEING AFRAID OF EVERYTHING. LIKE RIPPING OFF A BAND-AID. IF I DO IT FASTER, MAYBE IT WON'T BE SO BAD.
LIKE... IF MY LUCK'S GOING TO RUN OUT, I BETTER DO IT QUICKLY.
BUT I WAS ONLY THINKING OF MYSELF.
AH, CRAP.

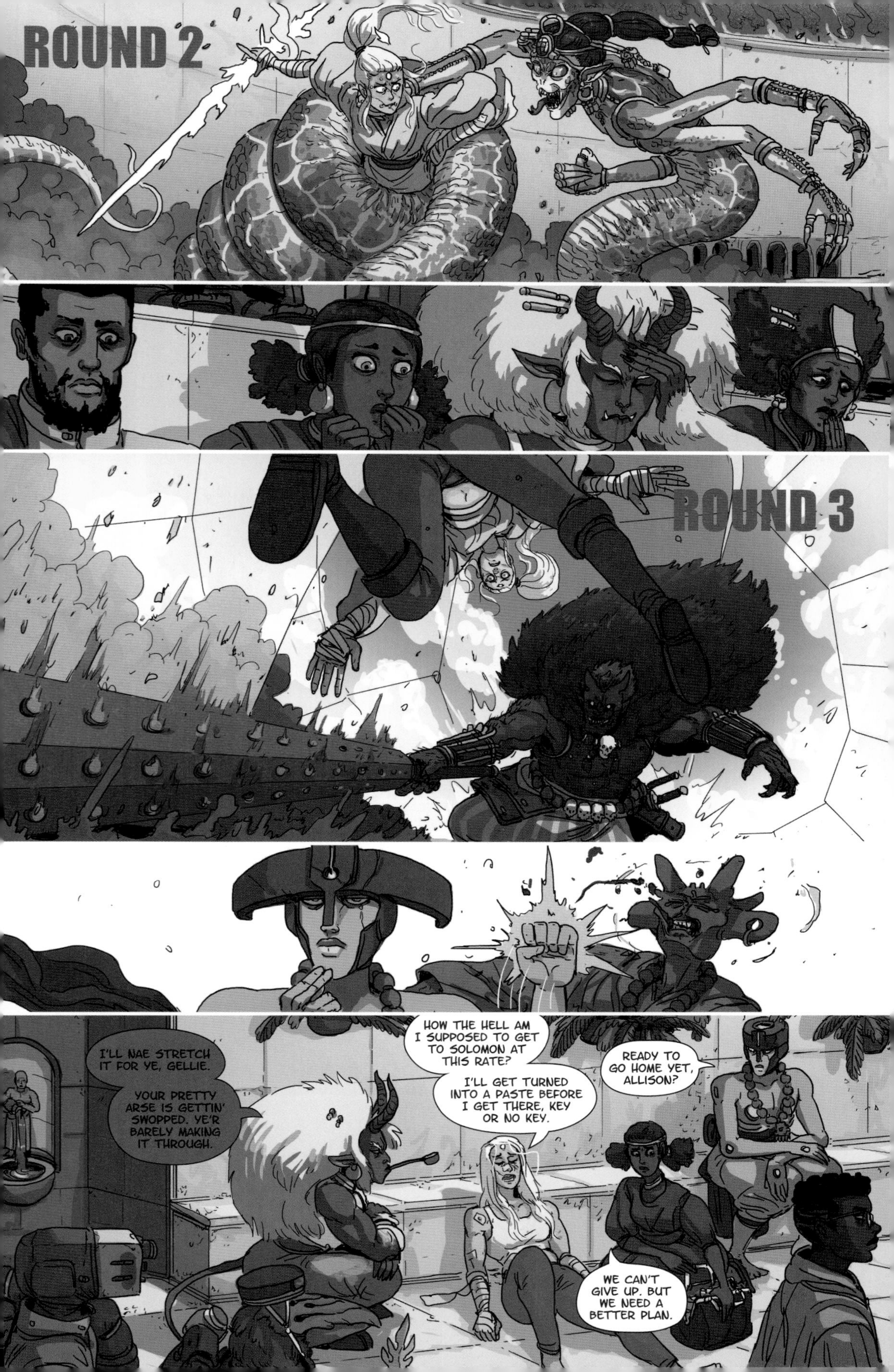
ROUND 2
ROUND 3
I'LL NAE STRETCH IT FOR YE, GELLIE.
YOUR PRETTY ARSE IS GETTIN' SWOPPED. YE'R BARELY MAKING IT THROUGH.
HOW THE HELL AM I SUPPOSED TO GET TO SOLOMON AT THIS RATE?
I'LL GET TURNED INTO A PASTE BEFORE I GET THERE, KEY OR NO KEY.
READY TO GO HOME YET, ALLISON?
WE CAN'T GIVE UP. BUT WE NEED A BETTER PLAN.

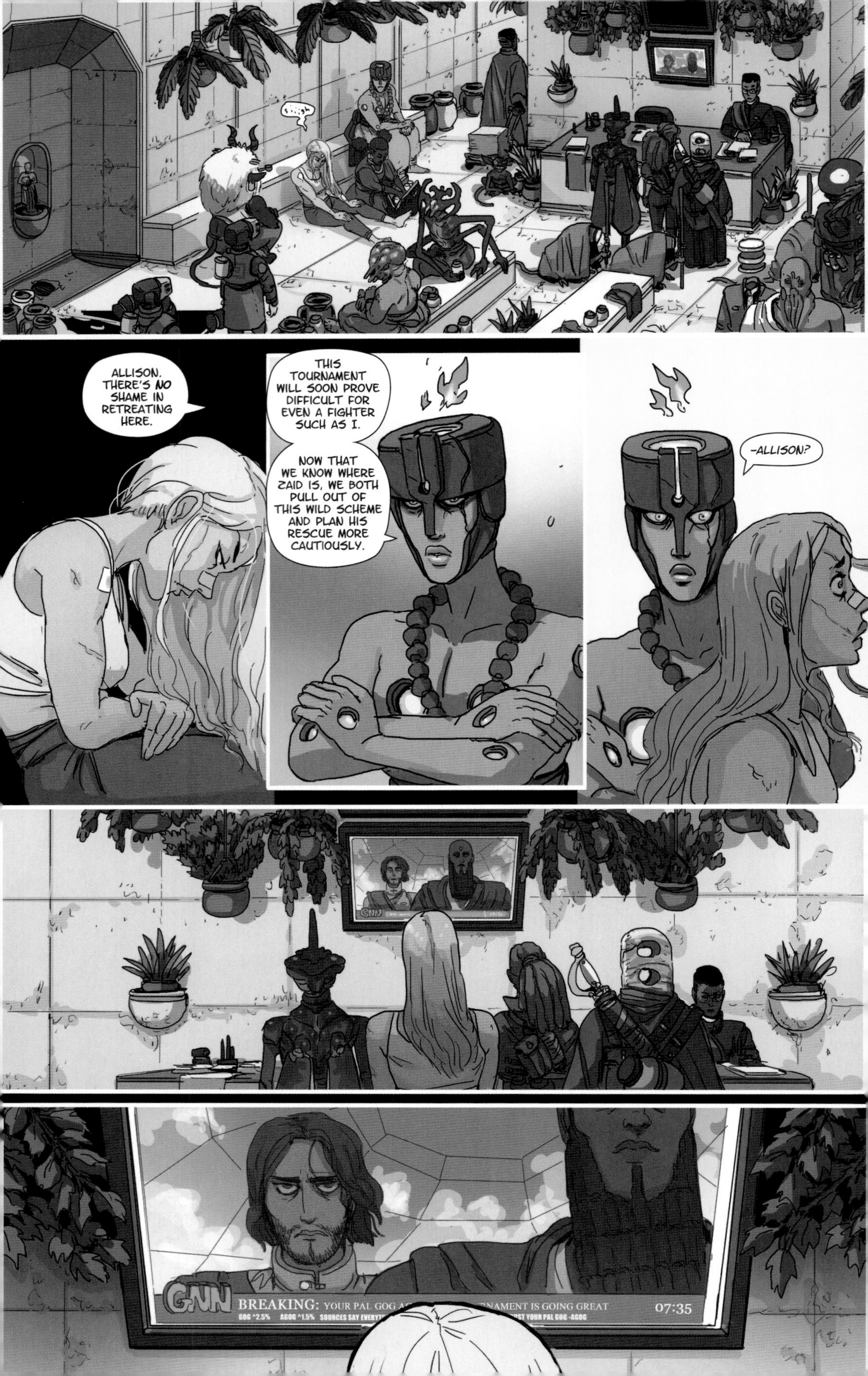
s...igh
ALLISON. THERE'S NO SHAME IN RETREATING HERE.
THIS TOURNAMENT WILL SOON PROVE DIFFICULT FOR EVEN A FIGHTER SUCH AS I.
NOW THAT WE KNOW WHERE ZAID IS, WE BOTH PULL OUT OF THIS WILD SCHEME AND PLAN HIS RESCUE MORE CAUTIOUSLY.
-ALLISON?
GNN
BREAKING: YOUR PAL GOG A
RNAMENT IS GOING GREAT
07:35
GOG ^2.5% AGOG ^1.5% SOURCES SAY EVERYT
UST YOUR PAL GOG -AGOG

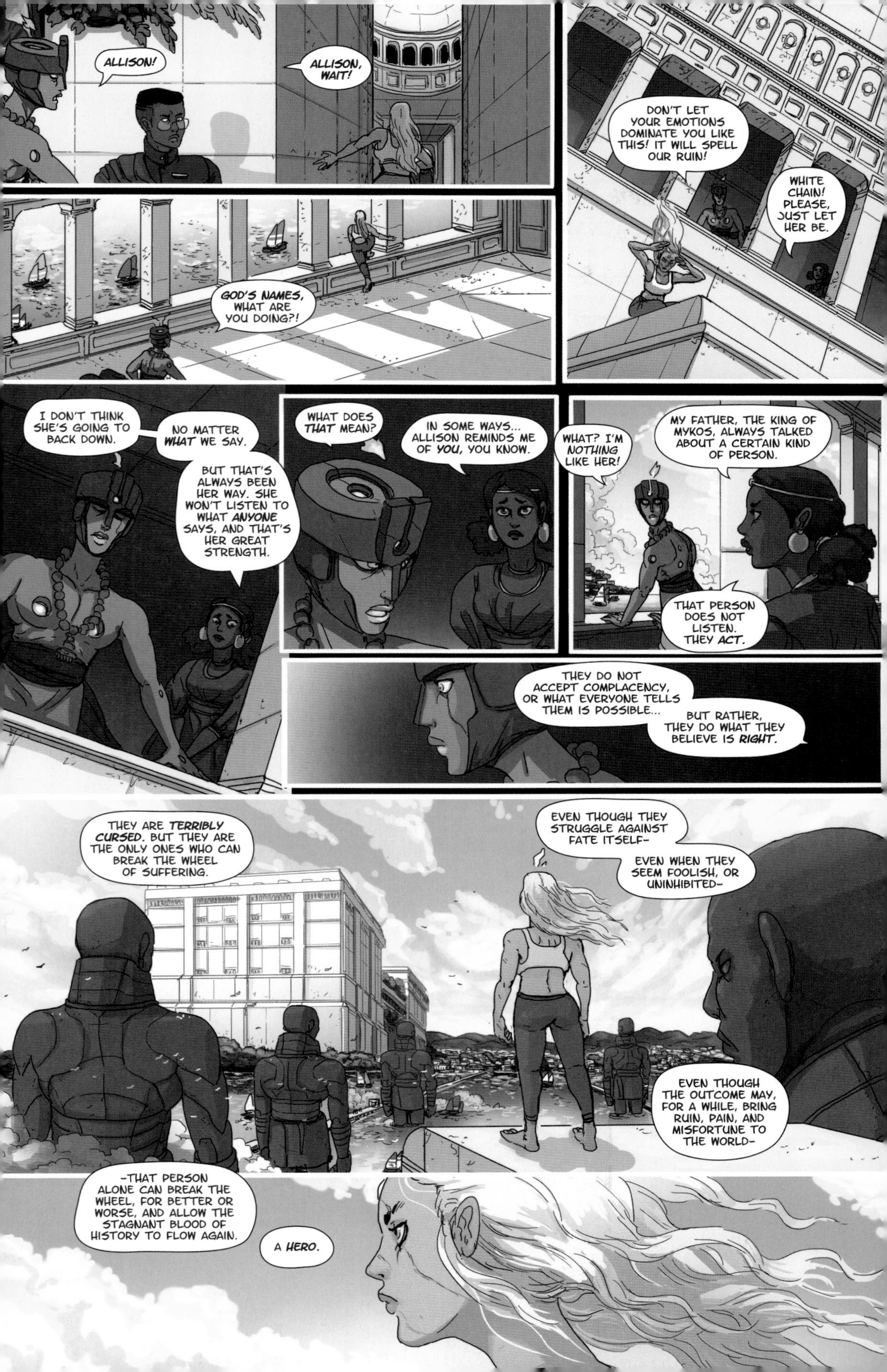

ALLISON!
ALLISON, WAIT!
DON'T LET YOUR EMOTIONS DOMINATE YOU LIKE THIS! IT WILL SPELL OUR RUIN!
WHITE CHAIN! PLEASE, JUST LET HER BE.
GOD'S NAMES, WHAT ARE YOU DOING?!
I DON'T THINK SHE'S GOING TO BACK DOWN.
NO MATTER WHAT WE SAY.
BUT THAT'S ALWAYS BEEN HER WAY. SHE WON'T LISTEN TO WHAT ANYONE SAYS, AND THAT'S HER GREAT STRENGTH.
WHAT DOES THAT MEAN?
IN SOME WAYS... ALLISON REMINDS ME OF YOU, YOU KNOW.
WHAT? I'M NOTHING LIKE HER!
MY FATHER, THE KING OF MYKOS, ALWAYS TALKED ABOUT A CERTAIN KIND OF PERSON.
THAT PERSON DOES NOT LISTEN. THEY ACT.
THEY DO NOT ACCEPT COMPLACENCY, OR WHAT EVERYONE TELLS THEM IS POSSIBLE...
BUT RATHER, THEY DO WHAT THEY BELIEVE IS RIGHT.
THEY ARE TERRIBLY CURSED. BUT THEY ARE THE ONLY ONES WHO CAN BREAK THE WHEEL OF SUFFERING.
EVEN THOUGH THEY STRUGGLE AGAINST FATE ITSELF-
EVEN WHEN THEY SEEM FOOLISH, OR UNINHIBITED-
EVEN THOUGH THE OUTCOME MAY, FOR A WHILE, BRING RUIN, PAIN, AND MISFORTUNE TO THE WORLD-
-THAT PERSON ALONE CAN BREAK THE WHEEL, FOR BETTER OR WORSE, AND ALLOW THE STAGNANT BLOOD OF HISTORY TO FLOW AGAIN.
A HERO.

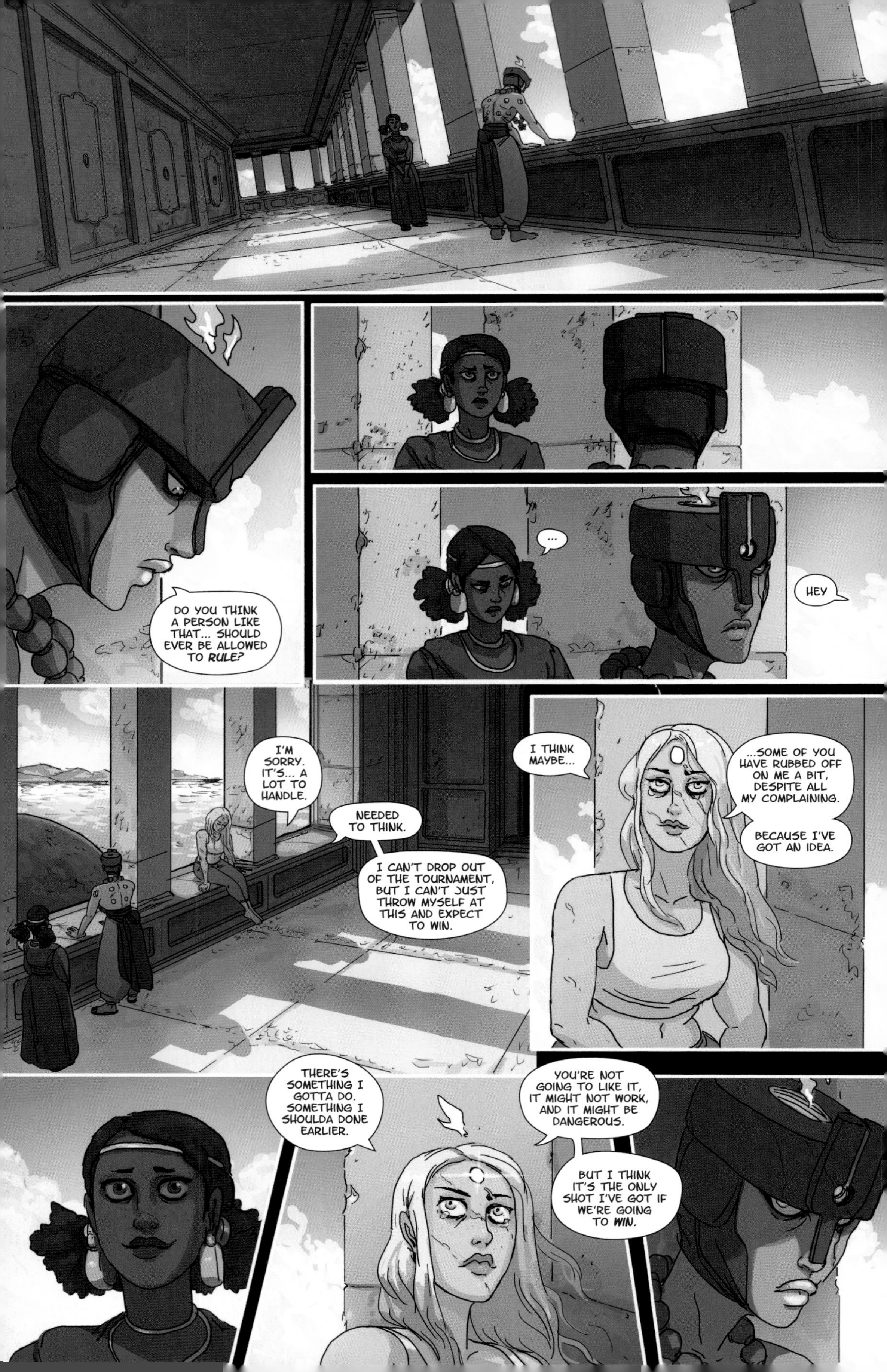
DO YOU THINK A PERSON LIKE THAT... SHOULD EVER BE ALLOWED TO *RULE?*
...
HEY
I'M SORRY. IT'S... A LOT TO HANDLE.
NEEDED TO THINK.
I CAN'T DROP OUT OF THE TOURNAMENT, BUT I CAN'T JUST THROW MYSELF AT THIS AND EXPECT TO WIN.
I THINK MAYBE...
...SOME OF YOU HAVE RUBBED OFF ON ME A BIT, DESPITE ALL MY COMPLAINING.
BECAUSE I'VE GOT AN IDEA.
THERE'S SOMETHING I GOTTA DO. SOMETHING I SHOULDA DONE EARLIER.
YOU'RE NOT GOING TO LIKE IT, IT MIGHT NOT WORK, AND IT MIGHT BE DANGEROUS.
BUT I THINK IT'S THE ONLY SHOT I'VE GOT IF WE'RE GOING TO *WIN.*

BUT AT THE MOMENT Het was sure he would spring forth, foaming at the mouth, the funeral was over, and the breaking of the bread began. It was then that Het jumped into action.

"May I have some bread?" she asked the fire-stoking woman, and was handed a thin and meager piece. She swallowed it down as the Sergeant watched, cold and irate, and then pulled herself up to her full height and planted her staff. In fact, Het was very tall, and her arms were corded like boughs, and her staff was so heavy that a rough man of the fields who worked a plough all day would scarcely be able to lift it. Even though she knew none of these things, everyone else recognized them very quickly, and so it grew very quiet indeed when she stood up.

"This bread is the finest I've had in my three years of service," she proclaimed, loudly and precisely. "Why, I'd deign to say it's better than the bread my grandmother baked." The assembled dwellers nodded in approval, even though they knew the bread was bitter and dry. The land may have been cold and harsh, but they were gracious for what they had. "How is your bread, auntie?" Het asked the fire-stoking woman. The woman caught the glint in Het's eye, and all of a sudden a wave of understanding and excitement passed around the gathered dwellers. "I'd deign to say it's the best bread I've baked yet," said the woman at the top of her voice, "The best bread in a century! There was a loud chorus of approval, and other voices joined in.

"The best bread on this side of the Wheel!"
"See how sweet and fresh it is!"
"They should serve it in the capital!"

More and more voices joined in until it was a cacophony of praise. Ridiculous, overfed, hyperbolic lies tumbled back and forth through the air, and Het stood at the center of it all, with her eye bright and sharp, and both hands on her quarterstaff. She was beginning to lose hope, when there was suddenly a shrill and piercing scream.

The scream came from an old and shriveled woman, who was bent double over the great table, and bile was pouring from her mouth and nose. For, as they all remembered then, the Rakshasa could not stand the sound of lies, and it crawled right out of the woman's mouth and writhed in a black and suppurating mass on the table. "Enough!" it shrieked, but Het scarcely gave it pause before she dashed forth and smashed its skull into five hundred pieces with a mighty blow of her quarterstaff. The blow was so powerful it split the table clean in two and sent echoes all the way up to the palace where it shattered the lord's prized crystal chandelier with the mere sound of its violence.

A great cheer went up and the broken body of the Rakshasa was beaten and bludgeoned by the furious crowd and dragged into the muck where it was later eaten by dogs. The old woman was brought immediately to the dwelling of a healer where she recovered through the healer's strong skill in herbal cleansing and lived another decade, demon free.

But it wasn't over for Het, by far. If anything, she gripped her quarterstaff even tighter, for while the crowd had been filling the air with lies, she had noticed something bizarre that filled her up to the brim with dread. The Sergeant had been trembling and quaking the entire time, just like the old woman, and his handsome face was lined with pain.

AND HET TURNED TO HIM IN FEAR AND SAID, "YOU TOO, HAVE A RAKSHASA INSIDE OF YOU."

"OF COURSE," CHOKED THE SERGEANT, "IT TAKES A DEMON TO FIND A DEMON, DIDN'T YOU KNOW? THAT'S WHY THEY MADE ME A SERGEANT."

"You don't have a Watchman's Eye at all," said Het, choking back tears, "You just know whether someone is lying or not."

"Yes," said the convulsing Sergeant, bile pouring from his nose and ruining his perfect mustache. "I am very good at catching liars and criminals. If you want to fraternize with the filthy, that is your business. I, however, am a

VI.

perfect policeman." Het had to admit, he was right. He was a very good policeman, with very clean fingernails. But he was a very poor person.

"Liars and criminals are not the same," said Het, and struck the Sergeant a mighty blow across the chest. At that, the Centurion, who had been waiting to kill someone all morning, sprung forth with a lustful, sputtering cry and drew his sword. But although he far outmatched Het at skill with the sword, he was a very poor swordsman. He got a few good cuts in on Het, which she bore for the rest of her life, but she was filled with the terrible fires of Will, and he was not. The moment she got a good blow on his over-swollen sword hand, it was over. He whined like a dog as Het gave him a thorough beating.

"Kill me," he begged, broken and bleeding, and cried piteously. It was the only thing he ever said to Het.

Het looked him over in pity, unbuckled her sword belt, and then threw it in the muck, for it was a killing weapon, unlike the stave. In this respect, Het was a very good swordswoman. She left the Centurion weeping and bade the dwellers teach him a more useful skill than killing. It was said he became a middling carpenter,

but that's a story for another time. Het turned back to the Sergeant. He had coughed his Rakshasa out into the dirt, and it was dragging itself feebly away from a ring of furious dwellers, who were harassing it with sticks and stones. The sight of it disgusted Het, for it was a greatly fattened and pampered thing. She bashed its brains out with very little thought and hurled its body into a sucking mire. When she returned, the Sergeant was bent over, quivering and cold. Without the demon inside of him, he was a small man, thin and sickly looking. Het was suddenly aware how much taller she was than him.

"You fool," babbled the Sergeant, "What will I do now? How will I make my living? How will I afford the money to keep my boots shined and my nails clean?"

Het looked at him, all clean-pressed and sharp, his eyes feverish and hateful, and over to the funeral pyre, which was burnt nearly to ashes, and the sorrowful gazes of the dwellers who bent there.

TRULY, SHE THOUGHT, SHE WOULD WASTE VERY LITTLE TIME ON THIS SMALL AND CRUEL MAN, SO SHE WALKED AWAY.

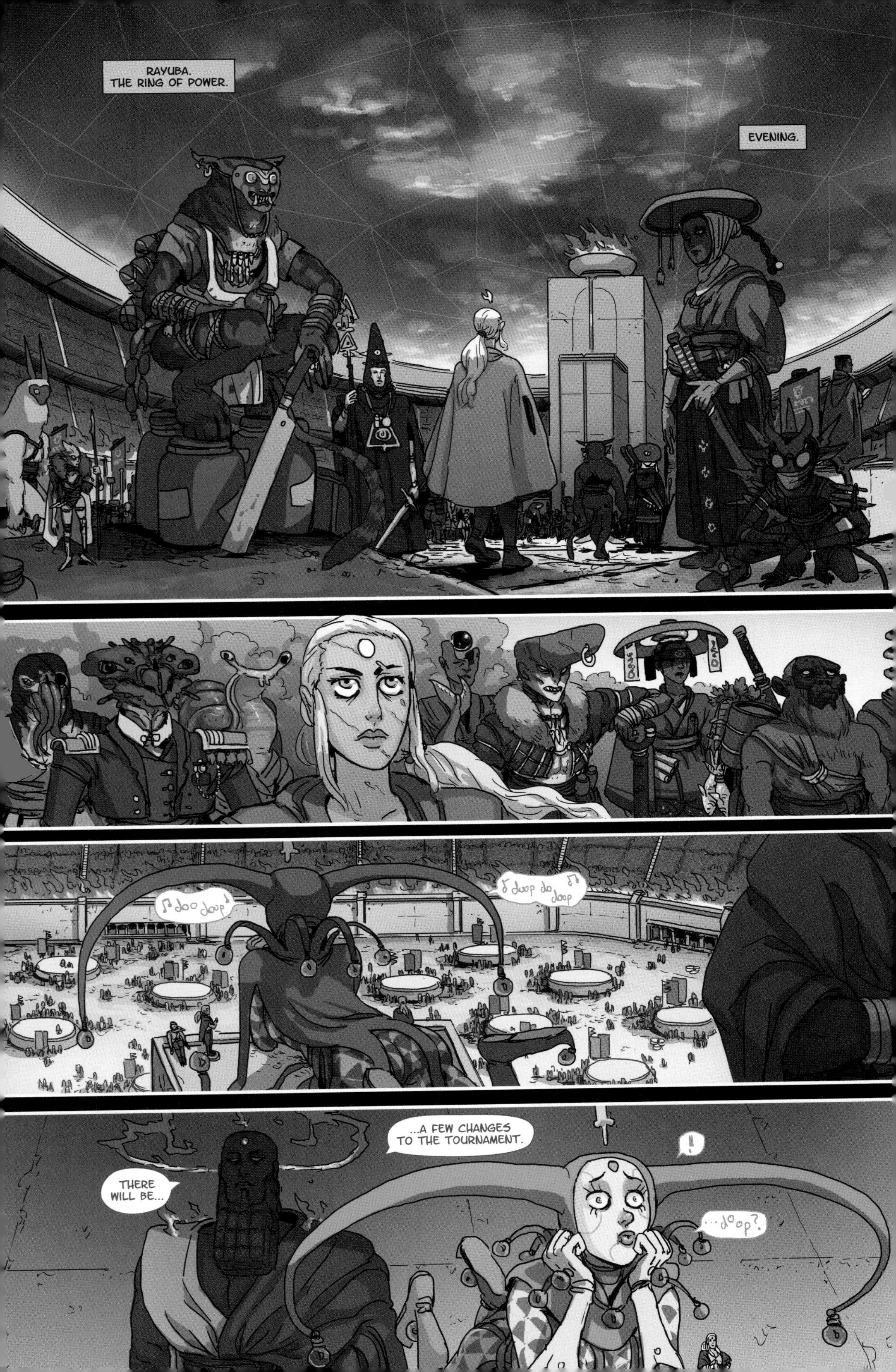

RAYUBA.
THE RING OF POWER.
EVENING.
doo doop
doop doo doop
THERE WILL BE...
...A FEW CHANGES TO THE TOURNAMENT.
!
...doop?

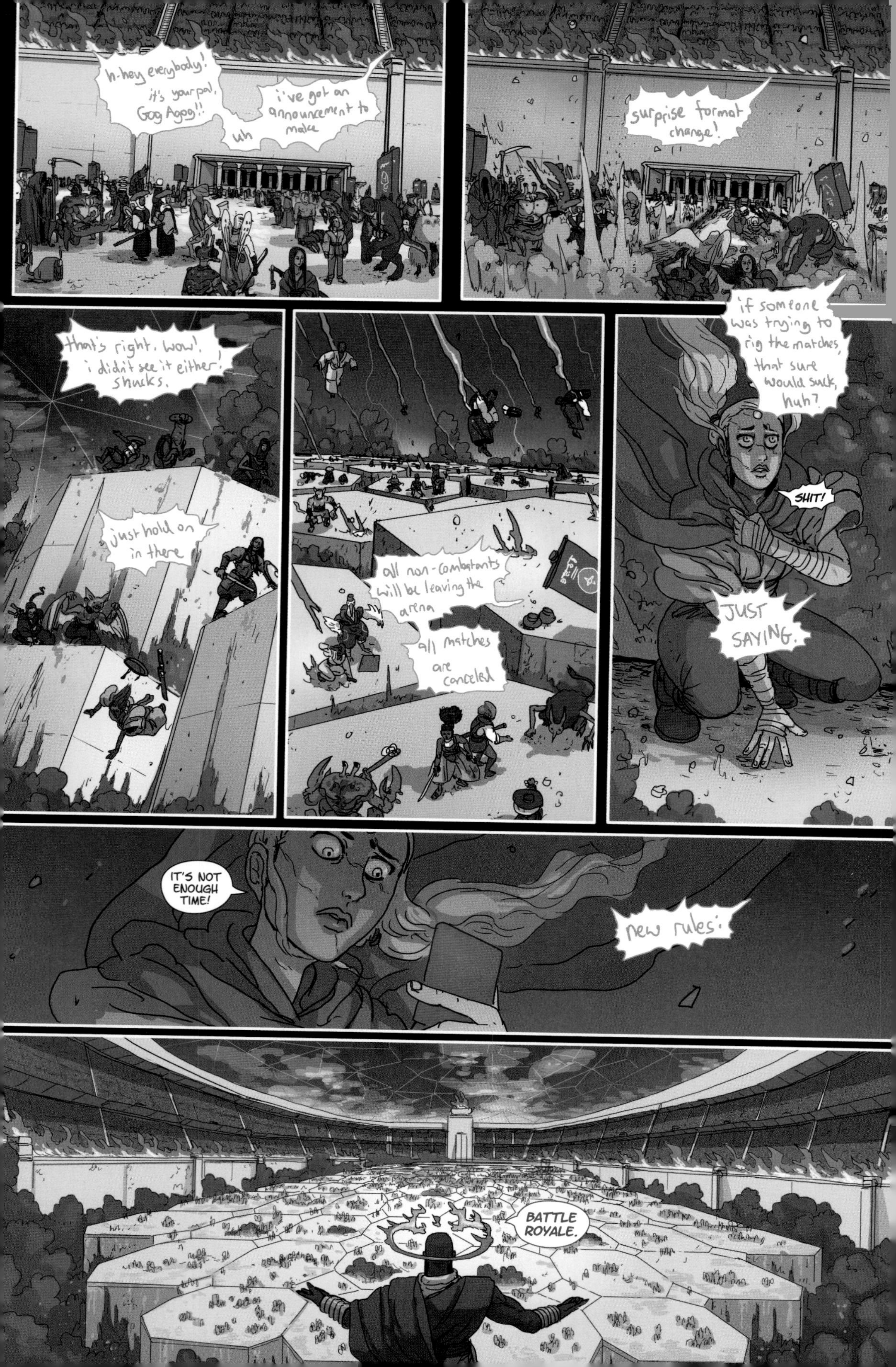
h-hey everybody! it's your pal, Gog Agog!!
uh
i've got an announcement to make
surprise format change!
that's right. wow! i didn't see it either! shucks.
just hold on in there
all non-combatants will be leaving the arena
all matches are canceled
if someone was trying to rig the matches, that sure would suck, huh?
SHIT!
JUST SAYING.
IT'S NOT ENOUGH TIME!
new rules:
BATTLE ROYALE.

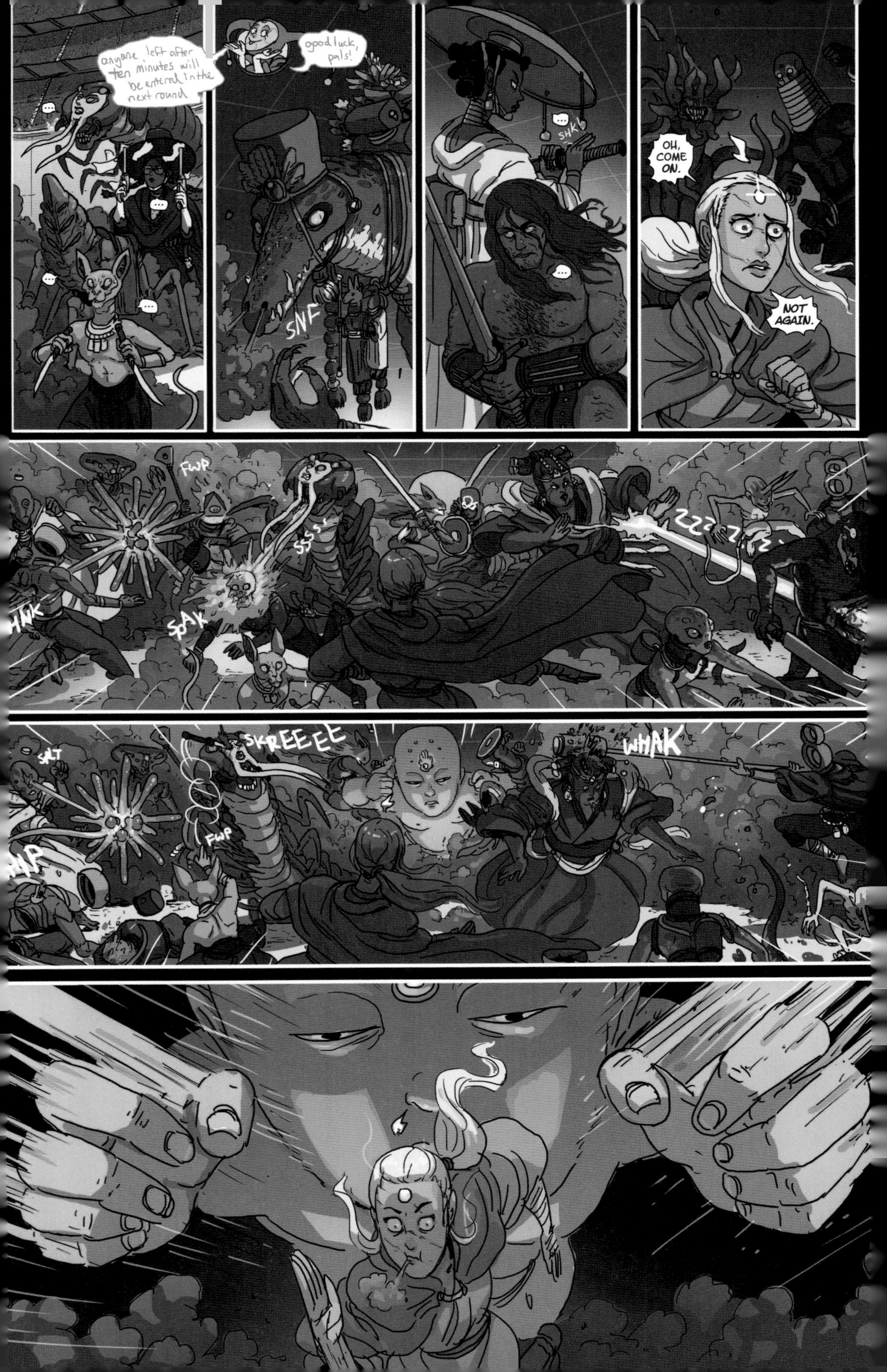
anyone left after ten minutes will be entered in the next round
good luck, pals!
...
...
...
...
SNF
...
SHK!
...
OH, COME ON.
NOT AGAIN.
FWP
SSSSS
ZZZZZZ
HWK
SPAK
SALT
SKREEEE
WHAK
FWP
HIP

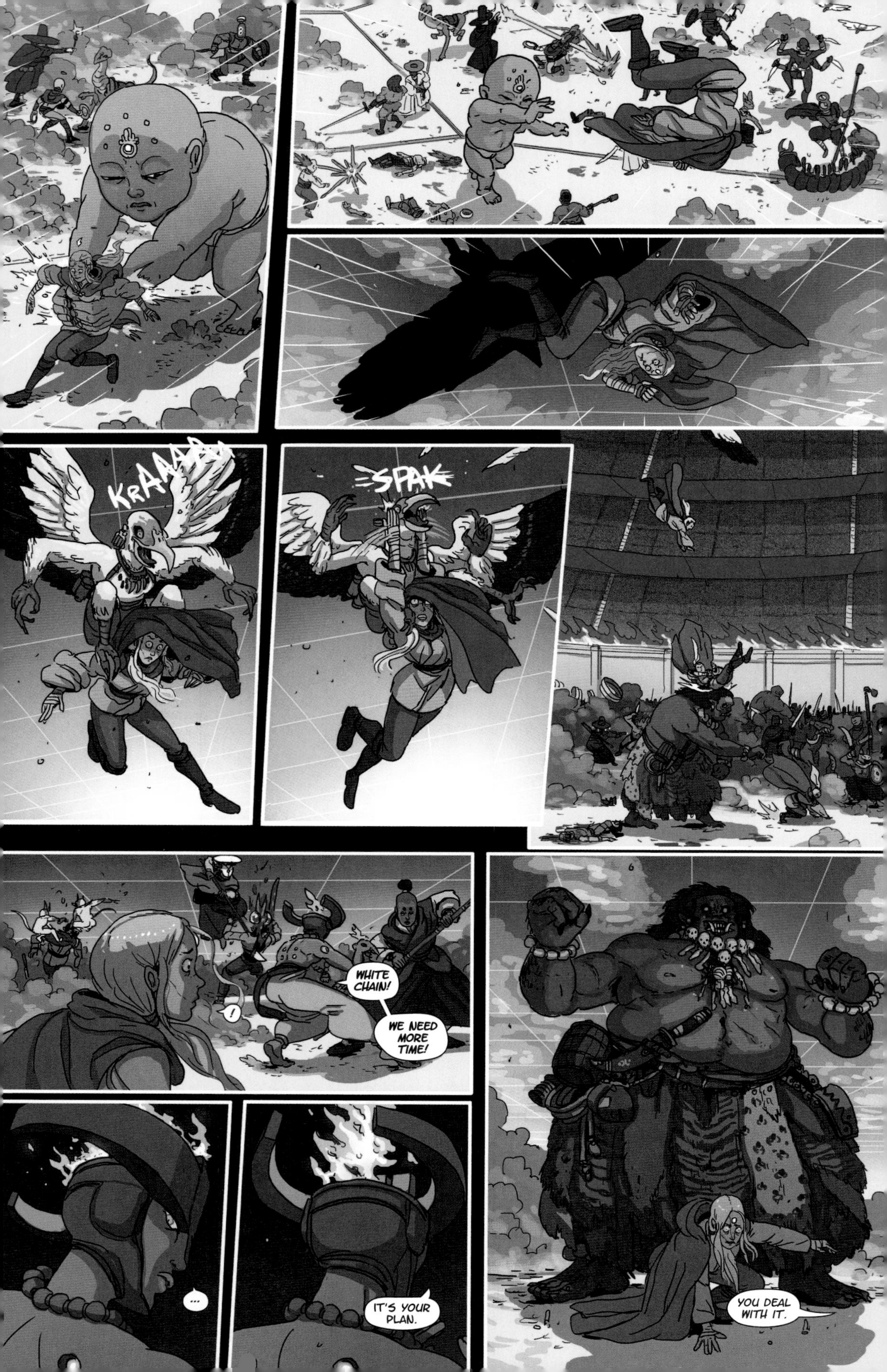
KRAAAB
SPAK
WHITE CHAIN!
WE NEED MORE TIME!
!
...
IT'S YOUR PLAN.
YOU DEAL WITH IT.

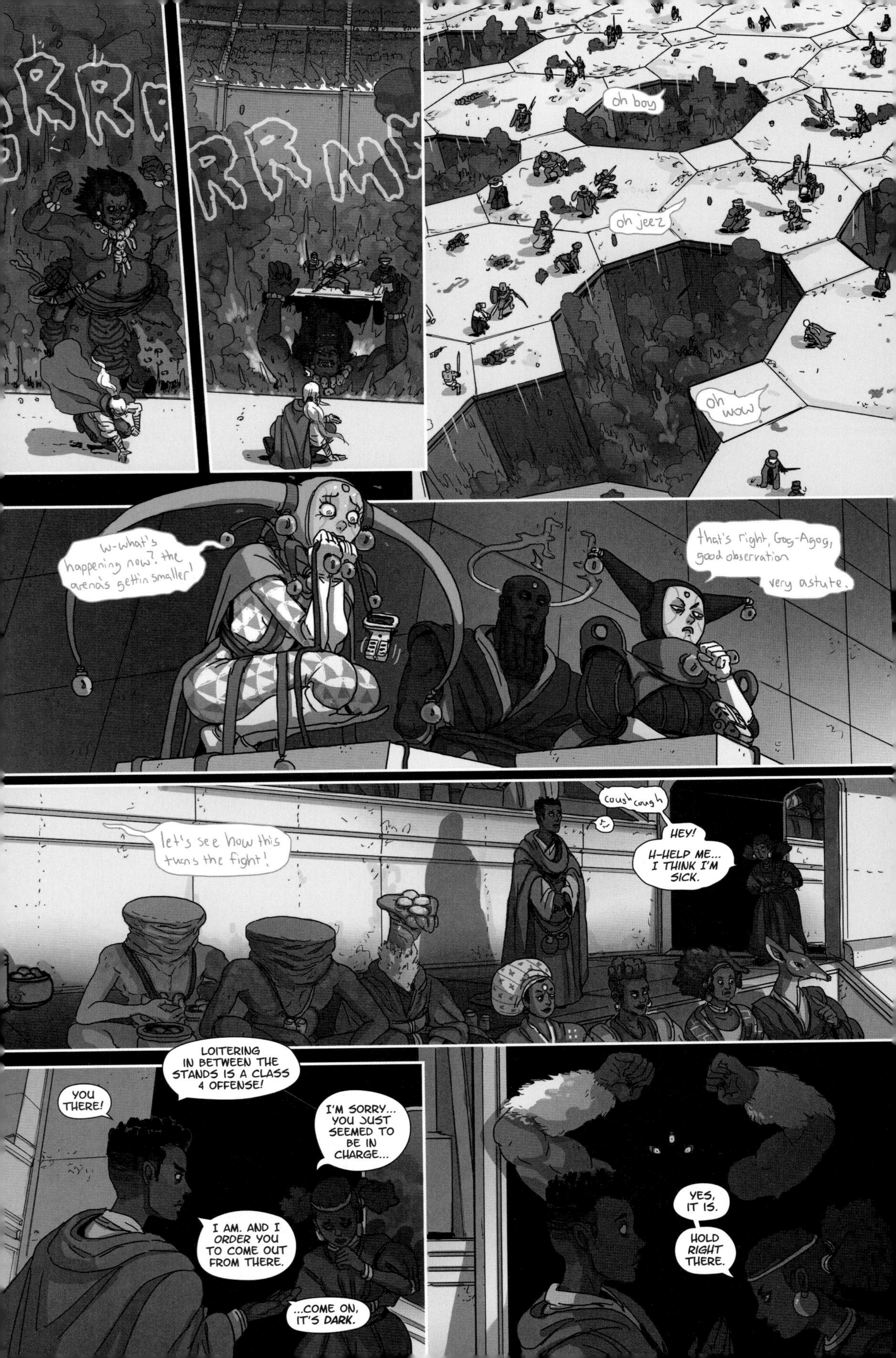
RRR
RRRMM
oh boy
oh jeez
oh wow
w-what's happening now? the arena's gettin smaller!
that's right, Gog-Agog, good observation
very astute.
let's see how this turns the fight!
cough cough
HEY!
H-HELP ME... I THINK I'M SICK.
YOU THERE!
LOITERING IN BETWEEN THE STANDS IS A CLASS 4 OFFENSE!
I'M SORRY... YOU JUST SEEMED TO BE IN CHARGE...
I AM. AND I ORDER YOU TO COME OUT FROM THERE.
...COME ON, IT'S DARK.
YES, IT IS.
HOLD RIGHT THERE.

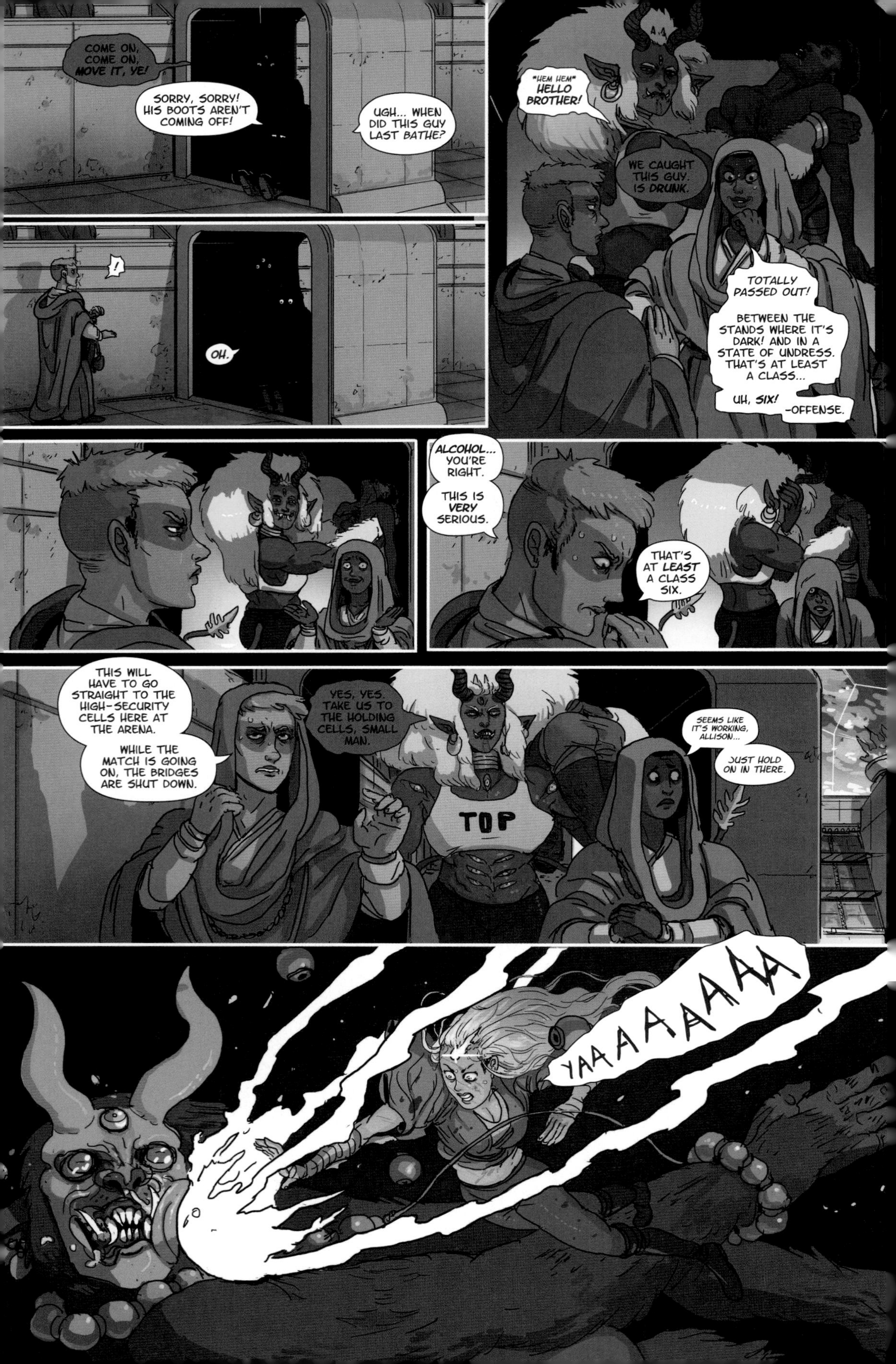

COME ON, COME ON, MOVE IT, YE!
SORRY, SORRY! HIS BOOTS AREN'T COMING OFF!
UGH... WHEN DID THIS GUY LAST BATHE?
!
OH.
HEM HEM HELLO BROTHER!
WE CAUGHT THIS GUY. IS DRUNK.
TOTALLY PASSED OUT!
BETWEEN THE STANDS WHERE IT'S DARK! AND IN A STATE OF UNDRESS. THAT'S AT LEAST A CLASS...
UH, SIX!
-OFFENSE.
ALCOHOL... YOU'RE RIGHT.
THIS IS VERY SERIOUS.
THAT'S AT LEAST A CLASS SIX.
THIS WILL HAVE TO GO STRAIGHT TO THE HIGH-SECURITY CELLS HERE AT THE ARENA.
WHILE THE MATCH IS GOING ON, THE BRIDGES ARE SHUT DOWN.
YES, YES. TAKE US TO THE HOLDING CELLS, SMALL MAN.
TOP
SEEMS LIKE IT'S WORKING, ALLISON...
JUST HOLD ON IN THERE.
YAAAAAAAA

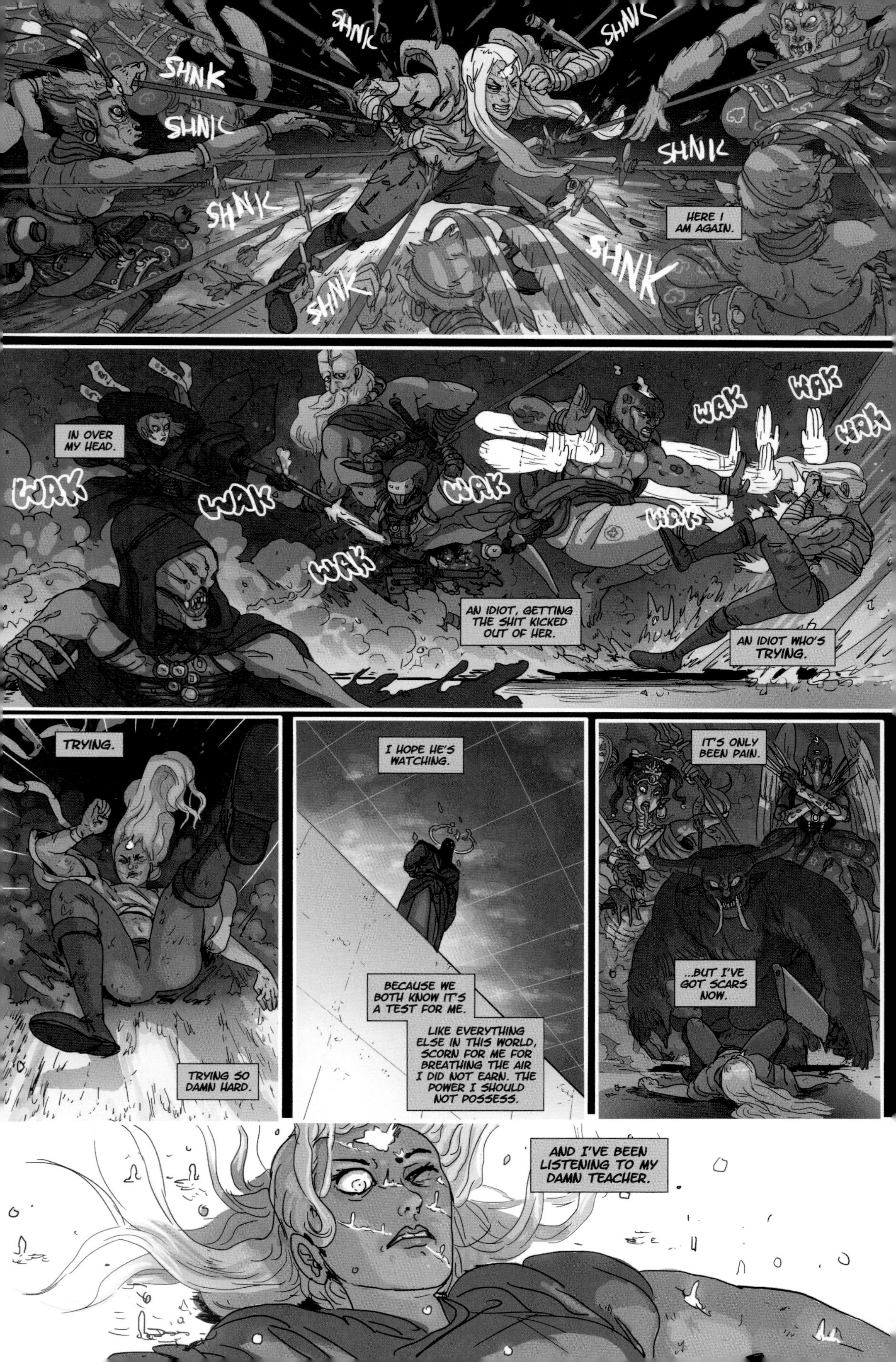
SHNK
SHNK
SHNK
SHNK
SHNK
SHNK
SHNK
SHNK
HERE I AM AGAIN.
IN OVER MY HEAD.
WAK
WAK
WAK
WAK
WAK
WAK
WAK
WAK
AN IDIOT, GETTING THE SHIT KICKED OUT OF HER.
AN IDIOT WHO'S TRYING.
TRYING.
TRYING SO DAMN HARD.
I HOPE HE'S WATCHING.
BECAUSE WE BOTH KNOW IT'S A TEST FOR ME.
LIKE EVERYTHING ELSE IN THIS WORLD, SCORN FOR ME FOR BREATHING THE AIR I DID NOT EARN. THE POWER I SHOULD NOT POSSESS.
IT'S ONLY BEEN PAIN.
...BUT I'VE GOT SCARS NOW.
AND I'VE BEEN LISTENING TO MY DAMN TEACHER.

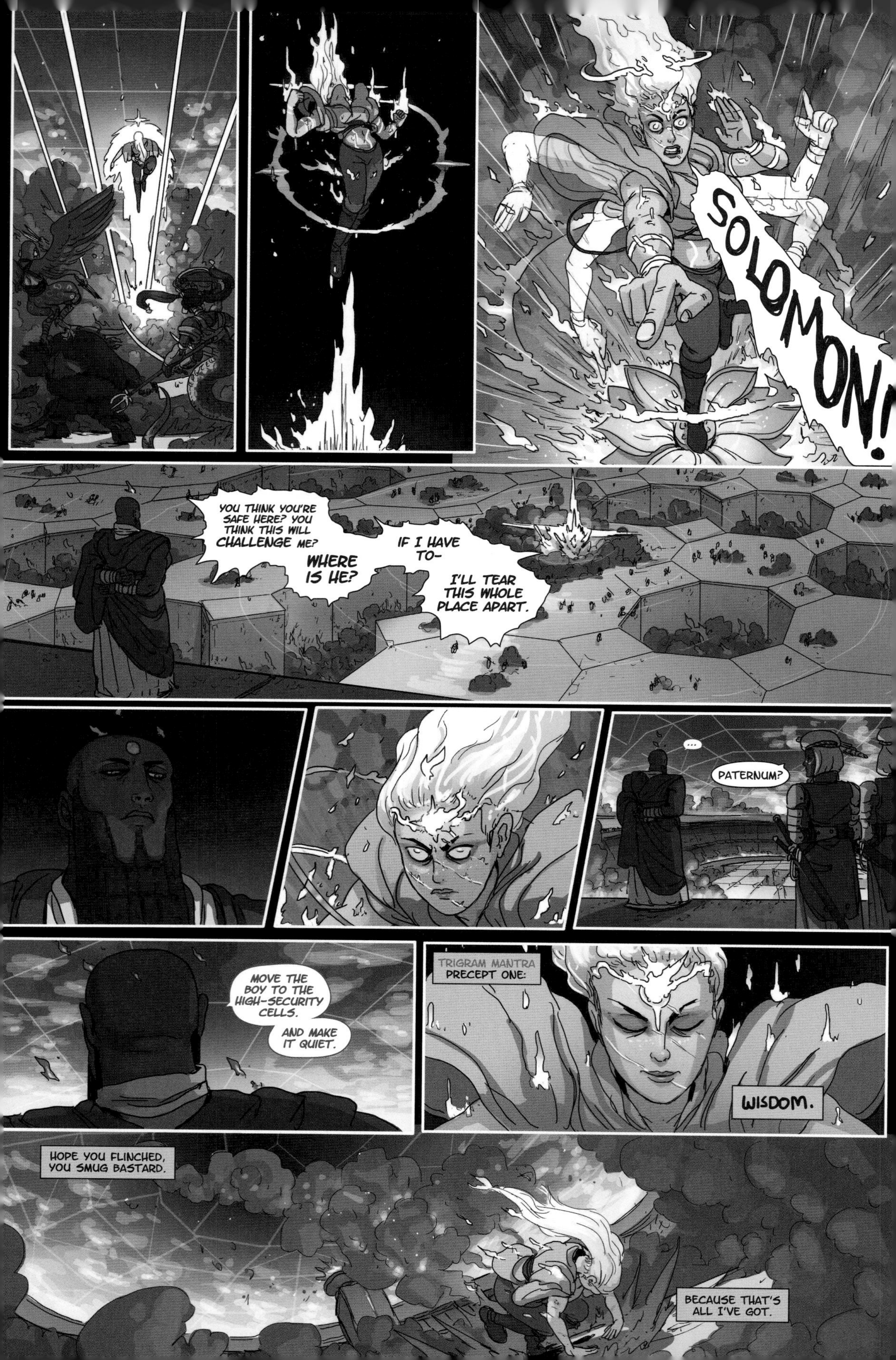
SOLOMON!!
YOU THINK YOU'RE SAFE HERE? YOU THINK THIS WILL CHALLENGE ME?
WHERE IS HE?
IF I HAVE TO-
I'LL TEAR THIS WHOLE PLACE APART.
...
PATERNUM?
MOVE THE BOY TO THE HIGH-SECURITY CELLS.
AND MAKE IT QUIET.
TRIGRAM MANTRA PRECEPT ONE:
WISDOM.
HOPE YOU FLINCHED, YOU SMUG BASTARD.
BECAUSE THAT'S ALL I'VE GOT.

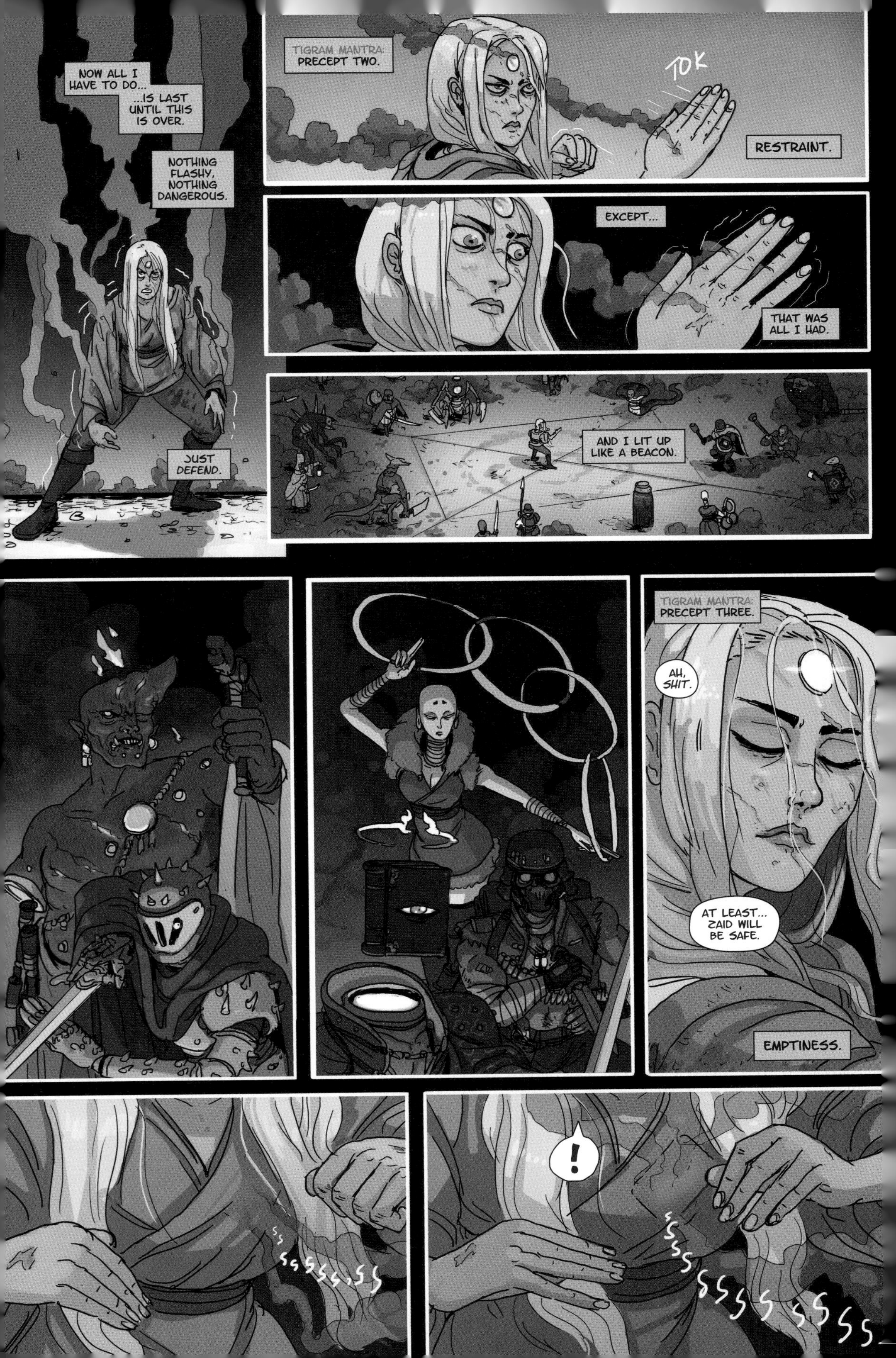

NOW ALL I HAVE TO DO...
...IS LAST UNTIL THIS IS OVER.
NOTHING FLASHY, NOTHING DANGEROUS.
JUST DEFEND.
TIGRAM MANTRA: PRECEPT TWO.
TOK
RESTRAINT.
EXCEPT...
THAT WAS ALL I HAD.
AND I LIT UP LIKE A BEACON.
TIGRAM MANTRA: PRECEPT THREE.
AH, SHIT.
AT LEAST... ZAID WILL BE SAFE.
EMPTINESS.
!

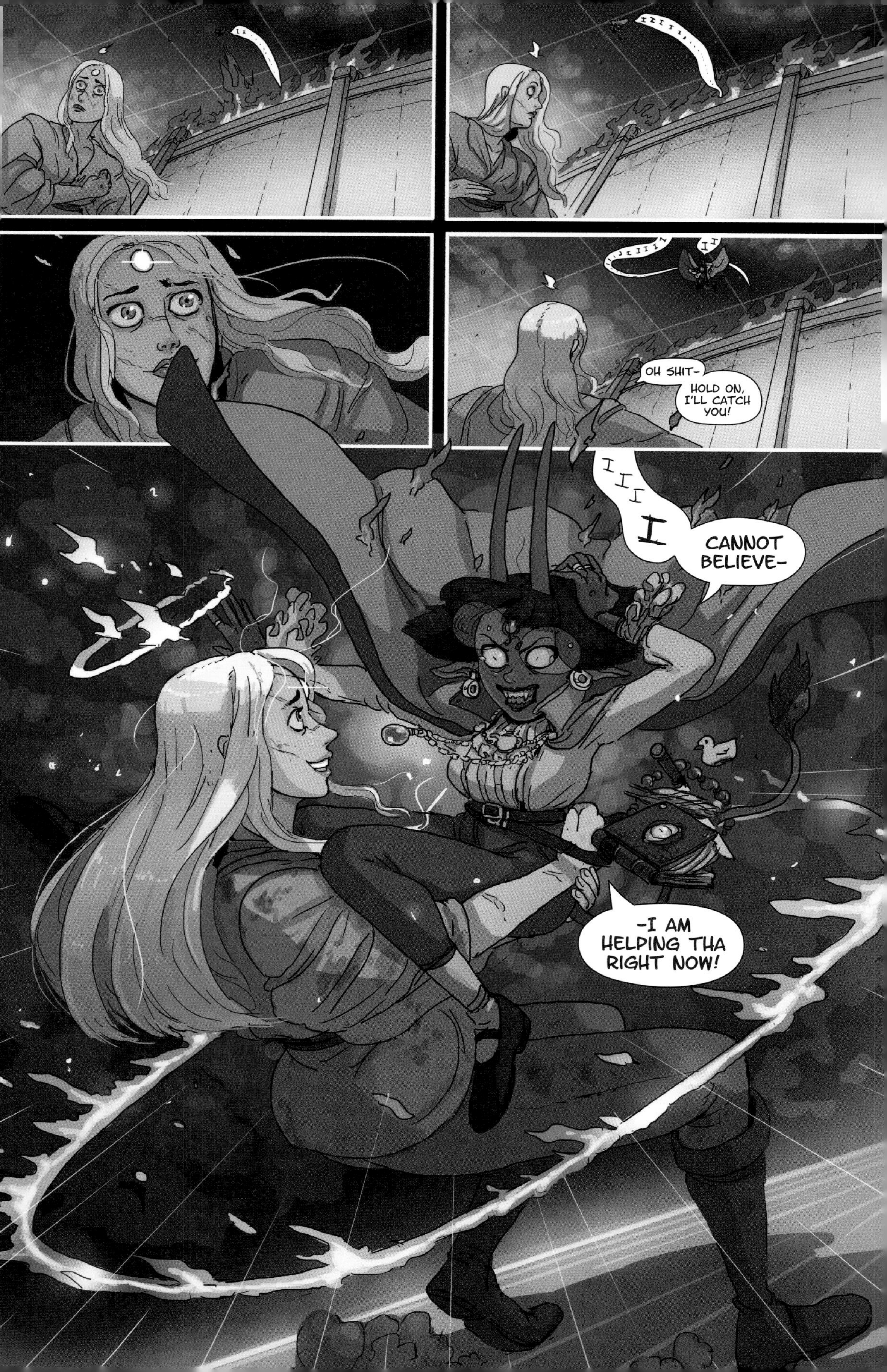
OH SHIT-
HOLD ON, I'LL CATCH YOU!
I I I I
CANNOT BELIEVE-
-I AM HELPING THA RIGHT NOW!

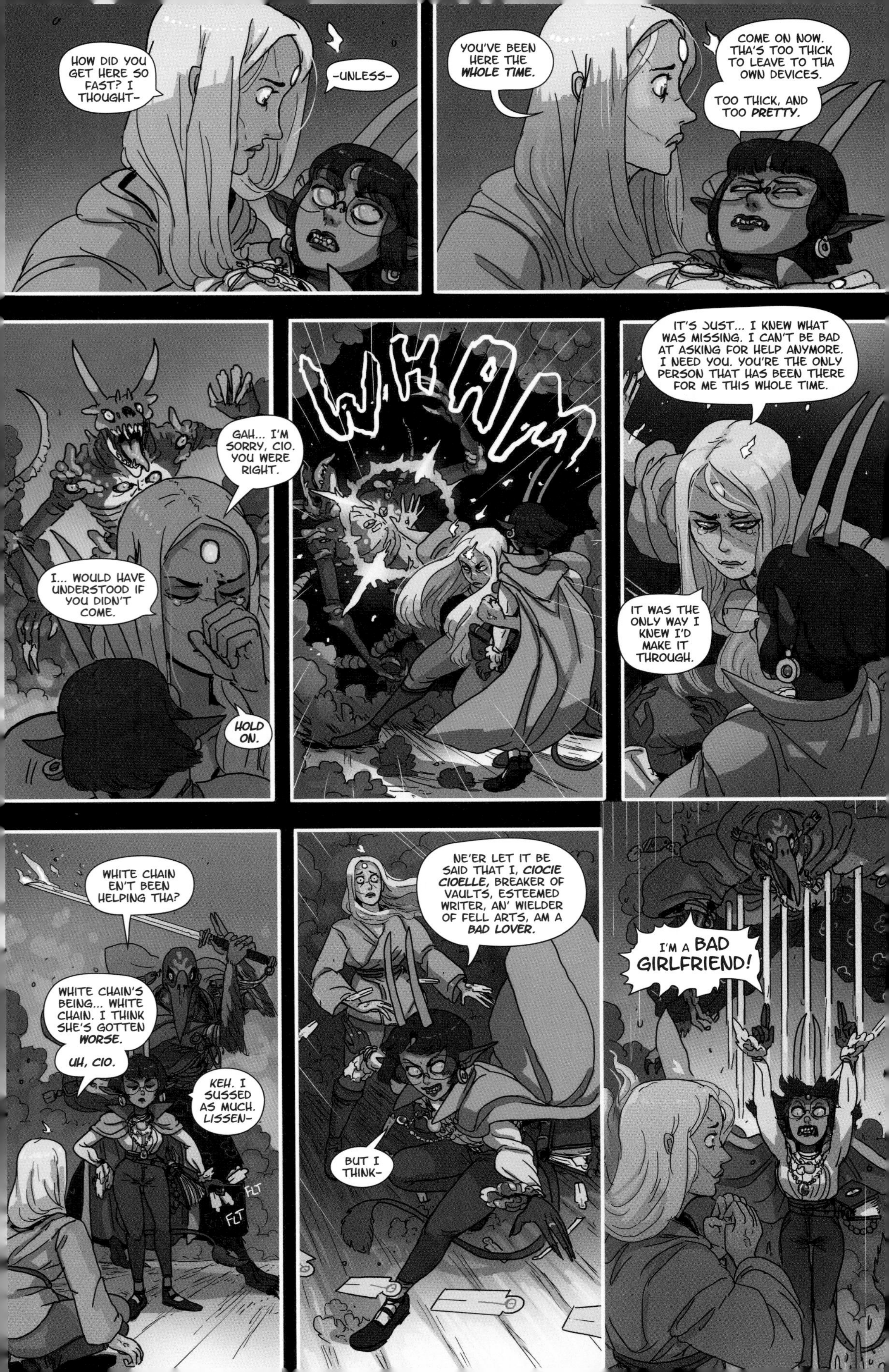

HOW DID YOU GET HERE SO FAST? I THOUGHT-
-UNLESS-
YOU'VE BEEN HERE THE WHOLE TIME.
COME ON NOW. THA'S TOO THICK TO LEAVE TO THA OWN DEVICES.
TOO THICK, AND TOO PRETTY.
GAH... I'M SORRY, CIO. YOU WERE RIGHT.
I... WOULD HAVE UNDERSTOOD IF YOU DIDN'T COME.
HOLD ON.
WHAM
IT'S JUST... I KNEW WHAT WAS MISSING. I CAN'T BE BAD AT ASKING FOR HELP ANYMORE. I NEED YOU. YOU'RE THE ONLY PERSON THAT HAS BEEN THERE FOR ME THIS WHOLE TIME.
IT WAS THE ONLY WAY I KNEW I'D MAKE IT THROUGH.
WHITE CHAIN EN'T BEEN HELPING THA?
WHITE CHAIN'S BEING... WHITE CHAIN. I THINK SHE'S GOTTEN WORSE.
UH, CIO.
KEH. I SUSSED AS MUCH. LISSEN-
FLT
FLT
NE'ER LET IT BE SAID THAT I, CIOCIE CIOELLE, BREAKER OF VAULTS, ESTEEMED WRITER, AN' WIELDER OF FELL ARTS, AM A BAD LOVER.
BUT I THINK-
I'M A BAD GIRLFRIEND!

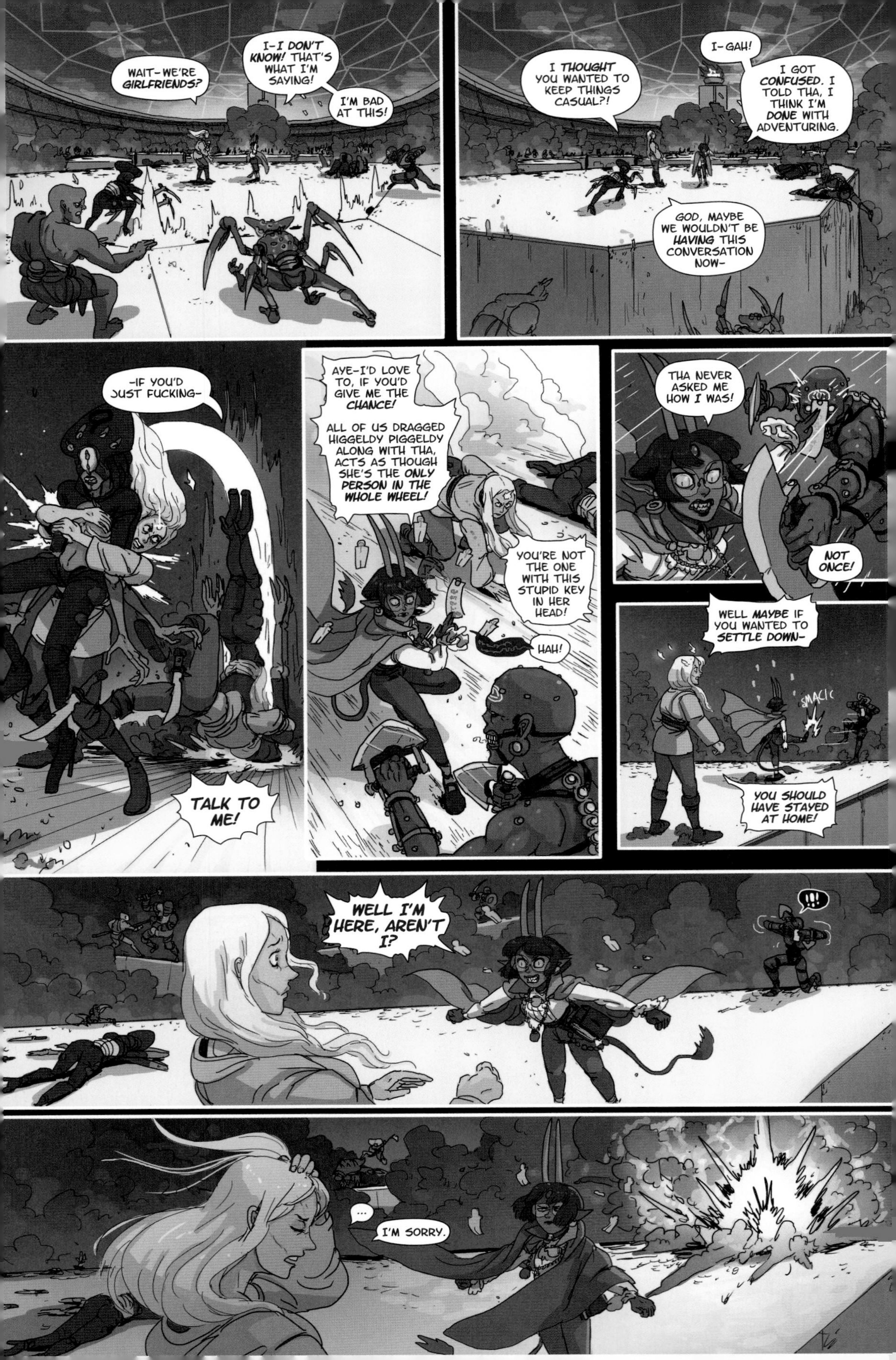
WAIT–WE'RE GIRLFRIENDS?
I–I DON'T KNOW! THAT'S WHAT I'M SAYING!
I'M BAD AT THIS!
I THOUGHT YOU WANTED TO KEEP THINGS CASUAL?!
I–GAH!
I GOT CONFUSED. I TOLD THA, I THINK I'M DONE WITH ADVENTURING.
GOD, MAYBE WE WOULDN'T BE HAVING THIS CONVERSATION NOW–
–IF YOU'D JUST FUCKING–
TALK TO ME!
AYE–I'D LOVE TO, IF YOU'D GIVE ME THE CHANCE!
ALL OF US DRAGGED HIGGELDY PIGGELDY ALONG WITH THA, ACTS AS THOUGH SHE'S THE ONLY PERSON IN THE WHOLE WHEEL!
YOU'RE NOT THE ONE WITH THIS STUPID KEY IN HER HEAD!
HAH!
THA NEVER ASKED ME HOW I WAS!
NOT ONCE!
WELL MAYBE IF YOU WANTED TO SETTLE DOWN–
SMACK
YOU SHOULD HAVE STAYED AT HOME!
WELL I'M HERE, AREN'T I?
!!!
...
I'M SORRY.

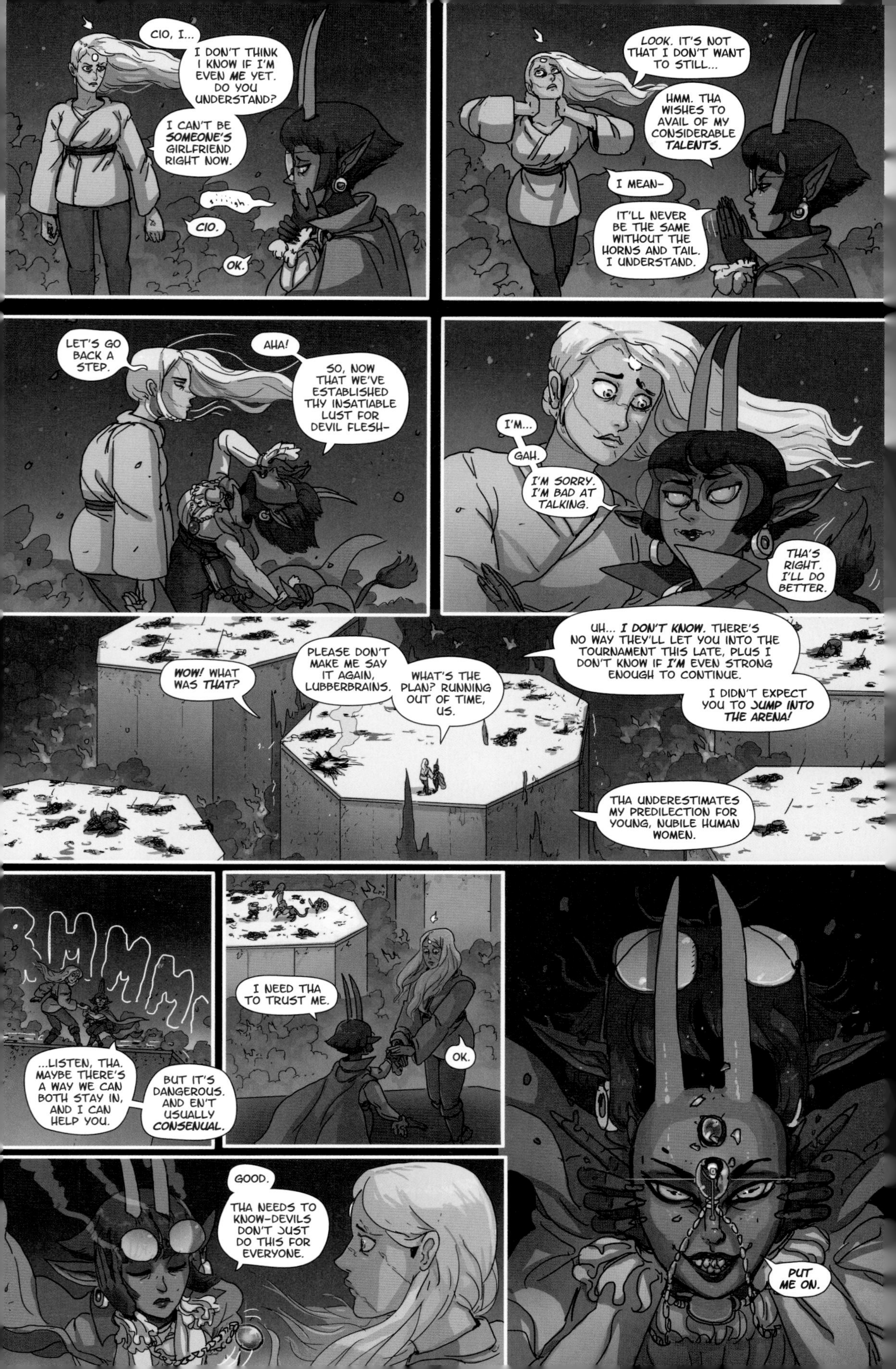
CIO, I...
I DON'T THINK I KNOW IF I'M EVEN *ME* YET. DO YOU UNDERSTAND?
I CAN'T BE *SOMEONE'S* GIRLFRIEND RIGHT NOW.
CIO.
OK.
LOOK. IT'S NOT THAT I DON'T WANT TO STILL...
HMM. THA WISHES TO AVAIL OF MY CONSIDERABLE *TALENTS.*
I MEAN-
IT'LL NEVER BE THE SAME WITHOUT THE HORNS AND TAIL. I UNDERSTAND.
LET'S GO BACK A STEP.
AHA!
SO, NOW THAT WE'VE ESTABLISHED THY INSATIABLE LUST FOR DEVIL FLESH-
I'M...
GAH.
I'M SORRY. I'M BAD AT TALKING.
THA'S RIGHT. I'LL DO BETTER.
WOW! WHAT WAS *THAT?*
PLEASE DON'T MAKE ME SAY IT AGAIN, LUBBERBRAINS.
WHAT'S THE PLAN? RUNNING OUT OF TIME, US.
UH... *I DON'T KNOW.* THERE'S NO WAY THEY'LL LET YOU INTO THE TOURNAMENT THIS LATE, PLUS I DON'T KNOW IF *I'M* EVEN STRONG ENOUGH TO CONTINUE.
I DIDN'T EXPECT YOU TO *JUMP INTO THE ARENA!*
THA UNDERESTIMATES MY PREDILECTION FOR YOUNG, NUBILE HUMAN WOMEN.
...LISTEN, THA. MAYBE THERE'S A WAY WE CAN BOTH STAY IN, AND I CAN HELP YOU.
BUT IT'S DANGEROUS. AND EN'T USUALLY *CONSENUAL.*
I NEED THA TO TRUST ME.
OK.
GOOD.
THA NEEDS TO KNOW-DEVILS DON'T JUST DO THIS FOR EVERYONE.
PUT ME ON.

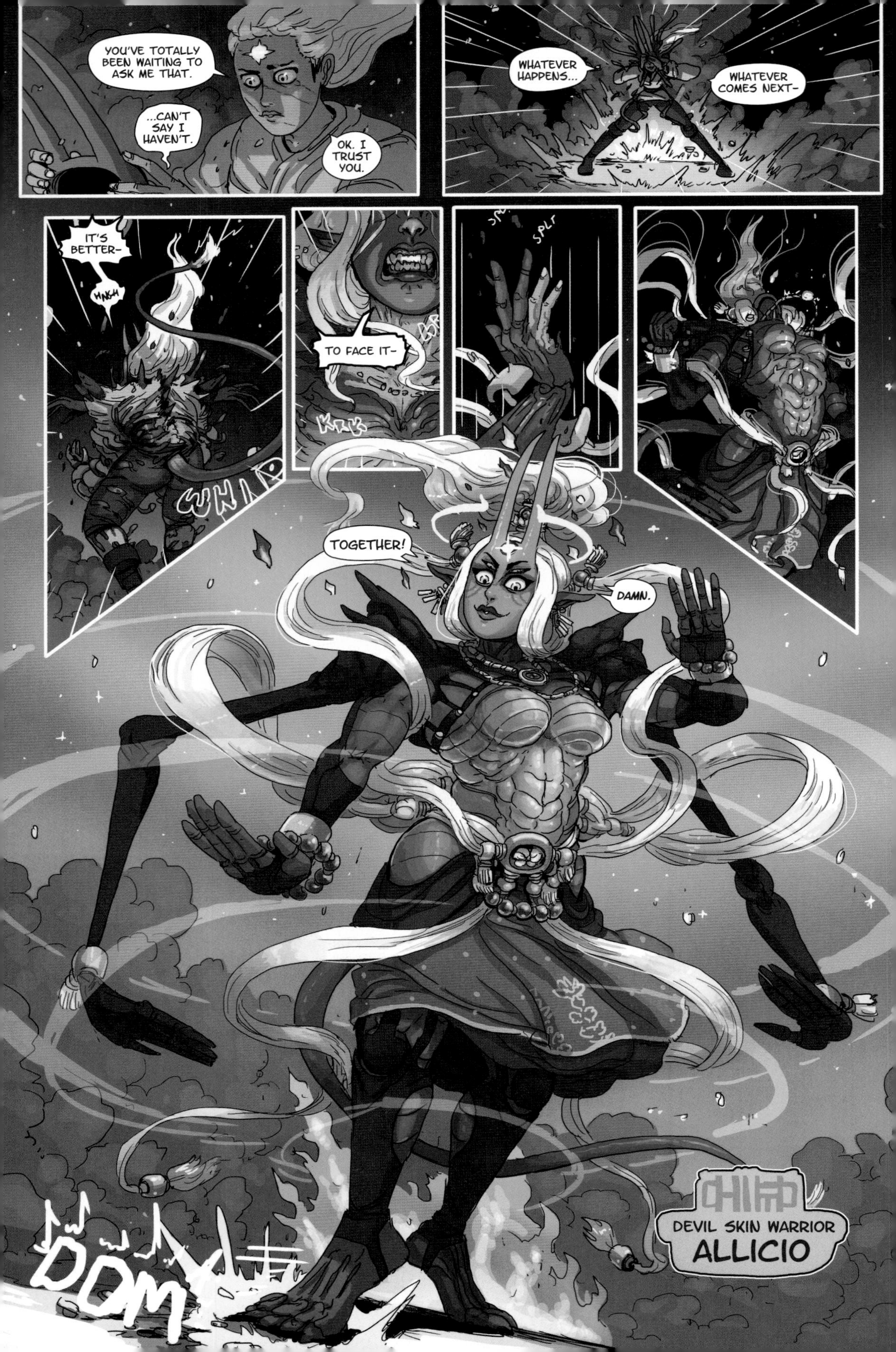

YOU'VE TOTALLY BEEN WAITING TO ASK ME THAT.
...CAN'T SAY I HAVEN'T.
OK. I TRUST YOU.
WHATEVER HAPPENS...
WHATEVER COMES NEXT-
IT'S BETTER-
MNGH
TO FACE IT-
KRK
SPLT
WHIP
TOGETHER!
DAMN.
DEVIL SKIN WARRIOR
ALLICIO
DOM

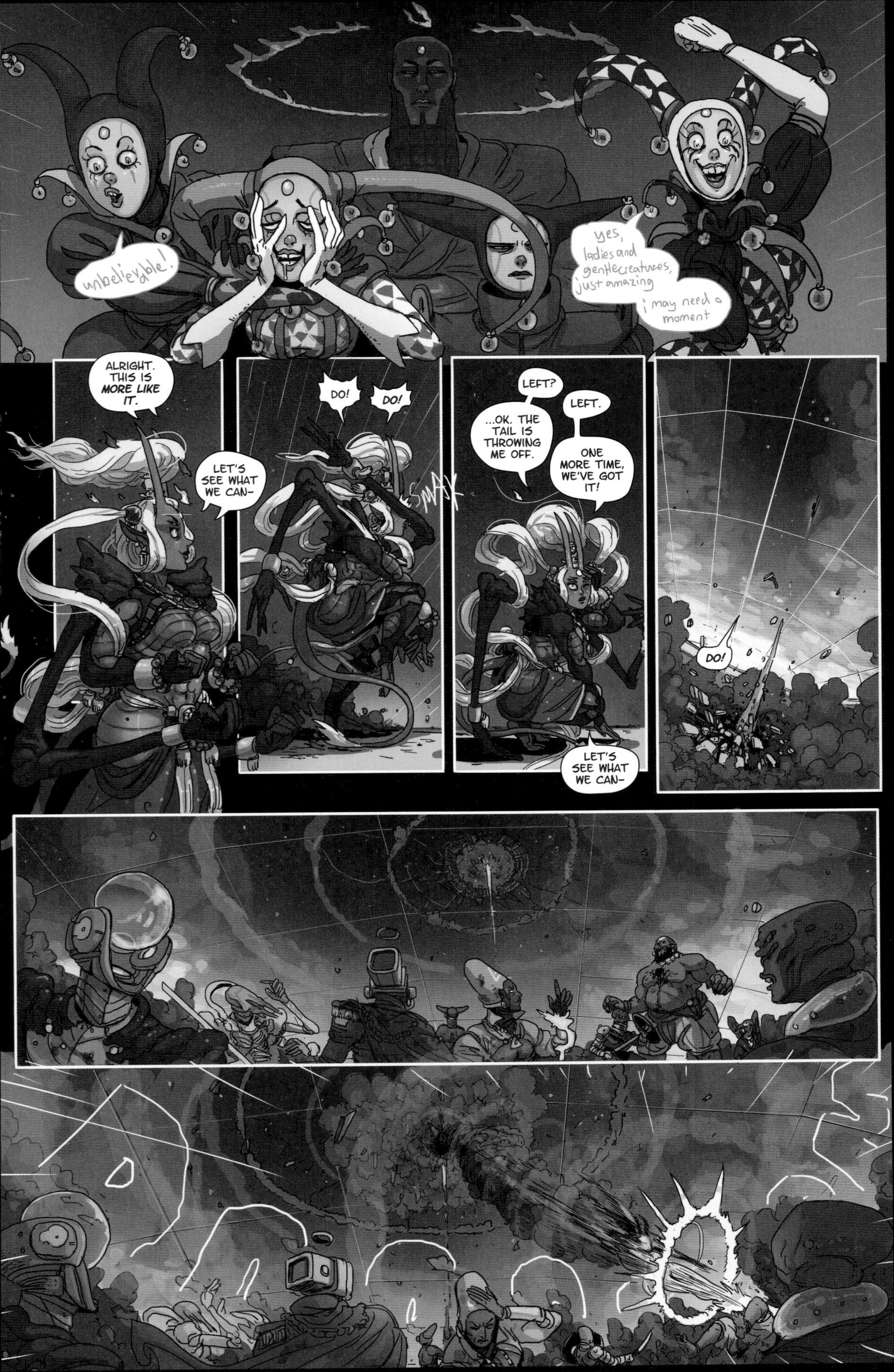
unbelievable!
yes, ladies and gentlecreatures, just amazing
i may need a moment
ALRIGHT. THIS IS MORE LIKE IT.
LET'S SEE WHAT WE CAN-
DO!
DO!
LEFT?
LEFT.
...OK. THE TAIL IS THROWING ME OFF.
ONE MORE TIME, WE'VE GOT IT!
LET'S SEE WHAT WE CAN-
DO!

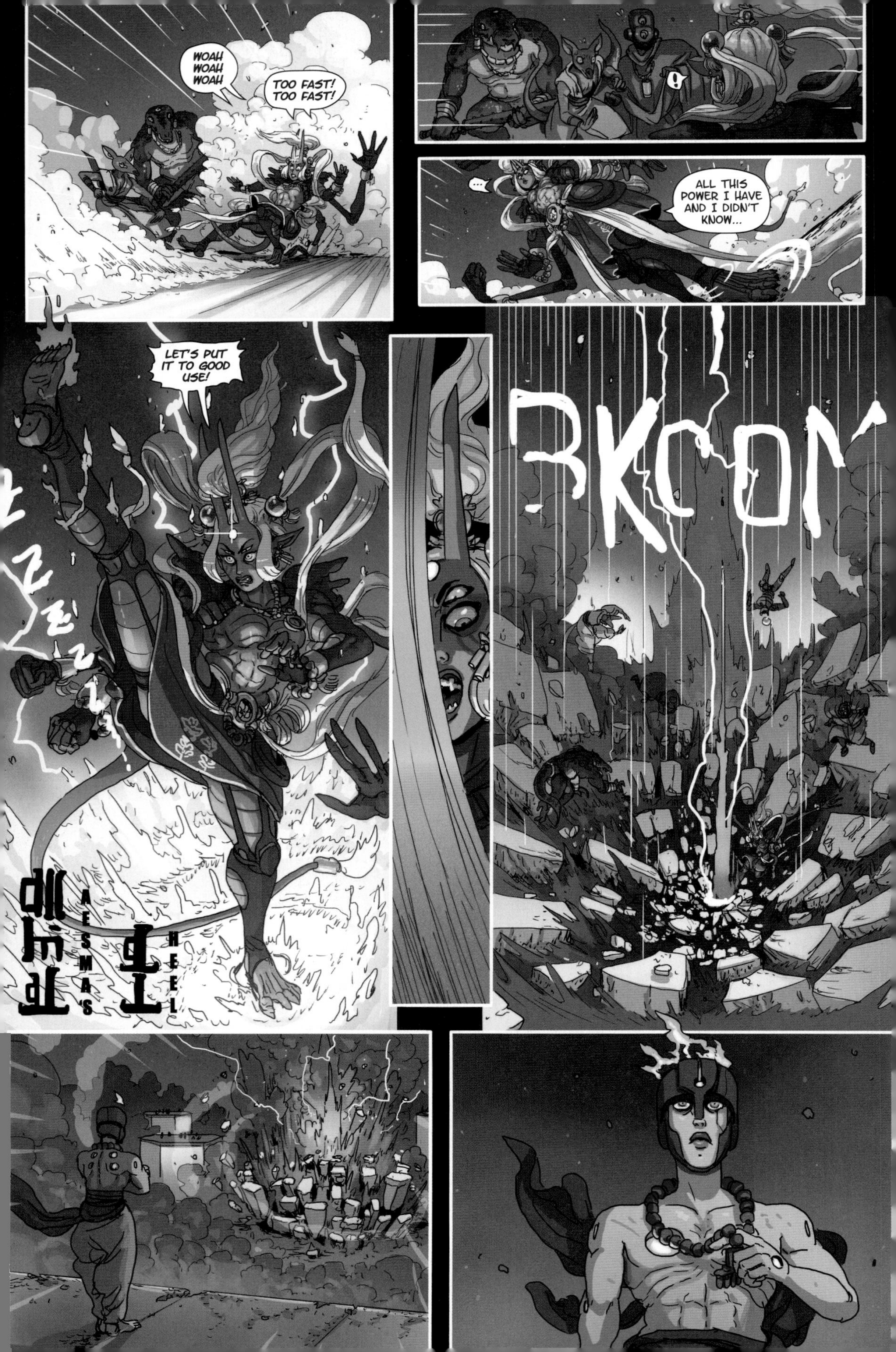
WOAH WOAH WOAH
TOO FAST! TOO FAST!
!
...
ALL THIS POWER I HAVE AND I DIDN'T KNOW...
LET'S PUT IT TO GOOD USE!
AESMA'S HEEL

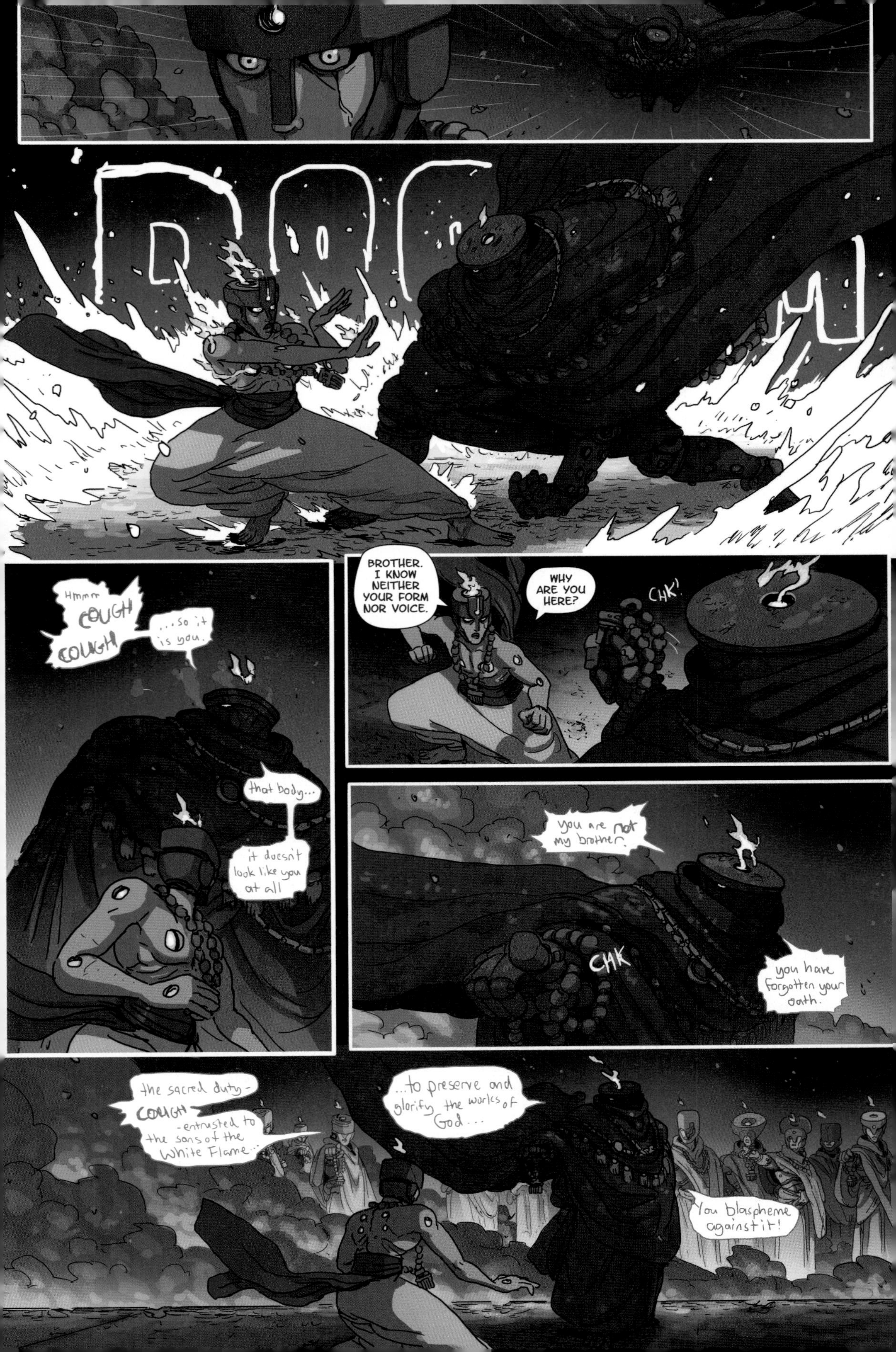

DOOM
Hmmm COUGH COUGH
...so it is you.
BROTHER. I KNOW NEITHER YOUR FORM NOR VOICE.
WHY ARE YOU HERE?
CHK!
that body...
it doesn't look like you at all
you are not my brother.
CHK
you have forgotten your oath.
the sacred duty- COUGH -entrusted to the sons of the White Flame...
...to preserve and glorify the works of God...
You blaspheme against it!

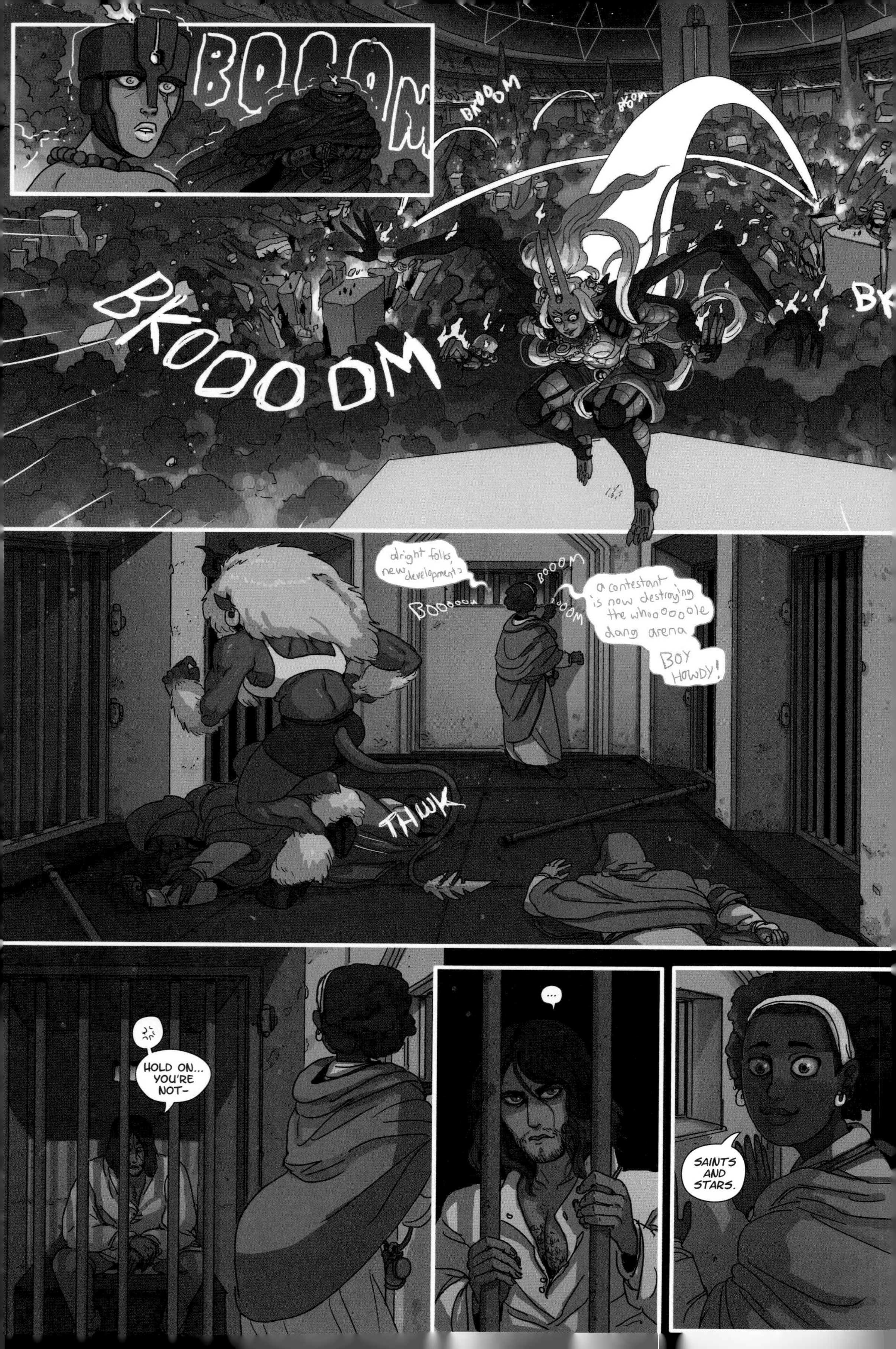
BOOOM
BROOOM
BOOM
BKOOOOM
BK
alright folks, new developments
BOOOOOM
BOOOM
a contestant is now destroying the whooooooole dang arena
BOY HOWDY!
THWK
HOLD ON... YOU'RE NOT-
...
SAINTS AND STARS.

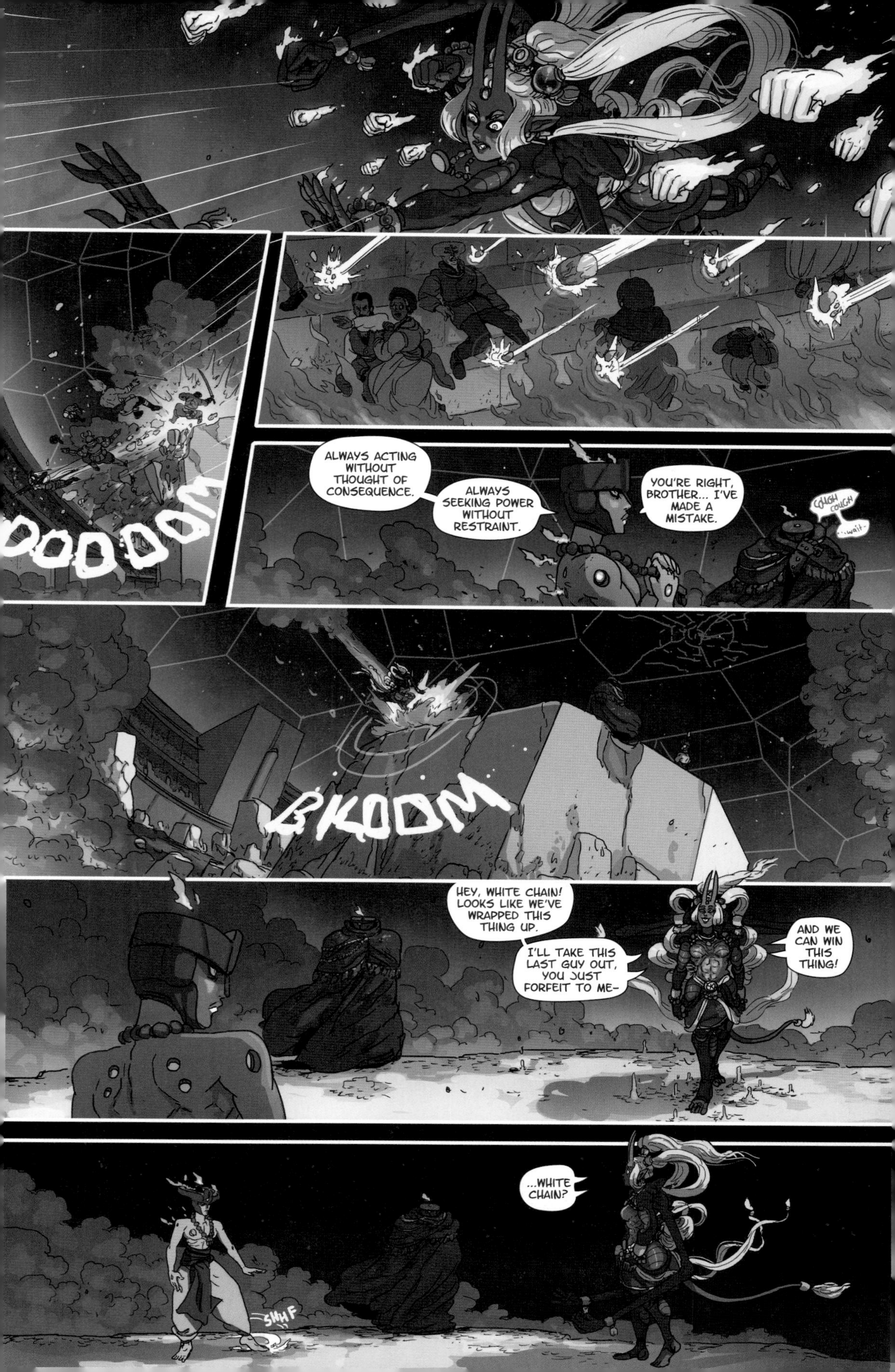
DOODOOM
ALWAYS ACTING WITHOUT THOUGHT OF CONSEQUENCE.
ALWAYS SEEKING POWER WITHOUT RESTRAINT.
YOU'RE RIGHT, BROTHER... I'VE MADE A MISTAKE.
COUGH COUGH
...wait...
BKOOM
HEY, WHITE CHAIN! LOOKS LIKE WE'VE WRAPPED THIS THING UP.
I'LL TAKE THIS LAST GUY OUT, YOU JUST FORFEIT TO ME-
AND WE CAN WIN THIS THING!
...WHITE CHAIN?
SHHF

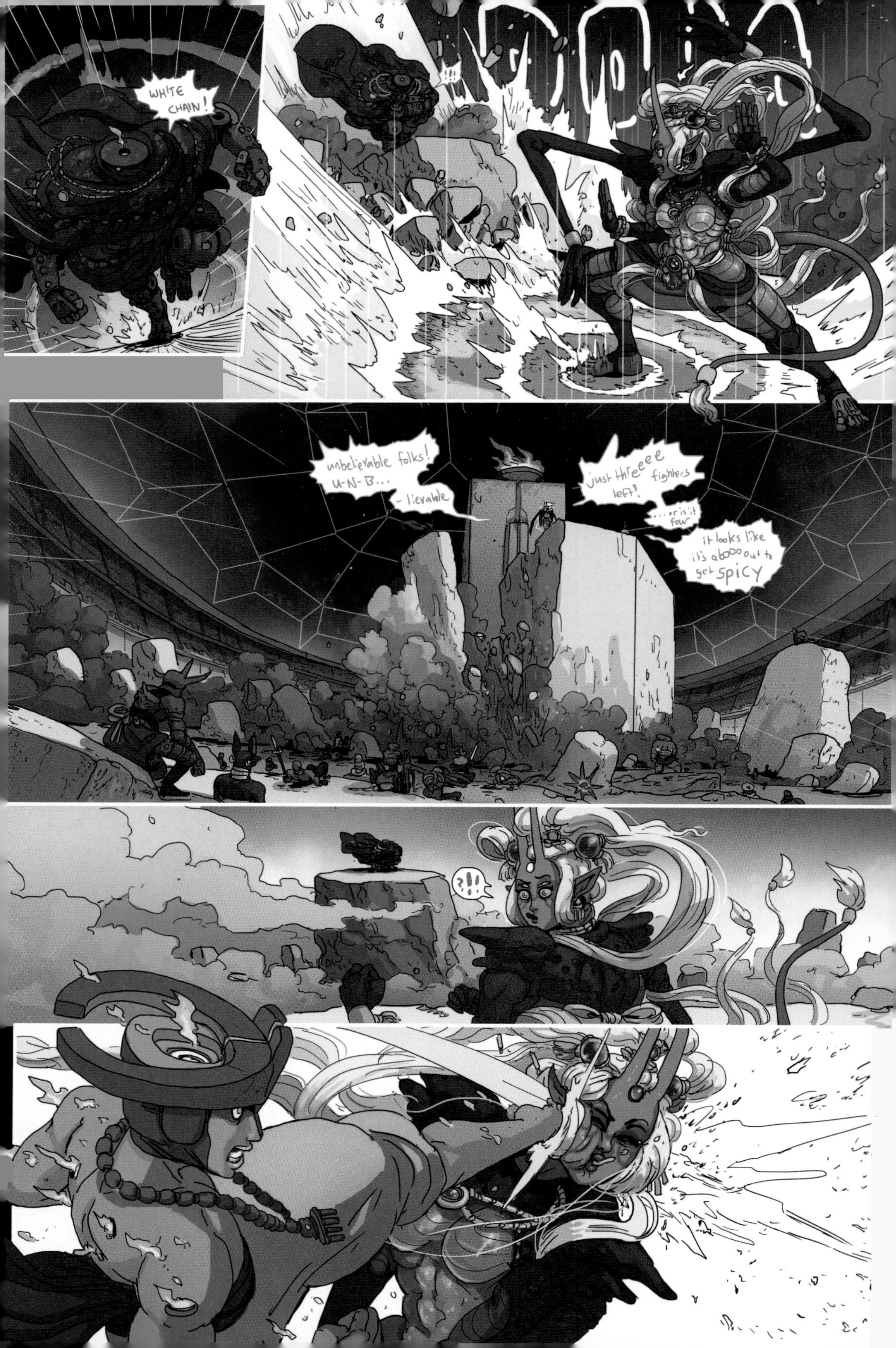
WHITE CHAIN!
!!!
unbelievable folks! U-N-B...
- lievable
just threeee fighters left!
...or is it four
it looks like it's aboooout to get SPICY
?!!

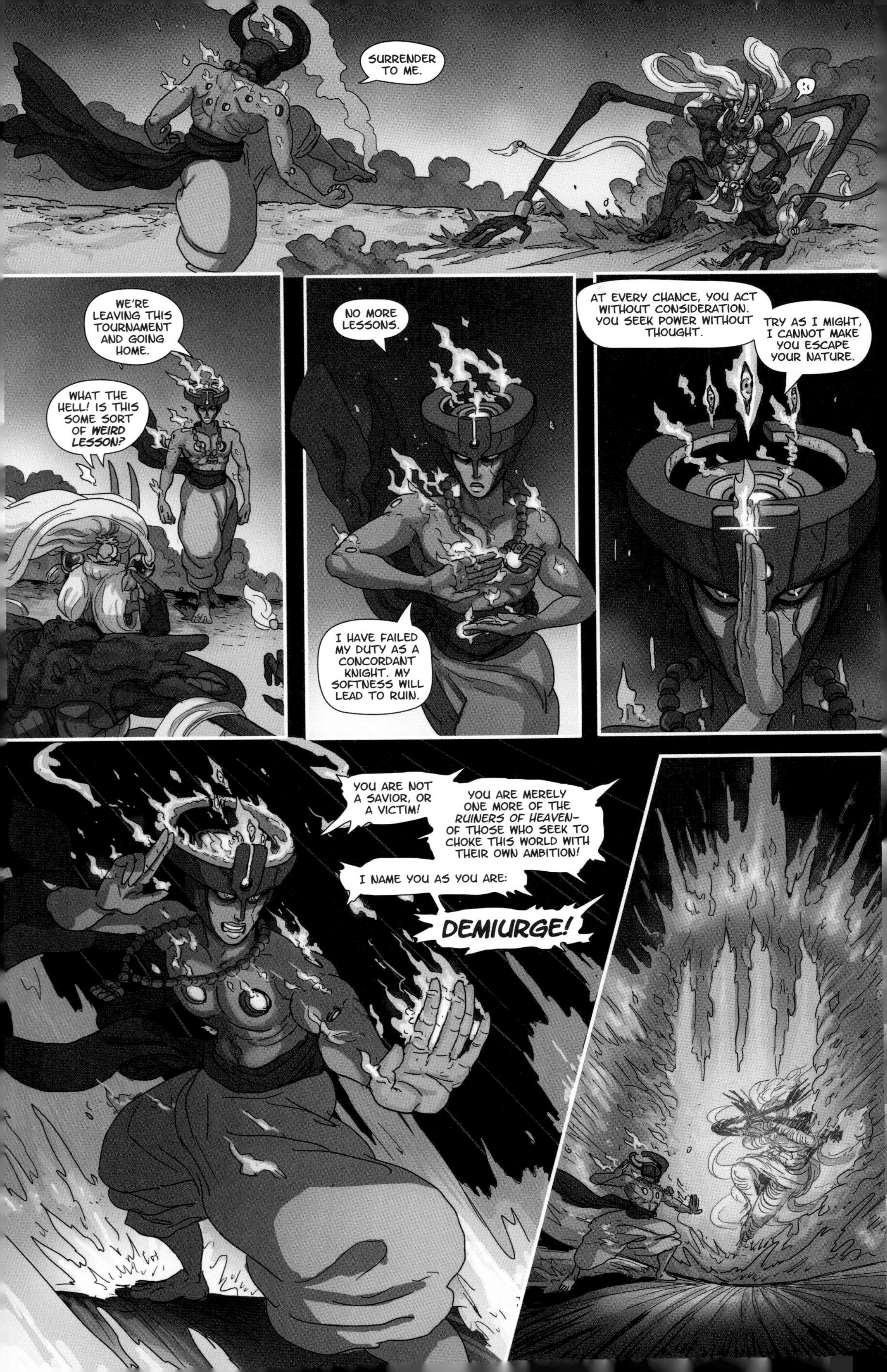
SURRENDER TO ME.
WE'RE LEAVING THIS TOURNAMENT AND GOING HOME.
WHAT THE HELL! IS THIS SOME SORT OF *WEIRD LESSON?*
NO MORE LESSONS.
I HAVE FAILED MY DUTY AS A CONCORDANT KNIGHT. MY SOFTNESS WILL LEAD TO RUIN.
AT EVERY CHANCE, YOU ACT WITHOUT CONSIDERATION. YOU SEEK POWER WITHOUT THOUGHT.
TRY AS I MIGHT, I CANNOT MAKE YOU ESCAPE YOUR NATURE.
YOU ARE NOT A SAVIOR, OR A VICTIM!
YOU ARE MERELY ONE MORE OF THE *RUINERS OF HEAVEN*-- OF THOSE WHO SEEK TO CHOKE THIS WORLD WITH THEIR OWN AMBITION!
I NAME YOU AS YOU ARE:
DEMIURGE!

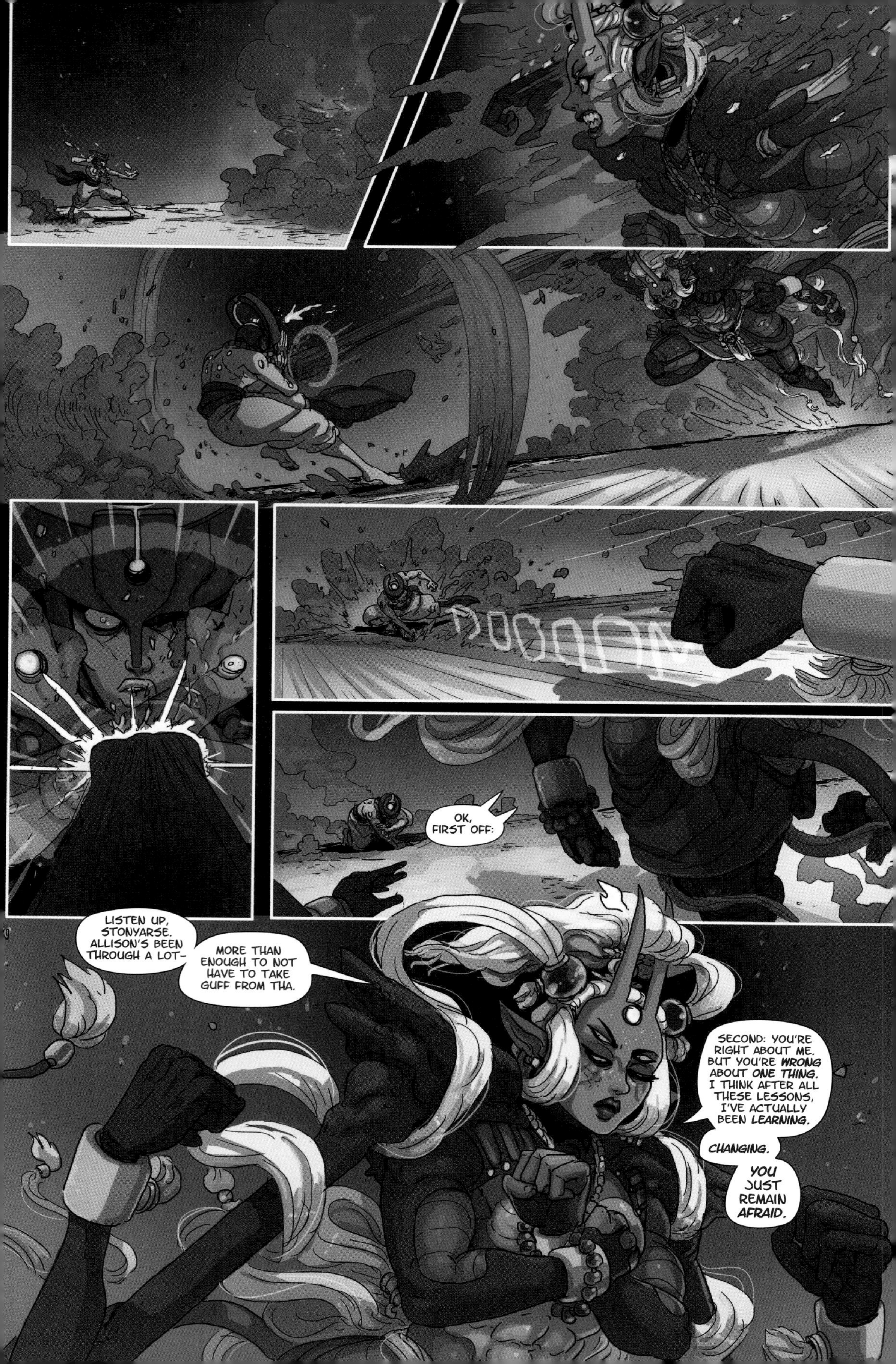
OK, FIRST OFF:
LISTEN UP, STONYARSE. ALLISON'S BEEN THROUGH A LOT-
MORE THAN ENOUGH TO NOT HAVE TO TAKE GUFF FROM THA.
SECOND: YOU'RE RIGHT ABOUT ME. BUT YOU'RE WRONG ABOUT ONE THING. I THINK AFTER ALL THESE LESSONS, I'VE ACTUALLY BEEN LEARNING.
CHANGING.
YOU JUST REMAIN AFRAID.

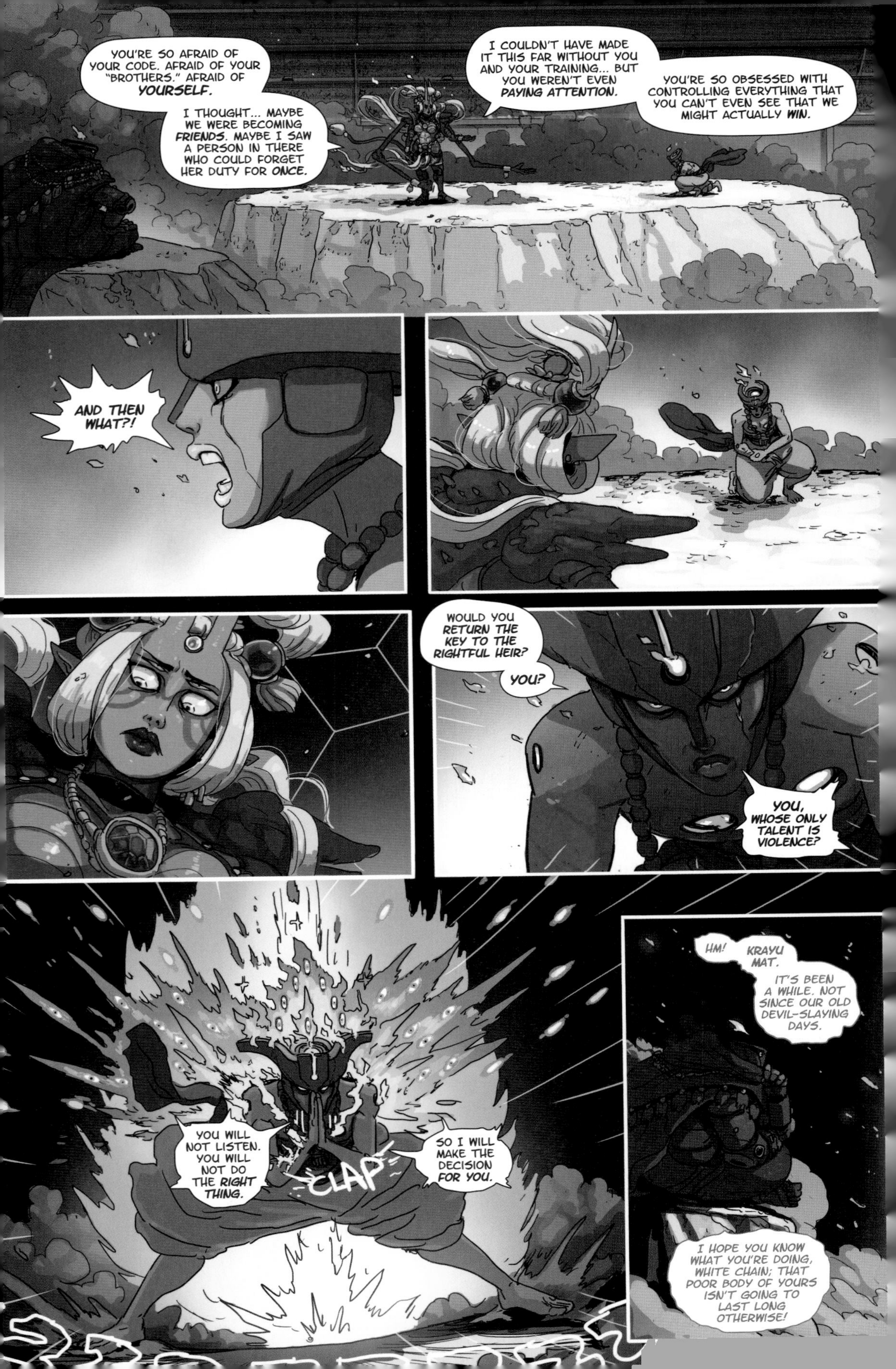
YOU'RE SO AFRAID OF YOUR CODE. AFRAID OF YOUR "BROTHERS." AFRAID OF YOURSELF.
I THOUGHT... MAYBE WE WERE BECOMING FRIENDS. MAYBE I SAW A PERSON IN THERE WHO COULD FORGET HER DUTY FOR ONCE.
I COULDN'T HAVE MADE IT THIS FAR WITHOUT YOU AND YOUR TRAINING... BUT YOU WEREN'T EVEN PAYING ATTENTION.
YOU'RE SO OBSESSED WITH CONTROLLING EVERYTHING THAT YOU CAN'T EVEN SEE THAT WE MIGHT ACTUALLY WIN.
AND THEN WHAT?!
WOULD YOU RETURN THE KEY TO THE RIGHTFUL HEIR?
YOU?
YOU, WHOSE ONLY TALENT IS VIOLENCE?
YOU WILL NOT LISTEN. YOU WILL NOT DO THE RIGHT THING.
CLAP
SO I WILL MAKE THE DECISION FOR YOU.
HM!
KRAYU MAT.
IT'S BEEN A WHILE. NOT SINCE OUR OLD DEVIL-SLAYING DAYS.
I HOPE YOU KNOW WHAT YOU'RE DOING, WHITE CHAIN; THAT POOR BODY OF YOURS ISN'T GOING TO LAST LONG OTHERWISE!

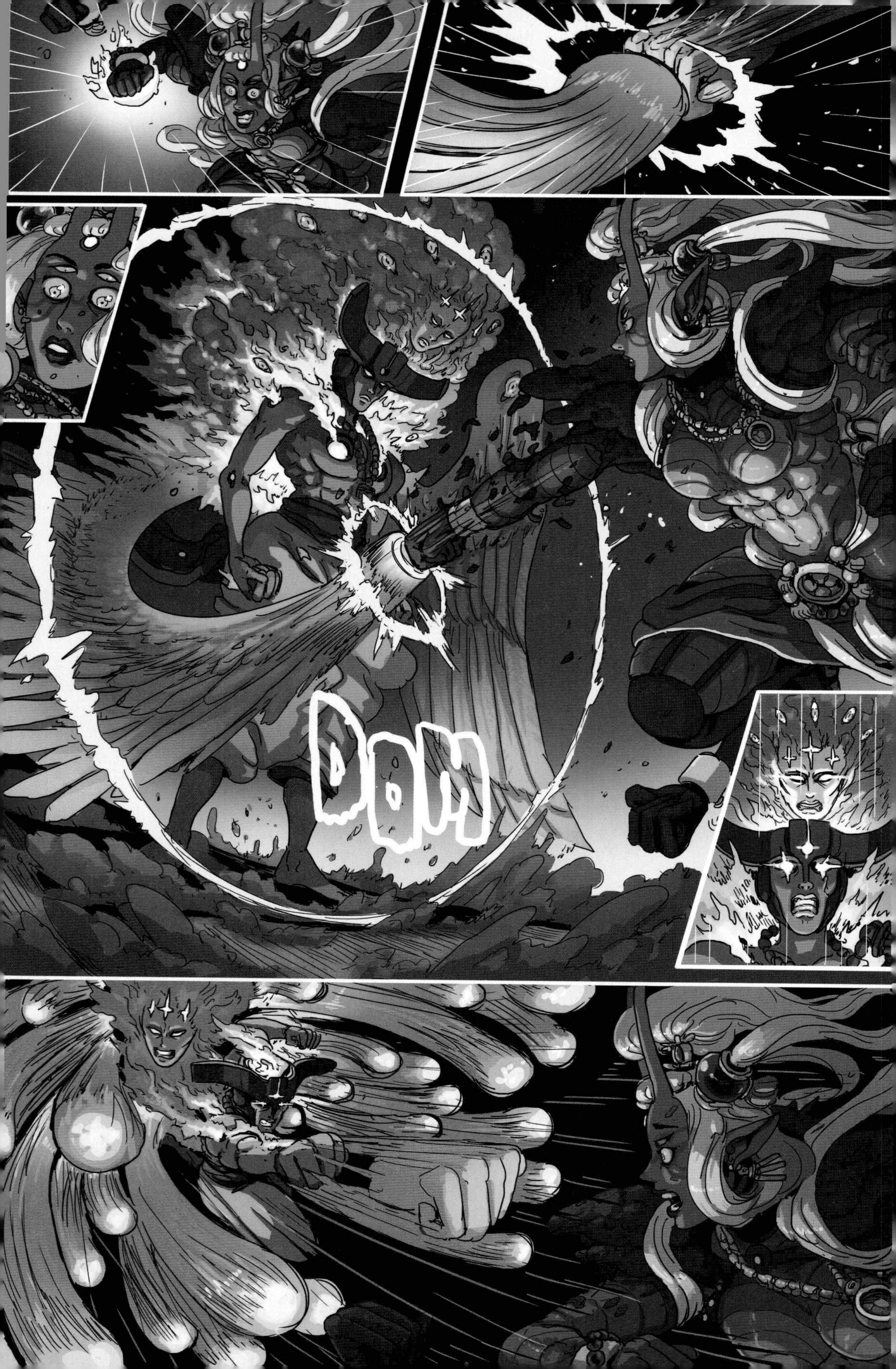
DOM

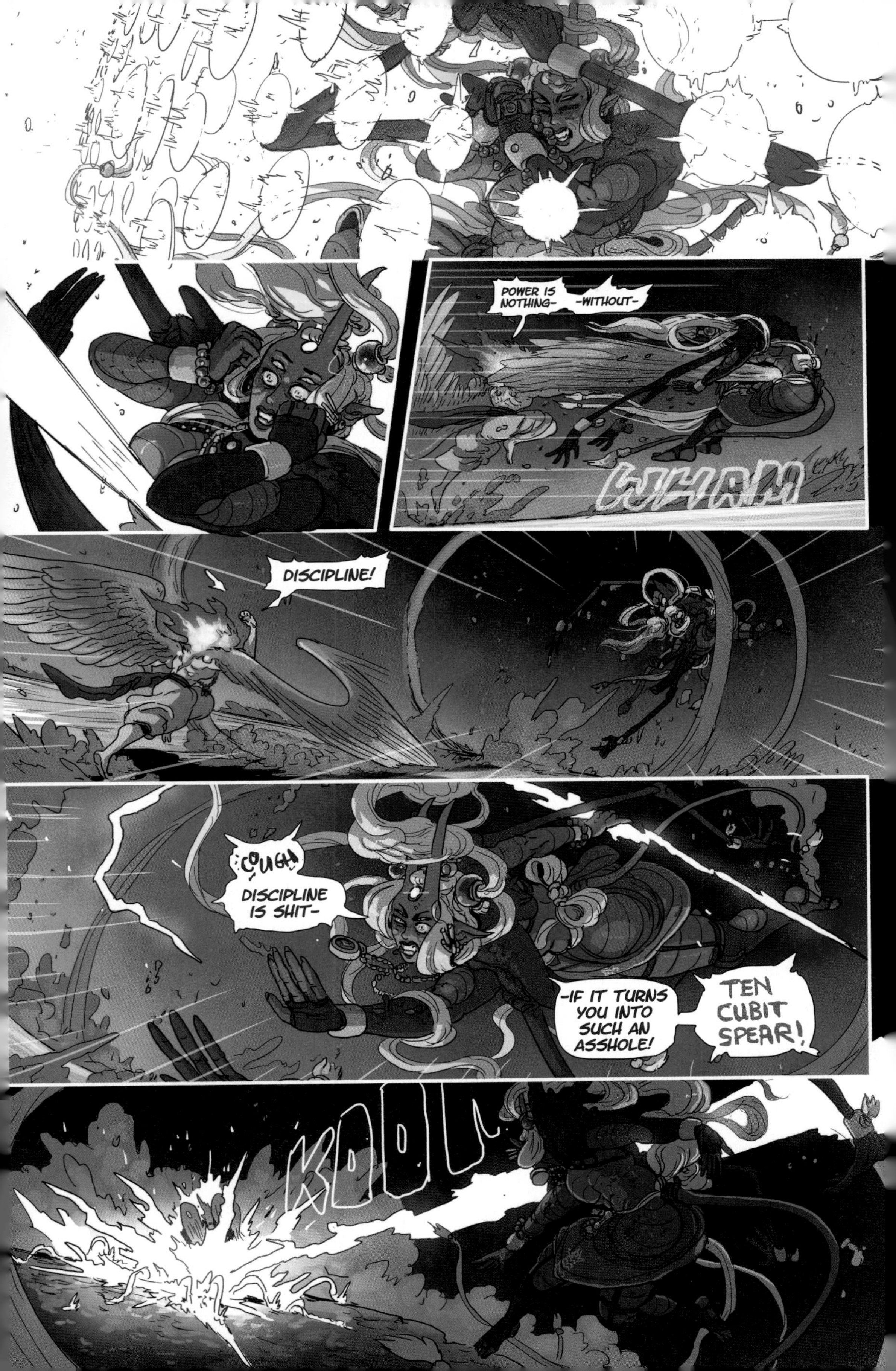
POWER IS NOTHING-
-WITHOUT-
WHAM
DISCIPLINE!
COUGH
DISCIPLINE IS SHIT-
-IF IT TURNS YOU INTO SUCH AN ASSHOLE!
TEN CUBIT SPEAR!
KOOL

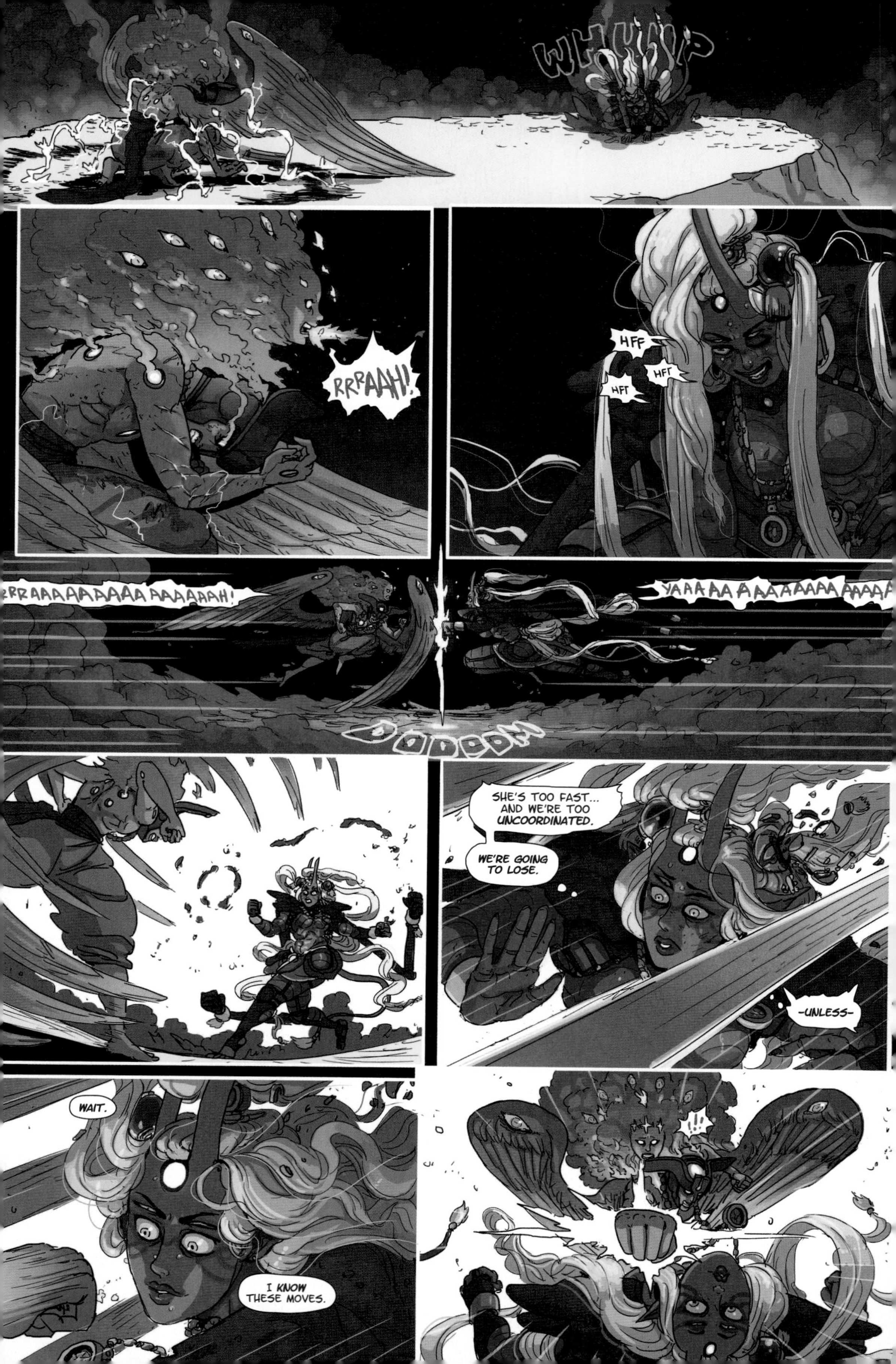

WHHHHP
RRRAAH!
HFF
HFT
HFT
RRRAAAAAAAAAAAA AAAAAAAH!
YAAA AA A AAAAAAA AAAA
SHE'S TOO FAST... AND WE'RE TOO UNCOORDINATED.
WE'RE GOING TO LOSE.
-UNLESS-
WAIT.
I KNOW THESE MOVES.
!!!

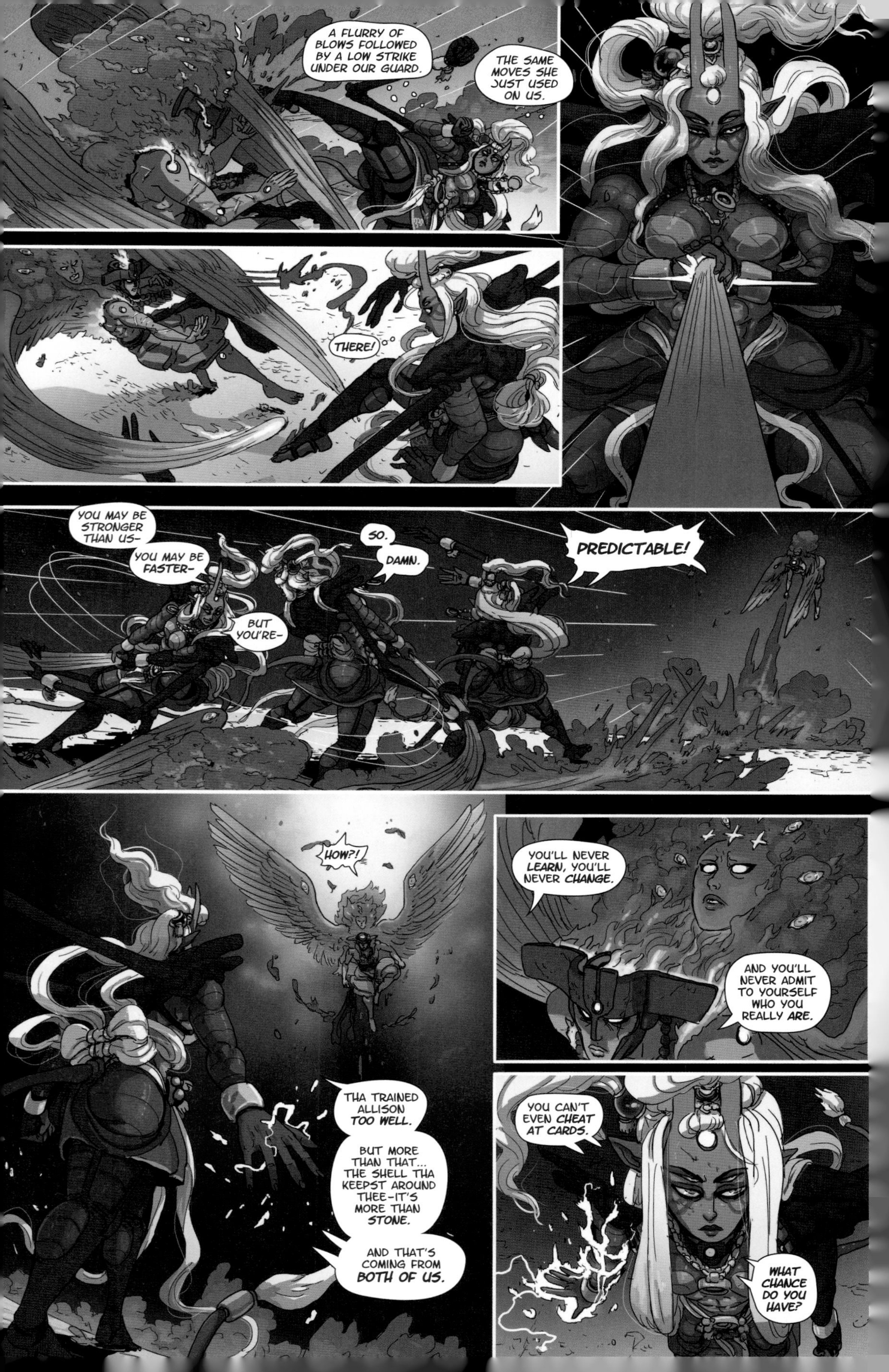
A FLURRY OF BLOWS FOLLOWED BY A LOW STRIKE UNDER OUR GUARD.
THE SAME MOVES SHE JUST USED ON US.
THERE!
YOU MAY BE STRONGER THAN US-
YOU MAY BE FASTER-
BUT YOU'RE-
SO.
DAMN.
PREDICTABLE!
HOW?!
THA TRAINED ALLISON TOO WELL.
BUT MORE THAN THAT... THE SHELL THA KEEPST AROUND THEE-IT'S MORE THAN STONE.
AND THAT'S COMING FROM BOTH OF US.
YOU'LL NEVER LEARN, YOU'LL NEVER CHANGE.
AND YOU'LL NEVER ADMIT TO YOURSELF WHO YOU REALLY ARE.
YOU CAN'T EVEN CHEAT AT CARDS.
WHAT CHANCE DO YOU HAVE?

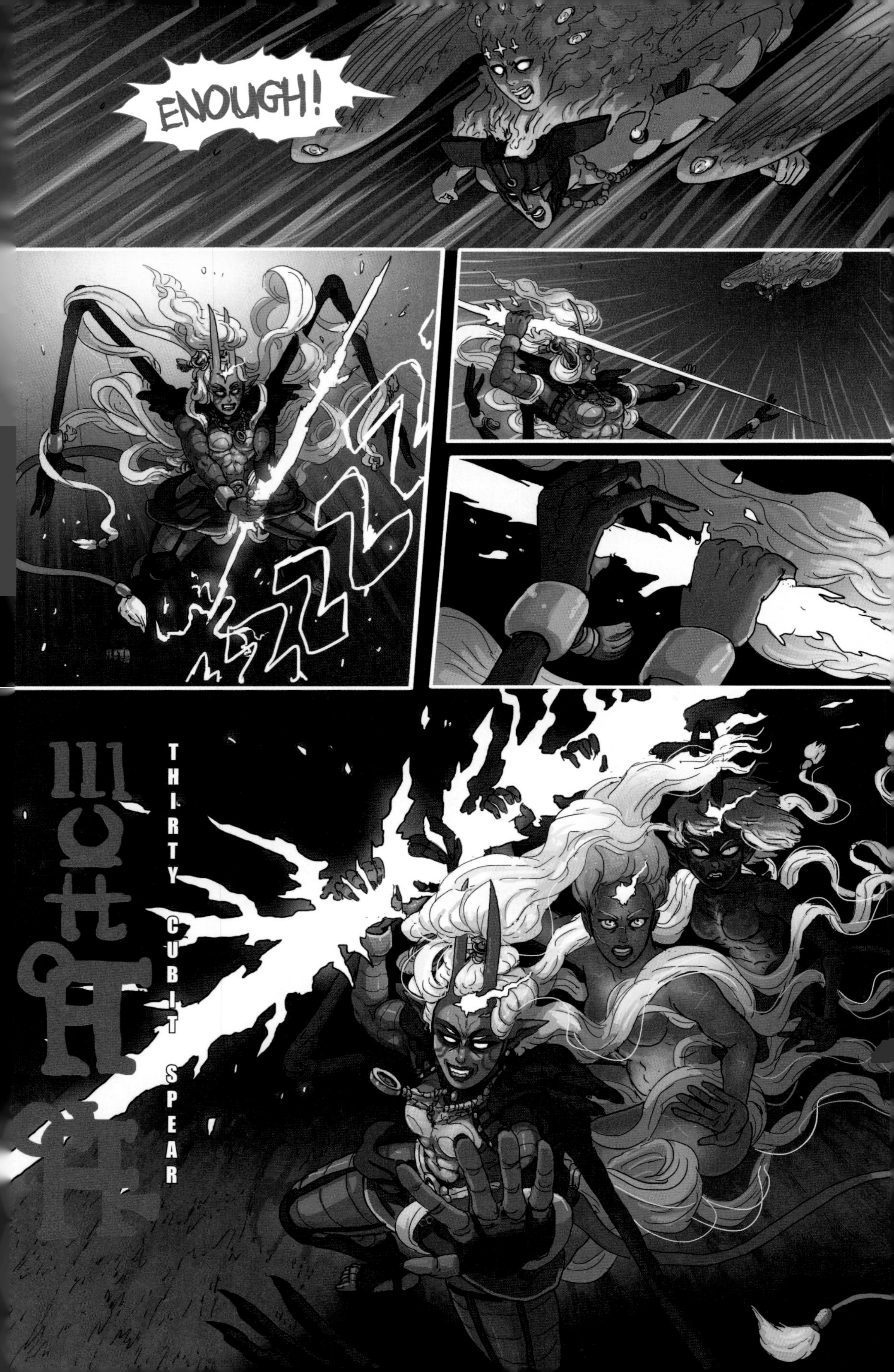
ENOUGH!
THIRTY CUBIT SPEAR

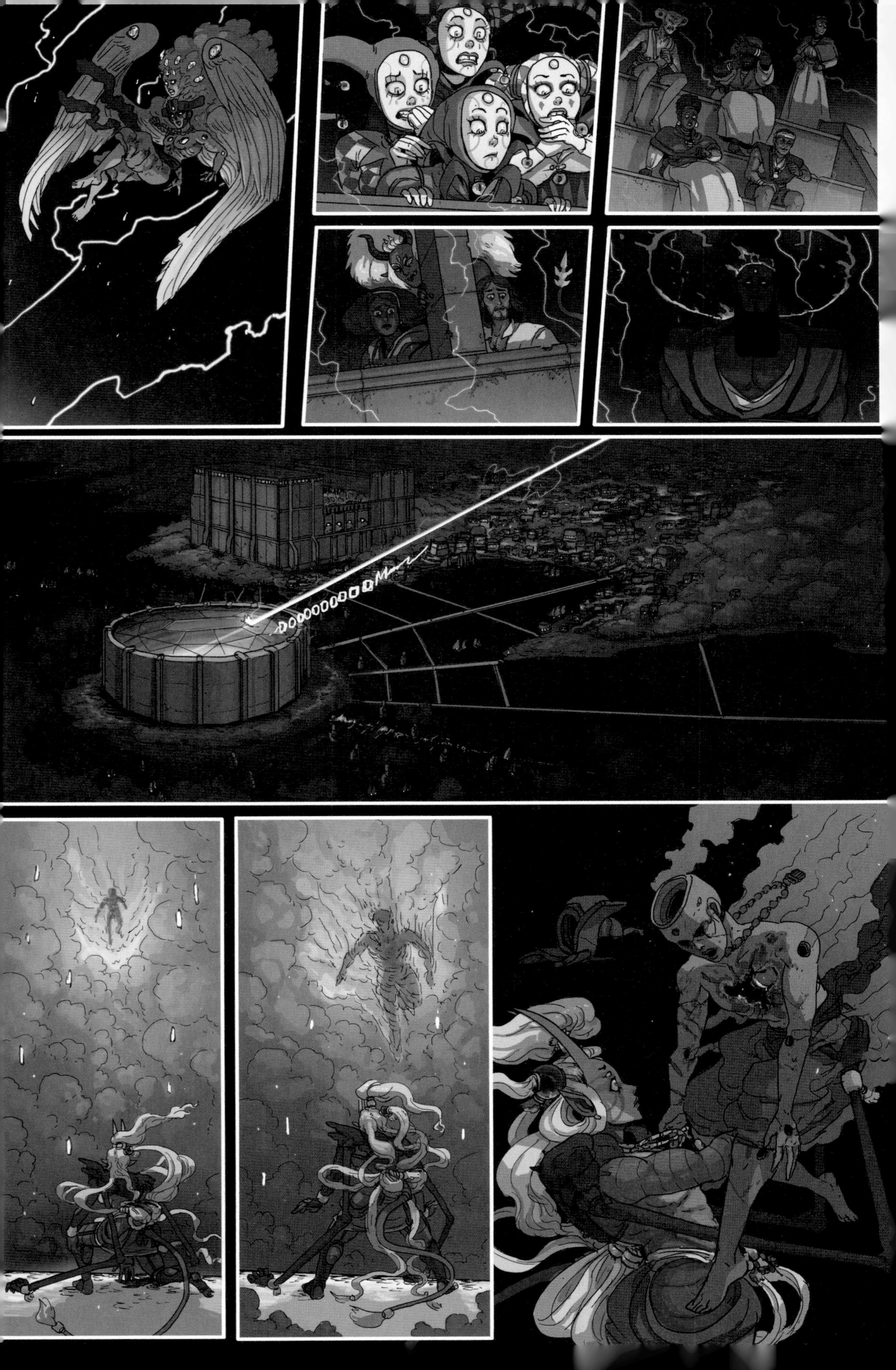
DOOOOOOOOOM

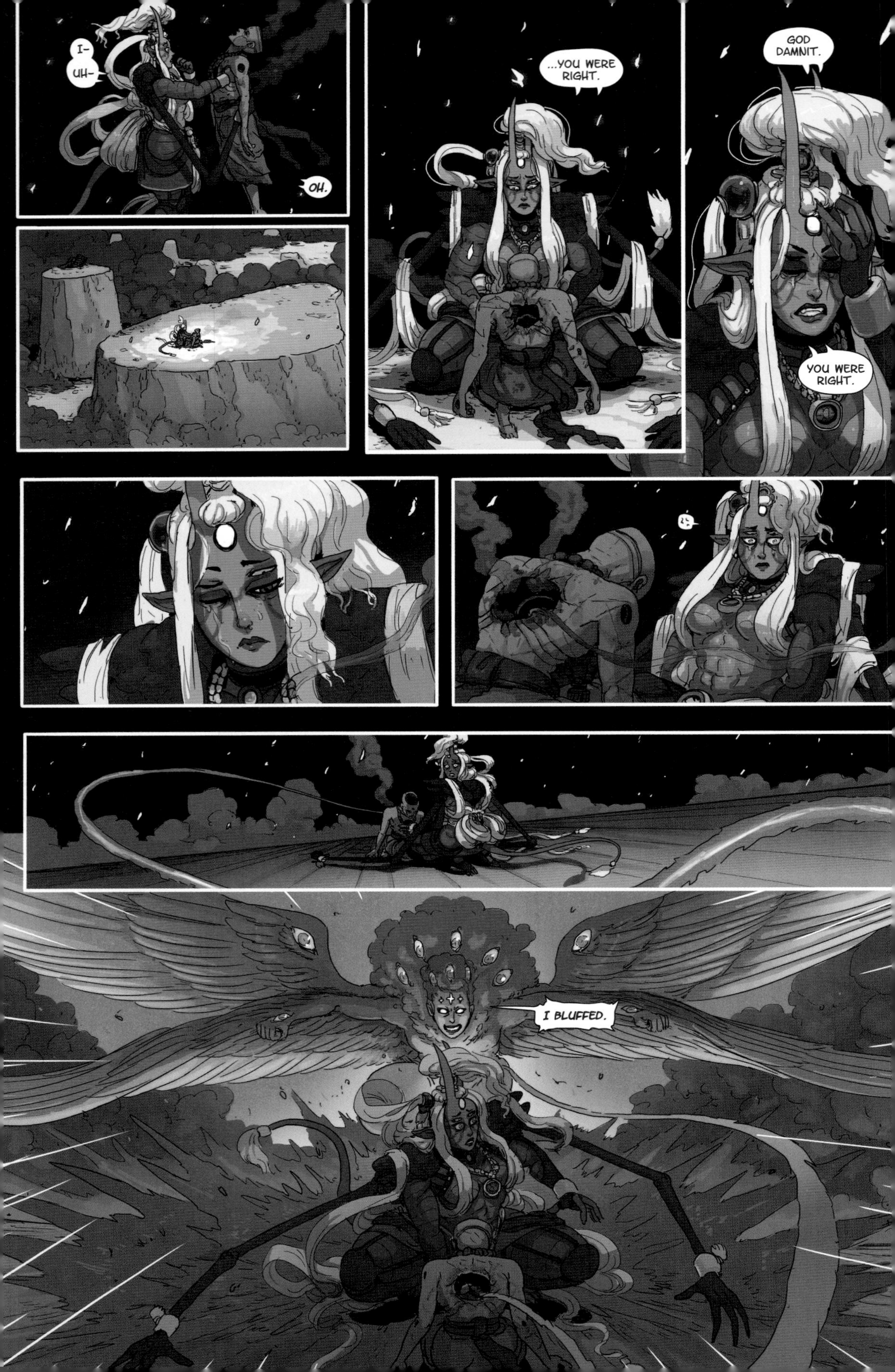
I-
UH-
OH.
...YOU WERE RIGHT.
GOD DAMNIT.
YOU WERE RIGHT.
I BLUFFED.

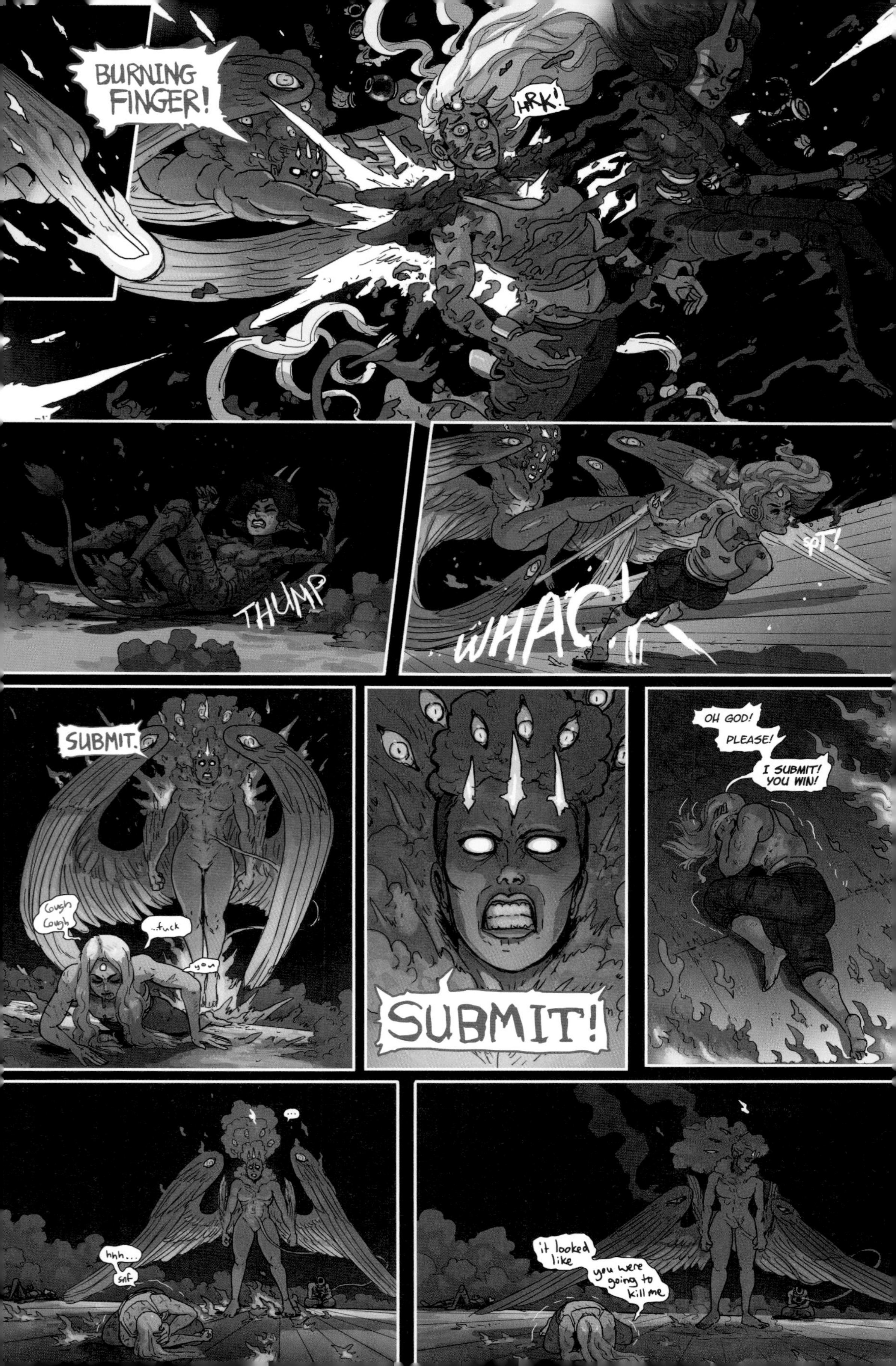
BURNING FINGER!
HRK!
THUMP
SPT!
WHAC
SUBMIT.
Cough Cough
...fuck
you
SUBMIT!
OH GOD!
PLEASE!
I SUBMIT! YOU WIN!
hhh...
snf
...
it looked like
you were going to kill me

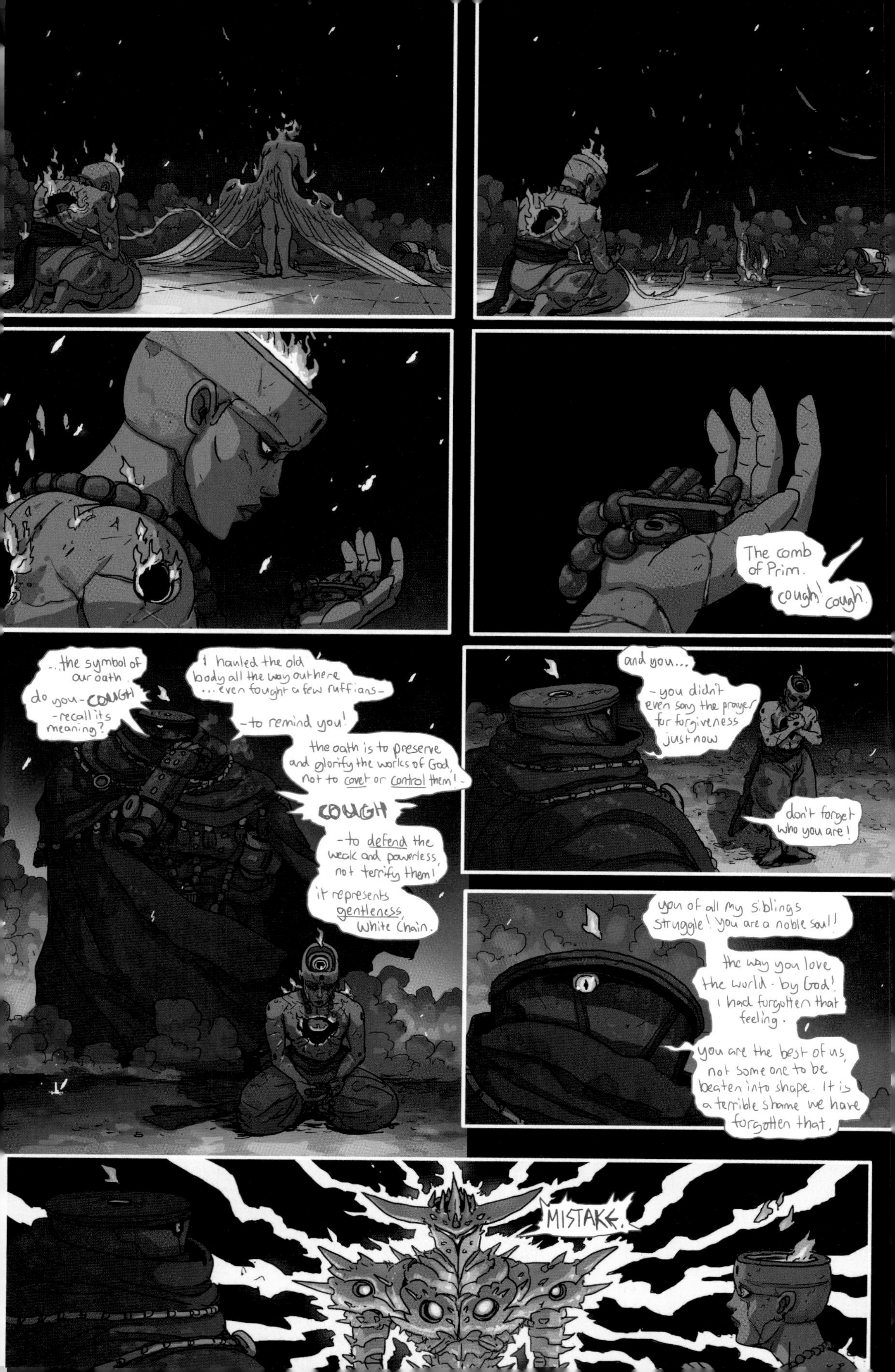
The comb of Prim.
cough! cough!
...the symbol of our oath.
do you-COUGH
-recall its meaning?
I hauled the old body all the way out here ...even fought a few ruffians-
-to remind you!
the oath is to preserve and glorify the works of God, not to covet or control them!
COUGH
-to defend the weak and powerless, not terrify them!
it represents gentleness, White Chain.
and you...
-you didn't even say the prayer for forgiveness just now
don't forget who you are!
you of all my siblings struggle! you are a noble soul!
the way you love the world - by God! I had forgotten that feeling.
you are the best of us, not some one to be beaten into shape. It is a terrible shame we have forgotten that.
MISTAKE.

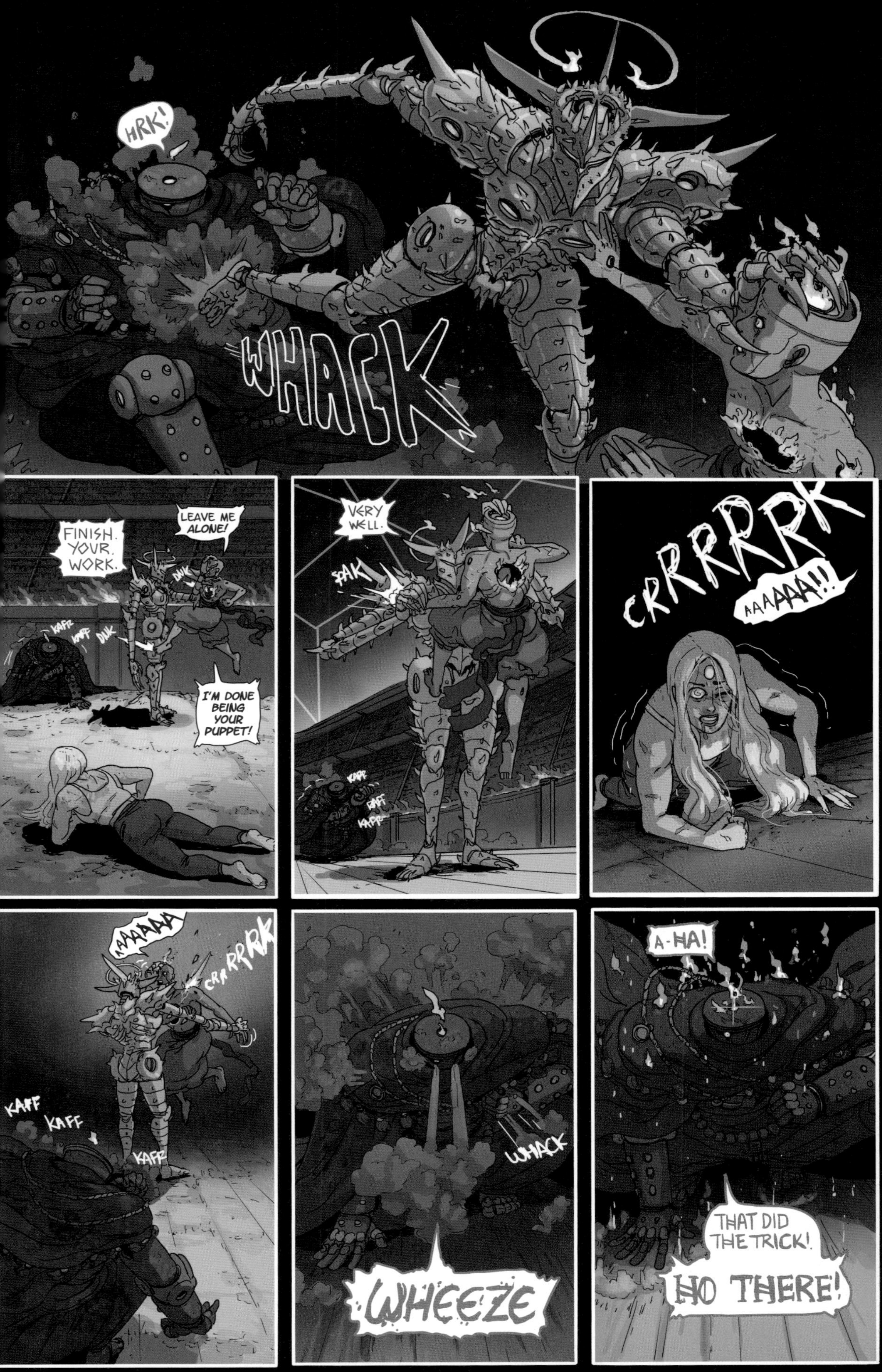
HRK!
WHACK
FINISH. YOUR. WORK.
LEAVE ME ALONE!
DUK
KAFF
KAFF
DUK
I'M DONE BEING YOUR PUPPET!
VERY WELL.
SPAK
CRRRRRK
AAAAAA!!
AAAAAA
CRRRRRK
KAFF
KAFF
KAFF
WHACK
WHEEZE
A-HA!
THAT DID THE TRICK!
HO THERE!

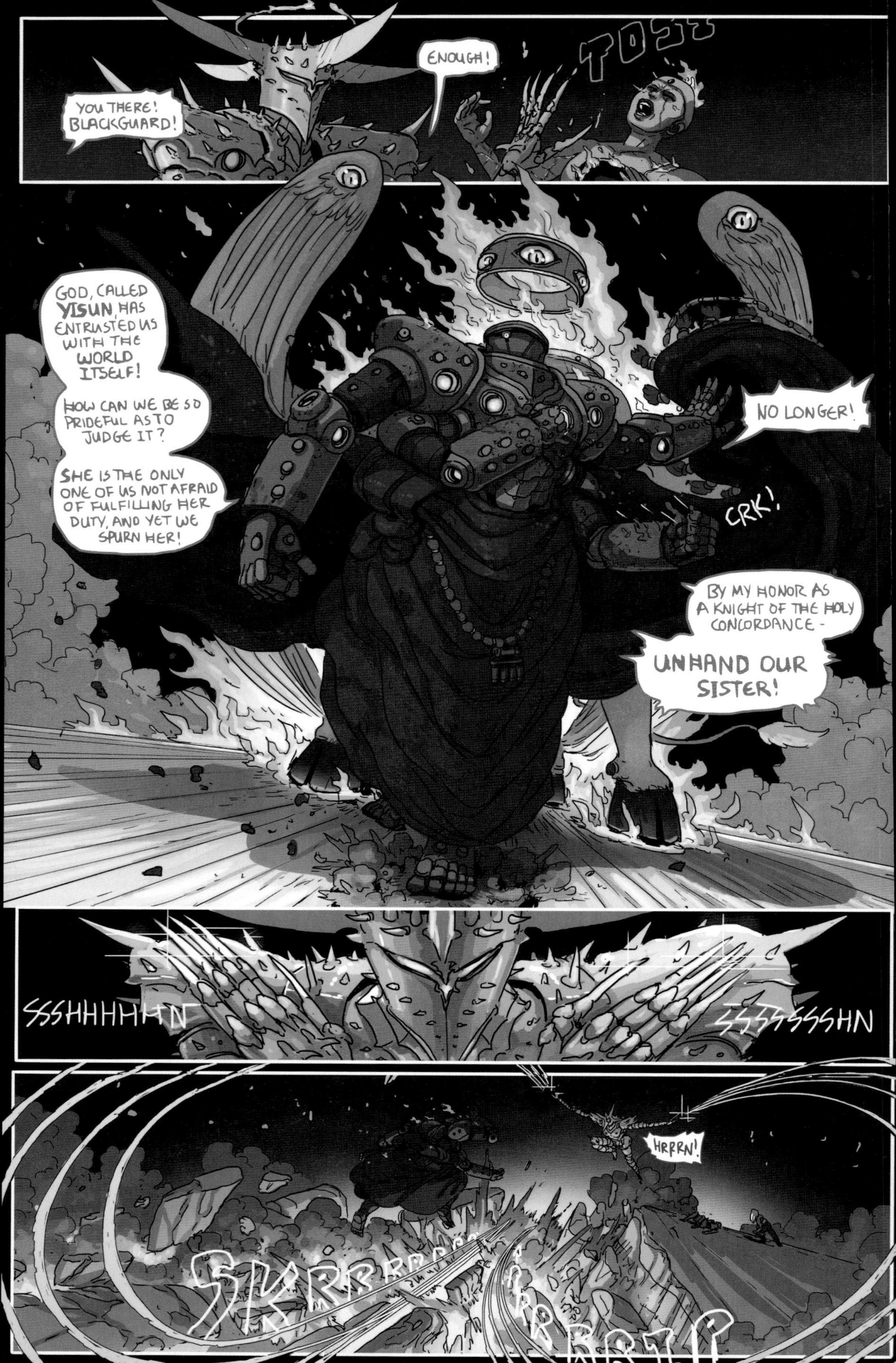
YOU THERE! BLACKGUARD!
ENOUGH!
GOD, CALLED YISUN, HAS ENTRUSTED US WITH THE WORLD ITSELF!
HOW CAN WE BE SO PRIDEFUL AS TO JUDGE IT?
SHE IS THE ONLY ONE OF US NOT AFRAID OF FULFILLING HER DUTY, AND YET WE SPURN HER!
NO LONGER!
CRK!
BY MY HONOR AS A KNIGHT OF THE HOLY CONCORDANCE -
UNHAND OUR SISTER!
SSSHHHHHN
SSSSSSSHN
HRRRN!
SKRRRRRRRRRRRRRIP

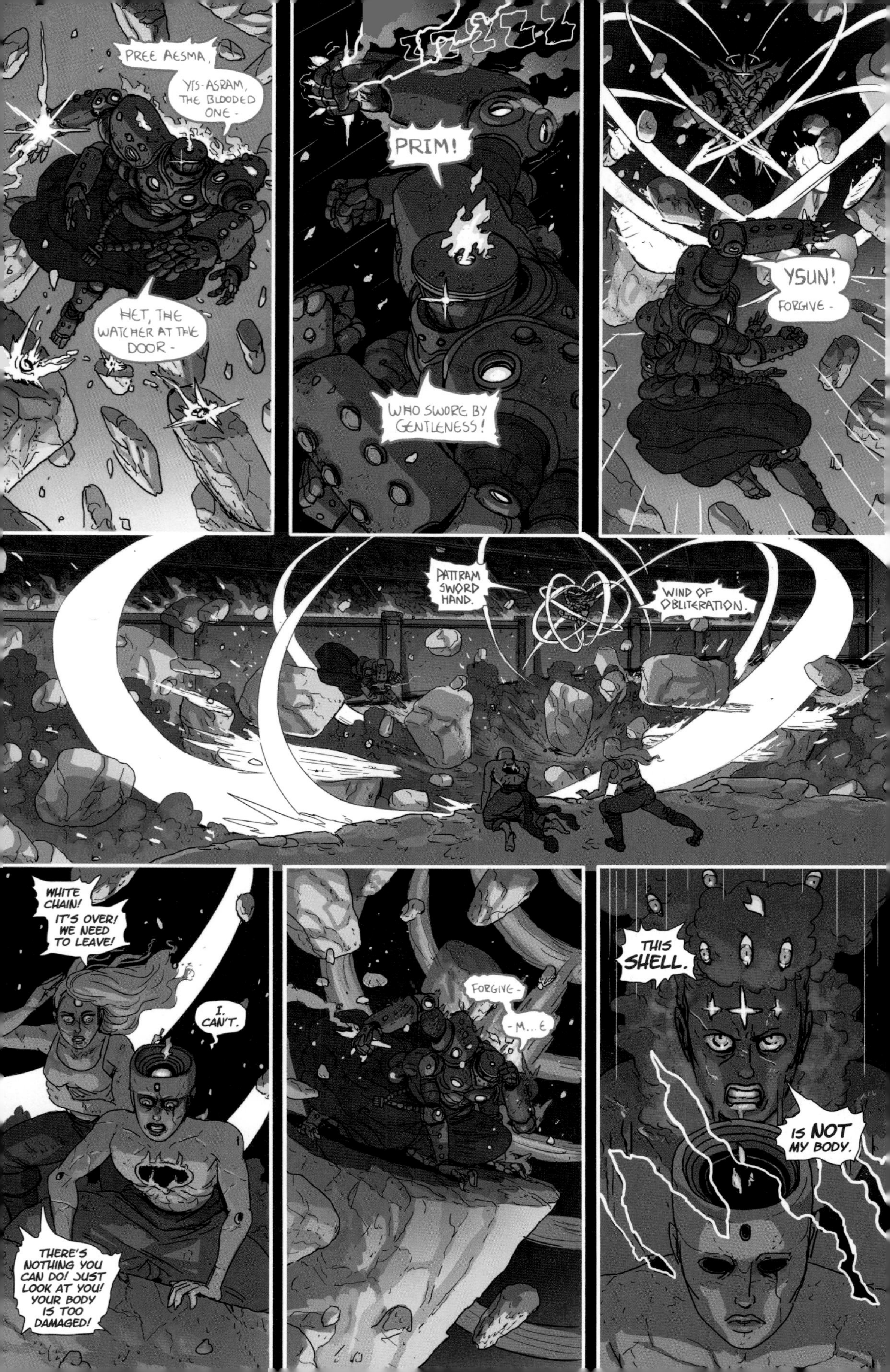
PREE AESMA,
YIS-ASRAM, THE BLOODED ONE-
HET, THE WATCHER AT THE DOOR-
PRIM!
WHO SWORE BY GENTLENESS!
YSUN!
FORGIVE-
PATTRAM SWORD HAND.
WIND OF OBLITERATION.
WHITE CHAIN! IT'S OVER! WE NEED TO LEAVE!
I. CAN'T.
THERE'S NOTHING YOU CAN DO! JUST LOOK AT YOU! YOUR BODY IS TOO DAMAGED!
FORGIVE-
-M... E
THIS SHELL.
IS NOT MY BODY.

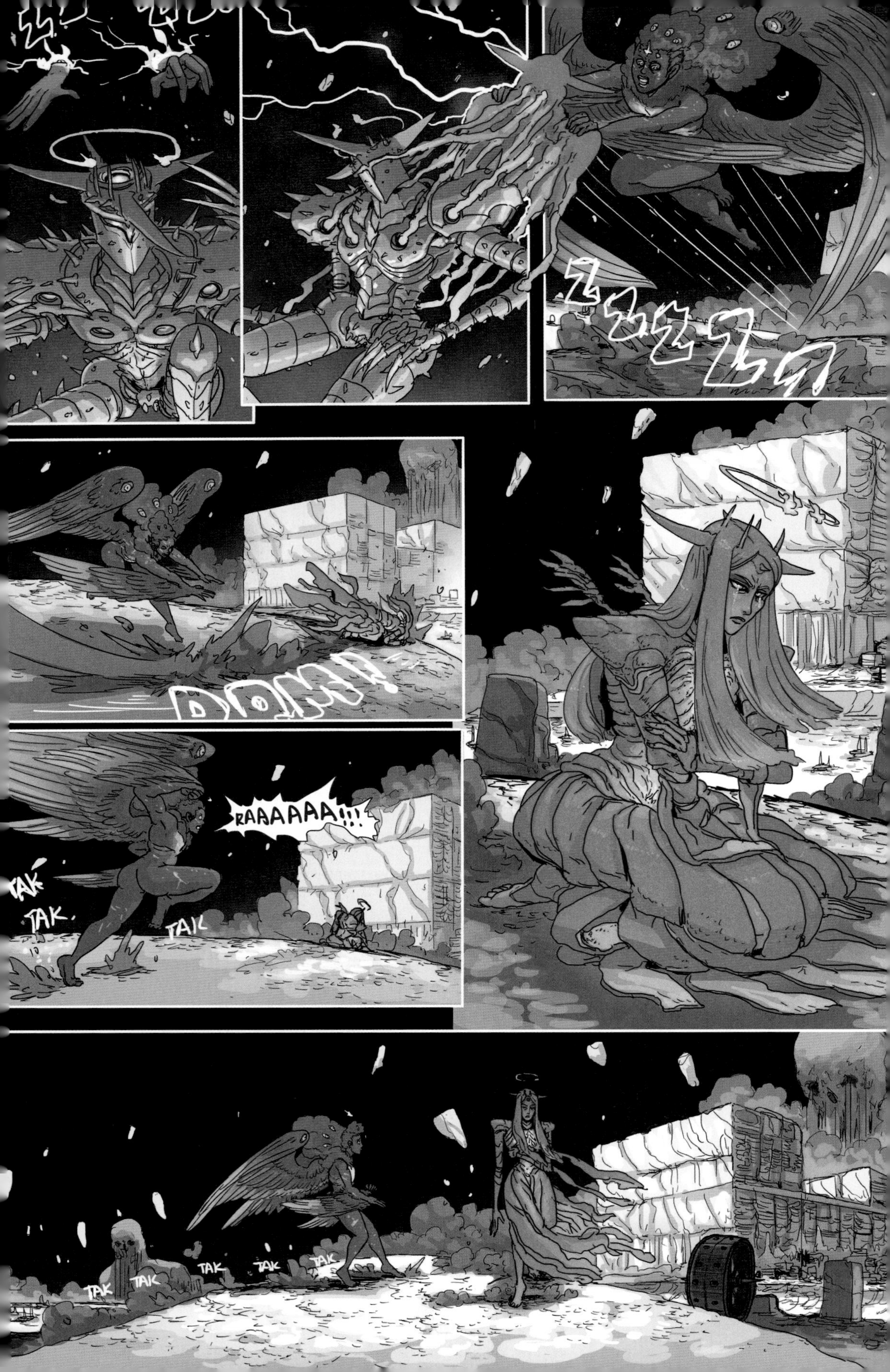
DOOM!!
RAAAAAA!!!
TAK
TAK
TAK
TAK
TAK
TAK
TAK
TAK

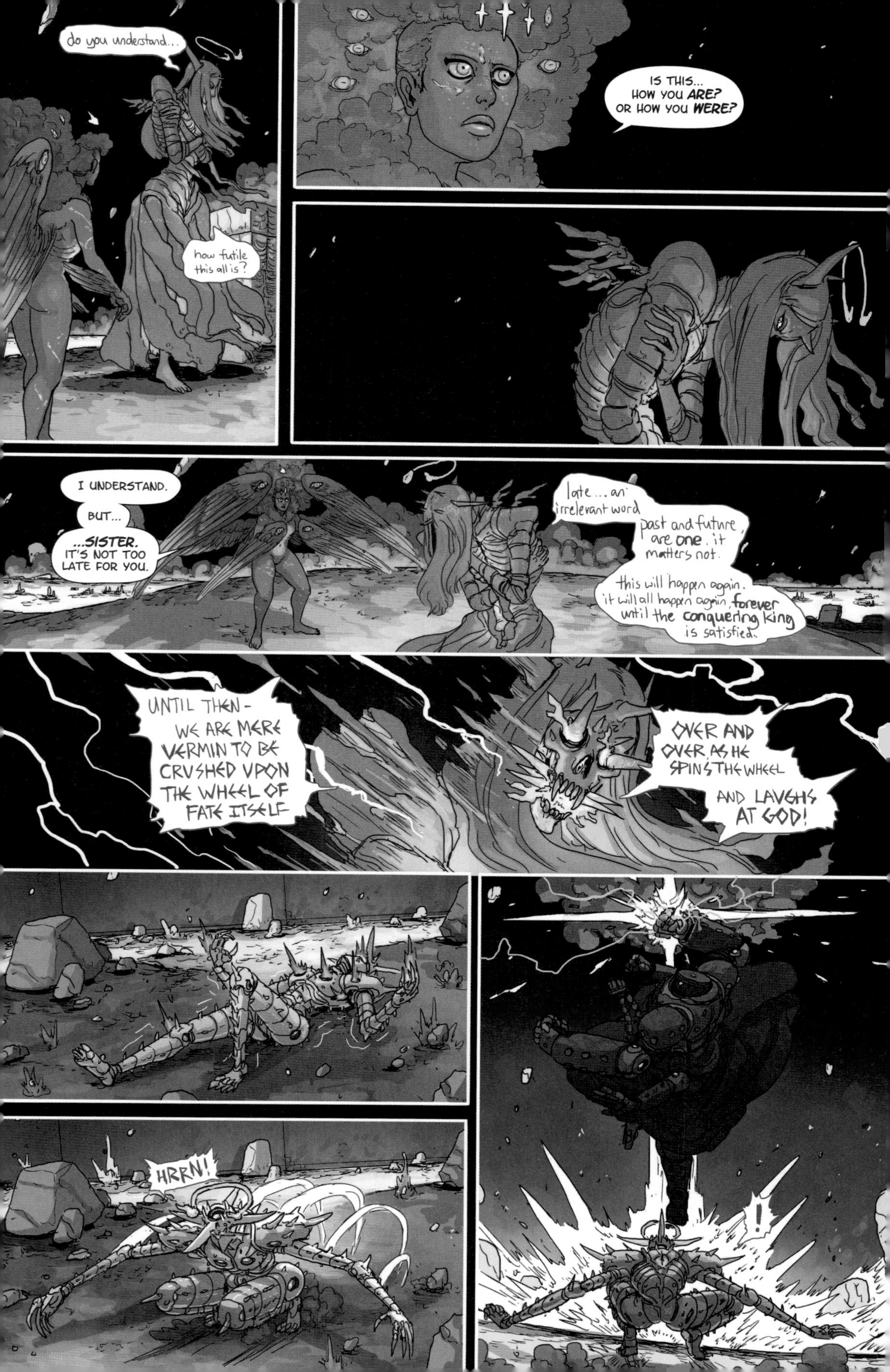
do you understand...
how futile this all is?
IS THIS... HOW YOU ARE? OR HOW YOU WERE?
I UNDERSTAND.
BUT...
...SISTER. IT'S NOT TOO LATE FOR YOU.
late... an irrelevant word
past and future, are one. it matters not.
this will happen again. it will all happen again, forever until the conquering king is satisfied.
UNTIL THEN - WE ARE MERE VERMIN TO BE CRUSHED UPON THE WHEEL OF FATE ITSELF
OVER AND OVER AS HE SPINS THE WHEEL
AND LAUGHS AT GOD!
HRRN!
!

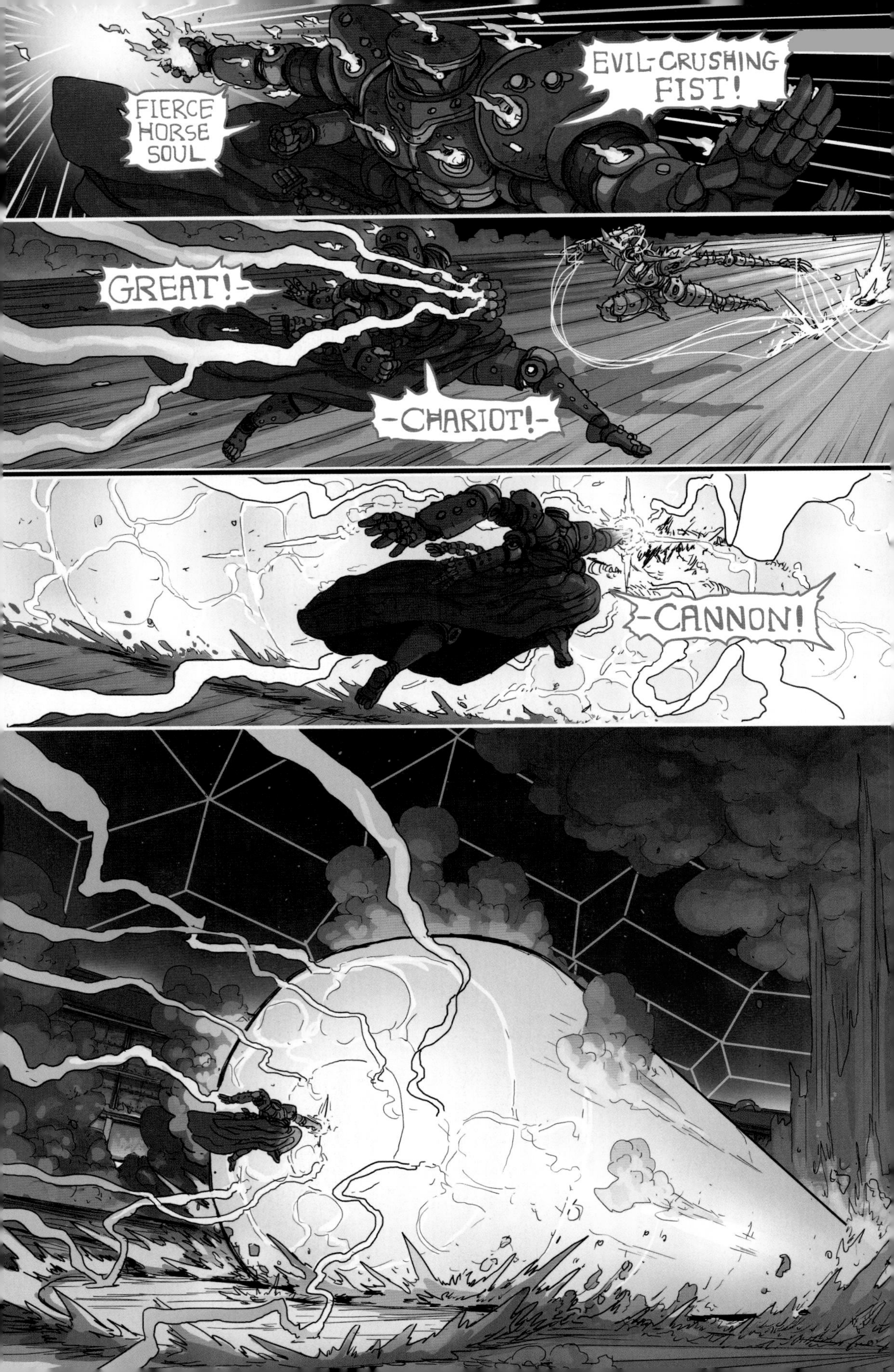
FIERCE HORSE SOUL
EVIL-CRUSHING FIST!
GREAT!-
-CHARIOT!-
-CANNON!

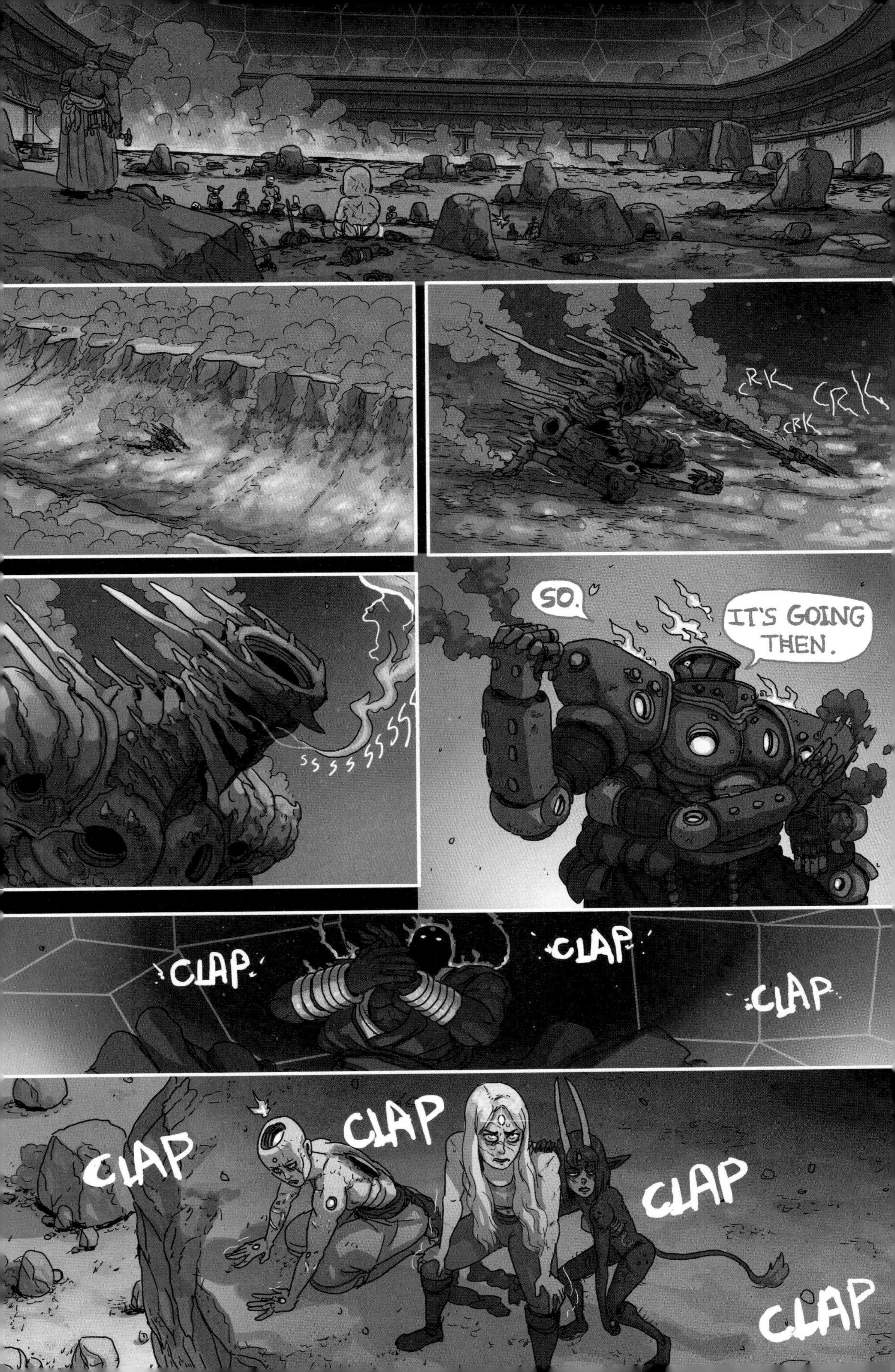
CRK
CRK
CRK
SSSSSSSSSS
SO.
IT'S GOING THEN.
CLAP
CLAP
CLAP
CLAP
CLAP
CLAP
CLAP

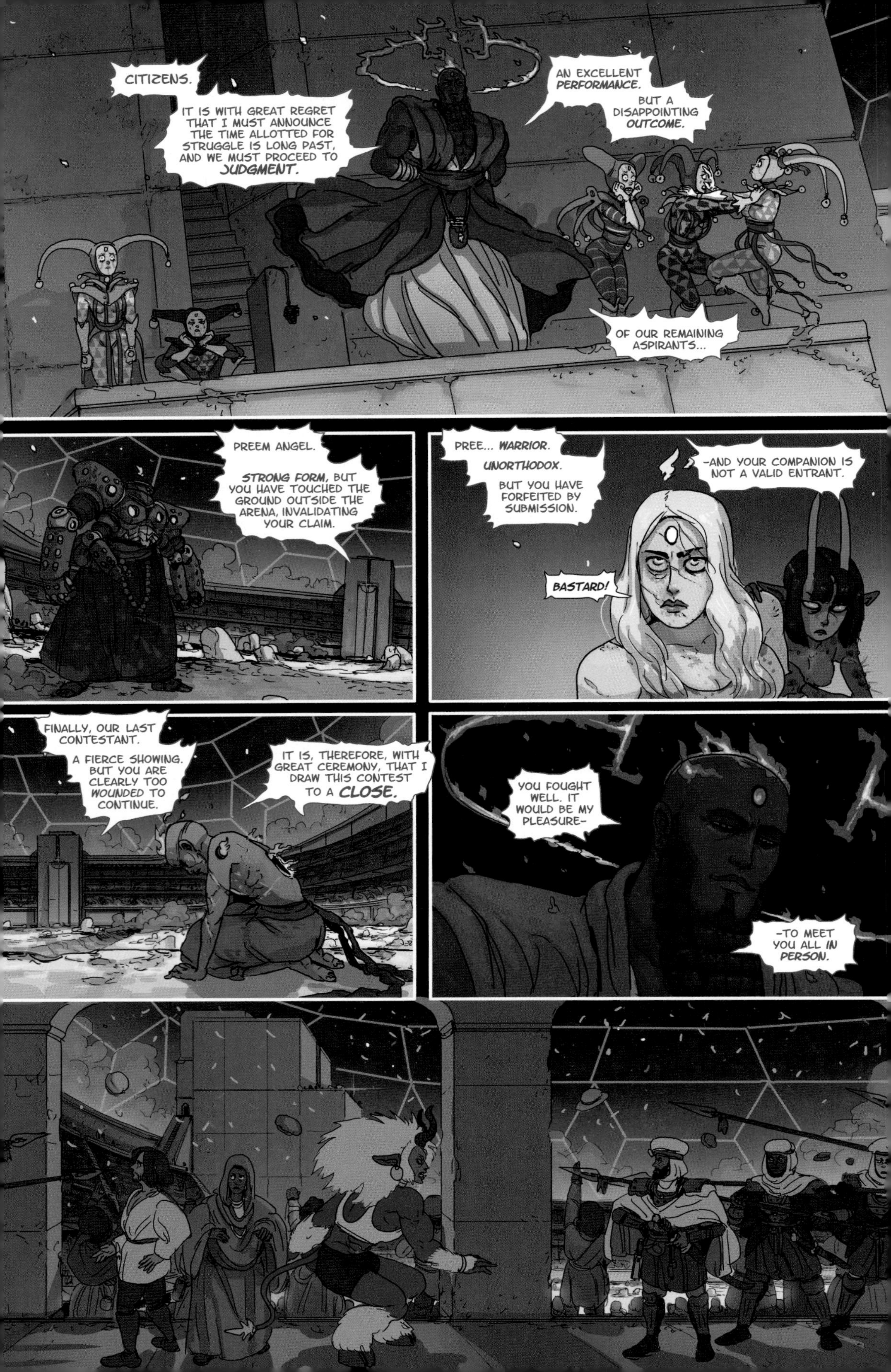
CITIZENS.
IT IS WITH GREAT REGRET THAT I MUST ANNOUNCE THE TIME ALLOTTED FOR STRUGGLE IS LONG PAST, AND WE MUST PROCEED TO JUDGMENT.
AN EXCELLENT PERFORMANCE.
BUT A DISAPPOINTING OUTCOME.
OF OUR REMAINING ASPIRANTS...
PREEM ANGEL.
STRONG FORM, BUT YOU HAVE TOUCHED THE GROUND OUTSIDE THE ARENA, INVALIDATING YOUR CLAIM.
PREE... WARRIOR.
UNORTHODOX.
BUT YOU HAVE FORFEITED BY SUBMISSION.
-AND YOUR COMPANION IS NOT A VALID ENTRANT.
BASTARD!
FINALLY, OUR LAST CONTESTANT.
A FIERCE SHOWING. BUT YOU ARE CLEARLY TOO WOUNDED TO CONTINUE.
IT IS, THEREFORE, WITH GREAT CEREMONY, THAT I DRAW THIS CONTEST TO A CLOSE.
YOU FOUGHT WELL. IT WOULD BE MY PLEASURE-
-TO MEET YOU ALL IN PERSON.

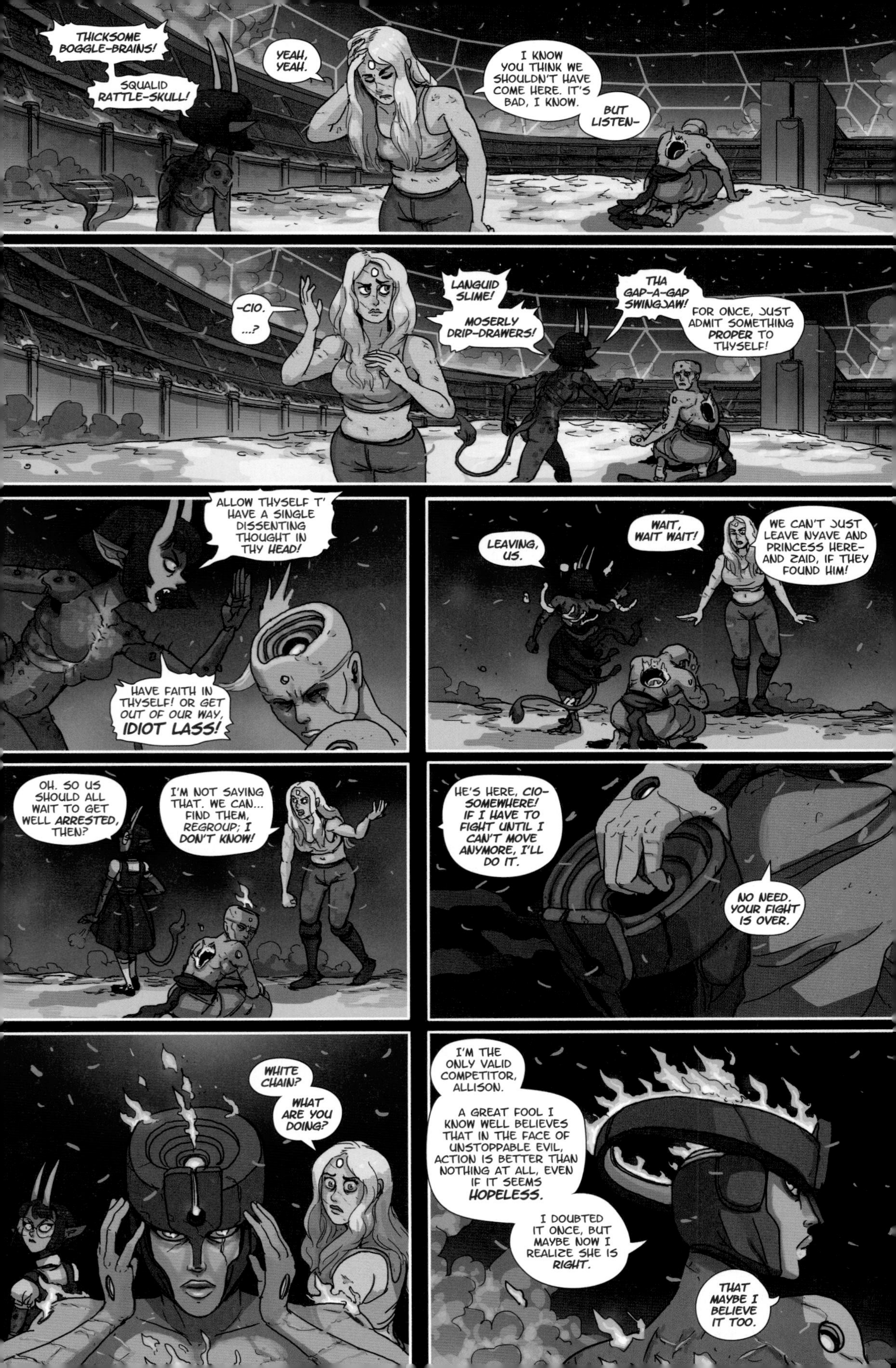
THICKSOME BOGGLE-BRAINS!
SQUALID RATTLE-SKULL!
YEAH, YEAH.
I KNOW YOU THINK WE SHOULDN'T HAVE COME HERE. IT'S BAD, I KNOW.
BUT LISTEN-
-CIO.
...?
LANGUID SLIME!
MOSERLY DRIP-DRAWERS!
THA GAP-A-GAP SWINGJAW!
FOR ONCE, JUST ADMIT SOMETHING PROPER TO THYSELF!
ALLOW THYSELF T' HAVE A SINGLE DISSENTING THOUGHT IN THY HEAD!
HAVE FAITH IN THYSELF! OR GET OUT OF OUR WAY, IDIOT LASS!
LEAVING, US.
WAIT, WAIT WAIT!
WE CAN'T JUST LEAVE NYAVE AND PRINCESS HERE- AND ZAID, IF THEY FOUND HIM!
OH. SO US SHOULD ALL WAIT TO GET WELL ARRESTED, THEN?
I'M NOT SAYING THAT. WE CAN... FIND THEM, REGROUP; I DON'T KNOW!
HE'S HERE, CIO- SOMEWHERE! IF I HAVE TO FIGHT UNTIL I CAN'T MOVE ANYMORE, I'LL DO IT.
NO NEED. YOUR FIGHT IS OVER.
WHITE CHAIN?
WHAT ARE YOU DOING?
I'M THE ONLY VALID COMPETITOR, ALLISON.
A GREAT FOOL I KNOW WELL BELIEVES THAT IN THE FACE OF UNSTOPPABLE EVIL, ACTION IS BETTER THAN NOTHING AT ALL, EVEN IF IT SEEMS HOPELESS.
I DOUBTED IT ONCE, BUT MAYBE NOW I REALIZE SHE IS RIGHT.
THAT MAYBE I BELIEVE IT TOO.

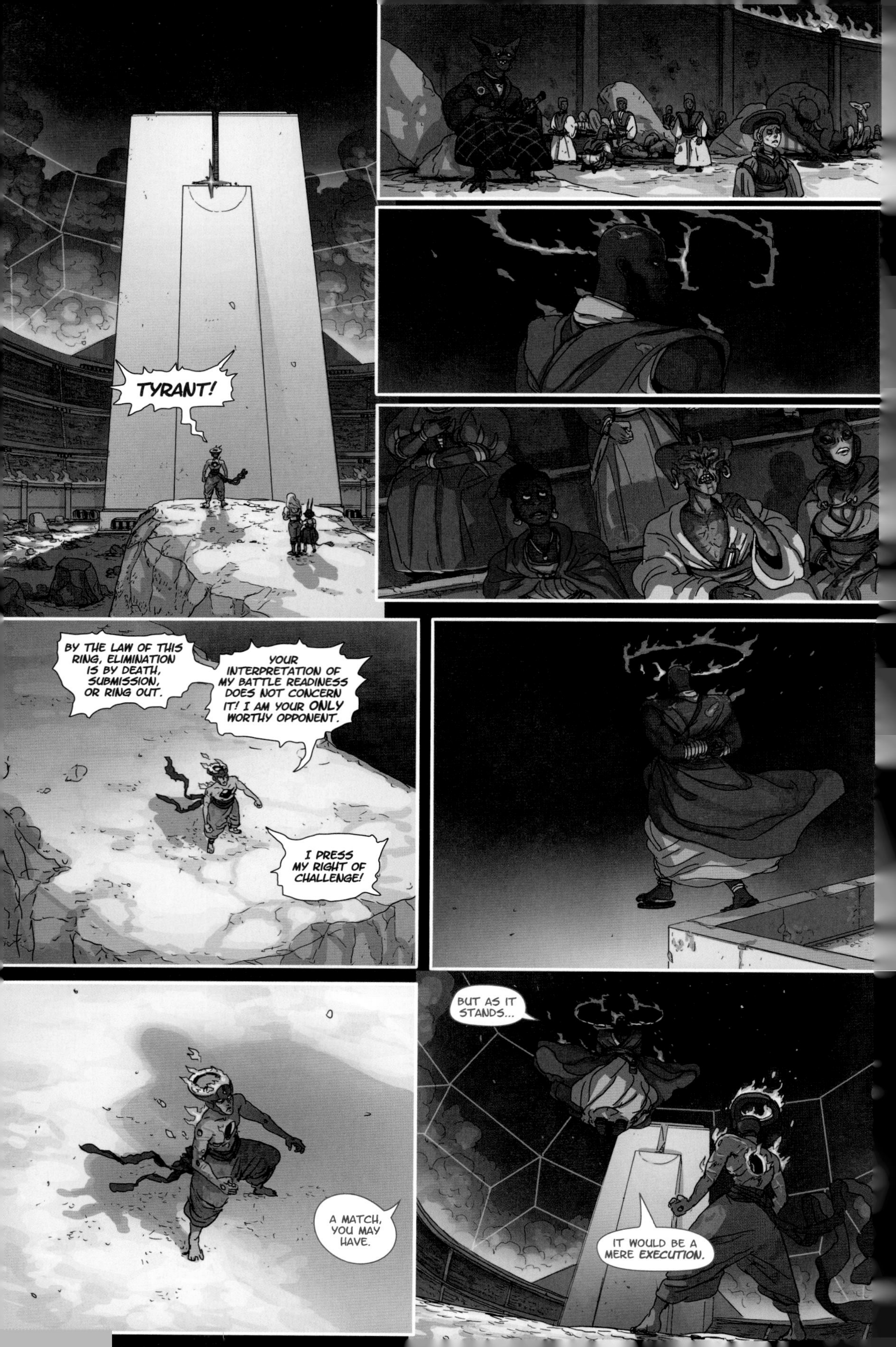
TYRANT!
BY THE LAW OF THIS RING, ELIMINATION IS BY DEATH, SUBMISSION, OR RING OUT.
YOUR INTERPRETATION OF MY BATTLE READINESS DOES NOT CONCERN IT! I AM YOUR ONLY WORTHY OPPONENT.
I PRESS MY RIGHT OF CHALLENGE!
A MATCH, YOU MAY HAVE.
BUT AS IT STANDS...
IT WOULD BE A MERE EXECUTION.

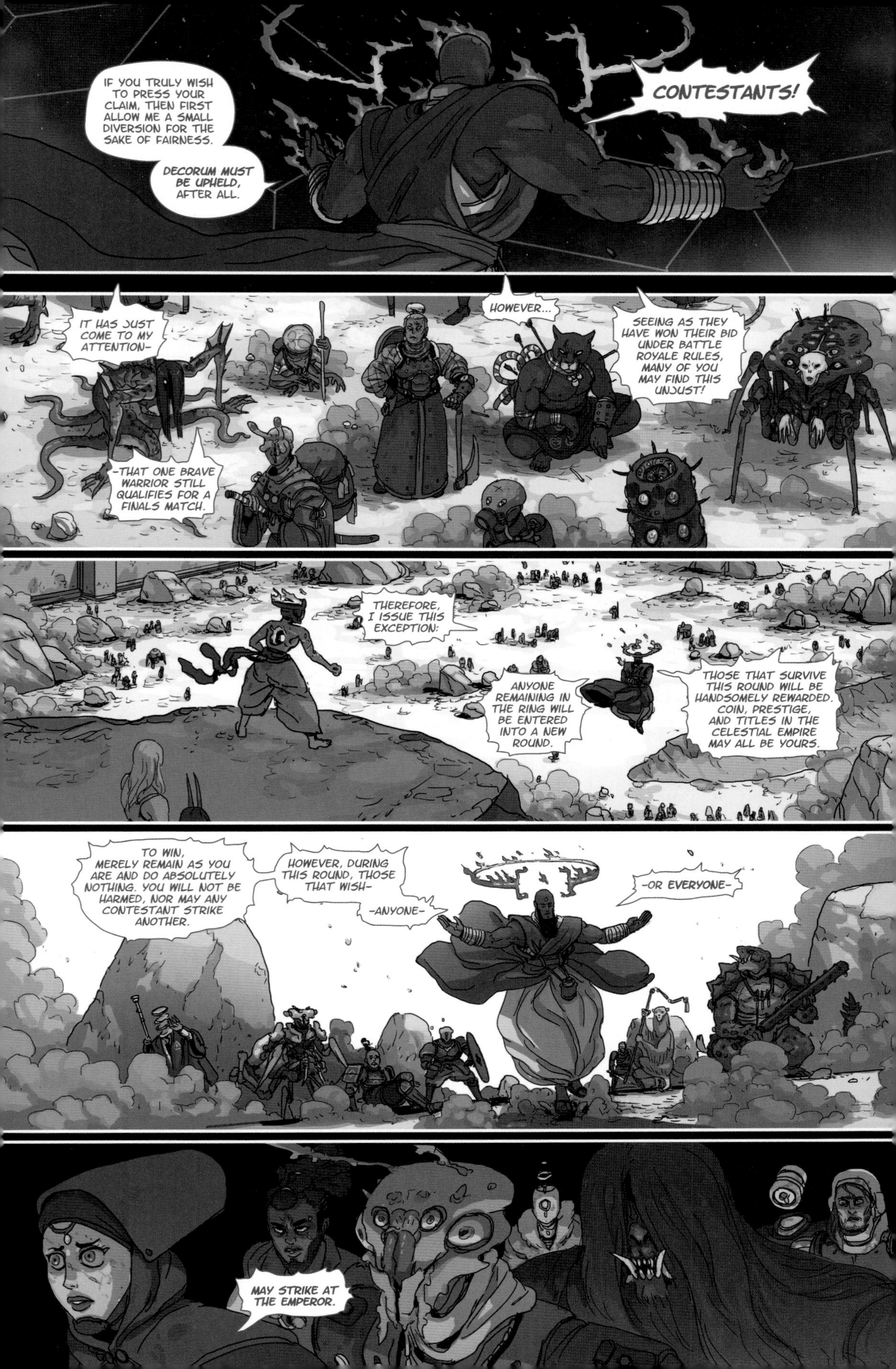
IF YOU TRULY WISH TO PRESS YOUR CLAIM, THEN FIRST ALLOW ME A SMALL DIVERSION FOR THE SAKE OF FAIRNESS.
DECORUM MUST BE UPHELD, AFTER ALL.
CONTESTANTS!
IT HAS JUST COME TO MY ATTENTION-
-THAT ONE BRAVE WARRIOR STILL QUALIFIES FOR A FINALS MATCH.
HOWEVER...
SEEING AS THEY HAVE WON THEIR BID UNDER BATTLE ROYALE RULES, MANY OF YOU MAY FIND THIS UNJUST!
THEREFORE, I ISSUE THIS EXCEPTION:
ANYONE REMAINING IN THE RING WILL BE ENTERED INTO A NEW ROUND.
THOSE THAT SURVIVE THIS ROUND WILL BE HANDSOMELY REWARDED. COIN, PRESTIGE, AND TITLES IN THE CELESTIAL EMPIRE MAY ALL BE YOURS.
TO WIN, MERELY REMAIN AS YOU ARE AND DO ABSOLUTELY NOTHING. YOU WILL NOT BE HARMED, NOR MAY ANY CONTESTANT STRIKE ANOTHER.
HOWEVER, DURING THIS ROUND, THOSE THAT WISH-
-ANYONE-
-OR EVERYONE-
MAY STRIKE AT THE EMPEROR.

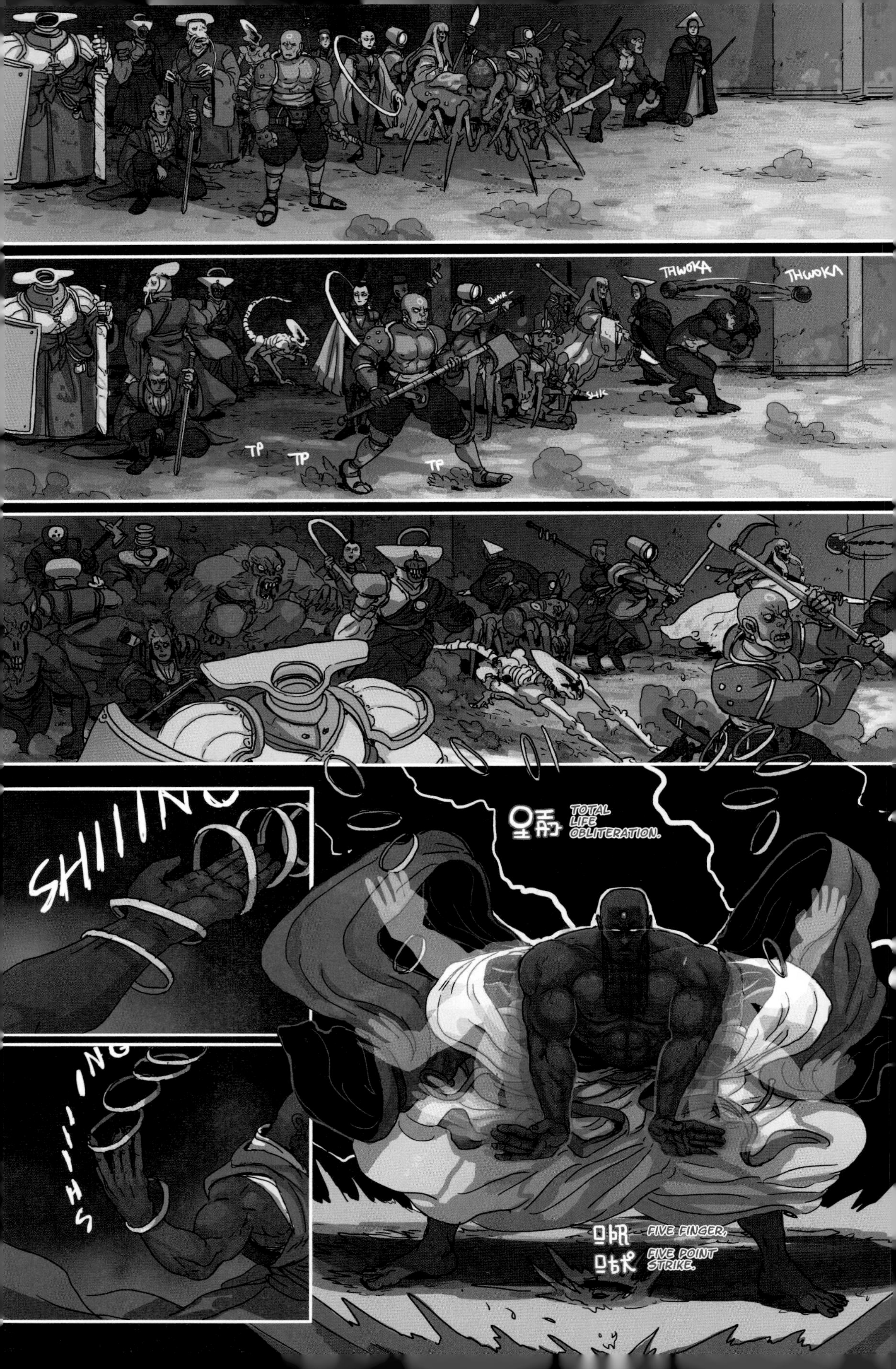

TP
TP
TP
SHIK
THWOKA
THWOKA
SHIIING
SHIIIING
TOTAL LIFE OBLITERATION.
FIVE FINGER,
FIVE POINT STRIKE.

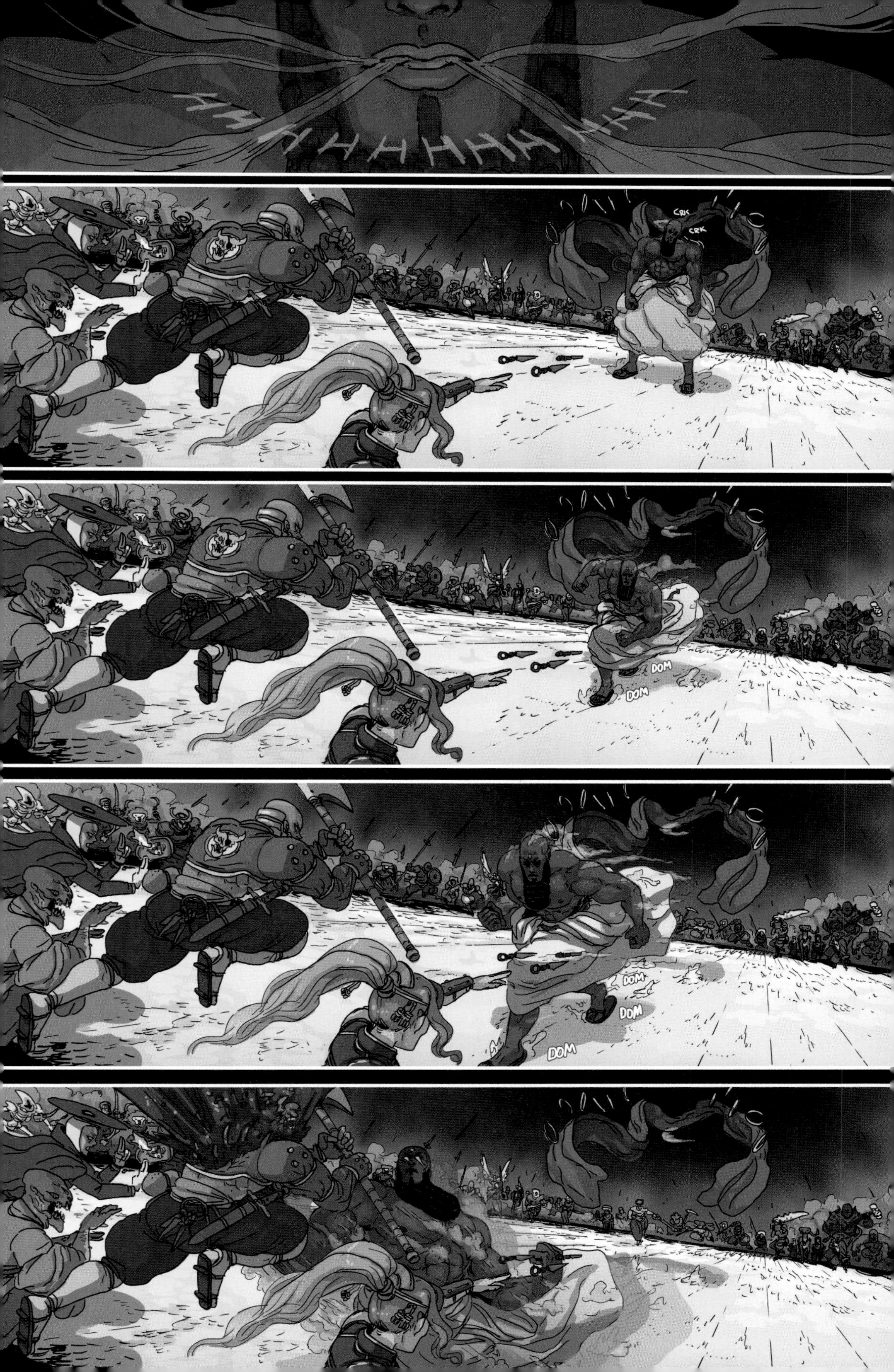
CRK
DOM
DOM
DOM
DOM
DOM

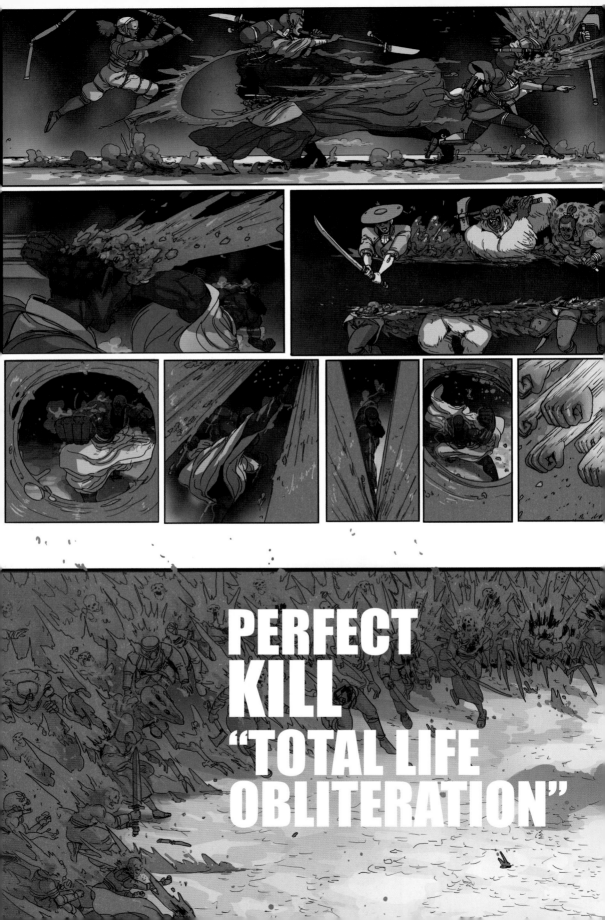

PERFECT
KILL
"TOTAL LIFE
OBLITERATION"

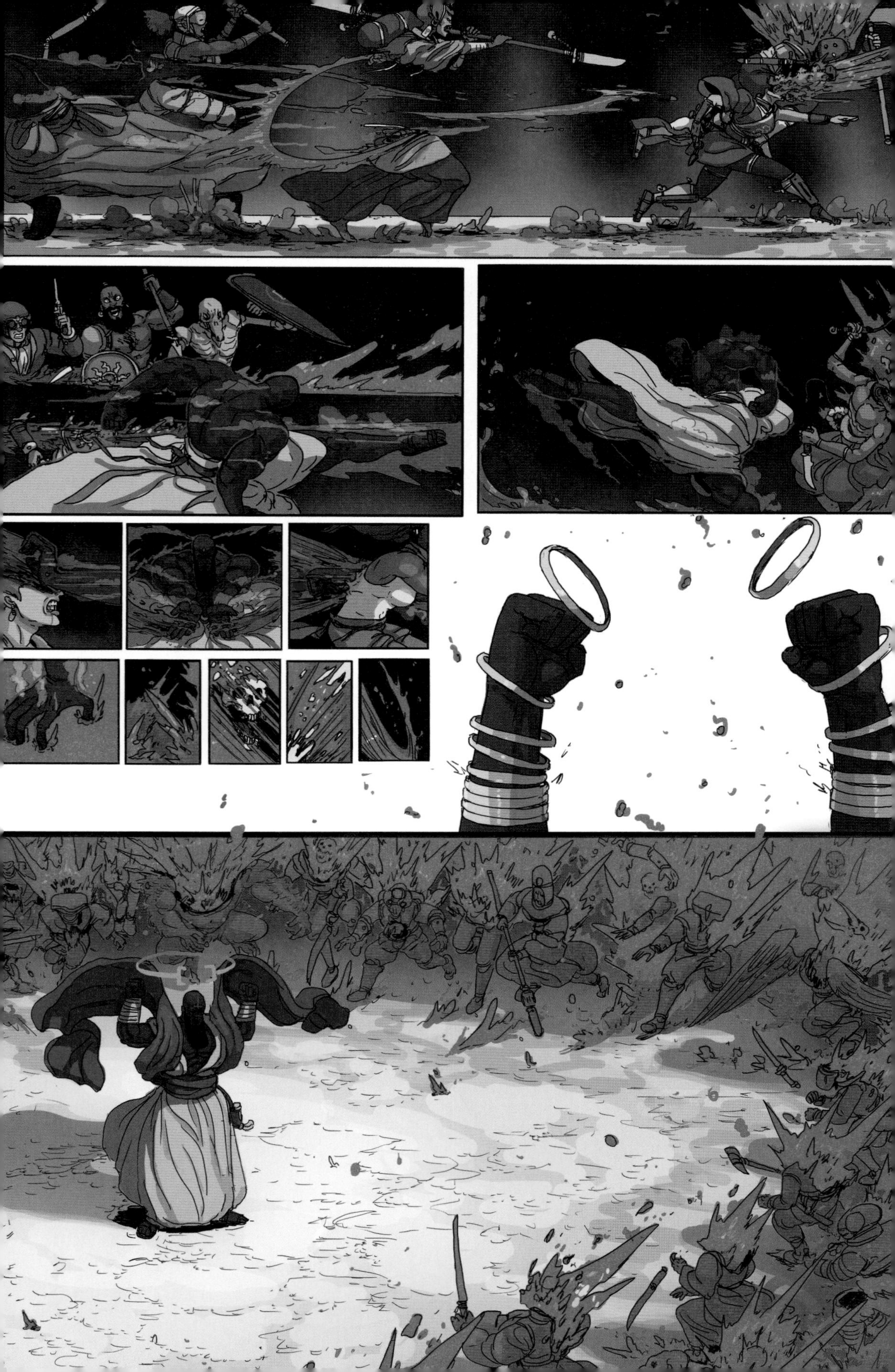

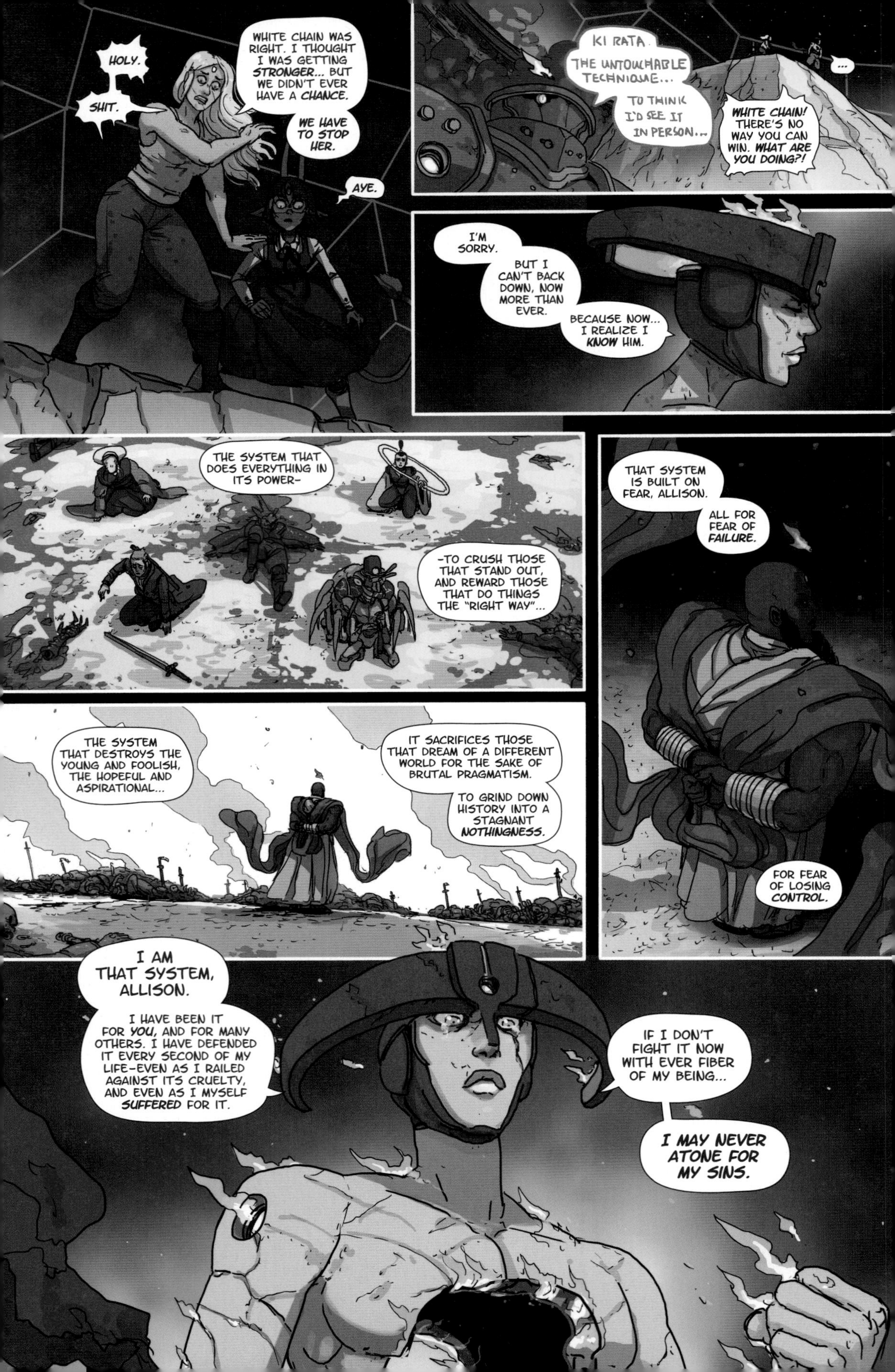
HOLY.
SHIT.
WHITE CHAIN WAS RIGHT. I THOUGHT I WAS GETTING **STRONGER**... BUT WE DIDN'T EVER HAVE A **CHANCE**.
WE HAVE TO STOP HER.
AYE.
KI RATA.
THE UNTOUCHABLE TECHNIQUE...
TO THINK I'D SEE IT IN PERSON...
...
WHITE CHAIN! THERE'S NO WAY YOU CAN WIN. **WHAT ARE YOU DOING?!**
I'M SORRY.
BUT I CAN'T BACK DOWN, NOW MORE THAN EVER.
BECAUSE NOW... I REALIZE I **KNOW** HIM.
THE SYSTEM THAT DOES EVERYTHING IN ITS POWER–
–TO CRUSH THOSE THAT STAND OUT, AND REWARD THOSE THAT DO THINGS THE "RIGHT WAY"...
THAT SYSTEM IS BUILT ON FEAR, ALLISON.
ALL FOR FEAR OF **FAILURE**.
THE SYSTEM THAT DESTROYS THE YOUNG AND FOOLISH, THE HOPEFUL AND ASPIRATIONAL...
IT SACRIFICES THOSE THAT DREAM OF A DIFFERENT WORLD FOR THE SAKE OF BRUTAL PRAGMATISM.
TO GRIND DOWN HISTORY INTO A STAGNANT **NOTHINGNESS**.
FOR FEAR OF LOSING **CONTROL**.
I AM THAT SYSTEM, ALLISON.
I HAVE BEEN IT FOR **YOU**, AND FOR MANY OTHERS. I HAVE DEFENDED IT EVERY SECOND OF MY LIFE–EVEN AS I RAILED AGAINST ITS CRUELTY, AND EVEN AS I MYSELF **SUFFERED** FOR IT.
IF I DON'T FIGHT IT NOW WITH EVER FIBER OF MY BEING...
I MAY NEVER ATONE FOR MY SINS.

VII.

HANK YOU FOR SLAYING THE RAKSHASA," said the dwellers, and went back to their harsh existence. They were gracious for it, nonetheless. Het shed her uniform and her boots and spent the last of her pay buying a good traveling cloak, a set of rough-spun clothing, and iron-nailed boots.

"Where will you go?" asked the fire-stoking woman. "To the Road, of course," said Het, for that was the nature of things.

Het abhorred violence. But there were Rakshasas about, and worse. Indeed, though her stave was very rarely used for cracking skulls, the skulls it cracked were very famous indeed. You may have heard of a few, and perhaps also how she came to be the doorkeeper of YISUN's speaking house, and how she met Prim once again on the road some time later.

BUT THOSE ARE STORIES FOR ANOTHER TIME.

Before she left, Het offered her old clothing to the dwellers, who declined.

"Your boots are very impractical for walking in the mud," they said, and Het had to agree. If you had to wash all the stains out every night, stains ceased to have meaning.

IT DIDN'T STOP HET FROM TAKING A BATH LATER, HOWEVER.

SOME HABITS DIE HARD.

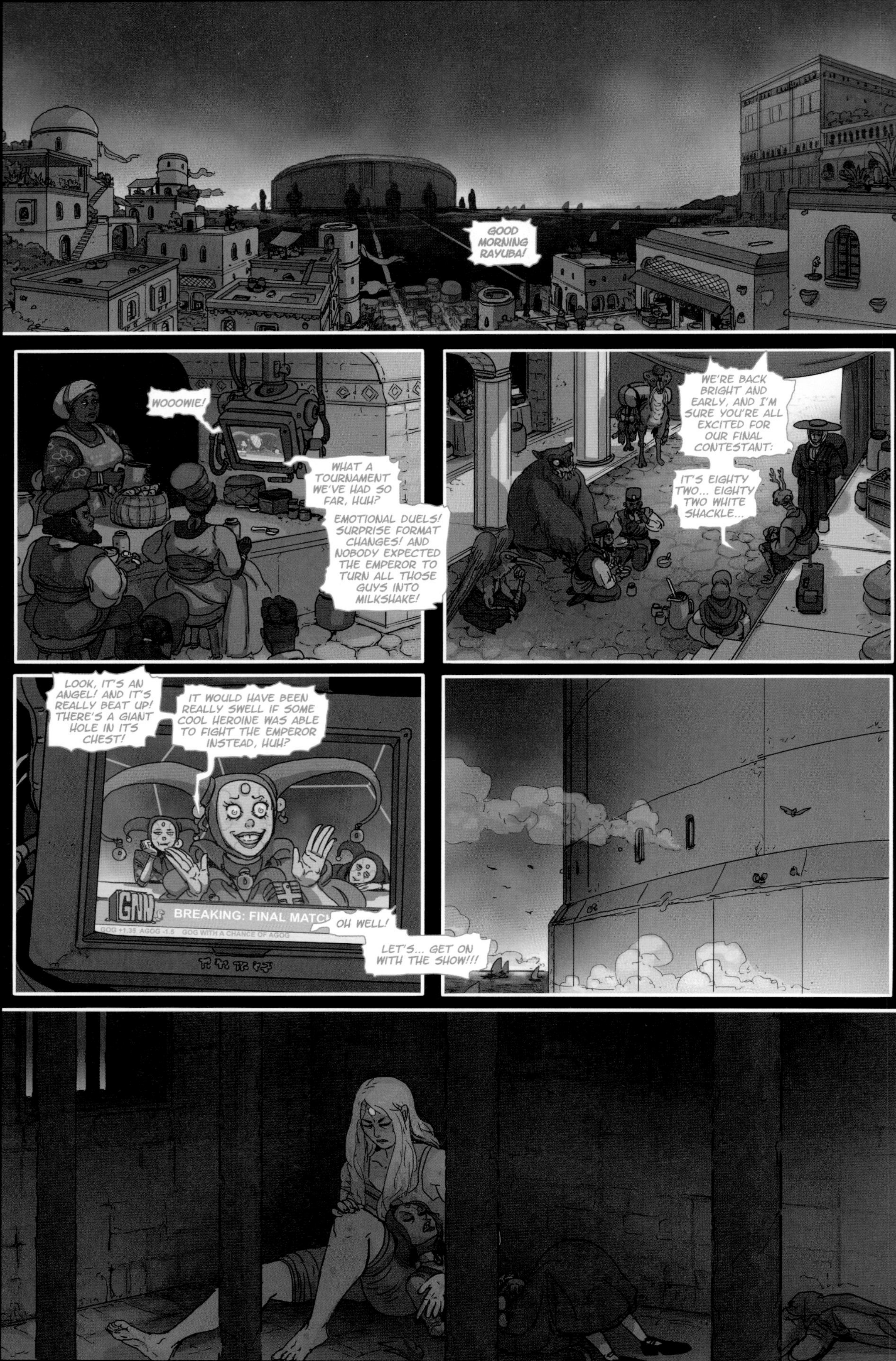
GOOD MORNING RAYUBA!
WOOOWIE!
WHAT A TOURNAMENT WE'VE HAD SO FAR, HUH?
EMOTIONAL DUELS! SURPRISE FORMAT CHANGES! AND NOBODY EXPECTED THE EMPEROR TO TURN ALL THOSE GUYS INTO MILKSHAKE!
WE'RE BACK BRIGHT AND EARLY, AND I'M SURE YOU'RE ALL EXCITED FOR OUR FINAL CONTESTANT:
IT'S EIGHTY TWO... EIGHTY TWO WHITE SHACKLE...
LOOK, IT'S AN ANGEL! AND IT'S REALLY BEAT UP! THERE'S A GIANT HOLE IN ITS CHEST!
IT WOULD HAVE BEEN REALLY SWELL IF SOME COOL HEROINE WAS ABLE TO FIGHT THE EMPEROR INSTEAD, HUH?
GNN
BREAKING: FINAL MATC
GOG +1.35 AGOG -1.5 GOG WITH A CHANCE OF AGOG
OH WELL!
LET'S... GET ON WITH THE SHOW!!!

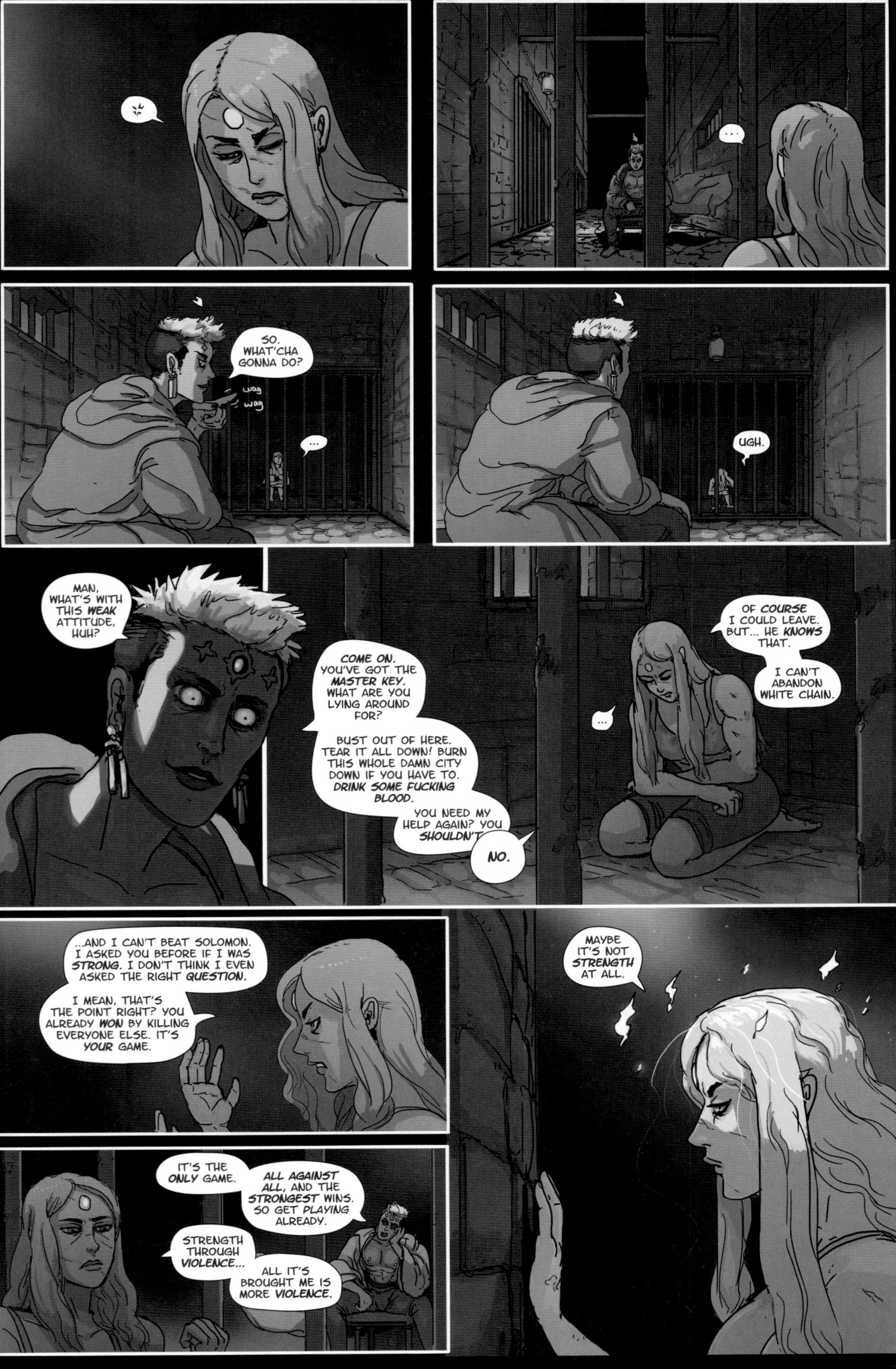

...
SO. WHAT'CHA GONNA DO?
wag wag
...
UGH.
MAN, WHAT'S WITH THIS WEAK ATTITUDE, HUH?
COME ON. YOU'VE GOT THE MASTER KEY. WHAT ARE YOU LYING AROUND FOR?
BUST OUT OF HERE. TEAR IT ALL DOWN! BURN THIS WHOLE DAMN CITY DOWN IF YOU HAVE TO. DRINK SOME FUCKING BLOOD.
YOU NEED MY HELP AGAIN? YOU SHOULDN'T
...
OF COURSE I COULD LEAVE. BUT... HE KNOWS THAT.
I CAN'T ABANDON WHITE CHAIN.
NO.
...AND I CAN'T BEAT SOLOMON. I ASKED YOU BEFORE IF I WAS STRONG. I DON'T THINK I EVEN ASKED THE RIGHT QUESTION.
I MEAN, THAT'S THE POINT RIGHT? YOU ALREADY WON BY KILLING EVERYONE ELSE. IT'S YOUR GAME.
IT'S THE ONLY GAME.
ALL AGAINST ALL, AND THE STRONGEST WINS. SO GET PLAYING ALREADY.
STRENGTH THROUGH VIOLENCE...
ALL IT'S BROUGHT ME IS MORE VIOLENCE.
MAYBE IT'S NOT STRENGTH AT ALL.

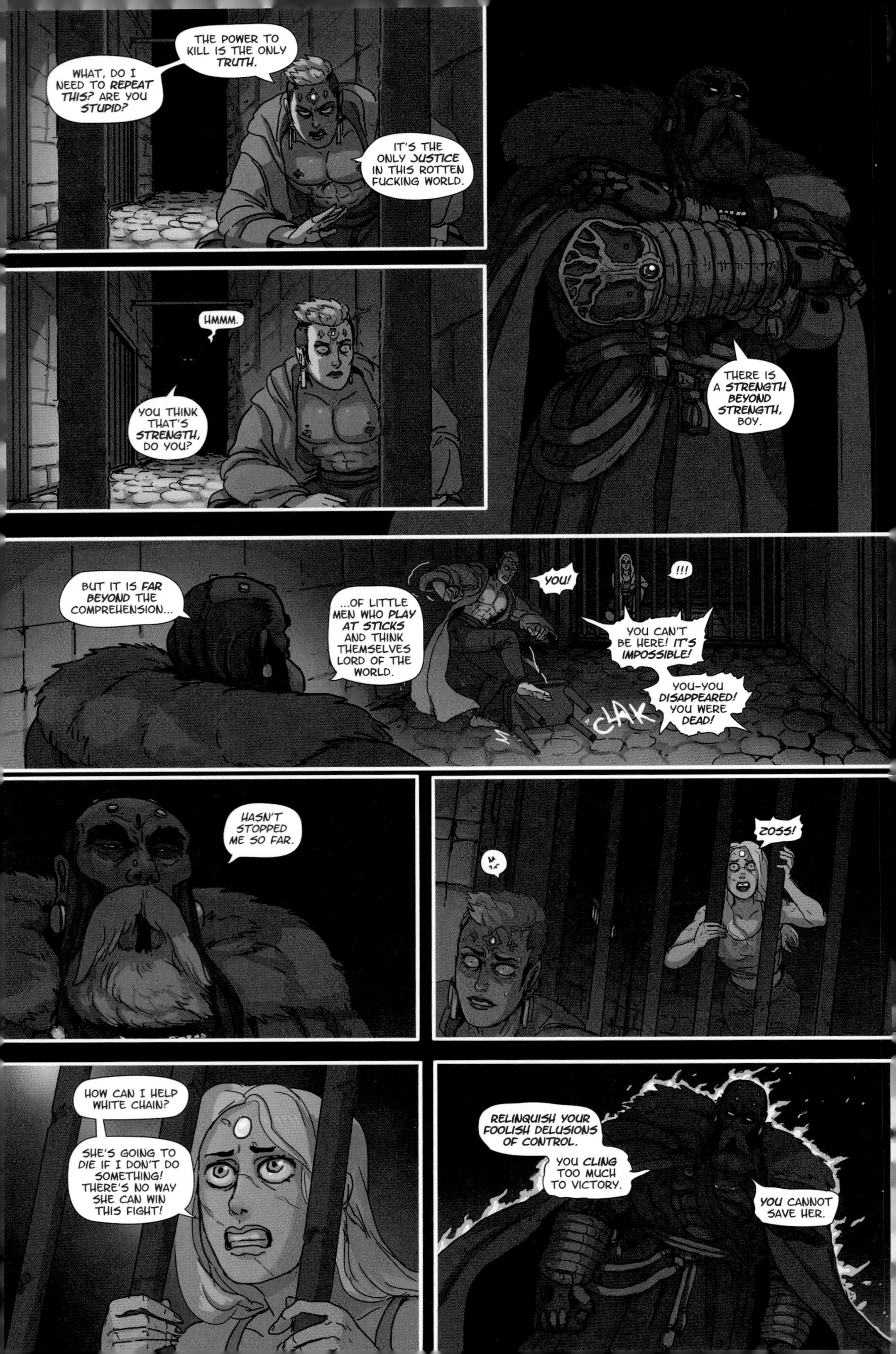
THE POWER TO KILL IS THE ONLY TRUTH.
WHAT, DO I NEED TO REPEAT THIS? ARE YOU STUPID?
IT'S THE ONLY JUSTICE IN THIS ROTTEN FUCKING WORLD.
HMMM.
YOU THINK THAT'S STRENGTH, DO YOU?
THERE IS A STRENGTH BEYOND STRENGTH, BOY.
BUT IT IS FAR BEYOND THE COMPREHENSION...
...OF LITTLE MEN WHO PLAY AT STICKS AND THINK THEMSELVES LORD OF THE WORLD.
YOU!
!!!
YOU CAN'T BE HERE! IT'S IMPOSSIBLE!
YOU-YOU DISAPPEARED! YOU WERE DEAD!
CLAK
HASN'T STOPPED ME SO FAR.
ZOSS!
HOW CAN I HELP WHITE CHAIN?
SHE'S GOING TO DIE IF I DON'T DO SOMETHING! THERE'S NO WAY SHE CAN WIN THIS FIGHT!
RELINQUISH YOUR FOOLISH DELUSIONS OF CONTROL.
YOU CLING TOO MUCH TO VICTORY.
YOU CANNOT SAVE HER.

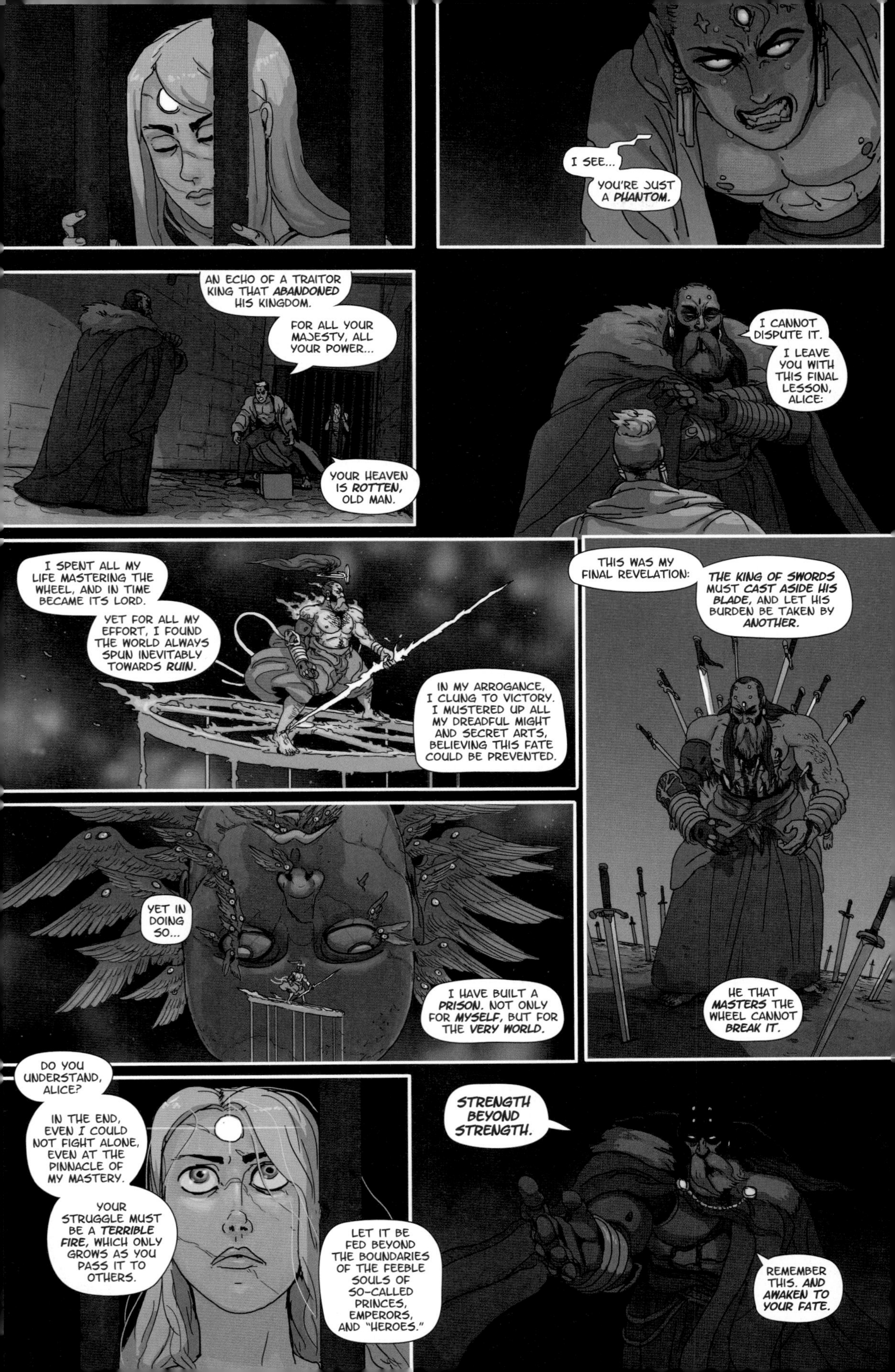
I SEE...
YOU'RE JUST A PHANTOM.
AN ECHO OF A TRAITOR KING THAT ABANDONED HIS KINGDOM.
FOR ALL YOUR MAJESTY, ALL YOUR POWER...
YOUR HEAVEN IS ROTTEN, OLD MAN.
I CANNOT DISPUTE IT.
I LEAVE YOU WITH THIS FINAL LESSON, ALICE:
I SPENT ALL MY LIFE MASTERING THE WHEEL, AND IN TIME BECAME ITS LORD.
YET FOR ALL MY EFFORT, I FOUND THE WORLD ALWAYS SPUN INEVITABLY TOWARDS RUIN.
IN MY ARROGANCE, I CLUNG TO VICTORY. I MUSTERED UP ALL MY DREADFUL MIGHT AND SECRET ARTS, BELIEVING THIS FATE COULD BE PREVENTED.
YET IN DOING SO...
I HAVE BUILT A PRISON. NOT ONLY FOR MYSELF, BUT FOR THE VERY WORLD.
THIS WAS MY FINAL REVELATION:
THE KING OF SWORDS MUST CAST ASIDE HIS BLADE, AND LET HIS BURDEN BE TAKEN BY ANOTHER.
HE THAT MASTERS THE WHEEL CANNOT BREAK IT.
DO YOU UNDERSTAND, ALICE?
IN THE END, EVEN I COULD NOT FIGHT ALONE, EVEN AT THE PINNACLE OF MY MASTERY.
YOUR STRUGGLE MUST BE A TERRIBLE FIRE, WHICH ONLY GROWS AS YOU PASS IT TO OTHERS.
LET IT BE FED BEYOND THE BOUNDARIES OF THE FEEBLE SOULS OF SO-CALLED PRINCES, EMPERORS, AND "HEROES."
STRENGTH BEYOND STRENGTH.
REMEMBER THIS. AND AWAKEN TO YOUR FATE.

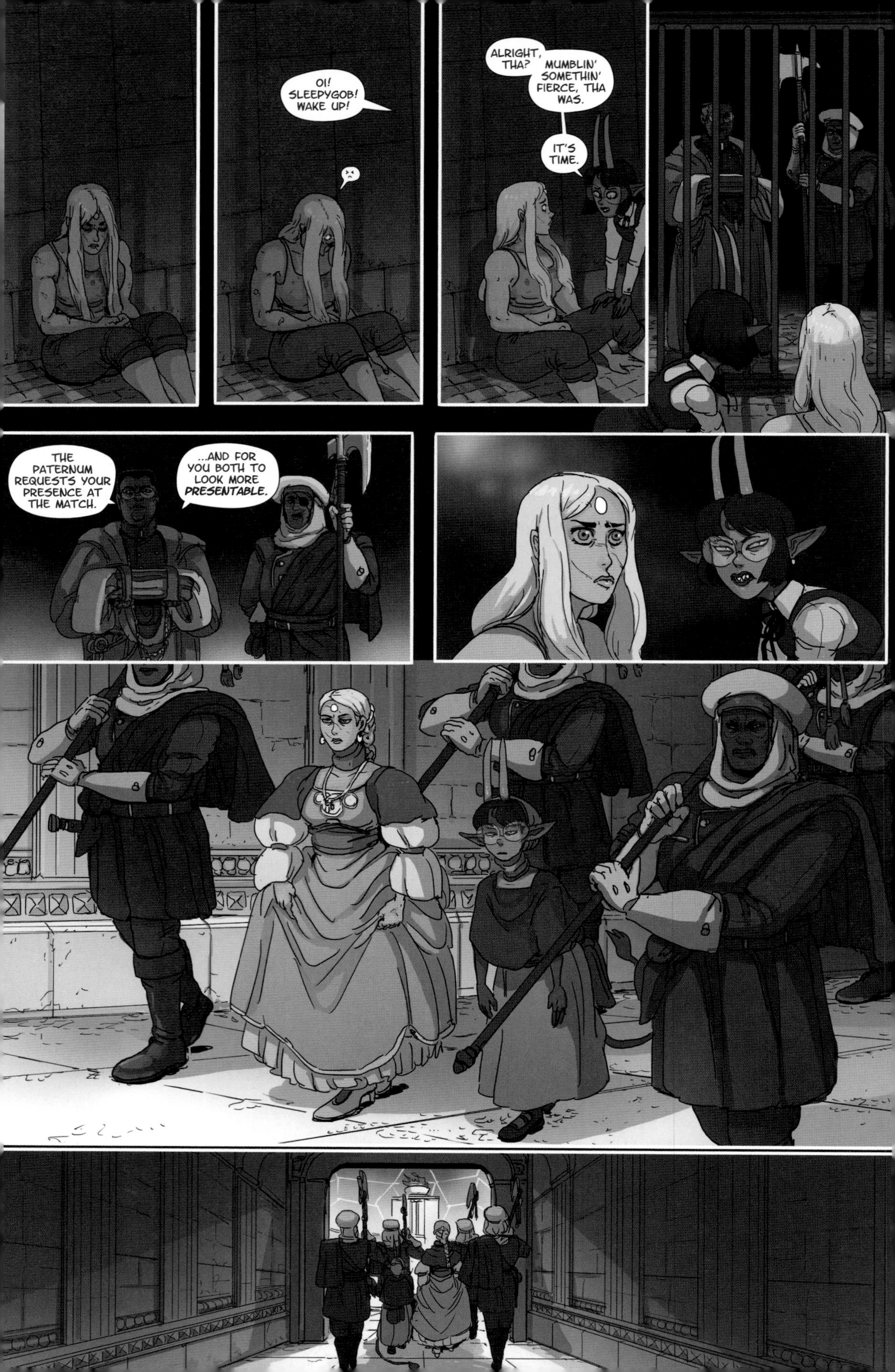
OI! SLEEPYGOB! WAKE UP!
ALRIGHT, THA?
MUMBLIN' SOMETHIN' FIERCE, THA WAS.
IT'S TIME.
THE PATERNUM REQUESTS YOUR PRESENCE AT THE MATCH.
...AND FOR YOU BOTH TO LOOK MORE PRESENTABLE.

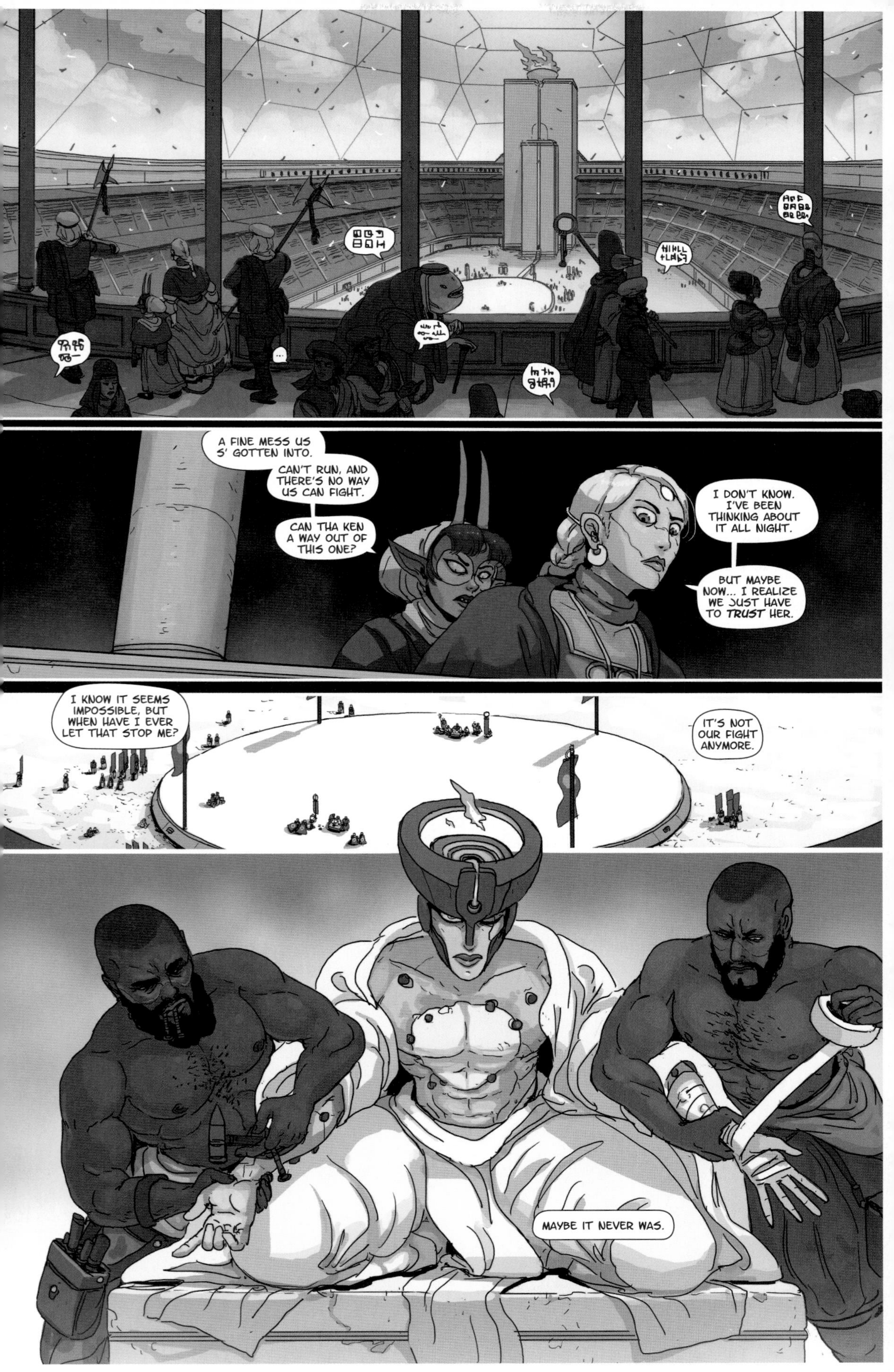
...
A FINE MESS US S' GOTTEN INTO.
CAN'T RUN, AND THERE'S NO WAY US CAN FIGHT.
CAN THA KEN A WAY OUT OF THIS ONE?
I DON'T KNOW. I'VE BEEN THINKING ABOUT IT ALL NIGHT.
BUT MAYBE NOW... I REALIZE WE JUST HAVE TO *TRUST* HER.
I KNOW IT SEEMS IMPOSSIBLE, BUT WHEN HAVE I EVER LET THAT STOP ME?
IT'S NOT OUR FIGHT ANYMORE.
MAYBE IT NEVER WAS.

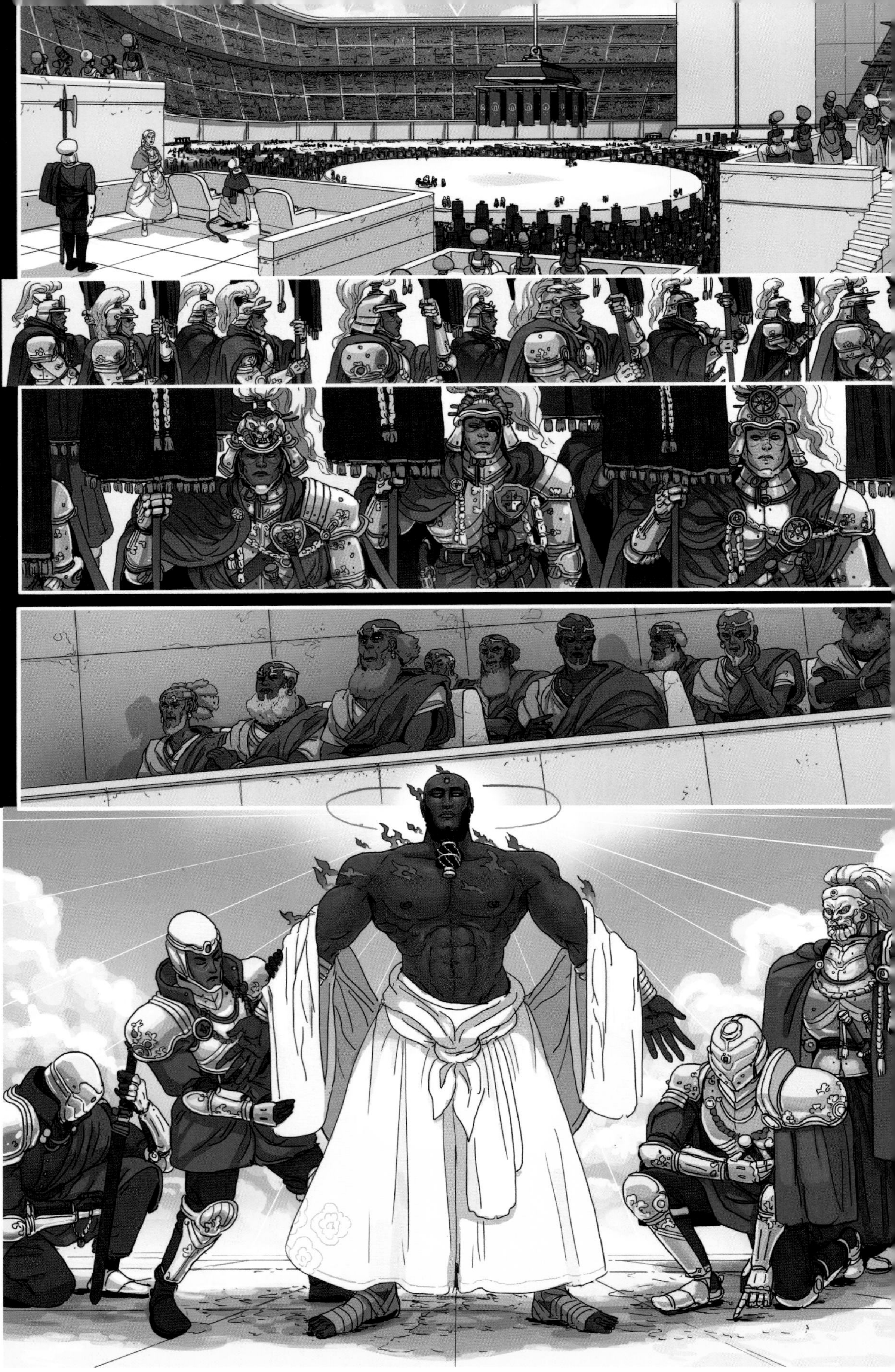

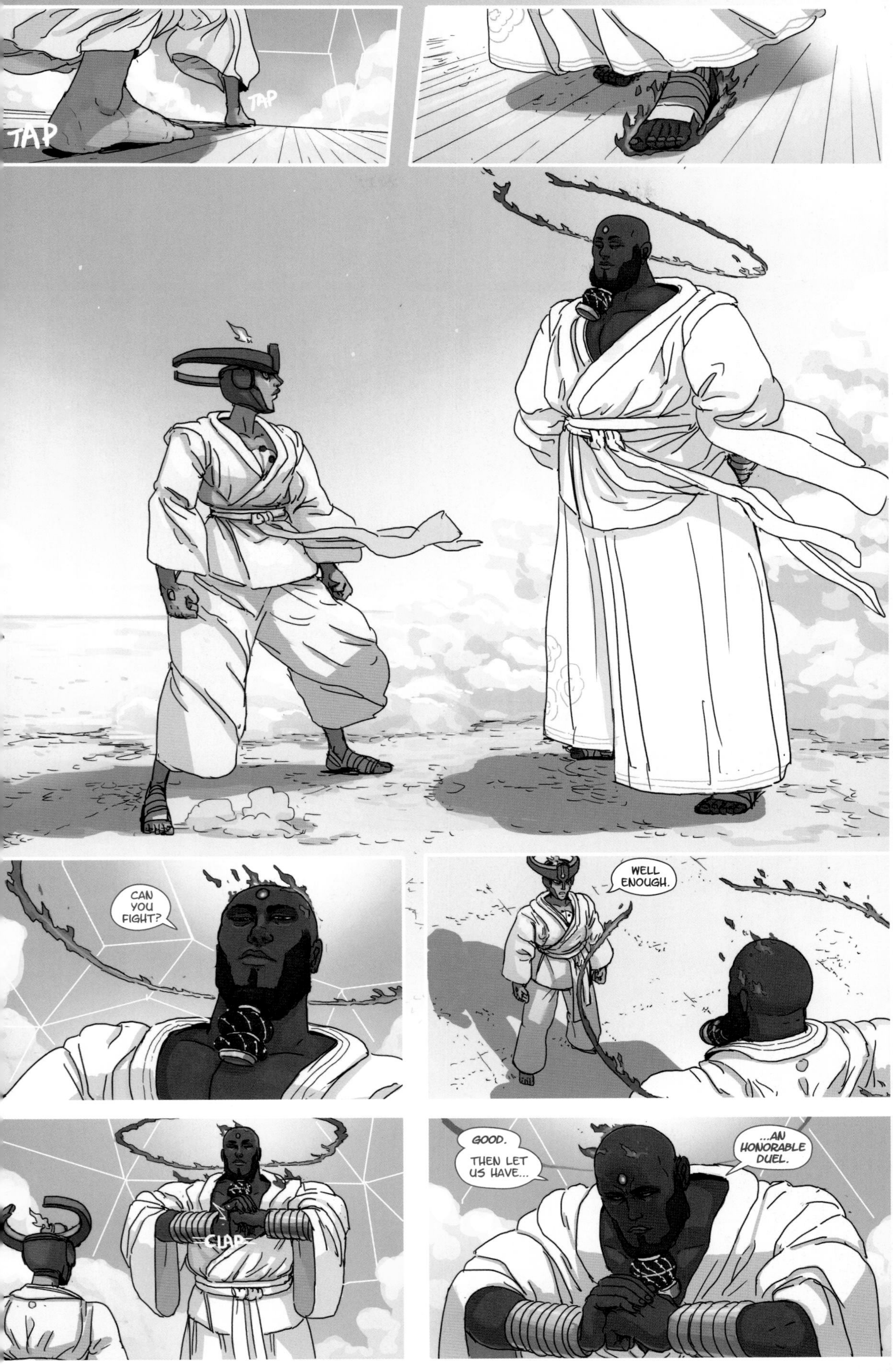
TAP
TAP
CAN YOU FIGHT?
WELL ENOUGH.
CLAP
GOOD.
THEN LET US HAVE...
...AN HONORABLE DUEL.

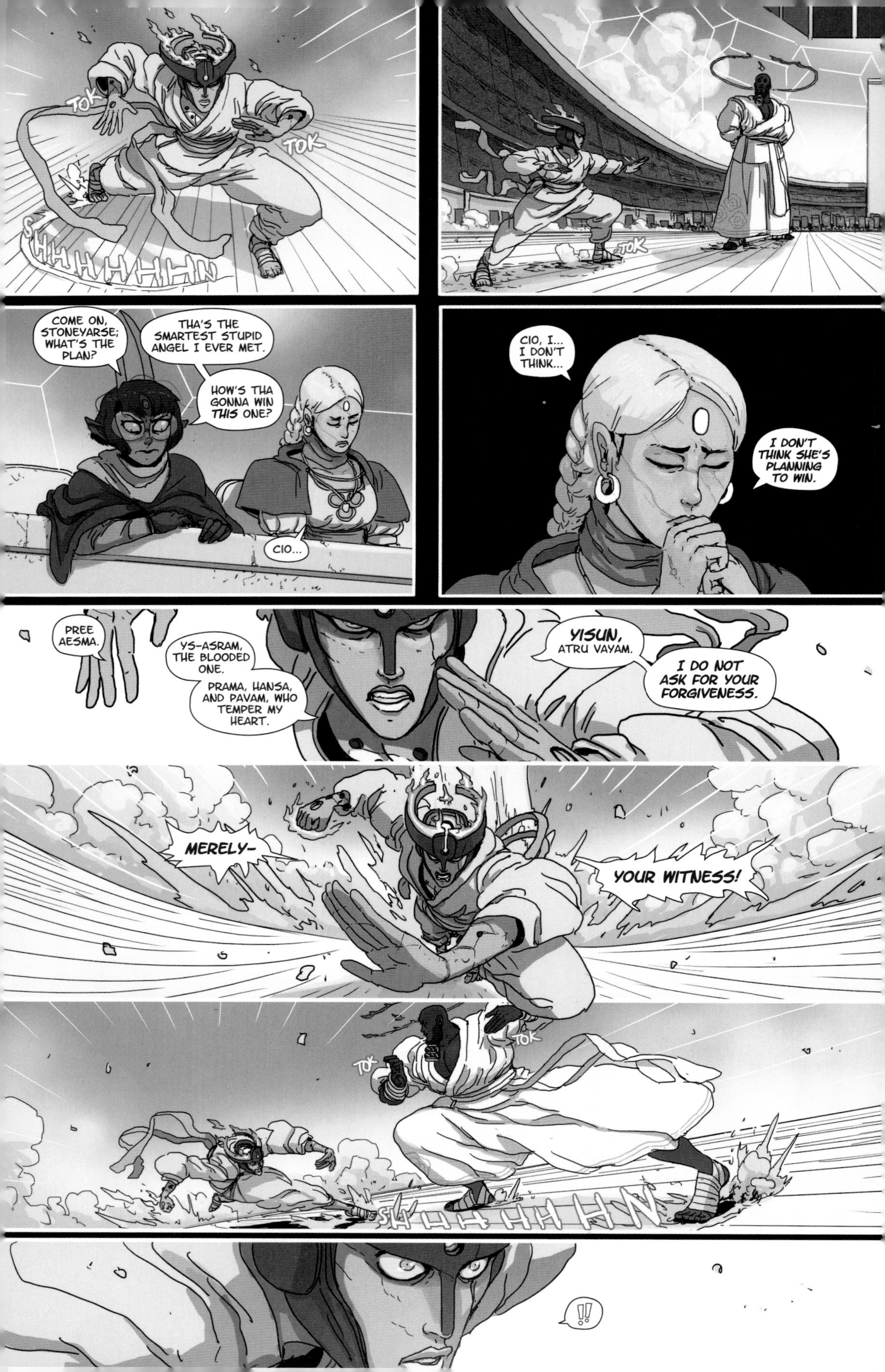
TOK
TOK
SHHHHHHHN
TOK
COME ON, STONEYARSE; WHAT'S THE PLAN?
THA'S THE SMARTEST STUPID ANGEL I EVER MET.
HOW'S THA GONNA WIN THIS ONE?
CIO...
CIO, I... I DON'T THINK...
I DON'T THINK SHE'S PLANNING TO WIN.
PREE AESMA.
YS-ASRAM, THE BLOODED ONE.
PRAMA, HANSA, AND PAVAM, WHO TEMPER MY HEART.
YISUN, ATRU VAYAM.
I DO NOT ASK FOR YOUR FORGIVENESS.
MERELY-
YOUR WITNESS!
TOK
TOK
SHHHHHHN
!!

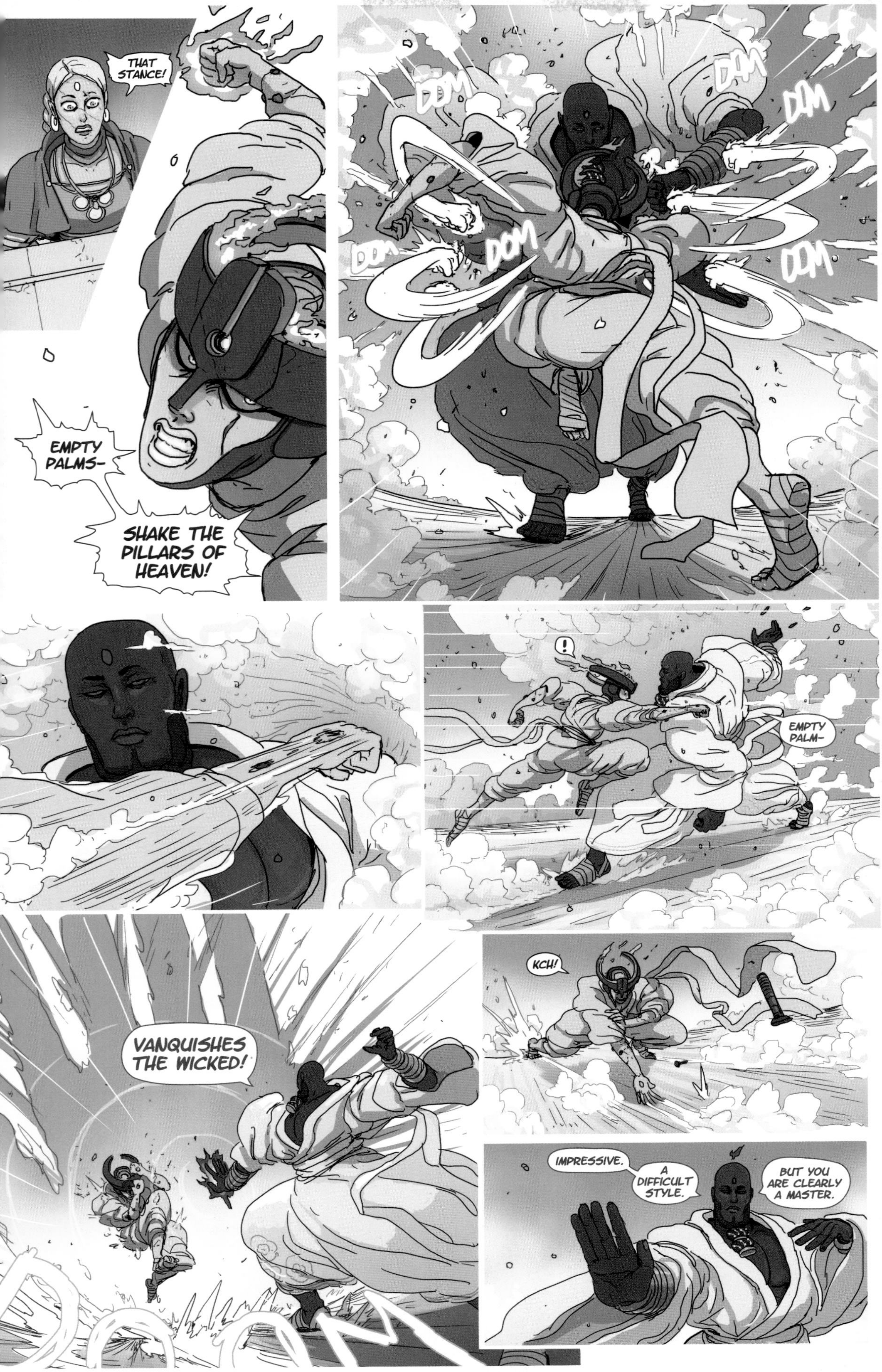
THAT STANCE!
EMPTY PALMS-
SHAKE THE PILLARS OF HEAVEN!
DOM
DOM
DOM
DOM
DOM
DOM
!
EMPTY PALM-
VANQUISHES THE WICKED!
DOOM
KCH!
IMPRESSIVE.
A DIFFICULT STYLE.
BUT YOU ARE CLEARLY A MASTER.

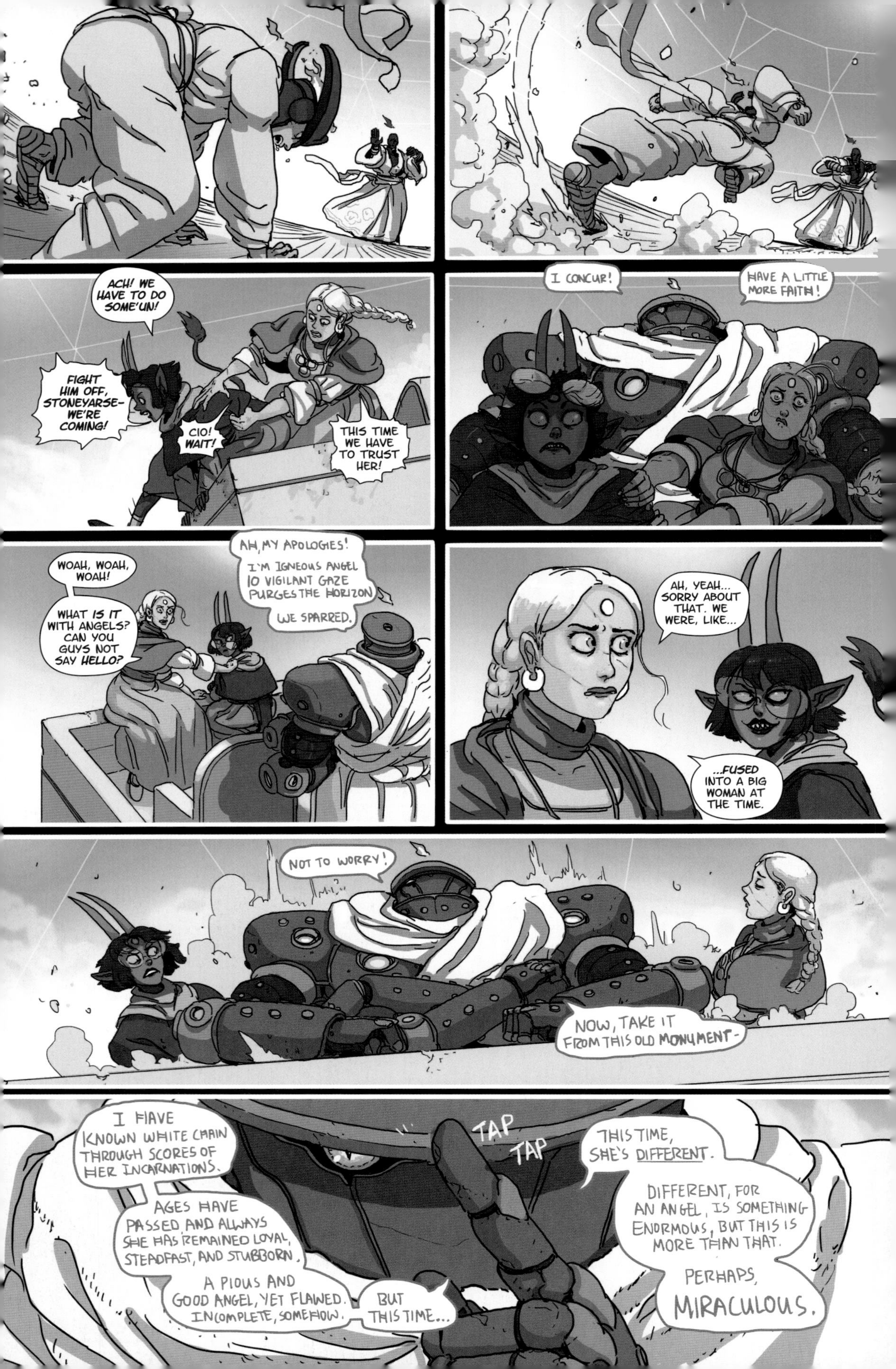
ACH! WE HAVE TO DO SOME'UN!
FIGHT HIM OFF, STONEYARSE- WE'RE COMING!
CIO! WAIT!
THIS TIME WE HAVE TO TRUST HER!
I CONCUR!
HAVE A LITTLE MORE FAITH!
WOAH, WOAH, WOAH!
WHAT IS IT WITH ANGELS? CAN YOU GUYS NOT SAY HELLO?
AH, MY APOLOGIES!
I'M IGNEOUS ANGEL 10 VIGILANT GAZE PURGES THE HORIZON
WE SPARRED.
AH, YEAH... SORRY ABOUT THAT. WE WERE, LIKE...
...FUSED INTO A BIG WOMAN AT THE TIME.
NOT TO WORRY!
NOW, TAKE IT FROM THIS OLD MONUMENT-
I HAVE KNOWN WHITE CHAIN THROUGH SCORES OF HER INCARNATIONS.
AGES HAVE PASSED AND ALWAYS SHE HAS REMAINED LOYAL, STEADFAST, AND STUBBORN.
A PIOUS AND GOOD ANGEL, YET FLAWED. INCOMPLETE, SOMEHOW.
BUT THIS TIME...
TAP
TAP
THIS TIME, SHE'S DIFFERENT.
DIFFERENT, FOR AN ANGEL, IS SOMETHING ENORMOUS, BUT THIS IS MORE THAN THAT.
PERHAPS, MIRACULOUS.

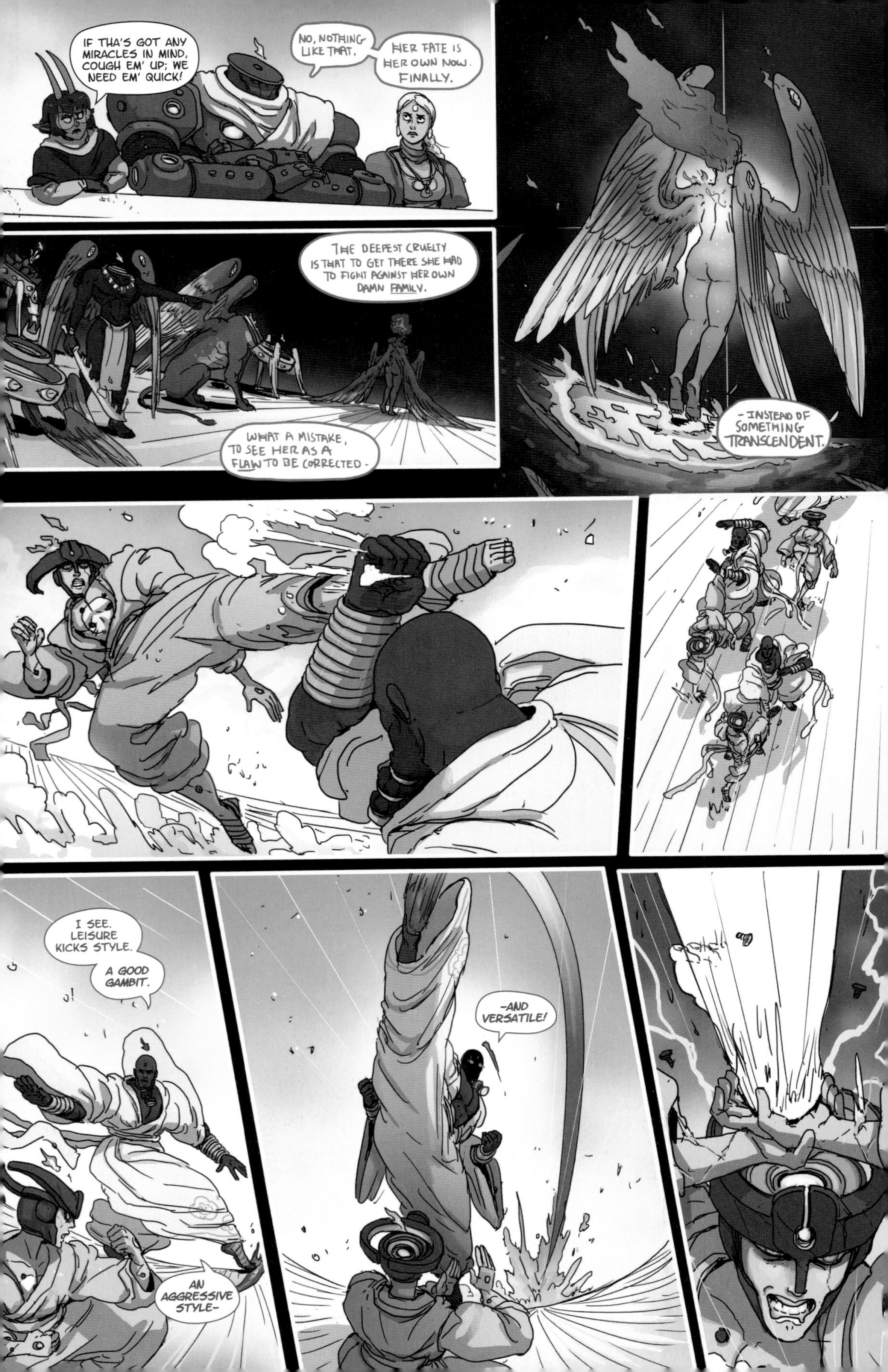
IF THA'S GOT ANY MIRACLES IN MIND, COUGH EM' UP; WE NEED EM' QUICK!
NO, NOTHING LIKE THAT.
HER FATE IS HER OWN NOW. FINALLY.
THE DEEPEST CRUELTY IS THAT TO GET THERE SHE HAD TO FIGHT AGAINST HER OWN DAMN FAMILY.
WHAT A MISTAKE, TO SEE HER AS A FLAW TO BE CORRECTED-
-INSTEAD OF SOMETHING TRANSCENDENT.
I SEE. LEISURE KICKS STYLE.
A GOOD GAMBIT.
AN AGGRESSIVE STYLE-
-AND VERSATILE!

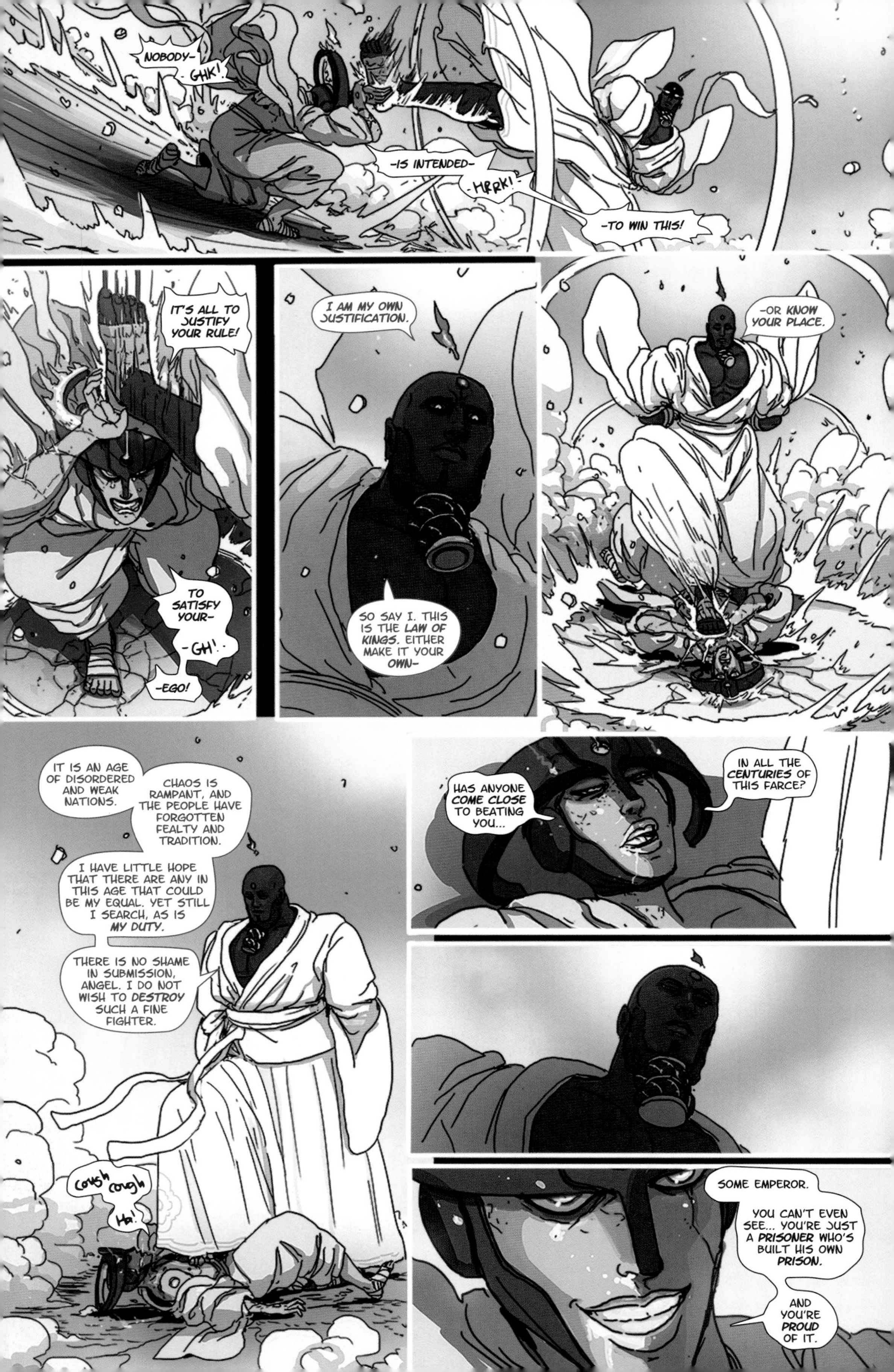
NOBODY-
-GHK!
-IS INTENDED-
-HRRK!-
-TO WIN THIS!
IT'S ALL TO JUSTIFY YOUR RULE!
TO SATISFY YOUR-
-GH!
-EGO!
I AM MY OWN JUSTIFICATION.
SO SAY I. THIS IS THE LAW OF KINGS. EITHER MAKE IT YOUR OWN-
-OR KNOW YOUR PLACE.
IT IS AN AGE OF DISORDERED AND WEAK NATIONS.
CHAOS IS RAMPANT, AND THE PEOPLE HAVE FORGOTTEN FEALTY AND TRADITION.
I HAVE LITTLE HOPE THAT THERE ARE ANY IN THIS AGE THAT COULD BE MY EQUAL. YET STILL I SEARCH, AS IS MY DUTY.
THERE IS NO SHAME IN SUBMISSION, ANGEL. I DO NOT WISH TO DESTROY SUCH A FINE FIGHTER.
cough cough
Ha!
HAS ANYONE COME CLOSE TO BEATING YOU...
IN ALL THE CENTURIES OF THIS FARCE?
SOME EMPEROR.
YOU CAN'T EVEN SEE... YOU'RE JUST A PRISONER WHO'S BUILT HIS OWN PRISON.
AND YOU'RE PROUD OF IT.

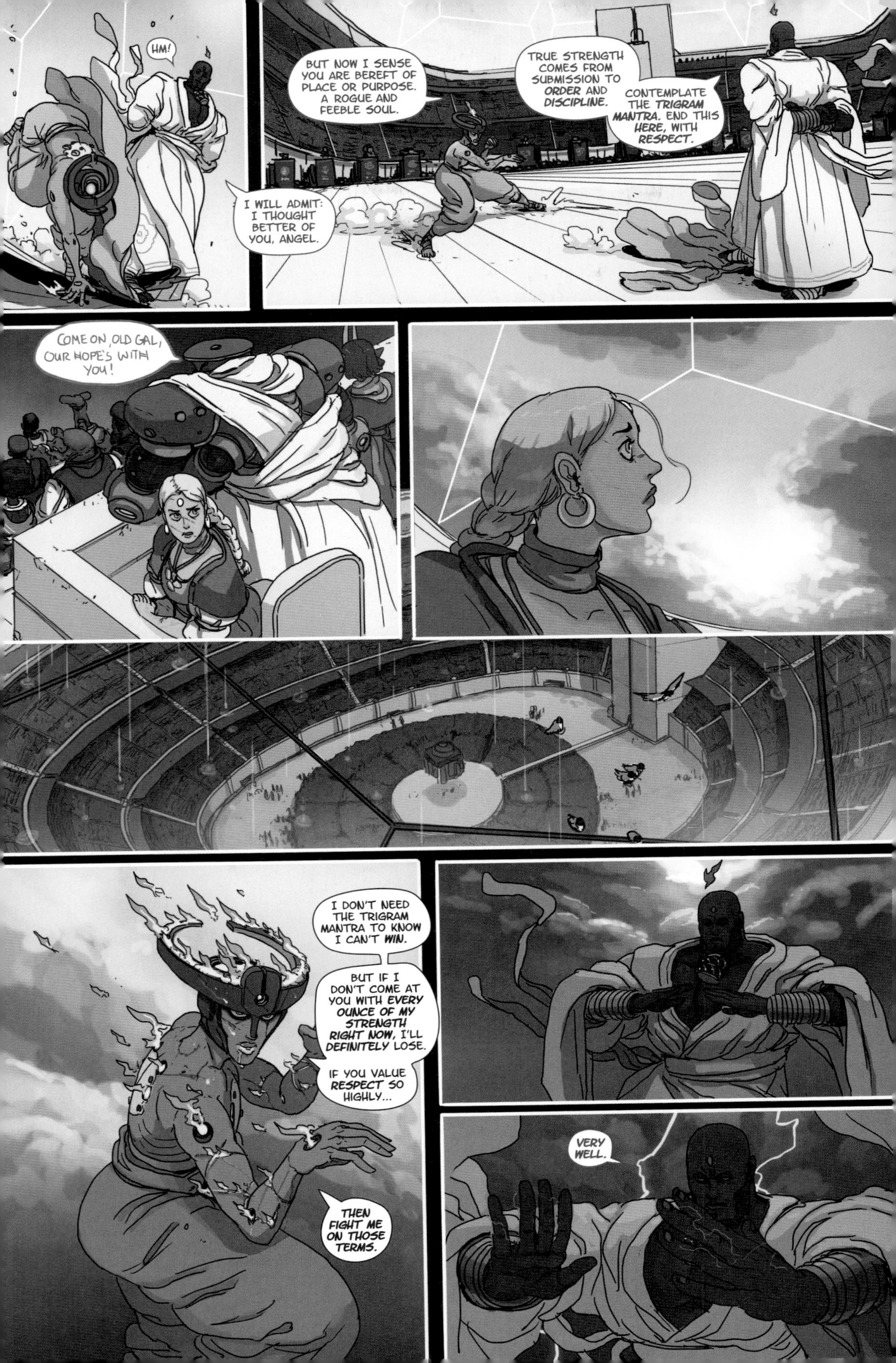
HM!
BUT NOW I SENSE YOU ARE BEREFT OF PLACE OR PURPOSE. A ROGUE AND FEEBLE SOUL.
TRUE STRENGTH COMES FROM SUBMISSION TO ORDER AND DISCIPLINE.
CONTEMPLATE THE TRIGRAM MANTRA. END THIS HERE, WITH RESPECT.
I WILL ADMIT: I THOUGHT BETTER OF YOU, ANGEL.
COME ON, OLD GAL, OUR HOPE'S WITH YOU!
I DON'T NEED THE TRIGRAM MANTRA TO KNOW I CAN'T WIN.
BUT IF I DON'T COME AT YOU WITH EVERY OUNCE OF MY STRENGTH RIGHT NOW, I'LL DEFINITELY LOSE.
IF YOU VALUE RESPECT SO HIGHLY...
THEN FIGHT ME ON THOSE TERMS.
VERY WELL.

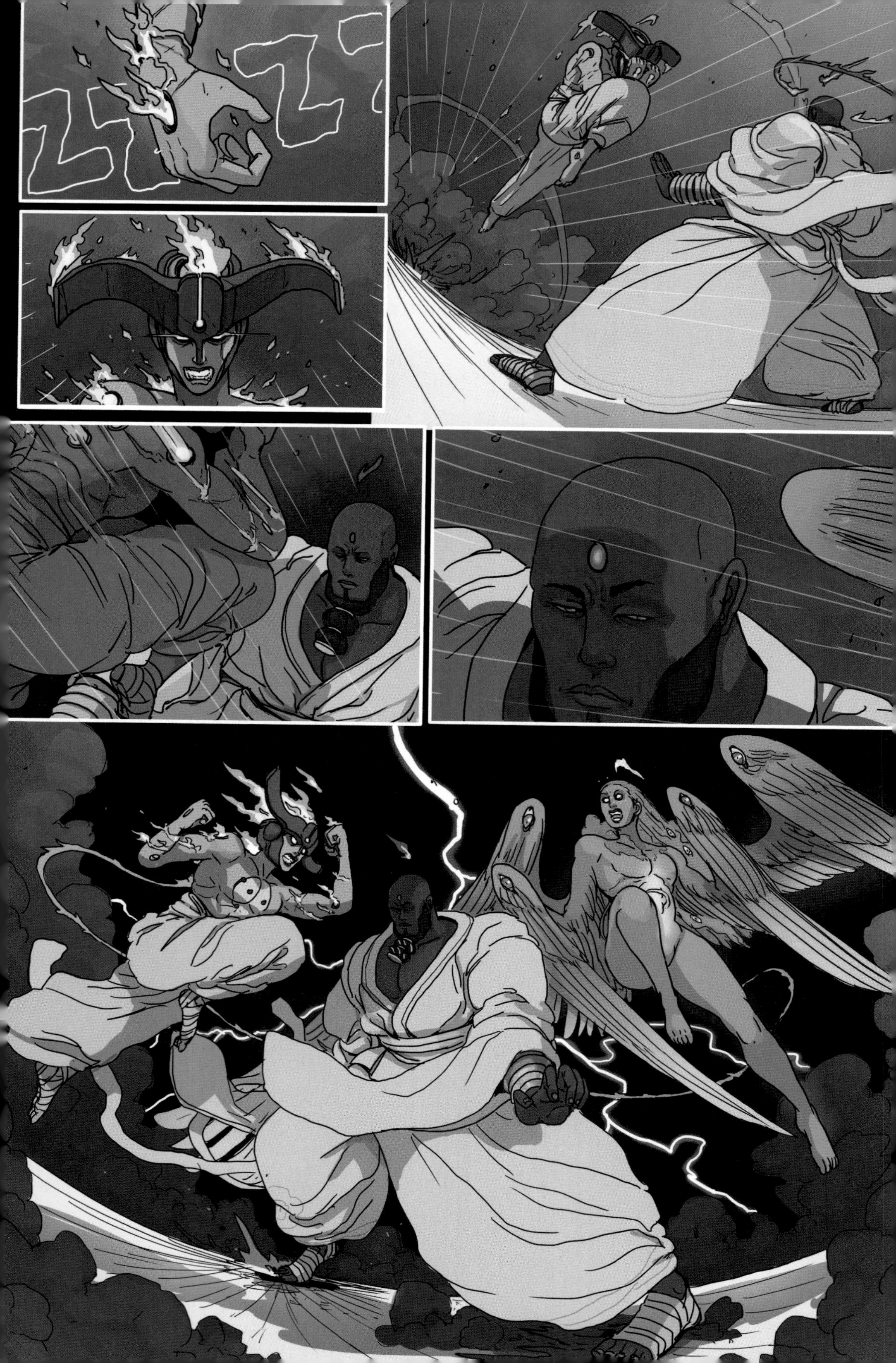

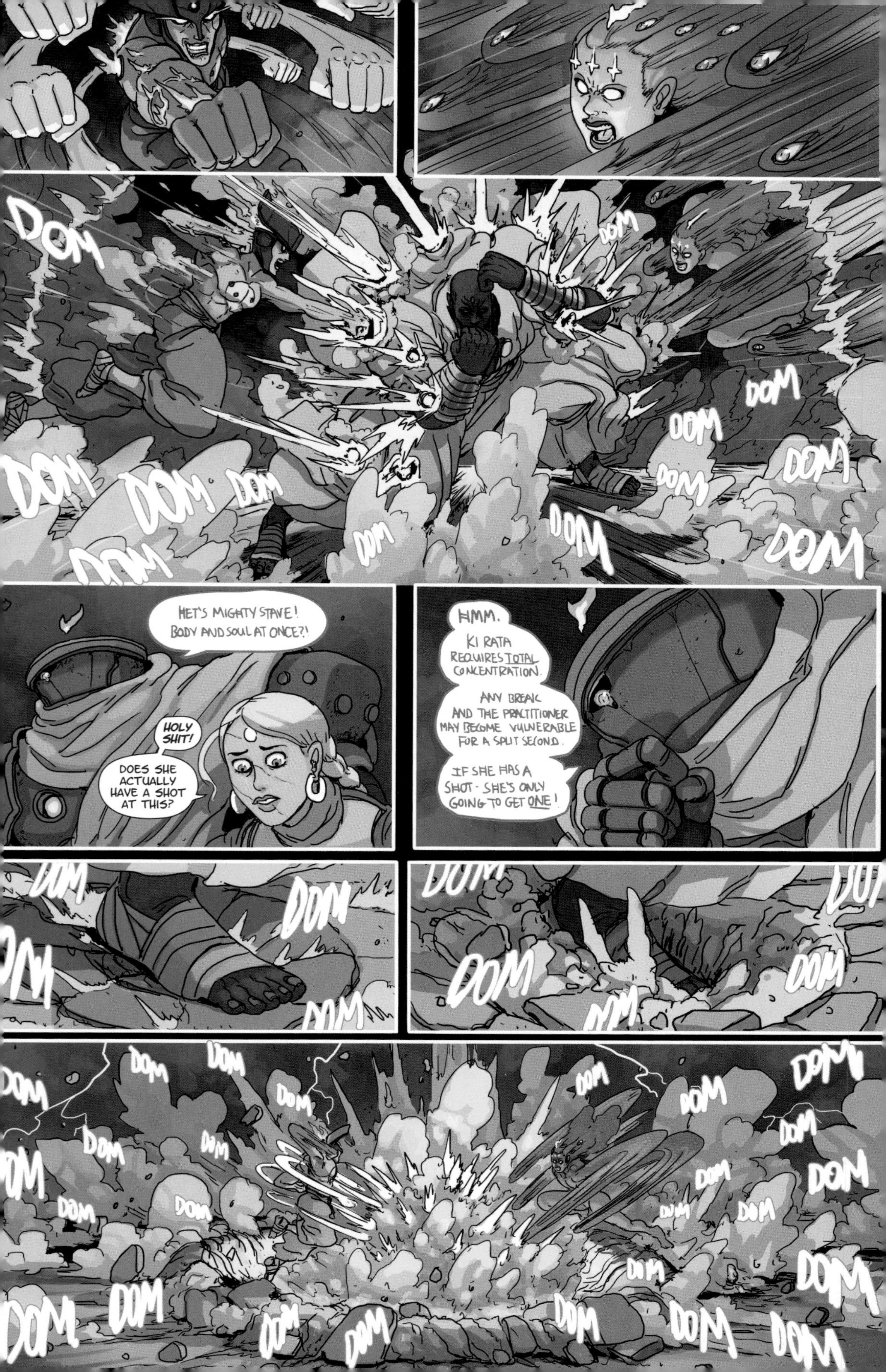
DOM
DOM
DOM
DOM
DOM
DOM
HET'S MIGHTY STAVE! BODY AND SOUL AT ONCE?!
HOLY SHIT!
DOES SHE ACTUALLY HAVE A SHOT AT THIS?
HMM.
KI RATA REQUIRES TOTAL CONCENTRATION.
ANY BREAK AND THE PRACTITIONER MAY BECOME VULNERABLE FOR A SPLIT SECOND.
IF SHE HAS A SHOT - SHE'S ONLY GOING TO GET ONE!
DOM
DOM
DOM
DOM
DOM
DOM

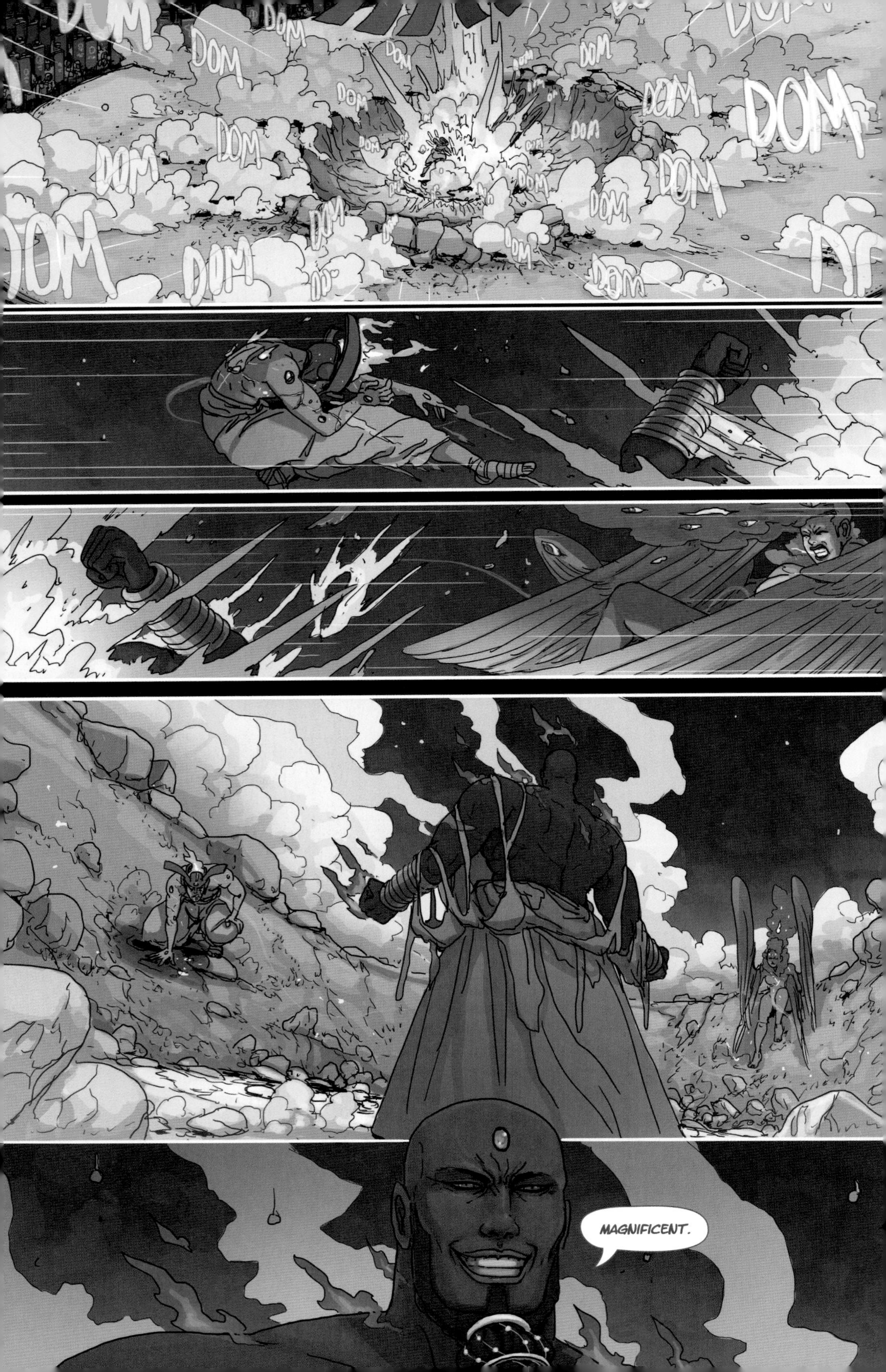

DOM
DOM
DOM
DOM
DOM
DOM
DOM
DOM
DOM
DOM
DOM
MAGNIFICENT.

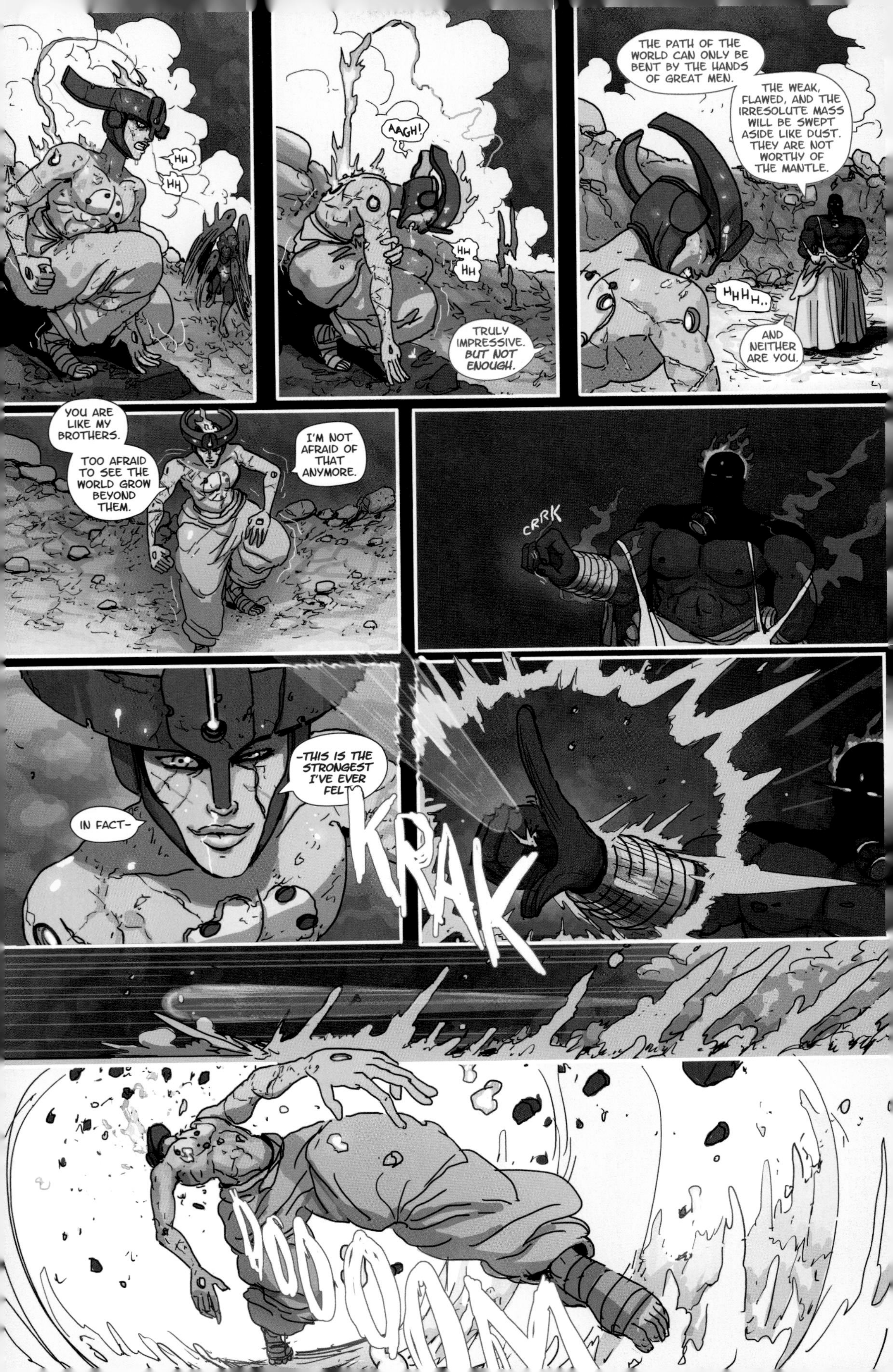
HH
HH
AAGH!
HH
HH
TRULY IMPRESSIVE. BUT NOT ENOUGH.
THE PATH OF THE WORLD CAN ONLY BE BENT BY THE HANDS OF GREAT MEN.
THE WEAK, FLAWED, AND THE IRRESOLUTE MASS WILL BE SWEPT ASIDE LIKE DUST. THEY ARE NOT WORTHY OF THE MANTLE.
HHHH..
AND NEITHER ARE YOU.
YOU ARE LIKE MY BROTHERS.
TOO AFRAID TO SEE THE WORLD GROW BEYOND THEM.
I'M NOT AFRAID OF THAT ANYMORE.
CRRK
IN FACT-
-THIS IS THE STRONGEST I'VE EVER FELT.
KRAK
DOOOOOM

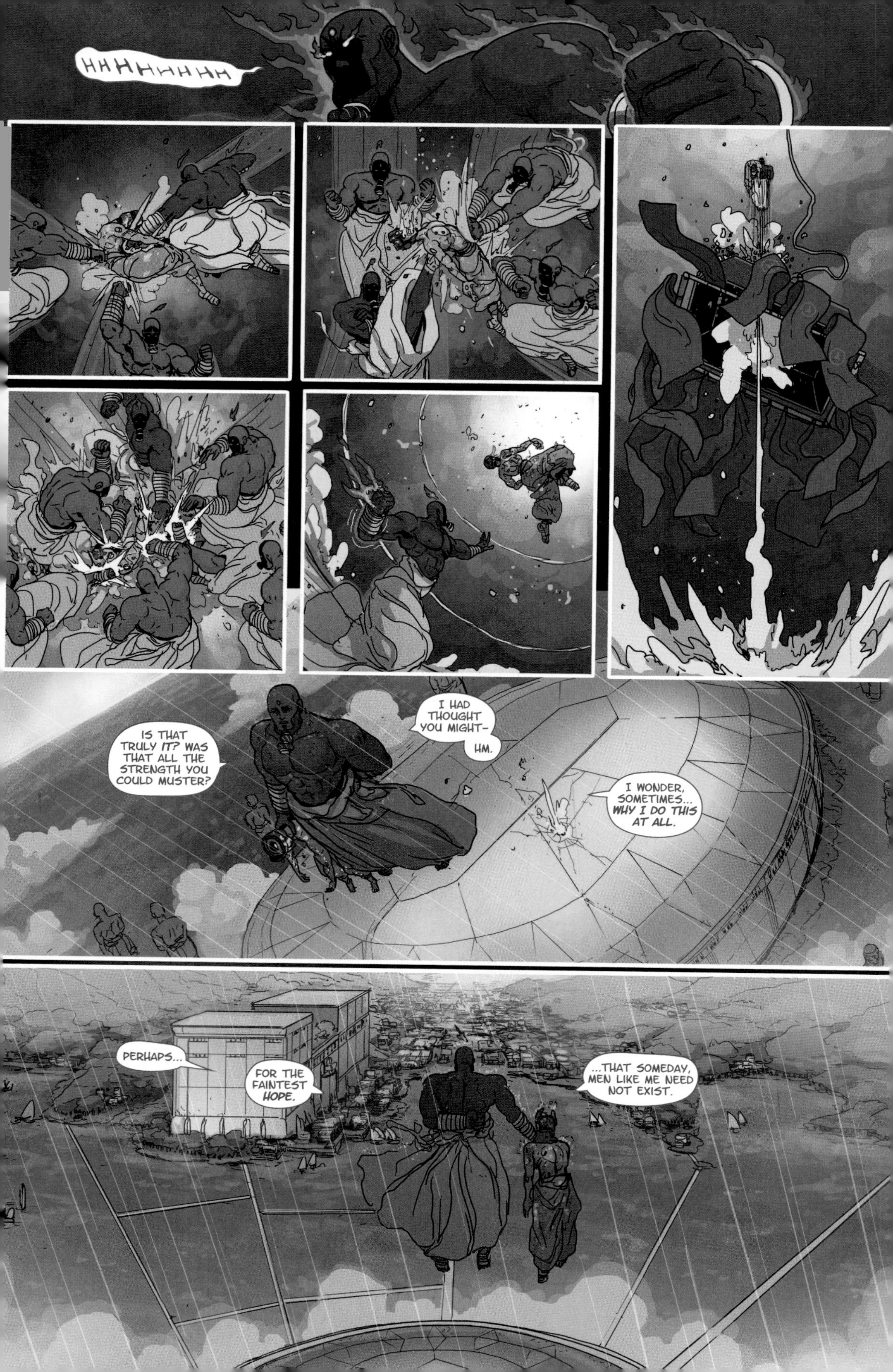
HHHHHHHH
IS THAT TRULY *IT*? WAS THAT ALL THE STRENGTH YOU COULD MUSTER?
I HAD THOUGHT YOU MIGHT-
HM.
I WONDER, SOMETIMES... ***WHY*** I DO THIS AT ALL.
PERHAPS...
FOR THE FAINTEST ***HOPE.***
...THAT SOMEDAY, MEN LIKE ME NEED NOT EXIST.

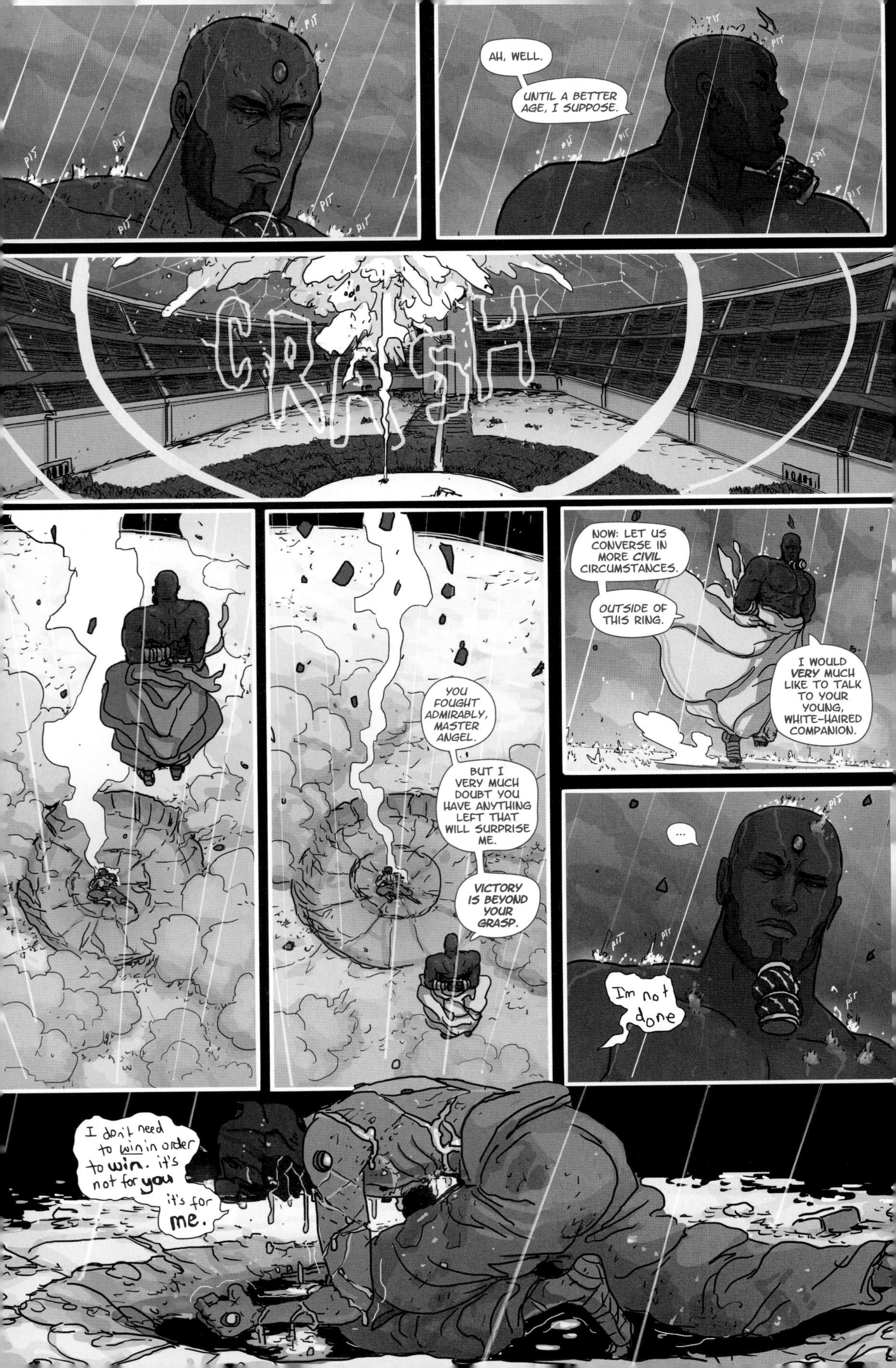
PIT
AH, WELL.
UNTIL A BETTER AGE, I SUPPOSE.
CRASH
YOU FOUGHT ADMIRABLY, MASTER ANGEL.
BUT I VERY MUCH DOUBT YOU HAVE ANYTHING LEFT THAT WILL SURPRISE ME.
VICTORY IS BEYOND YOUR GRASP.
NOW: LET US CONVERSE IN MORE CIVIL CIRCUMSTANCES.
OUTSIDE OF THIS RING.
I WOULD VERY MUCH LIKE TO TALK TO YOUR YOUNG, WHITE-HAIRED COMPANION.
...
I'm not done
I don't need to win in order to win. it's not for you it's for me.

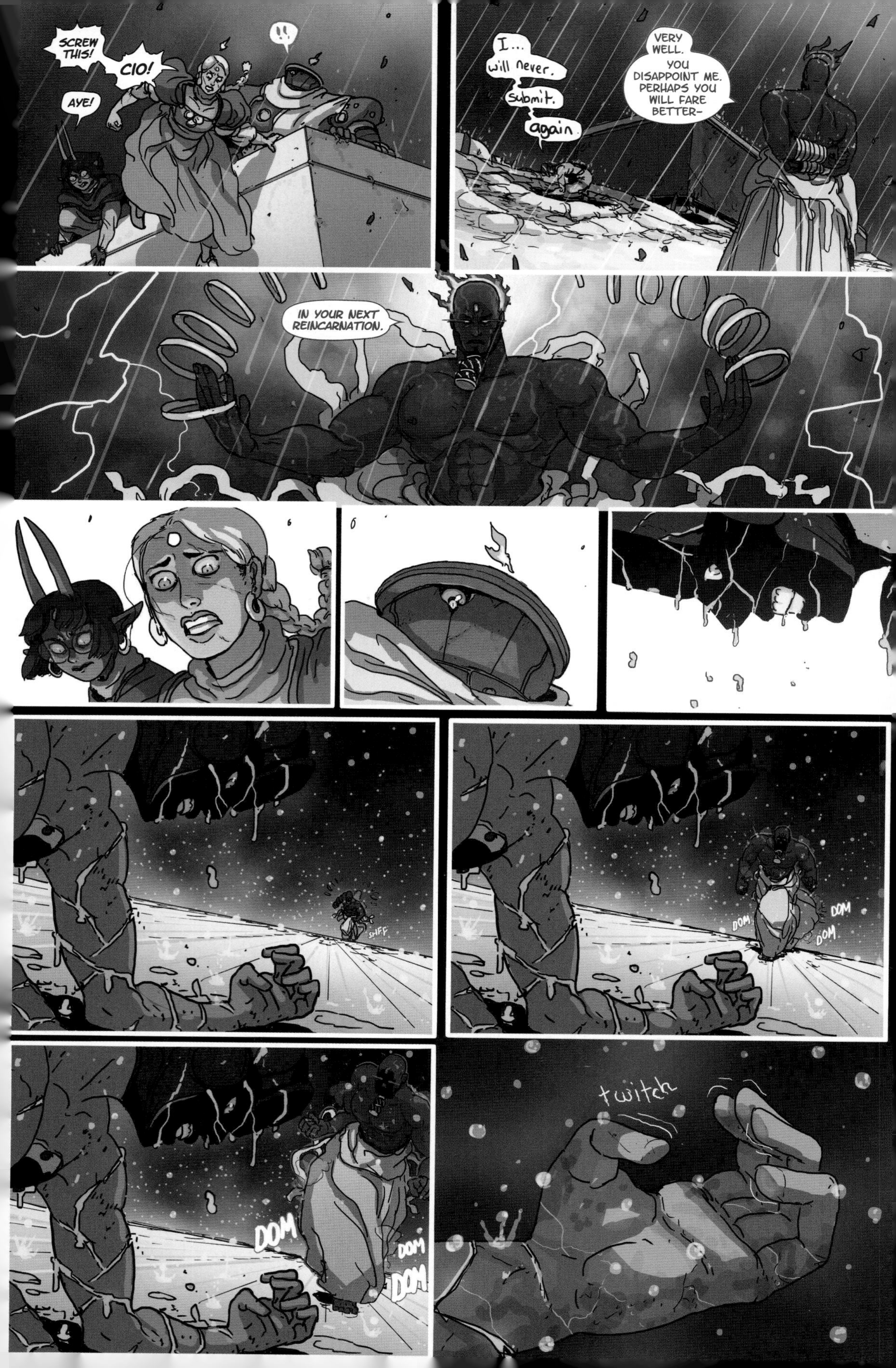
SCREW THIS!
CIO!
!!
AYE!
I... will never. submit. again.
VERY WELL. YOU DISAPPOINT ME. PERHAPS YOU WILL FARE BETTER-
IN YOUR NEXT REINCARNATION.
SHFF
DOM
DOM
DOM
DOM
DOM
DOM
twitch

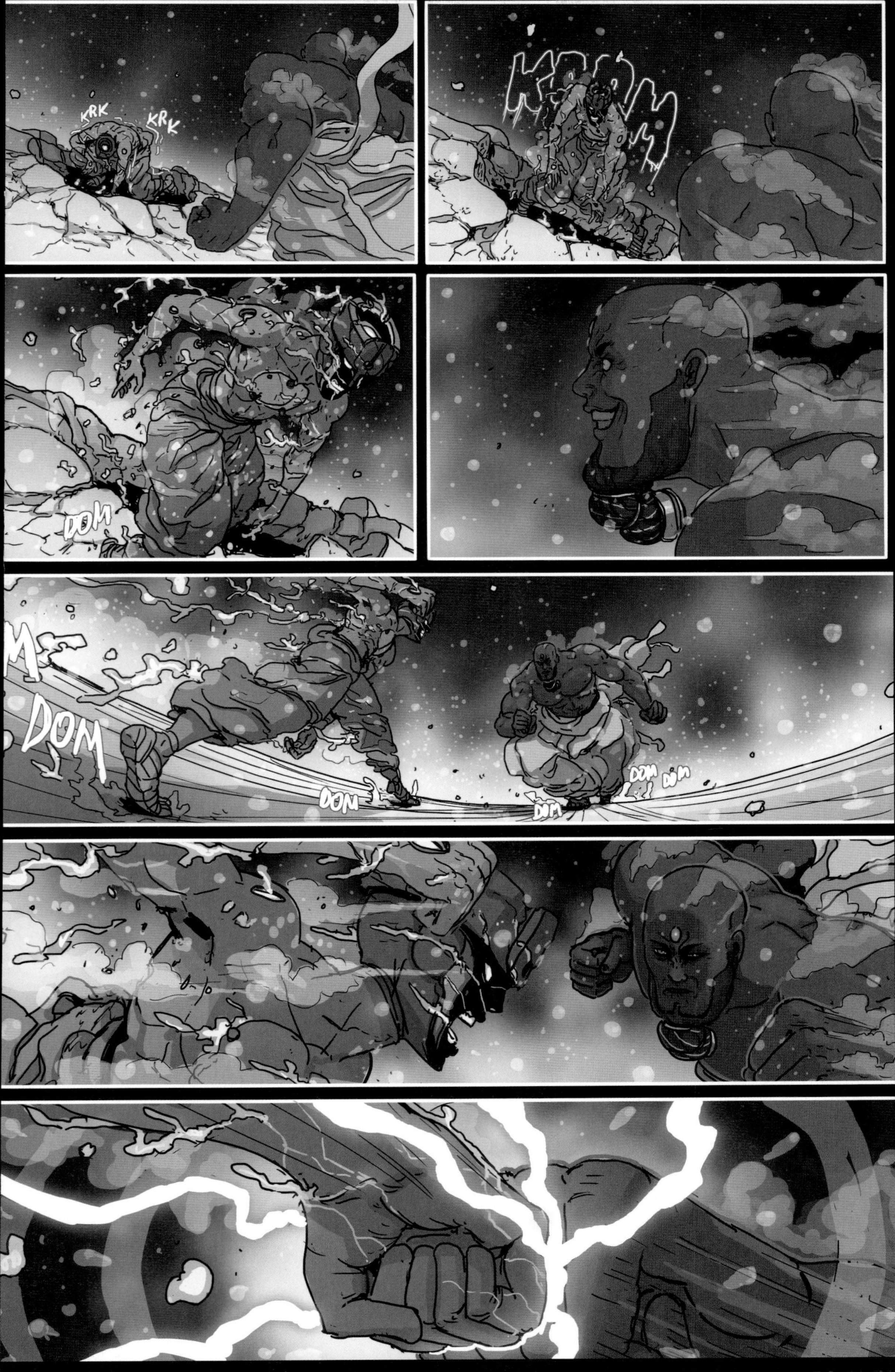
KRK
KRK
KROOM
DOM
M
DOM
DOM
DOM
DOM
DOM

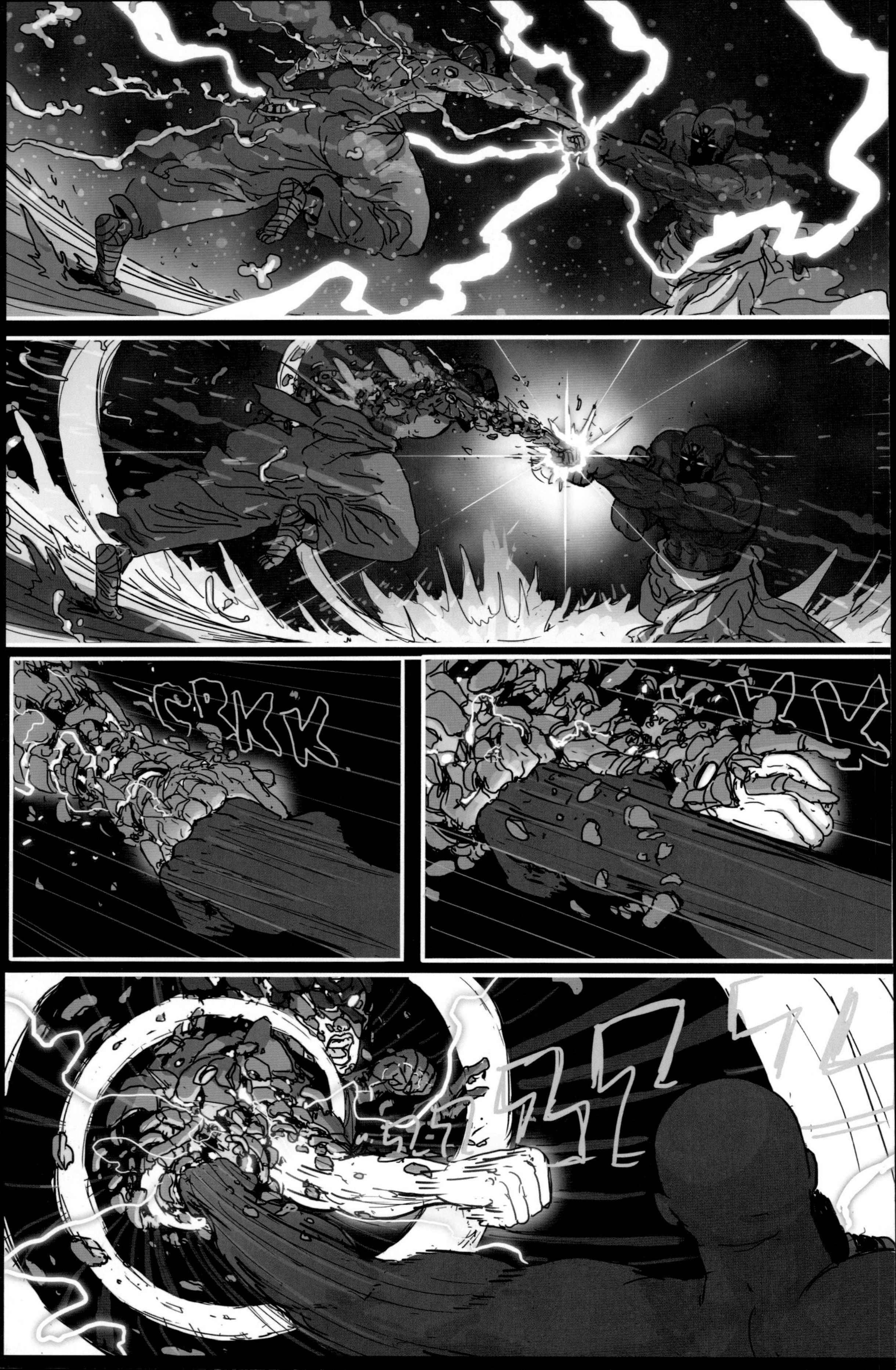
CRKK

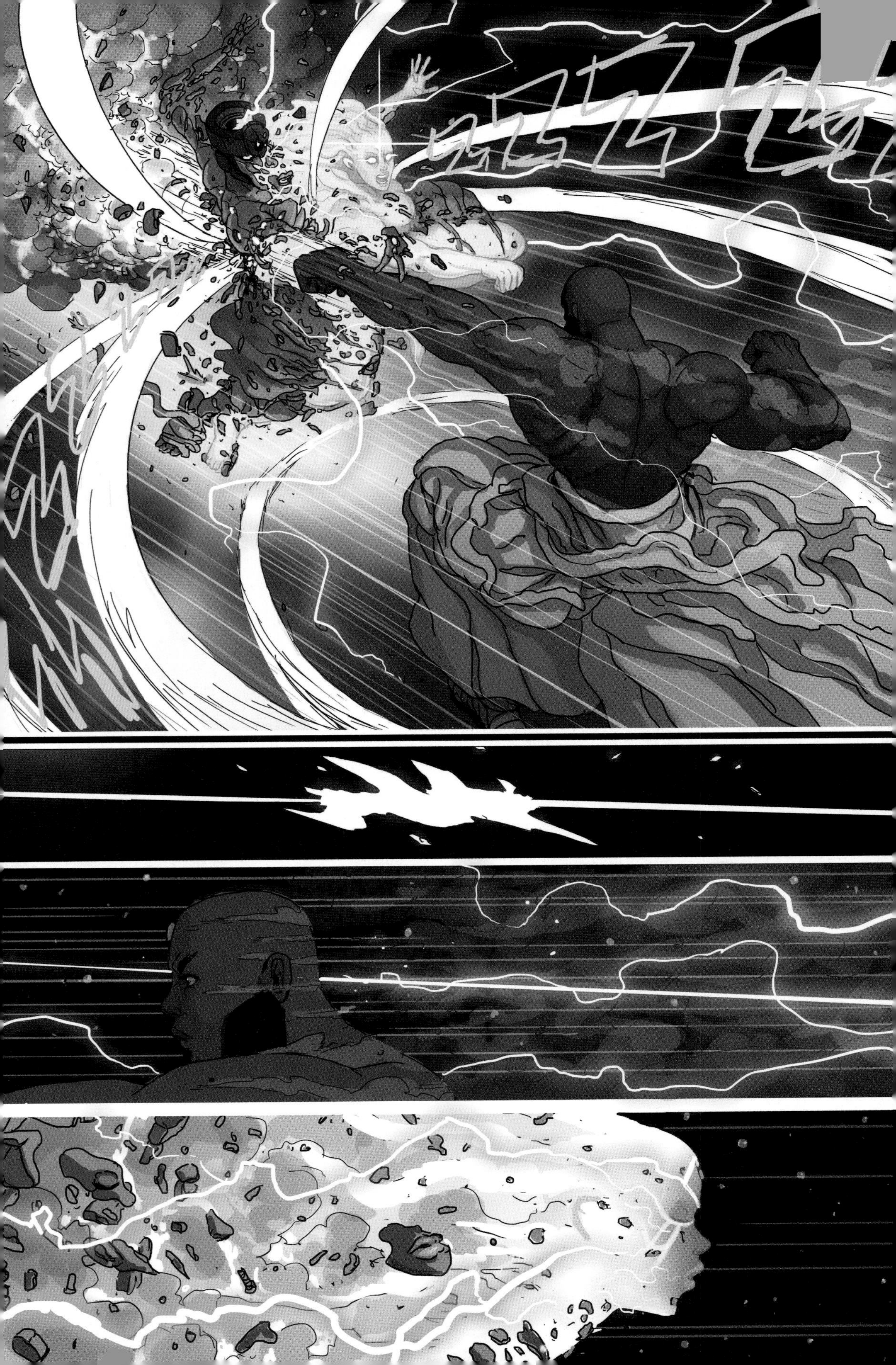

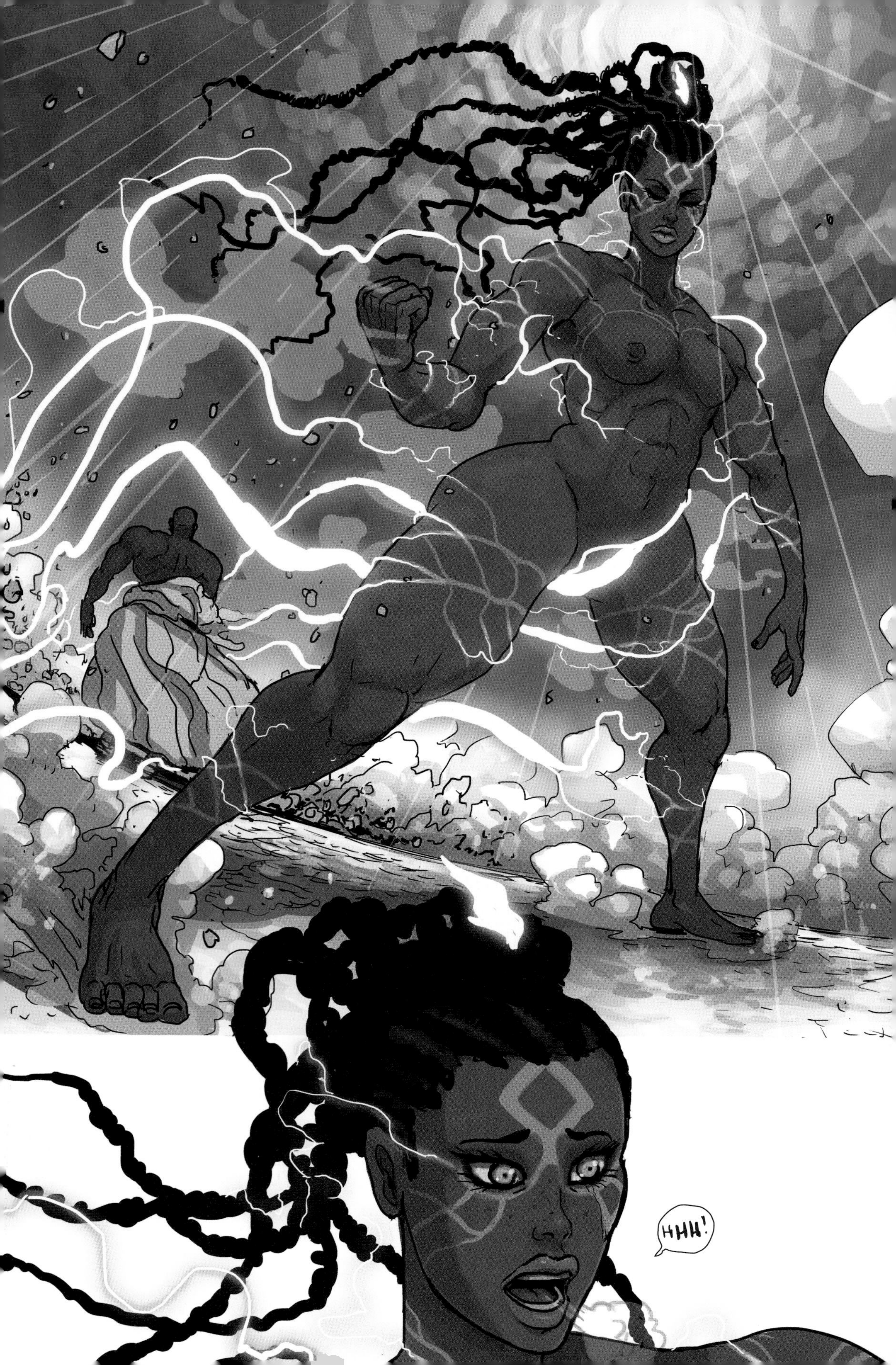
HHH!

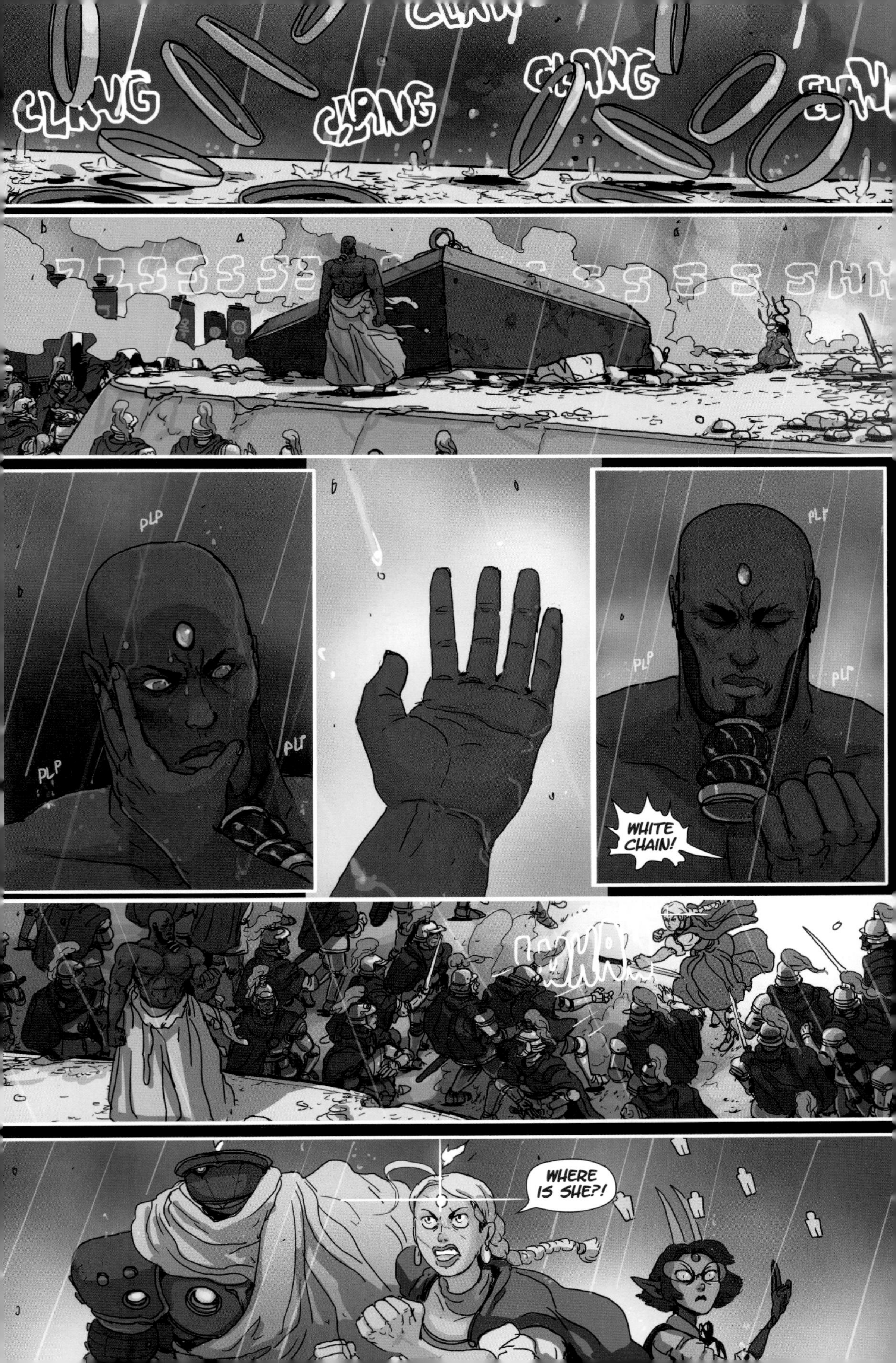
CLANG
CLANG
CLANG
ZSSSSSH
PLP
PLP
PLP
PLP
PLP
PLP
WHITE CHAIN!
WHERE IS SHE?!

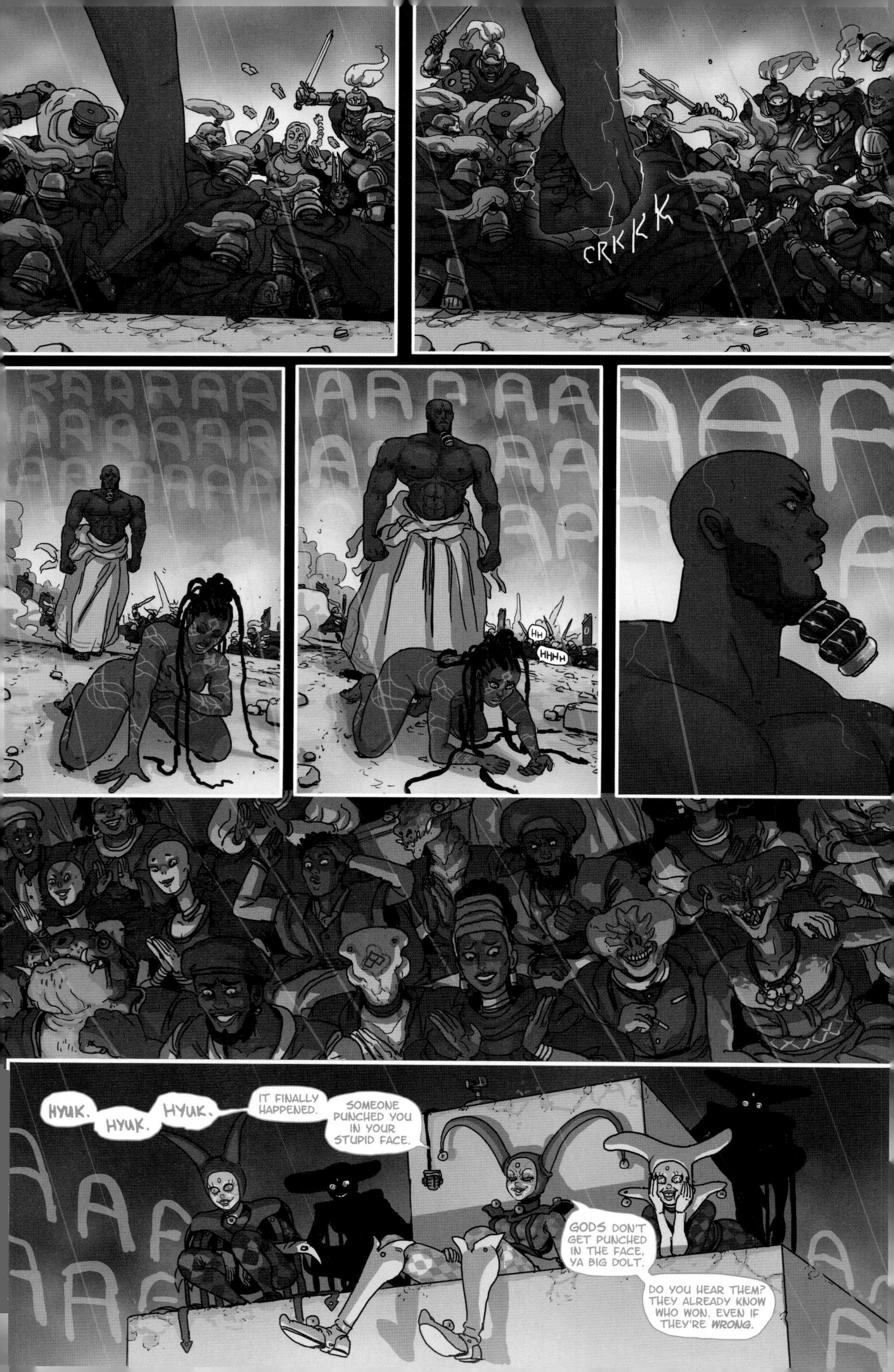
CRKKK
HH
HHHH
HYUK.
HYUK.
HYUK.
IT FINALLY HAPPENED.
SOMEONE PUNCHED YOU IN YOUR STUPID FACE.
GODS DON'T GET PUNCHED IN THE FACE, YA BIG DOLT.
DO YOU HEAR THEM? THEY ALREADY KNOW WHO WON. EVEN IF THEY'RE *WRONG*.

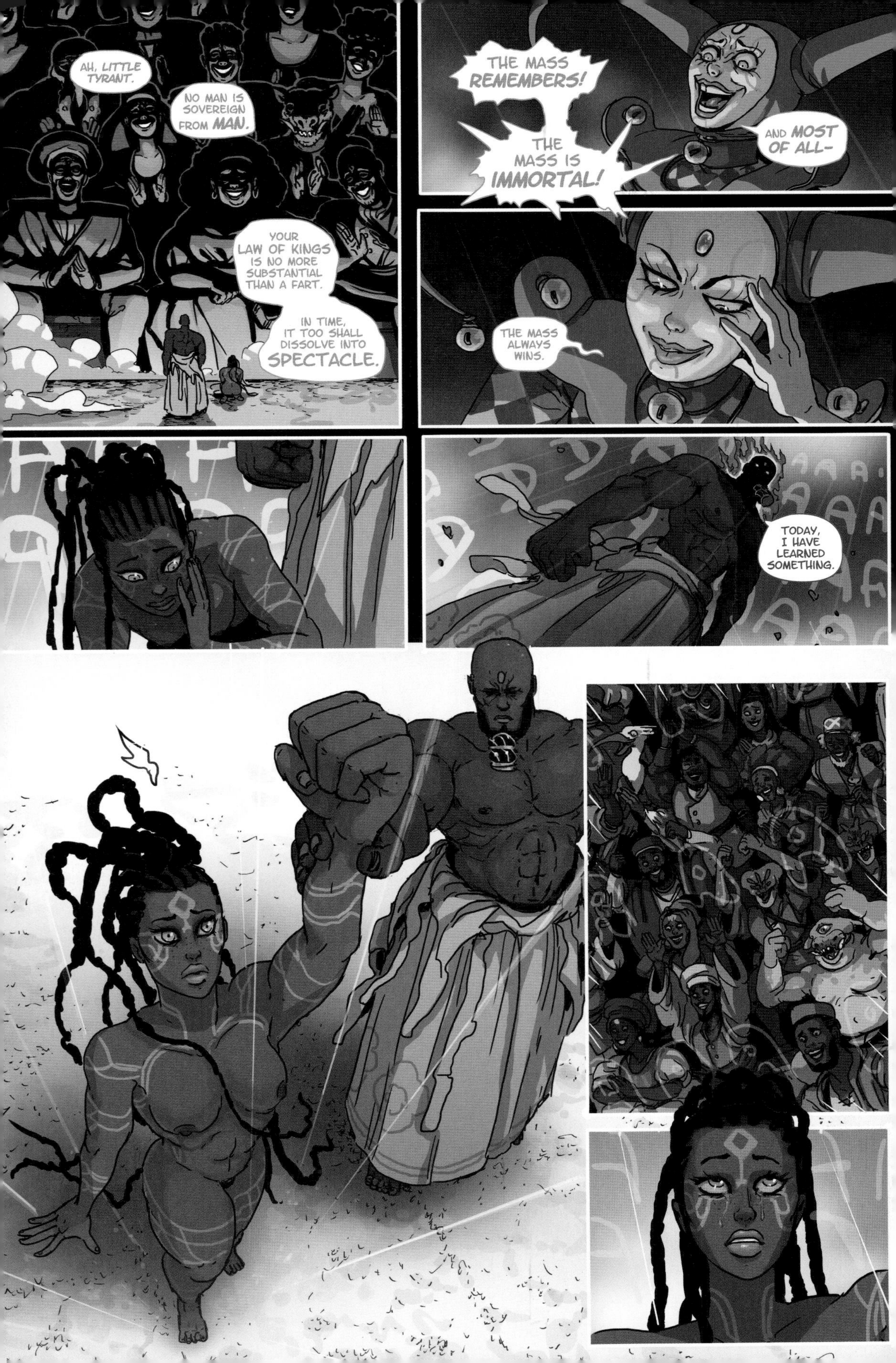
AH, LITTLE TYRANT.
NO MAN IS SOVEREIGN FROM MAN.
YOUR LAW OF KINGS IS NO MORE SUBSTANTIAL THAN A FART.
IN TIME, IT TOO SHALL DISSOLVE INTO SPECTACLE.
THE MASS REMEMBERS!
THE MASS IS IMMORTAL!
AND MOST OF ALL-
THE MASS ALWAYS WINS.
TODAY, I HAVE LEARNED SOMETHING.

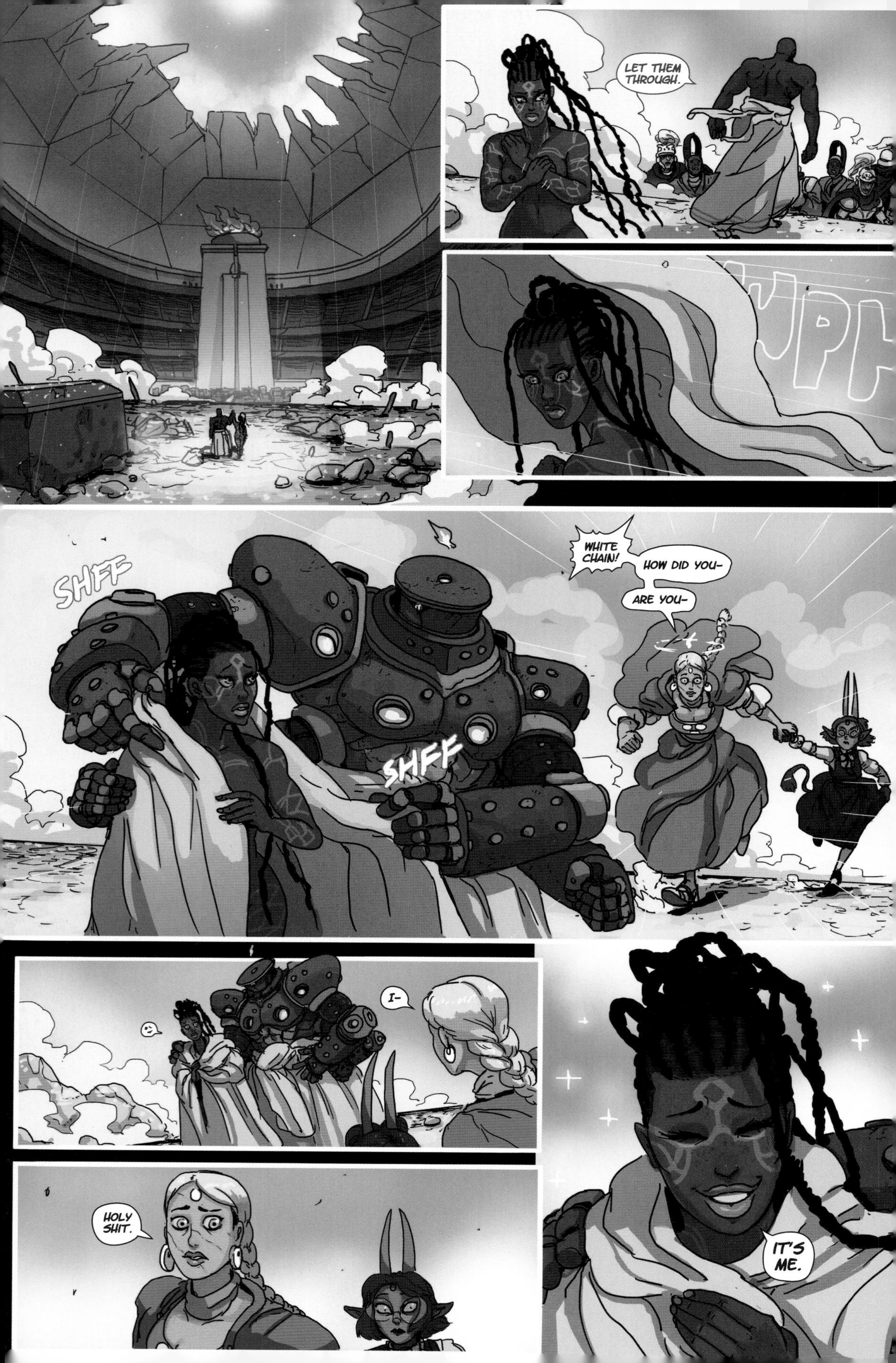
LET THEM THROUGH.
WHPCH
SHFF
WHITE CHAIN!
HOW DID YOU-
ARE YOU-
SHFF
I-
HOLY SHIT.
IT'S ME.

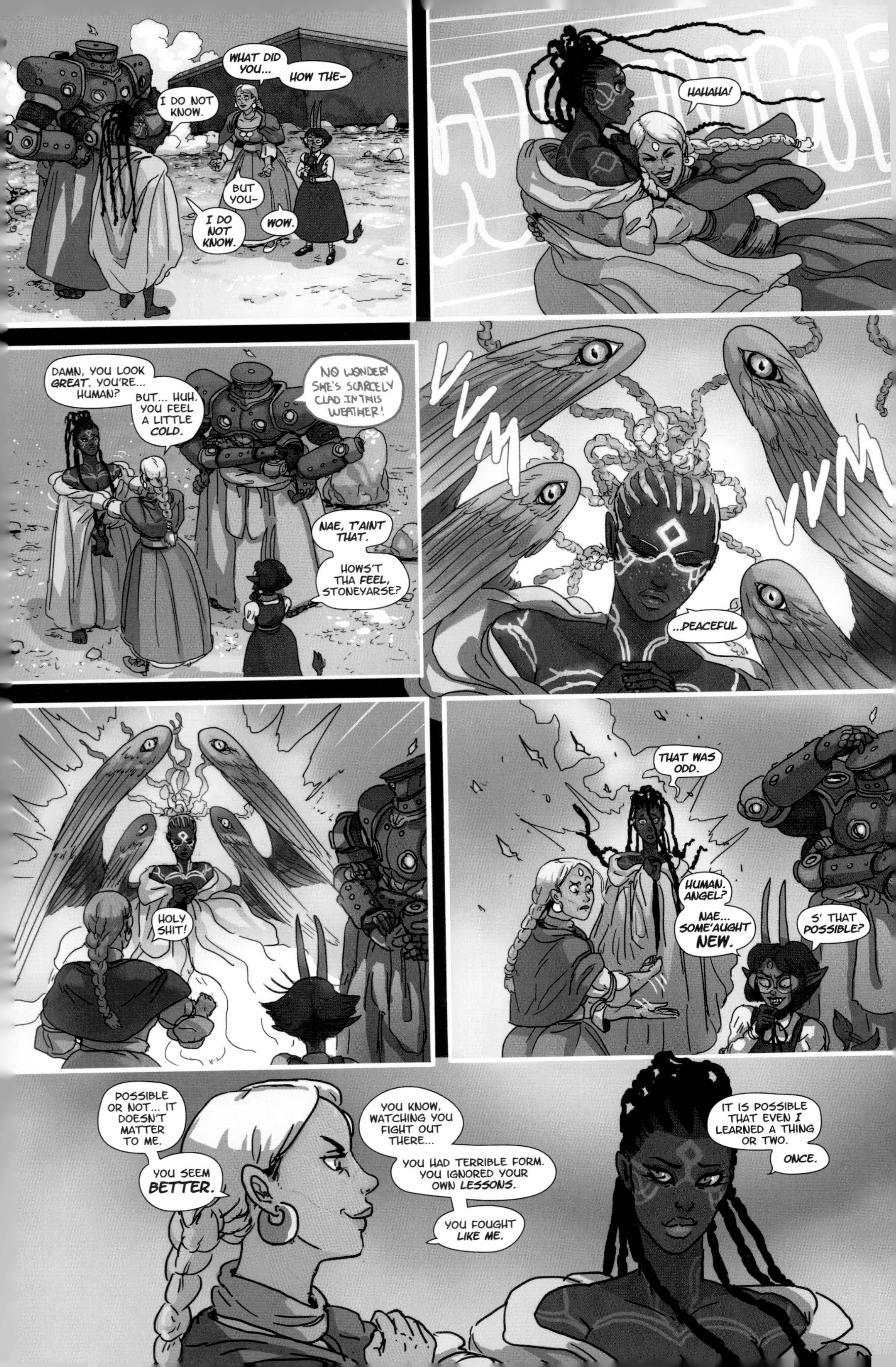
WHAT DID YOU...
HOW THE-
I DO NOT KNOW.
BUT YOU-
I DO NOT KNOW.
WOW.
HAHAHA!
DAMN, YOU LOOK GREAT. YOU'RE... HUMAN?
BUT... HUH. YOU FEEL A LITTLE COLD.
NO WONDER! SHE'S SCARCELY CLAD IN THIS WEATHER!
NAE, T'AINT THAT.
HOWS'T THA FEEL, STONEYARSE?
VVM
VVM
...PEACEFUL
HOLY SHIT!
THAT WAS ODD.
HUMAN. ANGEL?
NAE... SOME'AUGHT NEW.
S' THAT POSSIBLE?
POSSIBLE OR NOT... IT DOESN'T MATTER TO ME.
YOU SEEM BETTER.
YOU KNOW, WATCHING YOU FIGHT OUT THERE...
YOU HAD TERRIBLE FORM. YOU IGNORED YOUR OWN LESSONS.
YOU FOUGHT LIKE ME.
IT IS POSSIBLE THAT EVEN I LEARNED A THING OR TWO.
ONCE.

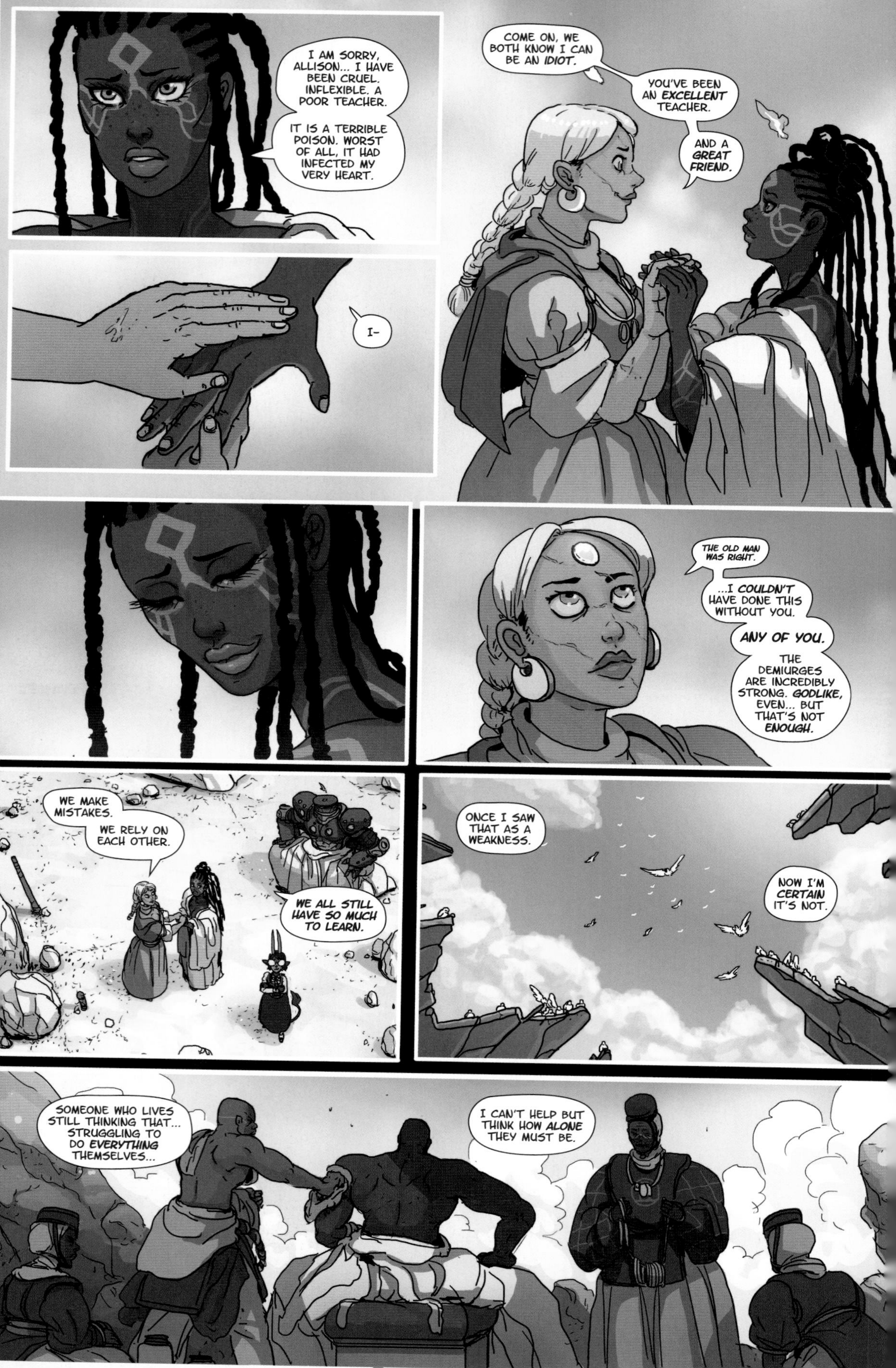
I AM SORRY, ALLISON... I HAVE BEEN CRUEL. INFLEXIBLE. A POOR TEACHER.
IT IS A TERRIBLE POISON. WORST OF ALL, IT HAD INFECTED MY VERY HEART.
I-
COME ON, WE BOTH KNOW I CAN BE AN IDIOT.
YOU'VE BEEN AN EXCELLENT TEACHER.
AND A GREAT FRIEND.
THE OLD MAN WAS RIGHT.
...I COULDN'T HAVE DONE THIS WITHOUT YOU.
ANY OF YOU.
THE DEMIURGES ARE INCREDIBLY STRONG. GODLIKE, EVEN... BUT THAT'S NOT ENOUGH.
WE MAKE MISTAKES.
WE RELY ON EACH OTHER.
WE ALL STILL HAVE SO MUCH TO LEARN.
ONCE I SAW THAT AS A WEAKNESS.
NOW I'M CERTAIN IT'S NOT.
SOMEONE WHO LIVES STILL THINKING THAT... STRUGGLING TO DO EVERYTHING THEMSELVES...
I CAN'T HELP BUT THINK HOW ALONE THEY MUST BE.

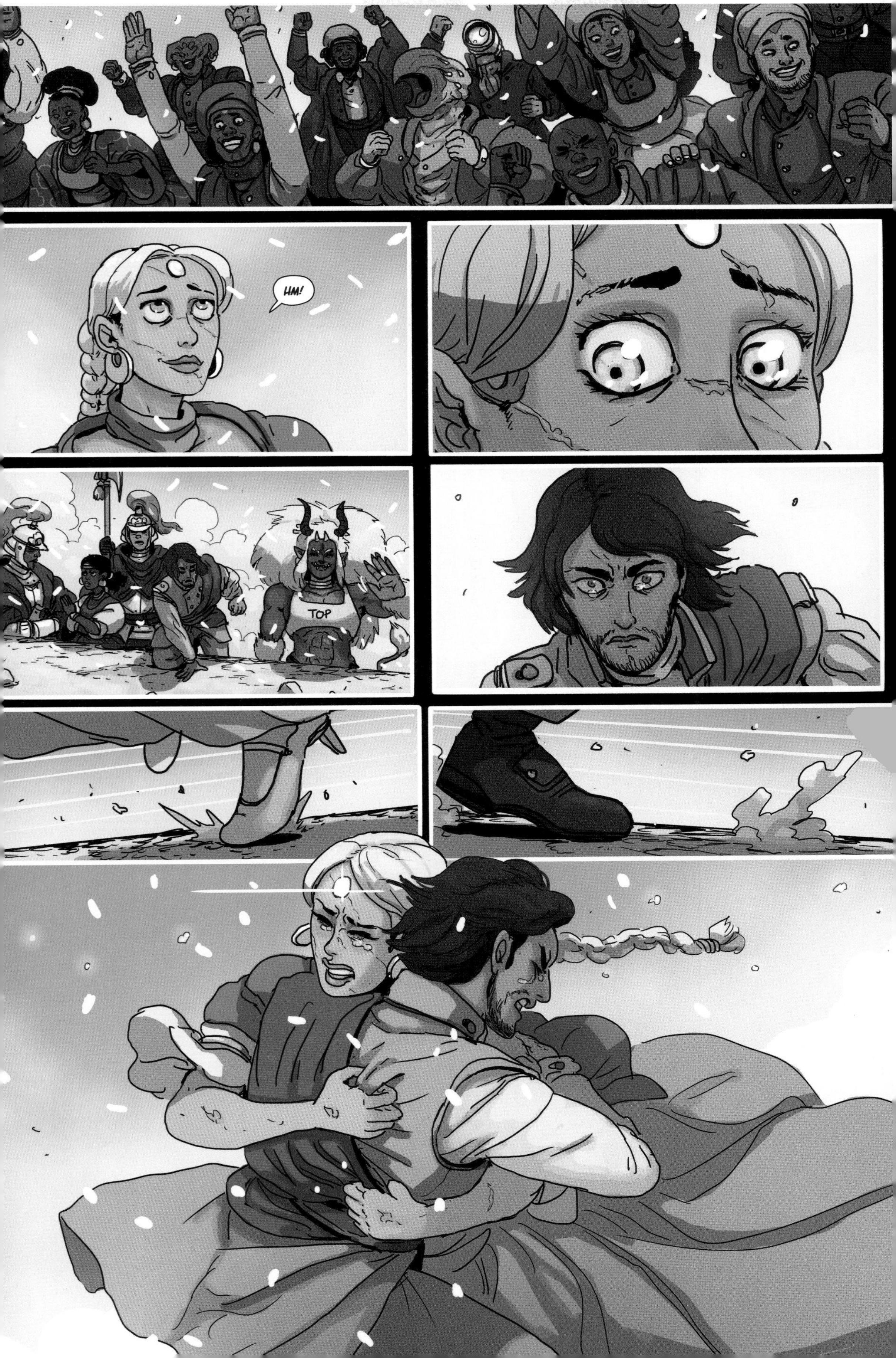
HM!
TOP

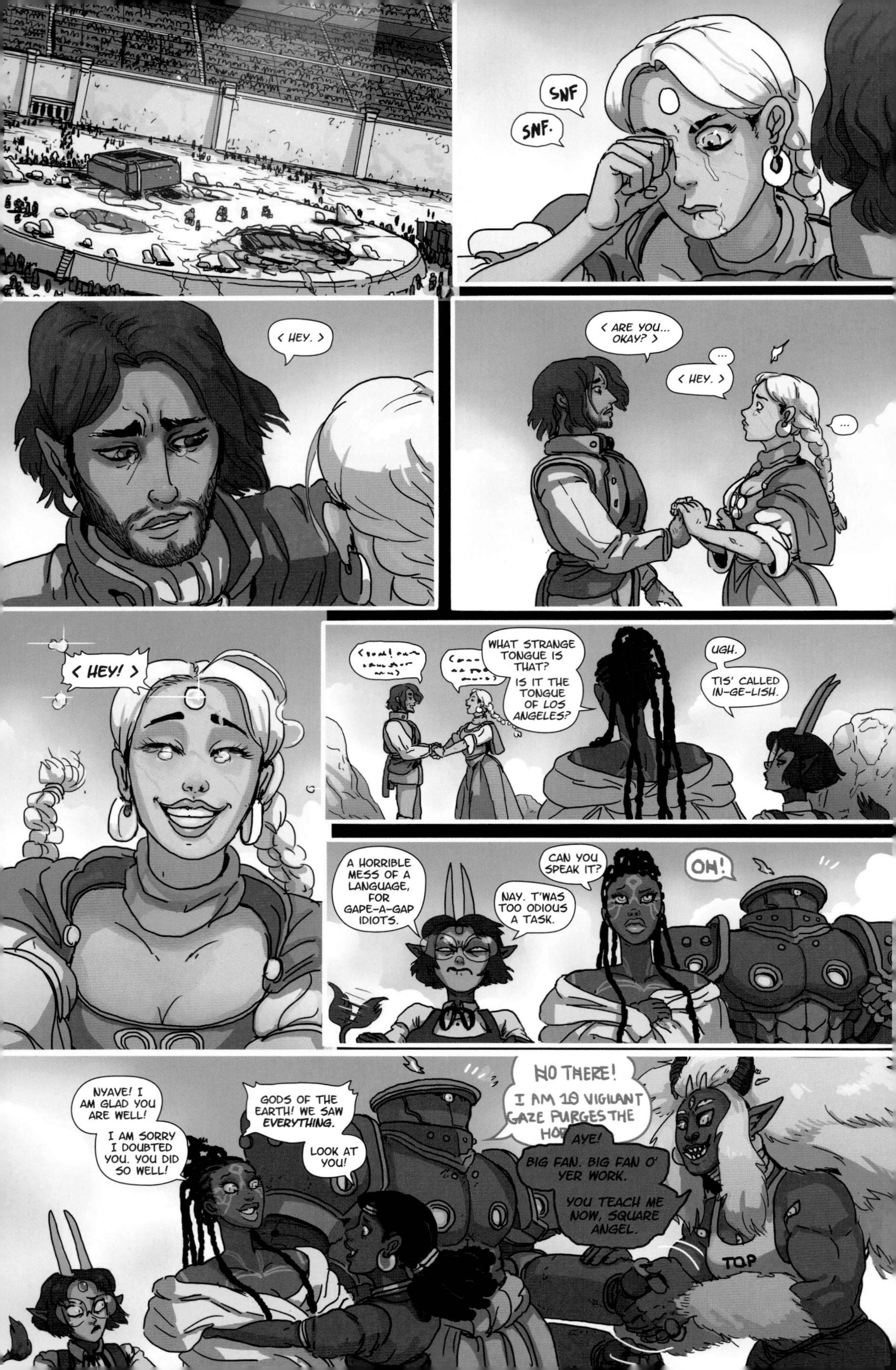
SNF
SNF.
< HEY. >
< ARE YOU... OKAY? >
...
< HEY. >
...
< HEY! >
WHAT STRANGE TONGUE IS THAT?
IS IT THE TONGUE OF LOS ANGELES?
UGH.
TIS' CALLED IN-GE-LISH.
A HORRIBLE MESS OF A LANGUAGE, FOR GAPE-A-GAP IDIOTS.
CAN YOU SPEAK IT?
NAY. T'WAS TOO ODIOUS A TASK.
OH!
NYAVE! I AM GLAD YOU ARE WELL!
I AM SORRY I DOUBTED YOU. YOU DID SO WELL!
GODS OF THE EARTH! WE SAW *EVERYTHING*.
LOOK AT YOU!
NO THERE!
I AM 10 VIGILANT GAZE PURGES THE HO
AYE!
BIG FAN. BIG FAN O' YER WORK.
YOU TEACH ME NOW, SQUARE ANGEL.
TOP

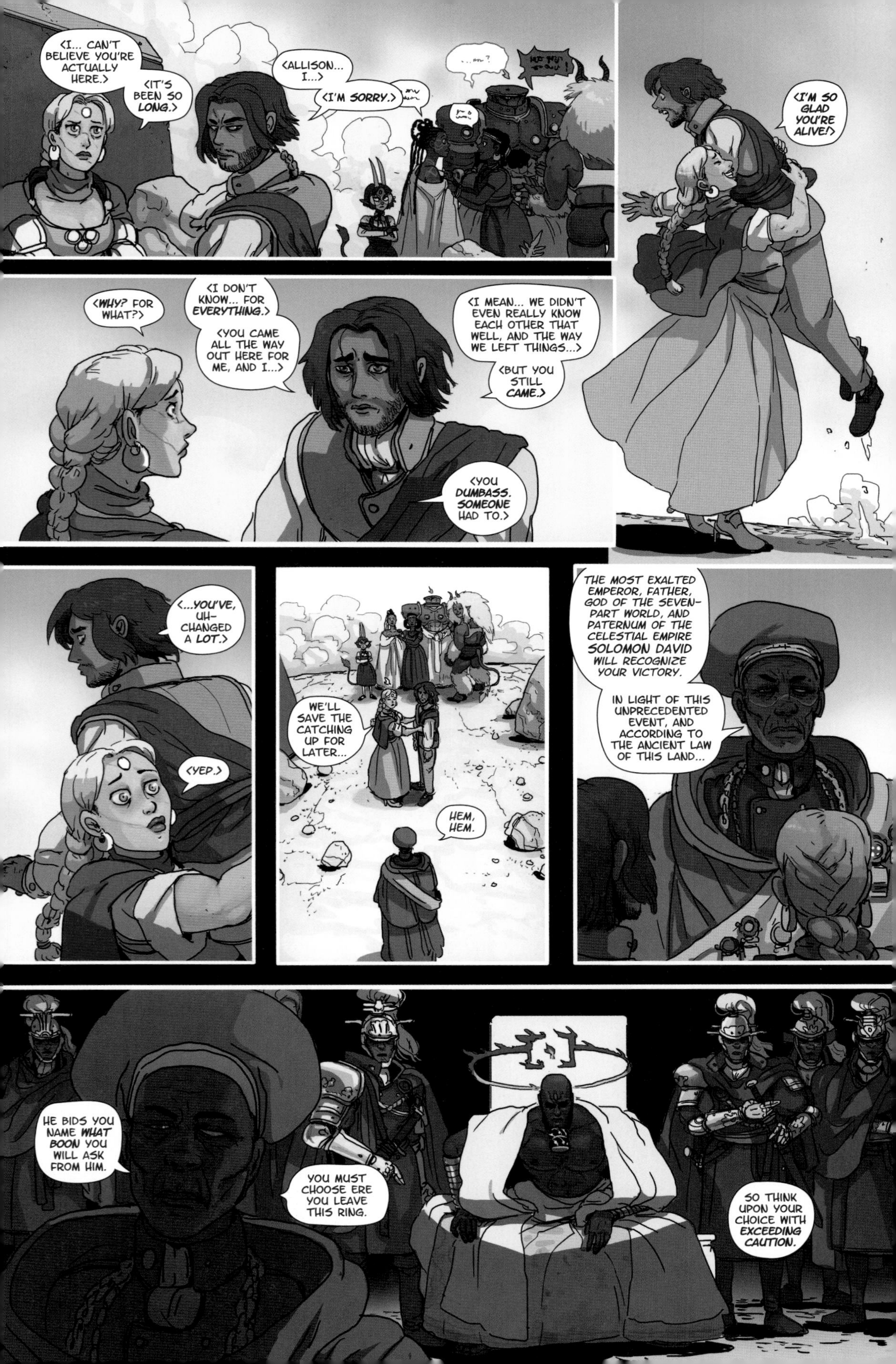
<I... CAN'T BELIEVE YOU'RE ACTUALLY HERE.>
<IT'S BEEN SO LONG.>
<ALLISON... I...>
<I'M SORRY.>
<WHY? FOR WHAT?>
<I DON'T KNOW... FOR EVERYTHING.>
<YOU CAME ALL THE WAY OUT HERE FOR ME, AND I...>
<I MEAN... WE DIDN'T EVEN REALLY KNOW EACH OTHER THAT WELL, AND THE WAY WE LEFT THINGS...>
<BUT YOU STILL CAME.>
<YOU DUMBASS. SOMEONE HAD TO.>
<I'M SO GLAD YOU'RE ALIVE!>
<...YOU'VE, UH- CHANGED A LOT.>
<YEP.>
WE'LL SAVE THE CATCHING UP FOR LATER...
HEM, HEM.
THE MOST EXALTED EMPEROR, FATHER, GOD OF THE SEVEN-PART WORLD, AND PATERNUM OF THE CELESTIAL EMPIRE SOLOMON DAVID WILL RECOGNIZE YOUR VICTORY.
IN LIGHT OF THIS UNPRECEDENTED EVENT, AND ACCORDING TO THE ANCIENT LAW OF THIS LAND...
HE BIDS YOU NAME WHAT BOON YOU WILL ASK FROM HIM.
YOU MUST CHOOSE ERE YOU LEAVE THIS RING.
SO THINK UPON YOUR CHOICE WITH EXCEEDING CAUTION.

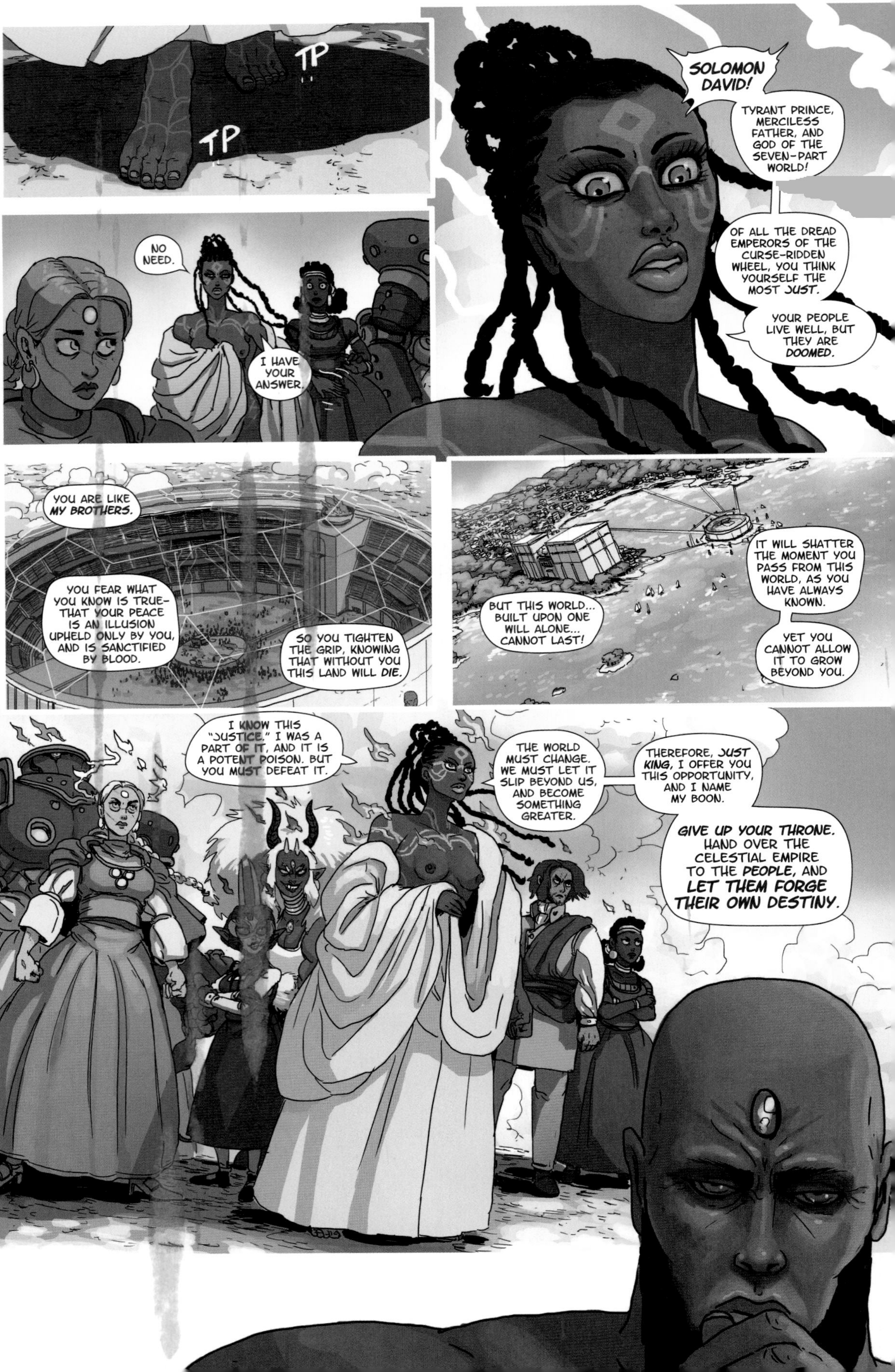
TP
TP
NO NEED.
I HAVE YOUR ANSWER.
SOLOMON DAVID!
TYRANT PRINCE, MERCILESS FATHER, AND GOD OF THE SEVEN-PART WORLD!
OF ALL THE DREAD EMPERORS OF THE CURSE-RIDDEN WHEEL, YOU THINK YOURSELF THE MOST JUST.
YOUR PEOPLE LIVE WELL, BUT THEY ARE DOOMED.
YOU ARE LIKE MY BROTHERS.
YOU FEAR WHAT YOU KNOW IS TRUE-THAT YOUR PEACE IS AN ILLUSION UPHELD ONLY BY YOU, AND IS SANCTIFIED BY BLOOD.
SO YOU TIGHTEN THE GRIP, KNOWING THAT WITHOUT YOU THIS LAND WILL DIE.
BUT THIS WORLD... BUILT UPON ONE WILL ALONE... CANNOT LAST!
IT WILL SHATTER THE MOMENT YOU PASS FROM THIS WORLD, AS YOU HAVE ALWAYS KNOWN.
YET YOU CANNOT ALLOW IT TO GROW BEYOND YOU.
I KNOW THIS "JUSTICE." I WAS A PART OF IT, AND IT IS A POTENT POISON. BUT YOU MUST DEFEAT IT.
THE WORLD MUST CHANGE. WE MUST LET IT SLIP BEYOND US, AND BECOME SOMETHING GREATER.
THEREFORE, JUST KING, I OFFER YOU THIS OPPORTUNITY, AND I NAME MY BOON.
GIVE UP YOUR THRONE. HAND OVER THE CELESTIAL EMPIRE TO THE PEOPLE, AND LET THEM FORGE THEIR OWN DESTINY.

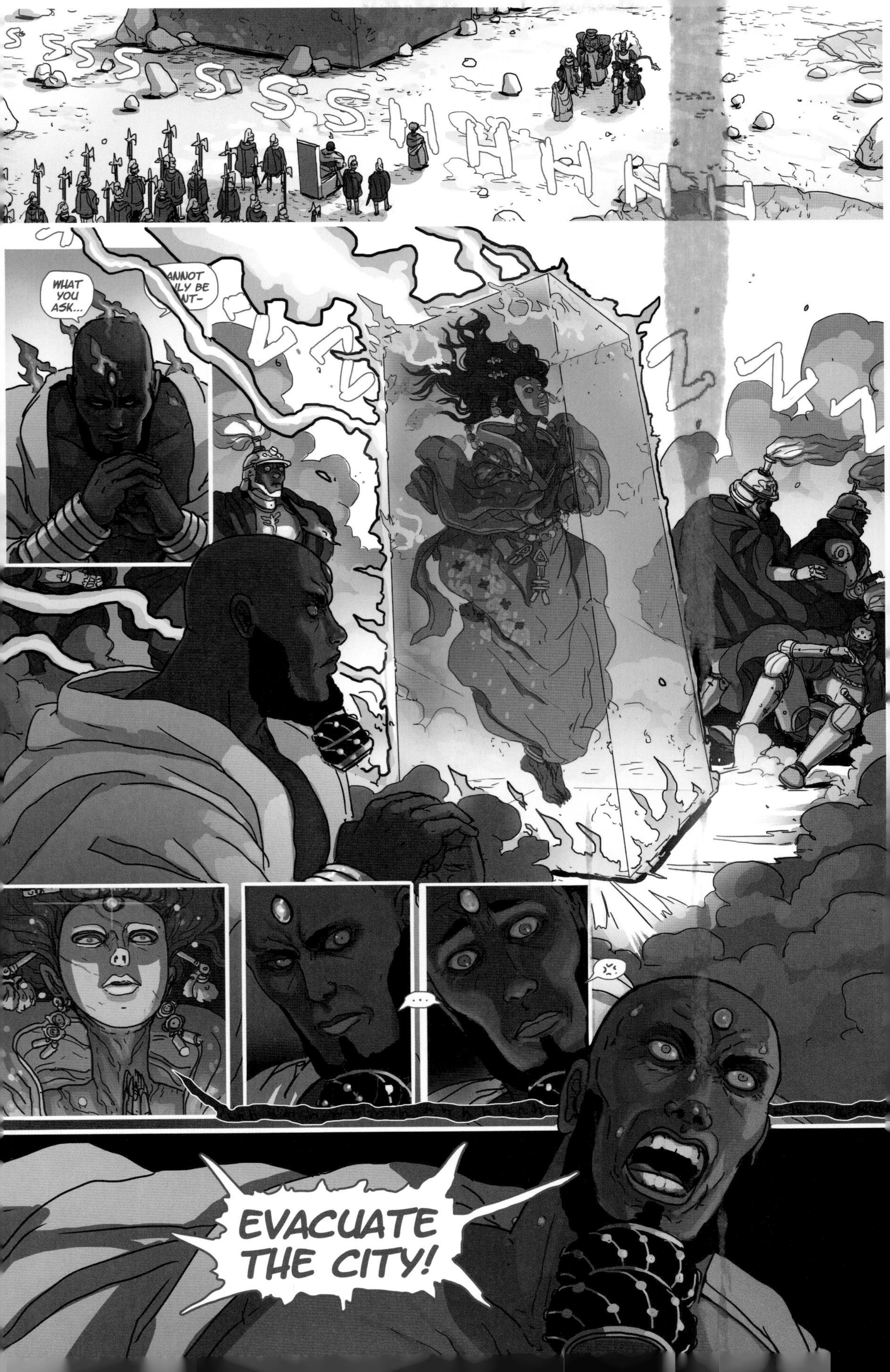

SSSSSSSHHHHH
WHAT YOU ASK...
ANNOT LY BE NT-
ZZZZ
...
EVACUATE THE CITY!

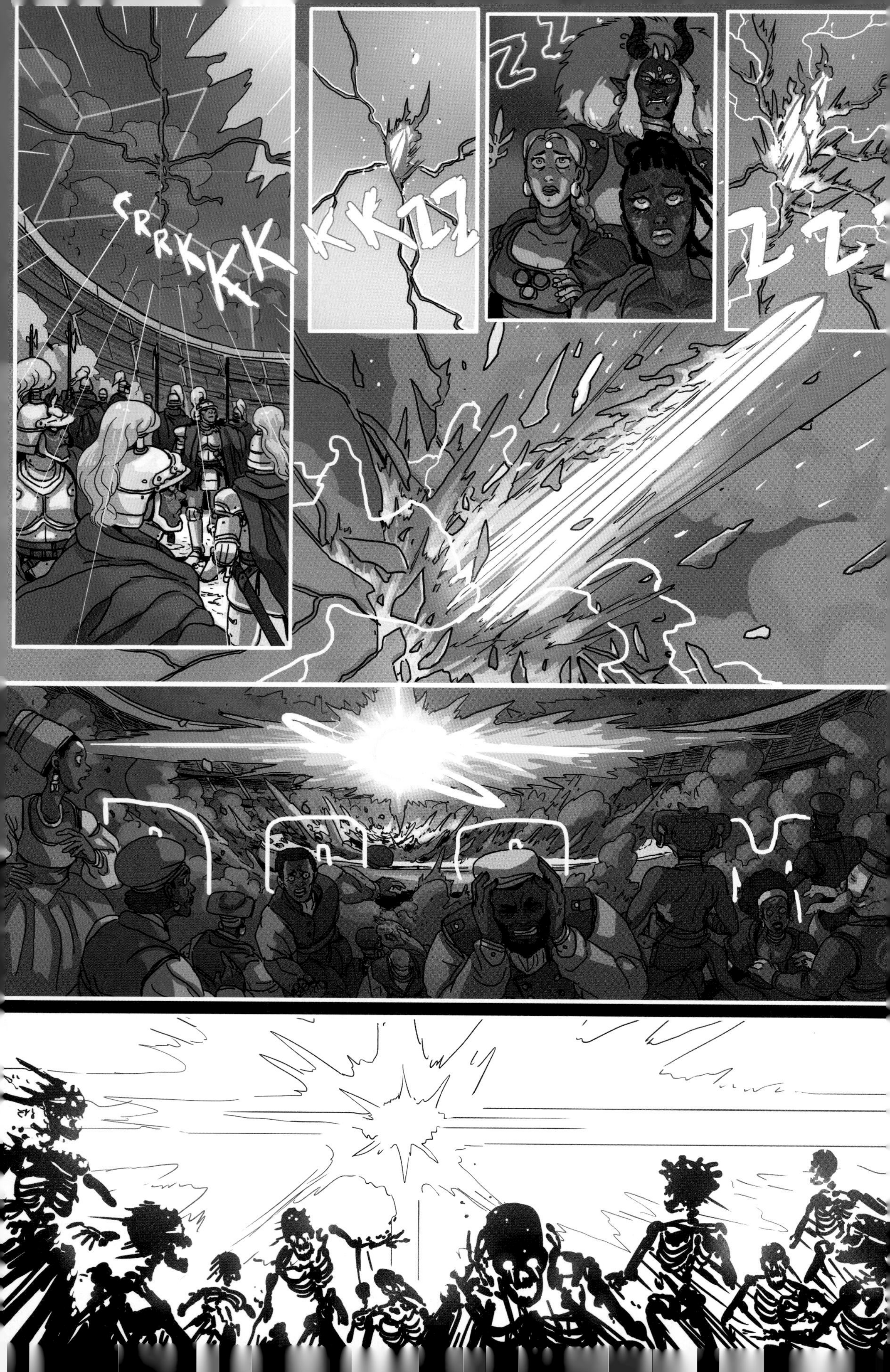
CRRKKKKKKZZZ
ZZ
ZZZ

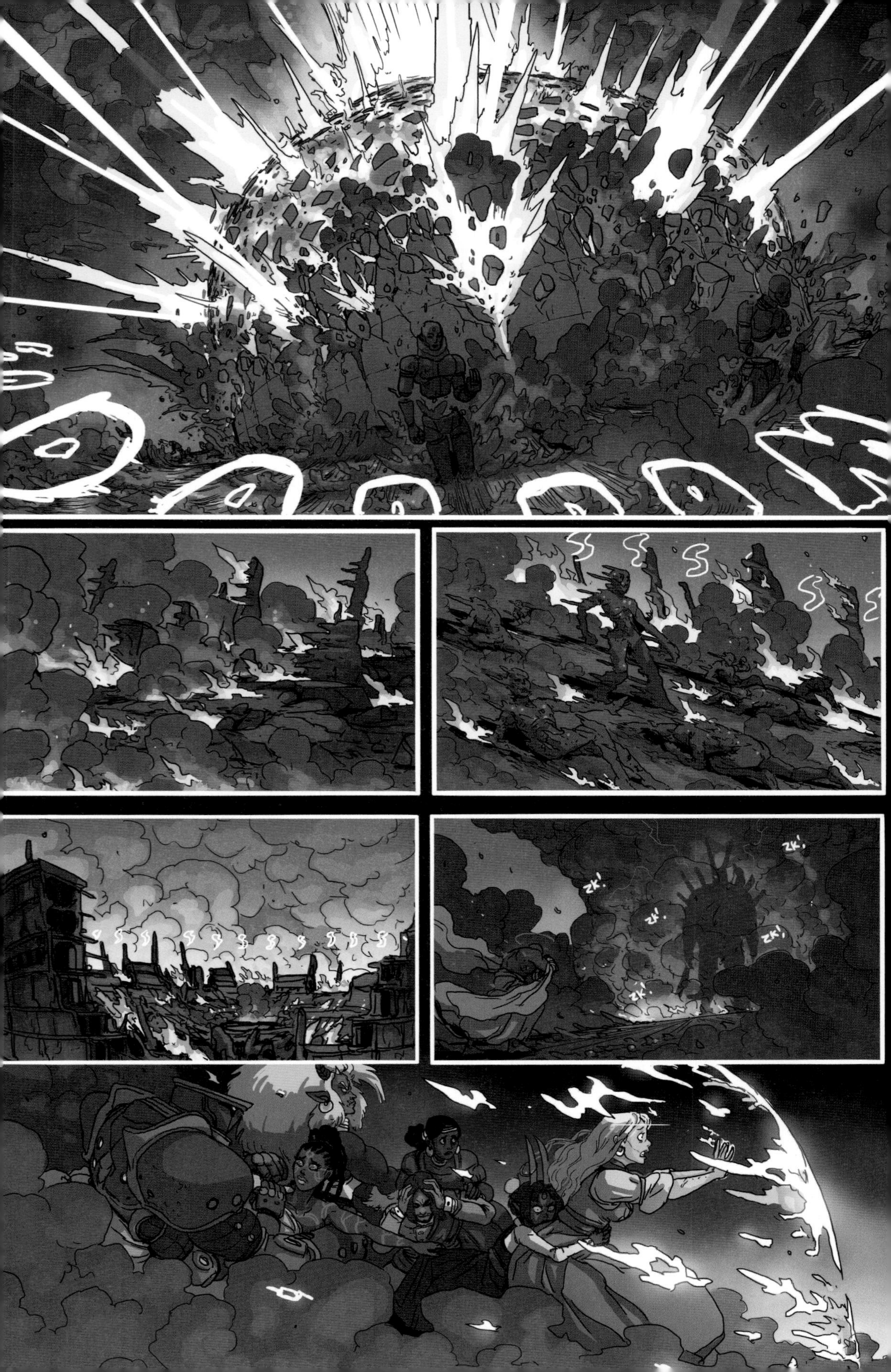
ZK!
ZK!
ZK!
ZK!
ZK!

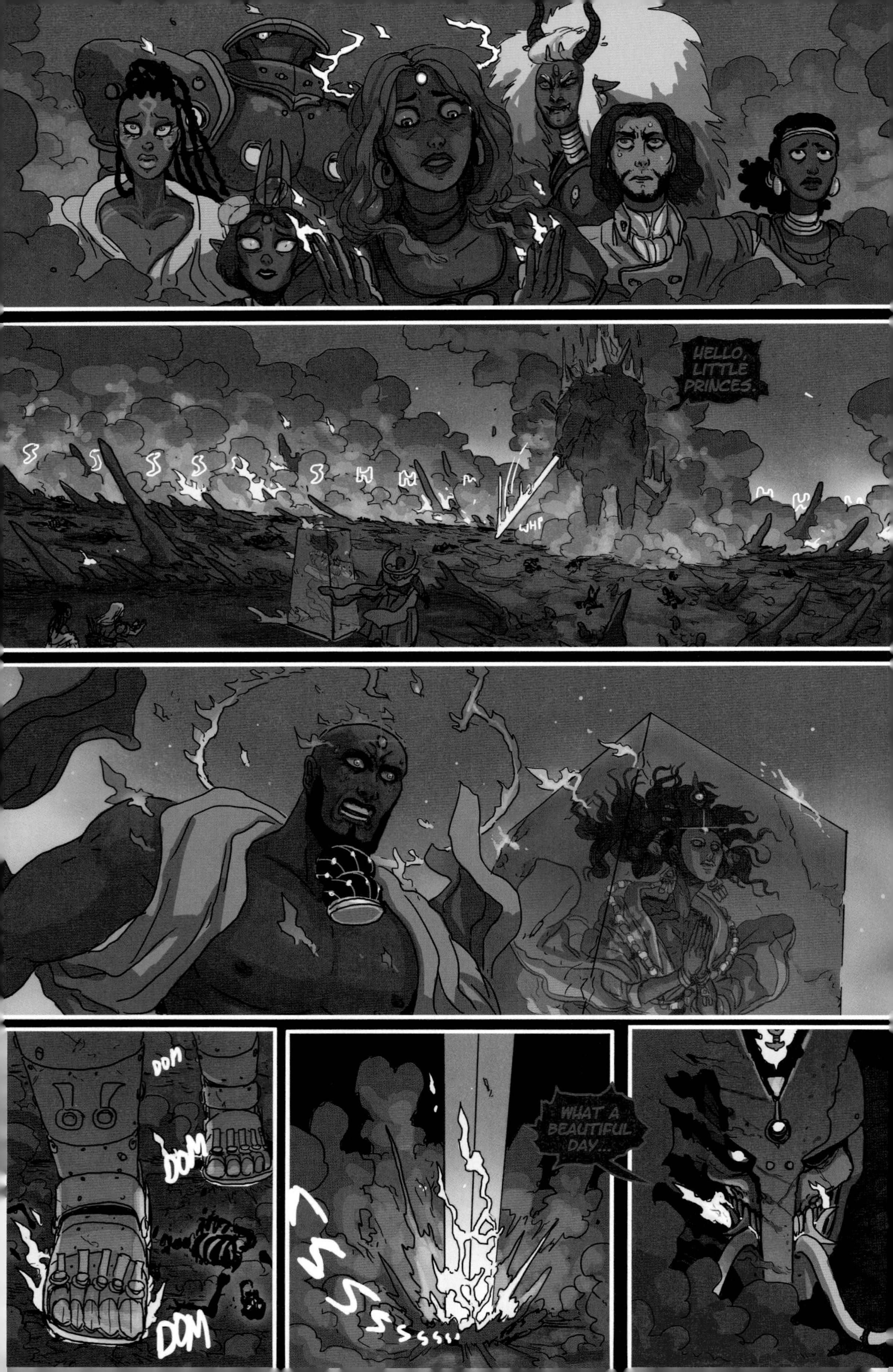
HELLO, LITTLE PRINCES.
SSSSSSHHMM
WHP
DOM
DOM
DOM
WHAT A BEAUTIFUL DAY...

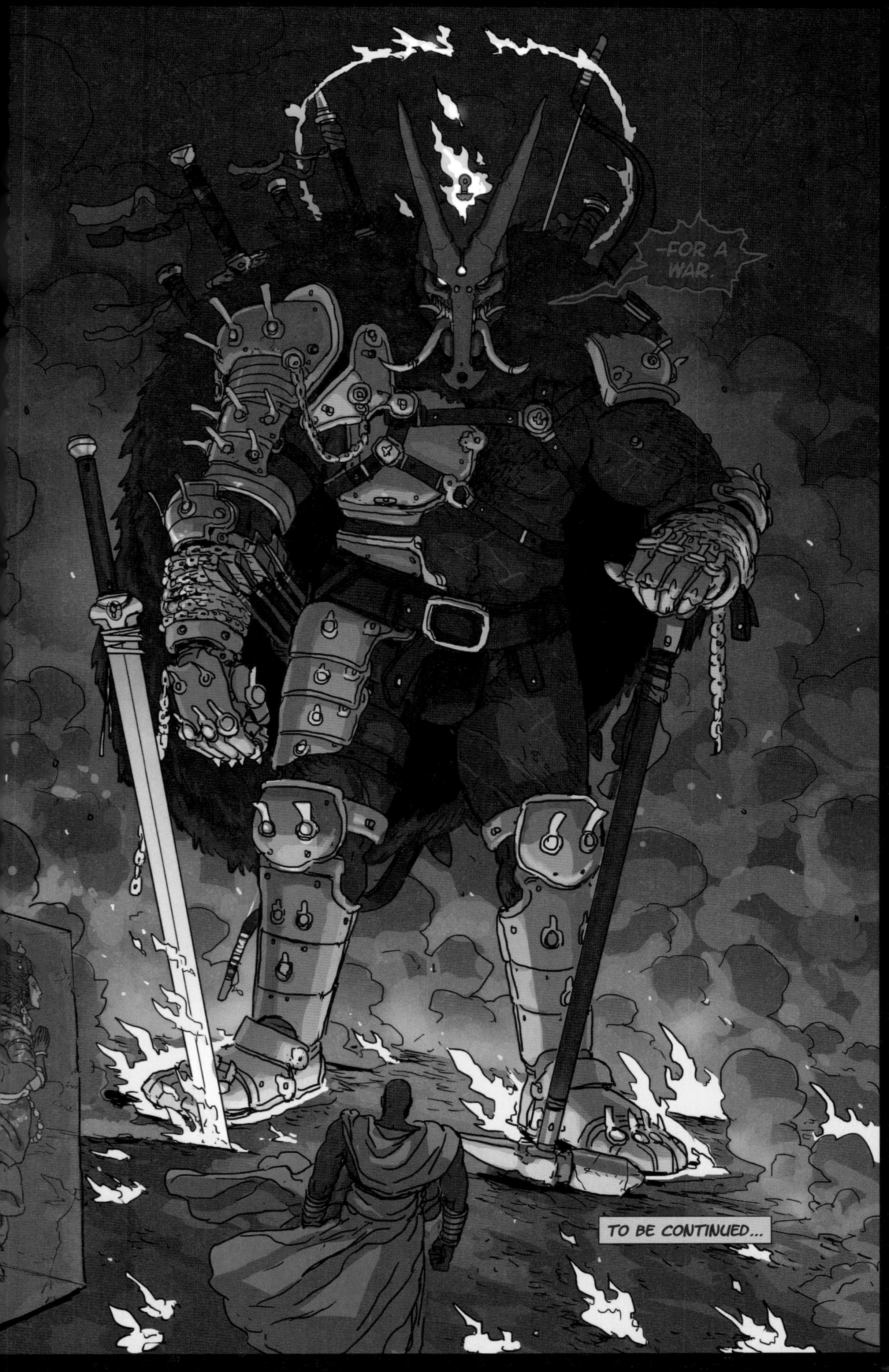
–FOR A WAR.
TO BE CONTINUED...

KILL 6 BILLION DEMONS